Andy McDermott is the bestselling author of the Nina Wilde & Eddie Chase adventure thrillers, which have been sold in over 30 countries and 20 languages. His debut novel, THE HUNT FOR ATLANTIS, was his first of several *New York Times* bestsellers. THE REVELATION CODE is the eleventh book in the series, and he has also written the explosive spy thriller THE PERSONA PROTOCOL.

A former journalist and movie critic, Andy is now a full-time novelist. Born in Halifax, he now lives in Bournemouth with his partner and son.

Praise for Andy McDermott:

'Adventure stories don't get much more epic than this' *Daily Mirror*

'If Wilbur Smith and Clive Cussler collaborated, they might have come up with a thundering big adventure blockbuster like this . . . a wide-screen, thrill-a-minute ride' *Peterborough Evening Telegraph*

'True Indiana Jones stuff with terrific pace' *Bookseller*

'A true blockbuster rollercoaster ride from start to finish . . . Popcorn escapism at its very best' *Crime and Publishing*

'A rip-roaring read and one which looks set to cement McDermott's place in the bestsellers list for years to come' *Bolton Evening News*

'Fast-moving, this is a pulse-racing adventure with action right down the line' *Northern Echo*

'A writer of rare, almost cinematic talent. Where others' action scenes limp along unconvincingly, his explode off the page in Technicolor' *Daily Express, Scotland*

'McDermott writes like Clive Cussler on speed. The action is non-stop' *Huddersfield Daily Examiner*

'An all-action cracker from one of Britain's most talented adventure writer

ANDY McDERMOTT

THE REVELATION CODE

headline

First published in 2015 by
HEADLINE PUBLISHING GROUP

First published in paperback in 2016 by
HEADLINE PUBLISHING GROUP

1

Cataloguing in Publication Data is available from the British Library

ISBN 978 0 7553 8078 7 (B format)
ISBN 978 1 4722 3236 6 (A format)

Typeset in Aldine 401BT by Avon DataSet Ltd, Bidford-on-Avon, Warwickshire

Printed and bound in Great Britain by Clays Ltd, St Ives plc

Headline's policy is to use papers that are natural, renewable and recyclable
products and made from wood grown in well-managed forests and other
controlled sources. The logging and manufacturing processes are expected to
conform to the environmental regulations of the country of origin.

HEADLINE PUBLISHING GROUP
An Hachette UK Company
Carmelite House
50 Victoria Embankment
London EC4Y 0DZ

www.headline.co.uk
www.hachette.co.uk

For Sebastian
and all the adventures that await

Prologue

Southern Iraq

The half-moon cast a feeble light over the desolate sand-swept plain. The region had been marshland not long ago, but war had changed that. Not directly; the islands spattering the expanse between the great rivers of the Tigris and the Euphrates had not been destroyed by shells and explosives. Instead spite had drained it, the dictator Saddam Hussein taking his revenge upon the Ma'dan people for daring to rise against him following the Gulf War. Dams and spillways had reduced the wetlands to a dustbowl, forcing the inhabitants to leave in order to survive.

That destruction was, ironically, making the mission of the trio of CIA operatives crossing the bleak landscape considerably easier. The no-fly zone established over southern Iraq gave the United States and its allies total freedom to operate, and the agents had parachuted to the Euphrates' northern bank earlier that night, their ultimate objective the toppling of the Iraqi leader. Had the marshes not been drained, they would have been forced to make a circuitous journey by boat, dragging it over reed-covered embankments whenever the water became too shallow to traverse. Instead, they had been able to drive the battered Toyota 4x4 waiting at their insertion point almost in a straight line across the lowlands.

'Not far now,' said the team's leader, Michael Rosemont, as

he checked a hand-held GPS unit. 'Two miles.'

The driver, Gabe Arnold, peered ahead through his night-vision goggles. He was driving without headlights to keep them hidden from potential observers. 'I can see the lake.'

'Any sign of Kerim and his people?'

'Not yet.'

'Might have known these Arabs would be late,' said the third man, from behind them. Ezekiel Cross was using a small flashlight to check a map, focusing it on an almost perfectly circular patch of pale blue marked *Umm al Binni*. 'Nobody in this part of the world can even do anything as basic as keep time. Savages.'

Rosemont let out a weary huff, but let the remark pass. 'How close is the nearest Iraqi unit, Easy?' he asked instead.

'Based on today's intel, about nine klicks to the north-east. Near the Tigris.' Cross's pale grey eyes flicked towards his superior. 'And I'd prefer not to be called that.'

'Okay, *Cross*,' Rosemont replied with a small shake of his head. Arnold suppressed a grin. 'Any other units nearby?'

'There's another fifteen klicks north of here. Forces have been building up there over the past week.'

'They know Uncle Sam's gonna come for 'em sooner or later,' said Arnold.

Cross made an impatient sound. 'We should have flattened the entire country the day after 9/11.'

'Iraq didn't attack us,' Rosemont pointed out.

'They're supporting al-Qaeda. And they're building weapons of mass destruction. To me, that justifies any action necessary to stop them.'

'Well, that's what we're waiting on the UN to confirm, ain't it?' Arnold said. 'Got to give 'em a chance to give up their WMDs before we put the hammer down.'

'The United Nations!' Cross spat. 'We should kick them out of our country. As if New York isn't enough of a pit of degeneracy already, we let a gang of foreign socialists and atheists squat there telling us what to do!'

'Uh-huh.' Rosemont had only known the Virginian for a few days, but that had been long enough to learn to tune out the agent's frequent rants about anything he considered an ungodly affront to his values – which, it seemed, was everything in the modern world. He turned his attention back to the driver. 'Still no sign of Kerim?'

'Nothing – no, wait,' replied Arnold, suddenly alert. 'I see a light.'

Cross immediately flicked off the flashlight, dropping the off-roader's interior into darkness. Rosemont narrowed his eyes and stared ahead. 'Where?'

'Twelve o'clock.'

'Is it them?' said Cross, wary.

The CIA leader picked out a tiny point of orange against the darkness. 'It's them. Right where they're supposed to be.'

'On schedule, too,' added Arnold. 'Guess they *can* keep time after all, huh?' Cross glowered at him.

The lake came into clearer view as the Toyota crested a low rise, a black disc against the moonlit wash covering the plain. Arnold surveyed it through his goggles. 'Man, that's weird. It looks like a crater or something.'

'That's the theory,' Rosemont told him. 'They think a meteorite made it a few thousand years ago; that's what the background data on the region said, anyhow. The lake used to be a lot bigger, but nobody knew that was at the bottom until Saddam drained the marshes.' His tone turned businesslike. 'Okay, this is it. I'll do the talking, get the intel off Kerim. You two ready the weapons for transfer.' He turned to regard the cases stacked in the Toyota's cargo bed.

'And after?' Cross asked.

'Depends on what Kerim tells me. If he's got new information

3

about the Iraqi defences, then we call it in and maybe go see for ourselves if HQ needs us to. If he doesn't, we give the Marsh Arab rebels their weapons and prep them for our invasion.'

'Assuming the UN doesn't try to stop us,' said Cross scathingly.

'Hey, hey,' Arnold cut in. 'There's something by the lake. Looks like a building, some ruins.'

Rosemont peered ahead, but there was not enough light to reveal any detail on the shore. 'There wasn't anything marked on the maps.'

'It's in the water. Musta been exposed when the lake dried up.'

'Are Kerim and his people by it?'

'No, they're maybe two hundred metres away.'

'It's not our problem, then.' Rosemont raised the M4 carbine on his lap and clicked off the safety. Cross did the same with his own weapon. They were meeting friendlies, but those at the sharp end of intelligence work in the CIA's Special Activities Division preferred to be ready for any eventuality.

Arnold brought the Toyota in. The point of orange light was revealed as a small campfire, figures standing around the dancing flames. All were armed, the fire's glow also reflecting dully off assorted Kalashnikov rifles. To Rosemont's relief, none were pointed at the approaching vehicle.

Yet.

The 4x4 halted. The men around the fire stood watching, waiting for its occupants to make the first move. 'All right,' said Rosemont. 'I'll go meet them.'

The CIA commander opened the door and stepped out. The action brought a response, some of the Ma'dan raising their guns. He took a deep breath. 'Kerim! Is Kerim here?'

Mutterings in Arabic, then a man stepped forward. 'I am Kerim. You are Michael?'

'Yes.'

Kerim waved him closer. The Ma'dan leader was in his early thirties, but a hard life in the marshes had added a decade of wear to his face. 'Michael, hello,' he said, before embracing the American and kissing him on both cheeks.

'Call me Mike,' Rosemont said with a smile.

The Arab returned it. 'It is very good to see you . . . Mike. We have waited a long time for this day. When you come to kill Saddam' – a spitting sound, echoed by the others as they heard the hated dictator's name – 'we will fight beside you. But his soldiers, they have tanks, helicopters. These are no good.' He held up his dented AK-47. 'We need more.'

'You'll have more.' Rosemont signalled to the two men in the Toyota. 'Bring 'em their toys!'

'You've got the intel?' asked Cross as he got out.

'Show of good faith. Come on.'

Cross was aggrieved by the change of plan, but he went with Arnold to the truck's rear. Each took out a crate and crunched through dead reeds to bring it to the group. 'This fire'll be visible for miles,' the Virginian complained. 'Stupid making it out in the open, real stupid.'

Kerim bristled. Rosemont shot Cross an irritated look, but knew he was right. 'You should put this out now we're here,' he told the Ma'dan leader. Kerim gave an order, and one of his men kicked dirt over the little pyre. 'Why didn't you set up in those ruins?'

The suggestion seemed to unsettle his contact. 'That is . . . not a good place,' said Kerim, glancing almost nervously towards the waterlogged structure. 'If it had been up to us, we would not have chosen to meet you here.'

'Why not?' asked Arnold, setting down his case.

'It is a place of death. Even before the water fell, all the marsh tribes stayed away from it. It is said that . . .' He hesitated.

'That the end of the world will begin there. Allah, praise be unto Him, will send out His angels to burn the earth.'

'You mean God,' snapped Cross.

Kerim was momentarily confused. 'Allah *is* God, yes. But it is a place we fear.'

With the fire extinguished, the ragged ruins were discernible in the moon's pallid light. They were not large, the outer buildings and walls having crumbled, but it seemed to Rosemont that the squat central structure had remained mostly intact. How long had it been submerged? Centuries, millennia? There was something indefinably ancient about it.

Not that it mattered. His only concerns were of the present. 'Well, here's something that'll make Saddam fear *you*,' he said, switching on a flashlight and opening one of the crates.

Its contents produced sounds of awe and excitement from the Ma'dan. Rosemont lifted out an olive-drab tube. 'This is an M72 LAW rocket – LAW stands for light anti-tank weapon. We'll show you how to use them, but if you can fire a rifle, you can fire one of these. We've also brought a couple thousand rounds of AK ammunition.'

'That is good. That is very good!' Kerim beamed at the CIA agent, then translated for the other Ma'dan.

'I guess they're happy,' said Arnold on seeing the enthusiastic response.

'Guess so,' Rosemont replied. 'Okay, Kerim, we need your intel on Saddam's local troops before—'

A cry of alarm made everyone whirl. The Marsh Arabs whipped up their rifles, scattering into the patches of dried-up reeds. 'What's going on?' Cross demanded, raising his own gun.

'Down, down!' Kerim called. 'The light, turn it off!'

Rosemont snapped off the torch and ducked. 'What is it?'

'Listen!' He pointed across the lake. 'A helicopter!'

The CIA operatives fell silent. Over the faint sigh of the wind, a new sound became audible: a deep percussive rumble. The chop of heavy-duty rotor blades.

Growing louder.

'Dammit, it's a Hind!' said Arnold, recognising the distinctive thrum of a Soviet-made Mil Mi-24 gunship. 'What the hell's it doing here? We're in the no-fly zone – why haven't our guys shot it down?'

'We first saw it two days ago,' said Kerim. 'It flies low, very low.'

'So it gets lost in the ground clutter,' said Arnold. 'Clever.'

'More like lucky,' Cross corrected. 'Our AWACS should still pick it up.'

'We've got some new intel, then,' Rosemont said with a wry smile. 'They need to point their radar in this direction.'

Arnold tried to locate the approaching gunship. 'Speaking of direction, is it comin' in ours?'

'Can't tell. Get the NVGs from the truck . . . Shit!' A horrible realisation hit Rosemont. 'The truck, we've got to move it! If they see it—'

'On it!' cried Arnold, sprinting for the Toyota. 'I'll hide it in the ruins.'

'They might still see its tracks,' warned Cross.

'We'll have to chance it,' Rosemont told him. 'Kerim! Get your men into cover over there.' He pointed towards the remains of the building.

The Ma'dan leader did not take well to being given orders. 'No! We will not go into that place!'

'Superstition might get you killed.'

'The helicopter will not see us if we hide in the reeds,' Kerim insisted.

'Let them stay,' said Cross dismissively. 'We need to move.'

'Agreed,' said Rosemont, putting the LAW back into its case.

The Toyota's engine started, then sand kicked from its tyres as Arnold swung it towards the ruins. 'Come on.'

Gear jolting on their equipment webbing, they ran after the 4x4, leaving the Marsh Arabs behind. It took almost half a minute over the uneven ground to reach cover, the outer edge of the ruins marked by the jagged base of a pillar sticking up from the sands like a broken tooth. By now, Arnold had stopped the Toyota beside the main structure, its wheels in the water. He jumped out. 'Where's the chopper?'

Rosemont looked over a wall. He couldn't see the helicopter itself, but caught the flash of its navigation lights. A reflection told him that it was less than thirty feet above the water. A couple of seconds later, the lights flared again, revealing that while the Hind wasn't heading straight at them, it would make landfall a couple of hundred metres beyond Kerim's position.

'If it's got its nav lights on, they don't know we're here,' said Cross. 'They'd have gone dark if they were on an attack run.'

'Yeah, but they gotta be using night vision to fly that low without a spotlight,' Arnold warned. 'They might still see us.'

The helicopter neared the shore, the roar of its engines getting louder. Tension rose amongst the three men. The Hind was travelling in a straight line; if it suddenly slowed or altered course, they would know they had been spotted.

The gunship's thunder reached a crescendo . . .

And passed. It crossed the shore and continued across the barren plain, a gritty whirlwind rising in its wake.

Arnold blew out a relieved whistle. 'God damn. That was close.'

Rosemont kept watching the retreating strobes. 'Let's give it a minute to make sure it's gone – Cross, what the hell? Turn that light out!'

Cross was shining his flashlight over the ruined structure. 'I want to see this.'

'Yeah, and the guys in that chopper might see *you*!'

'They won't. Look, there's a way in.' A dark opening was revealed in the dirty stone; an arched entrance, still intact. Cross waded into the lake, the water rising up his shins as he approached the passage. 'There's something written above it.' Characters carved into the stonework stood out in the beam from his flashlight.

'What does it say?' asked Arnold, moving to the water's edge.

Rosemont reluctantly joined him. 'I don't know what language that is,' he said, indicating a line of angular runes running across the top of the opening, 'but the letters above it? I think they're Hebrew. No idea what they say, though.'

'We should find out.' Cross aimed his light into the entrance, revealing a short tunnel beyond, then stepped deeper into the water.

'Cross, get back – God damn it,' Rosemont growled as the other man ducked through the entrance. He traded exasperated looks with Arnold. 'Wait here and watch for the chopper. I'll get him.'

He splashed into the lake. Cross had by now disappeared inside the ruined structure, spill from his flashlight washing back up the tunnel. 'Cross! Get out of there. We've got a job to do.'

There was no reply. Annoyed, Rosemont sluiced through the opening and made his way into the building's heart, turning on his own flashlight. The water rose to his knees. 'Hey! When I tell you to—'

He stopped in amazement.

The room was not large, only a few metres along each wall. But it had clearly been a place of great importance to its builders. Stone columns coated in flaked gilding supported each corner of the ceiling, bands of pure gold and silver around them inset with numerous gemstones. Not even the grime left by the long submersion in the lake could diminish their splendour. The walls themselves were covered in the skeletal ancient text he had seen outside. There were more Hebrew passages too, but the other language occupied so much space that these were relegated to separate tablets laid out around the room's waterlogged perimeter.

It was obvious what the temple had been built to house. The wall opposite the entrance contained a niche a little over a foot high, more gold lining it. Above it was a faded painting, a stylised seven-branched menorah – a Hebrew lampstand – with several letters over it. Carvings resembling the sun's rays directed Rosemont's eyes to its contents.

A strange stone figure filled the nook. Its body was human – but the head was that of a lion. Wrapped tightly around the statuette's torso, shrouding it like wings, were several metal sheets embossed with a pattern resembling eyes.

Cross stood at the alcove, examining the artefact. 'Do you see it?' he gasped. 'Do you *see* it?'

'Yeah, I see it,' Rosemont replied. There was a new edge to the other man's voice that he had never heard before, a breathless excitement – no, *wonderment*. 'What is it?'

Cross gave his superior a glance that was somewhere between pity and disdain. 'You *don't* see it, otherwise you'd know.'

'Okay, then enlighten me.'

'An apt choice of words.' He leaned closer for a better look at the leonine head. 'It's an angel.'

'Yeah, I can see that, I guess. It does kinda look like an angel.'

'No, you don't understand. It doesn't just *look* like an angel. It *is* an angel! Exactly as described in the Book of Revelation! Chapter four, verse six – "Four beasts full of eyes before and behind. And the first beast was like a lion." And there's more: "And the four beasts had each of them six wings about him."' He crouched, the water sloshing up to his chest. 'There's something written on its side. I know what it says.'

'You can read it?' asked Rosemont, surprised.

'No – but I still know what it says. Revelation chapter four, verse eight – "And they rest not, day and night, saying 'Holy, holy, holy, Lord God Almighty, which was, and is, and is to come.'" They aren't *speaking* day and night – the words are written on them, always visible. That's what it means!'

'That's what *what* means?'

'Revelation! I understand it, it's all coming to me . . .' Cross stared at the angel, then turned to face Rosemont. The older agent was momentarily startled by his expression, an almost messianic light burning in his eyes. 'You said this lake was a meteorite crater. Revelation chapter eight, verse ten – "There fell a great star from heaven, burning as if it were a lamp." Wormwood, the falling star; it's describing a fireball, a meteor strike – and this is it, this is where it landed! It's the bottomless pit!' He faced the alcove once more. 'The prophecy, it's true . . .'

'All right, so you've had a vision from God,' said Rosemont, his discomfort replaced by impatience. 'We've still got a mission to carry out. This is a job for archaeologists, not the CIA – let Indiana Jones take care of it. We need to get Kerim's intel on those Iraqi positions.'

'You do that,' Cross replied as he took out a compact digital camera. 'This is more important.'

'The hell it is.' Rosemont stepped closer as Cross took a photo of the alcove and the surrounding text-covered wall. 'You're coming with me, right now—'

'Mike!' Arnold's shout reached them from outside. 'The chopper, it's coming back!'

'Shit,' said Rosemont. The Iraqis had probably spotted the Toyota's tracks cutting across the dried-up marshlands. 'Okay, Bible study's over – move out!'

He splashed back down the tunnel, readying his rifle. Cross hesitated, then almost reverently took the angel from its niche, finding it surprisingly heavy for its size, and followed.

The two men joined Arnold near the broken pillar. 'They've turned out their nav lights,' he warned.

Rosemont listened. The pulsing thunder again grew louder, coming from somewhere to the south-east. He couldn't see the aircraft, but with night-vision gear, its pilot's view of the lake would be as clear as in daylight. 'We need to get away from the ruins.'

'You sure? The walls'll give us cover—'

'Not against rockets. The moment they see the truck, they'll assume we're inside and blow the hell out of the place! Spread out and try to reach Kerim's people.' He started to move, then caught sight of what Cross was carrying. 'What the hell are you doing?'

'I can't leave it behind,' Cross replied.

'Put it down and take up your weapon! That's an order, Cross!'

The two men glared at each other, neither willing to back down . . . then the deadlock was broken by Arnold's cry. '*Incoming!*'

A flash of fiery light in the sky – and something streaked overhead. The CIA agents threw themselves flat—

The rocket hit the Toyota, the truck exploding in a dazzling fireball. Two more missiles hit the temple itself, shattering stonework and causing the roof to collapse with a crash that shook the surrounding sands. Then the gunship blasted over the ruin, swinging into a wide loop above the lake.

'Is everyone okay?' Rosemont called. His two companions responded in the affirmative.

'We lost the truck,' said Arnold unhappily, looking back at the burning wreck. 'How are we gonna get out of here?'

'We'll walk if we have to,' said Rosemont, 'but let's worry about staying alive first.' He glanced towards Kerim's position.

'We've still got two LAWs over there. We might be able to bring down that chopper.'

Arnold was not convinced. 'It'd take a miracle.'

'God's on our side,' said Cross, unshakeable conviction in his voice. He held up the angel. 'We found this for a reason. The Lord won't let us die now.'

'We need firepower, not faith!' said Rosemont. 'Leave that damn thing here – we've got to get those rockets.' Cross gave him an affronted look, then reluctantly placed the angel at the foot of the pillar. 'Okay, Gabe, find Kerim. Cross, with me.'

The agents set off at a run. Rosemont searched for the Hind over the dark water, but saw nothing. He could tell from the changing pitch of its engine note that it was turning around, though – another attack could come at any moment—

More fire in the sky – and dusty geysers erupted as cannon fire ripped across the shoreline. The gunner had spotted the Ma'dan and opened up as the Mi-24 swept in. The Marsh Arabs returned fire, muzzle flashes bursting from the reeds, but the AKs were useless against the Hind's thick armour. Tracer rounds homed in on the gunmen and hit home, screams rising over the helicopter's clamour as bodies were shredded by a storm of explosive shells.

Cross and Rosemont dived to the ground. The gunship roared over the shore, then vanished into the blackness once again. Kalashnikovs crackled after it in futile rage.

Rosemont raised his head. 'Jesus Christ!' He felt Cross bristle at the blasphemy, but had no time or inclination to consider anyone's religious sensitivities. 'We've got to get those LAWs before these bastards cut us to pieces.'

They ran again, men racing past them in the other direction; fear of whatever haunted the temple had been overpowered by an instinctive urge to seek cover behind solid stone. The two agents vaulted the torn remains of several Ma'dan. 'There!'

said Cross, spotting the campfire's still-glowing embers.

Rosemont picked out the two crates in the moonlight. 'We only get one chance at this.'

'We'll do it.' Cross snatched up the LAW from the open case as Rosemont retrieved the second weapon from the other. Both tugged out the pins to release their launchers' rear covers, then pulled hard to extend the firing tubes—

'*Incoming!*' Arnold cried.

The agents dropped again as the Hind swept in along the lake's edge. Rockets lanced from its wing pods, explosions ripping down the shore. More screams, some abruptly cut off as another fusillade scattered mangled bodies.

'*No!*' Cross cried as the line of detonations reached the ruins—

The saw-toothed pillar disintegrated in a flash of flame. More rockets hammered what remained of the temple into rubble, then the Mi-24 veered back out over the lake.

Rosemont jumped up, raising the LAW to his shoulder. He peered through the sight, fingers resting on the rubber trigger bar. 'Cross! It's coming back around – get ready!'

But the other man was staring in horror towards the ruins. 'No,' he whispered. 'The angel can't have been destroyed. It *can't*!'

'Worry about your damn angel later. We've got—' Rosemont broke off as a new sight was picked out by the flickering light of burning reeds.

Something was swelling on the shore, a dirty mustard-yellow mass. It took a moment for the CIA leader to realise that it was a *cloud*, some sort of gas boiling up from the edge of the ruins. But it was like nothing he had ever seen before; far thicker and heavier than the smoke from the vegetation, almost like a liquid as it churned and spread outwards.

It reached a dazed Ma'dan, roiled around him – and the man

screamed. Clutching at his face, he tried to run, but could only manage a drunken stagger before collapsing. The still-expanding cloud swallowed him, and his cries became a gurgling wail of agony before abruptly falling silent. Other men nearby joined the terrifying chorus as the gas reached them.

Rosemont's eyes widened in fear. 'Holy shit, they're using *chemical weapons*! MOPP gear – suit up! *Suit up!*'

The United States had long accused Saddam's regime of possessing weapons of mass destruction, and now it appeared that the proof was rolling towards them as the deadly cloud kept growing. The CIA agents had come prepared, their webbing holding a pack containing Mission-Oriented Protective Posture clothing – an oversuit, gloves and mask to protect against nuclear, chemical and biological agents – but they had not expected to need them.

Panic rose in both men as they dropped the LAWs, shrugged off their gear and tore open the pouches. More sounds of terror and death reached them as the sulphurous fog spread, swamping the fleeing tribesmen. Cross worked his arms into the thick nylon overalls and tugged them up over his shoulders, then hurriedly pulled on the gas mask before zipping up the garment and drawing the hood over his head. Rosemont sealed his own outer covering a few seconds later, closing the hood tightly around his mask before starting to don his gloves. He looked back down the shore—

'Gabe!' he cried, seeing a familiar figure in the firelight.

Arnold was thirty metres away, desperately trying to secure his gas mask as he ran. Its straps were twisted, costing valuable seconds as he attempted to straighten them. At last he managed it and raised the hood, but his hands were still uncovered.

He pulled on one glove, fumbling with the other as the cloud reached him—

Contact with exposed skin was enough to kill, Rosemont saw

with horror. Arnold suddenly grabbed at his unprotected hand, clawing it as if being bitten by a million insects. His shriek was clearly audible even through the mask. Then he dropped, writhing in the sand before the yellow haze consumed him.

The Marsh Arabs all suffered the same fate as the wind carried the cloud along the lake's edge. Kerim was among the last to fall, firing his AK-47 into the malevolent yellow mass in a final act of defiance before he too succumbed.

His second glove secured, Rosemont was about to run from the approaching miasma when he remembered that there were still other threats to deal with. The Hind's roar grew louder. 'The rockets!' he yelled to the fully suited Cross. 'Get the rockets!'

They retrieved the LAWs. There was nothing to aim at in the black sky, and with their thickly lined hoods up, it was hard to pinpoint the source of the noise. Rosemont took his best guess and stared down the sights, the mask's eyepiece smearing his vision. 'Wait for it,' he told his companion. 'Wait . . .'

Staccato bursts of flame as the Mil's cannon fired—

'Now!'

Rosemont squeezed the trigger bar. The rocket shot from the launcher with a loud bang, the back-blast smacking up a rooster tail of dust behind him.

But Cross hadn't moved. 'Fire, *now!*' Rosemont shouted, watching the orange spot of the rocket's motor race towards the gunship—

The Hind suddenly banked hard. The pilot had seen the incoming missile and was taking evasive action. Rosemont cursed as he realised his shot was going to miss . . .

Cross finally fired – and Rosemont realised why he had hesitated for a crucial moment. The Hind had swerved away from the first missile . . . but would fly right into the path of the second.

The cannon fire ceased, the Hind disappearing against the black sky. The first rocket continued pointlessly along its course, but the second was still angling to meet the aircraft. The engine note changed, the pilot applying full power as he tried to climb away from the incoming missile—

A flash – and for a split-second the Hind was fully illuminated as the LAW struck home.

It exploded against the helicopter's tail boom. The Mil's heaviest armour was concentrated around the cockpit and engines, but even if it had covered the entire fuselage it would not have been enough to stop a dedicated anti-tank round. The warhead ripped a jagged hole through the chopper's flank, severing the mechanical linkage to the tail rotor.

The result was instantaneous.

Without the smaller rotor to counteract the enormous torque of the main blades, the Hind was hurled into an uncontrollable spin. Engines screaming, the helicopter cartwheeled overhead, Cross and Rosemont both ducking as it hurtled past. It smashed into the ground barely fifty metres beyond them, the mangled remains tumbling through the sand in a searing ball of flaming aviation fuel.

Rosemont lifted his head, heart pounding at the close call – only to freeze in fear as the yellow cloud rolled over the two men.

Everything went dark. He didn't dare move, or even breathe, terrified that doing so would open up a gap in his hastily donned protective gear and let in the poisonous fog . . .

Seconds passed. No pain. He risked a breath. The mysterious chemical agent had not found a way to his lungs. 'Cross!' he gasped. 'Are you okay?'

No reply. Worry rose at the thought of being trapped far behind enemy lines, alone – then he heard a voice. 'Yeah. I'm fine.'

Another gasp, this time of relief. 'That was a hell of a shot.'

'I was a championship hunter before I joined the Marines. I hit what I aim at.'

'Good to know. Your suit's holding?'

'So far.'

'Whatever this stuff is, MOPP-1 can resist it.' He carefully moved in the direction of the other man's voice until his fingertips made contact with Cross's suit. 'I guess we've got our smoking gun. Saddam *has* got chemical weapons, and is willing to use them. We have to call this in.' He reached for his radio before remembering that it had been attached to his discarded webbing.

'I don't think this was anything to do with Saddam,' said Cross thoughtfully.

'What do you mean? You saw it – one of that 'copter's rockets blew up and released it.'

'No, it blew up, but the gas came from something else.' Cross suddenly gripped his wrist. 'It came from the angel! We've got to find it.'

'If it got hit by a rocket, there won't be anything left bigger than your pinky,' Rosemont pointed out. He made out the other man's shape as visibility started to return. 'Help me find the radio.'

'This is more important. Don't you see? Revelation chapter nine, verse two – "And there arose a smoke out of the pit—"'

'I don't give a damn what the Book of Revelations says!' Rosemont barked. 'This isn't Sunday school; this is a Special Activities Division operation. You're an agent, not a preacher; now shut the hell up and carry out the mission!'

Cross regarded him for a moment, his face unreadable behind the mask, then he turned away. 'Don't you walk away from – son of a bitch!' Rosemont yelled after him. 'You're finished, you hear me?'

★ ★ ★

Cross ignored Rosemont's angry shouts as he jogged back towards the ruins. The wind had shifted, wafting the yellow mass off the shore and out over the lake. The fires from the crashed helicopter and the burning reed beds cast a hellish glow across the landscape.

Appropriate, he thought. From the moment he first saw the angel inside the temple, he was absolutely sure, more than he had ever been about anything, that he knew what he had found – and what it meant.

But there had been only one angel. According to the Book of Revelation, there were three more. So where were they?

He approached the spot where the broken pillar had stood. The only thing there now was a rubble-strewn crater.

From which the gas was still rising.

He reached the edge of the gouge in the earth. A shallow pool of dark water was at the bottom. Amongst the debris around it, his light picked out a shape that was clearly not natural. Part of the statue. One of its wings was still attached, but the embossed metal that had been wrapped around the angel's body was now twisted and torn where the figure had been smashed by the explosion, exposing a darker core hidden inside.

The strange gas was belching from this black stone. The wind was enough to blow it clear, though he resisted the temptation to remove his mask for a better look. The sight put him in mind of a smoke grenade, but . . .

'Where's it all coming from?' he whispered. Smoke grenades contained enough chemicals to produce a screen for ninety seconds at most, but this was pumping out a colossal volume, and showed no signs of stopping.

He stepped down cautiously into the pit. A sound became audible even through his hood's charcoal-impregnated lining, a sizzling like fatty bacon on a grill. The dark material at the statue's heart almost appeared to be boiling, blistering with countless tiny bubbles, each releasing more gas as it burst.

Another wisp of the gas to one side caught his eye. A chunk of the broken statue, smaller than his little finger, had landed at the very edge of the pool. He crouched to examine it. There was a sliver of the dark material embedded in the cracked ceramic shell, partially beneath the water's surface. The exposed section was burning away just like its larger counterpart, consuming itself in some reaction with the air. As he watched, the top of the splinter spat and bubbled to nothingness . . . and the thin line of yellow smoke died away.

Intrigued, Cross gently lifted the fragment from the water. It was warm, even through his glove. After a moment, the strange substance fizzed and puffed a new strand of yellow fumes into the wind. He dipped it back into the puddle. The reaction stopped.

A light swept over him. 'Cross!' called Rosemont from the crater's lip. 'What the hell are you doing?'

'I found the angel,' Cross replied, climbing out to meet him and indicating the larger hunk of the statue. 'That's where the smoke's coming from. It wasn't a chemical weapon; it was here all along, hidden in the temple. Waiting for us to find it. Waiting for *me* to find it.'

Rosemont shone his flashlight over the broken figure. It was still belching out its seemingly endless plume of oily yellow gas. 'Damn. What the hell *is* that?'

'It's a messenger from God. Look.' Cross illuminated the little pool. The dark water was revealed as a bloody red, the discoloration spreading outwards from the fragment like ink across damp paper. '"And the third part of the sea became blood . . ."'

The lead agent snapped his light at Cross's face. 'I don't want to hear one more goddamn Bible quote out of you, okay? This whole situation has gotten way out of control.'

'I know what we have to do. We have to take the angel out of here.'

'Are you out of your mind?' Rosemont protested. 'It killed Gabe, it killed Kerim and all his men! We're not taking it anywhere.'

'Putting it in water stops the smoke. If we find a container, we can transport it—'

'Water, huh?' Rosemont jumped into the crater. Before Cross could intervene, he had hauled the remains of the angel from the ground. The toxic gas swirled around him as he stomped back out of the pit, heading to the lake's edge.

'What are you doing?' Cross demanded as he followed.

'Making this safe.' He drew back his arm – and hurled the statue out into the water.

'No!' yelled Cross, but it was too late. The broken figure spun through the air, a poisonous vortex spiralling in its wake, before it splashed down some sixty feet from the shoreline. Both men stared at the water until the ripples subsided.

Rosemont turned back to Cross. 'Right. Now we radio in and—'

He froze. Cross had raised his gun and was pointing it at his chest. 'You shouldn't have done that,' said the Virginian in a voice that, while level, was straining with anger. 'You've just interfered with God's plan.'

'God's plan?' said Rosemont, trying to control his fear. 'What the hell are you talking about?'

'The Day of Judgement. It's coming. The first angel bound at the Euphrates has been released. The seals will be broken, the seven trumpets will sound, and . . .' He paused, new realisation filling him with greedy wonder. 'And the mystery of God should be finished . . .'

Rosemont shook his head. 'You're crazy. Lower your weapon, right now, or—'

Cross pulled the trigger.

A single bullet ripped through Rosemont's heart and exploded out from his back. Eyes wide in shock behind his mask, he crumpled to the ground.

Cross stared at the dead man, his face unreadable, then bent to take his radio. He set it to an emergency frequency. 'Wintergreen, Wintergreen, this is Maven,' he said, using the operation's code names. 'Wintergreen, this is Maven. Come in.'

A female voice responded. 'This is Wintergreen. We read you, Maven. Sitrep.'

'Mission failure, I repeat, mission failure. We were ambushed – the Iraqis had a gunship on patrol. Rosemont and Arnold are dead. So are our contacts.'

A pause. When the woman replied, it was with clear concern even through the fuzz of the scrambled transmission. 'Everyone's dead?'

'Yes, everyone but me. Our transport was destroyed. I need immediate evac.'

'We can't give you evac with a gunship in the air.'

'It's been shot down. I need to get out of here before they come to see what happened to it.'

A long silence as the controller conferred with a superior. Finally, she responded: 'Okay, Maven, can you reach Point Charlie?' A backup rendezvous point some miles to the south. 'If you hole up there, we'll get an extraction team to you asap.'

'I'll make it,' Cross answered. 'I'll contact you when I arrive.'

'Roger that, Maven. Good luck.' She paused again, then added in a softer voice: 'I'm sorry about Mike and Gabe.'

'So am I,' said Cross, giving Rosemont's corpse an emotionless glance. 'Maven out.'

He switched off the radio, then surveyed the area. The cloud had now mostly dispersed, but he didn't risk removing his MOPP gear; there were still drifting patches of haze in the air.

Instead he returned to where he had donned the suit to retrieve his equipment webbing. There was a water flask attached; he took it, then went back to the crater.

The small sliver of the angel was still submerged in the blood-red water. He removed the flask's cap, then carefully picked up the shard and dropped it inside before it started to smoke again. The thought occurred that he should find one of the dead agents' canteens, as there was no way of knowing how long it would be before he was rescued, but he dismissed it. He knew he would find what he needed to survive. "'For the Lamb which is in the midst of the throne shall lead them unto living fountains of waters . . .'" he said quietly as he firmly refastened the cap.

His cargo secured, he set out into the wilderness.

1

New York City

Twelve Years Later

'Has everything I've done in my life been worth it?'
Nina Wilde sat facing Dr Elaine Senzer, but her eyes were lowered, avoiding the psychiatrist's gaze. Instead she fixated on small, irrelevant details – a scuff on the other woman's shoe, indentations on the carpet where her chair had been moved – as she tried to put her fears into words. 'That's the question I've been asking myself recently,' she went on. 'And the thing that's worrying me is . . . is that I'm not sure it has.'

Elaine leaned forward, adjusting her glasses. 'I'm curious why you'd say that. You've already achieved more in your life than most people – I mean, it's fair to say that you're the most famous archaeologist in the world. You found Atlantis, you discovered the lost city of El Dorado and a hidden Egyptian pyramid, and all those other amazing things. That's something to be proud of, surely?'

'Is it?' Nina caught herself leaning back in her seat, as if subconsciously trying to maintain the distance between them. 'Yeah, I found all those things – and I got a lot of people killed in the process. Too many people.'

'You didn't kill them personally.'

'Some of them I did.' Even without looking directly at Elaine, she could sense the psychiatrist's shock at the revelation. 'They were trying to kill *me*, it was always in self-defence . . . but yeah, I've killed people. And you know what's really scary? I've lost count of how many.'

Elaine hurriedly scribbled a note. 'I see.'

Nina gave her a grim smile. 'You're not going to have me committed to Bellevue, are you?'

'No, no,' the dark-haired woman hastily assured her. 'I actually think it's good that you feel able to tell me about it at this relatively early stage. If you remember, when we started these sessions last month, it was quite a challenge for you to open up about anything at all. The very nature of post-traumatic stress causes sufferers to try to internalise it – there's a great deal of anger, guilt—'

'Tell me about it,' Nina muttered.

'I'm afraid it doesn't work that way,' said Elaine, with sympathy. 'You have to tell me.'

'You want me to tell you about my guilt?' Nina snapped. 'Okay – about four months ago, one of my friends was murdered right in front of me. And it was all my fault! Macy wouldn't have been there if not for me . . .' Her voice faded to inaudibility.

A long silence was eventually broken by the psychiatrist. 'Nina . . . are you okay?'

'If I was okay, I wouldn't be seeing a shrink, would I?' the redhead replied, wiping her eyes. 'What kind of a stupid question is that?'

Elaine shrugged off the insult with professional calm. 'Tell me about Macy. I know you're reluctant, but I really think it would help. Please,' she added, seeing her patient clench her fists. 'In your own time; you don't have to say anything if you don't want to.'

'For a hundred and fifty bucks an hour, I'm not going to sit here in silence. I could do that for free at Starbucks, and the coffee would be better.' Nina took a deep breath, then a second, before continuing. 'Macy . . . she was an archaeology student when I first met her. She had a case of' – a brief smile at the memory – 'hero worship.' Her expression darkened once more. 'Spending time with me soon cured her of that.'

'But she *was* your friend,' Elaine said.

'Yes. She could be annoying – God, she could be annoying! – but yeah, she was. She was young, that was all. And she thought life was there to be enjoyed, so she went all out to enjoy it.'

'Whereas you . . . ?'

A wry shake of the head, her shoulder-length hair swinging. 'I'm not exactly a party animal. Never have been. But Macy threw herself head-first into everything. And that . . .' Her voice broke. 'That got her killed.'

'How so?'

'She invited herself along on my last job for the International Heritage Agency. I could have said no, sent her home. But I didn't. I don't know why, maybe because . . . maybe because I was afraid it might be the last chance I had to spend time with her.'

Elaine flicked back through her notebook. 'Your illness – you thought it was terminal at that point?'

Nina nodded. She had been under a slow death sentence, poisoned by a toxin from deep within the earth. 'Yeah. There was a treatment, but I didn't know about it then.' She kept the full truth to herself: that the 'treatment' was nothing less than the legendary fountain of immortality sought by Alexander the Great. After the horrors she had been through to find it, she had vowed to keep its location a secret, to prevent the inevitable further bloodshed if others fought to control it. 'So I let Macy come with us, and . . .' She choked up.

'Are you all right?' Elaine asked. 'Do you need a Kleenex or something?'

Nina rubbed away a tear. 'No, no. I'm okay. It's just, talking about it . . .'

'I understand.'

'It's . . .' Nina sat sharply upright, looking Elaine straight in the eye for the first time. 'It's not *fair*! She was so young, she was practically still a kid! And this man, this *bastard*, killed her like she was nothing – just to get to me. If I hadn't gotten involved, or if I'd done what I should have done and told Macy to go home, she'd still be alive! I got her *killed*!'

She slumped forward, head in her hands, trying to hold in her sobs. Elaine looked on with concern. 'Nina, I'm so, so sorry. But you must know deep down that's not true. You didn't kill your friend. Someone else did.'

Nina forced out a reply. 'If it wasn't for me, she'd still be alive. The same goes for Rowan Sharpe, and Jim McCrimmon, and Ismail Assad and Hector Amoros and Chloe Lamb and – and so many others I can't even remember all their names!' She looked up in despair. 'This is what I mean, Elaine. Yes, I made all those discoveries – but this was the cost. Hundreds of people have died because of me.'

'It can't be that many,' Elaine said, though with uncertainty.

'Trust me, I was there. My whole career, everything I've accomplished, has been surrounded by death and destruction. Even when I was still a kid, my parents died – were murdered – while they were hunting for Atlantis. Which is why I've been asking: was it all worth it?' She looked down at her abdomen, where a small but distinct swelling revealed the presence of her unborn child. 'Do I want to bring a kid into my world? What right have I got to put a baby at that kind of risk?'

'But you're not working for the IHA any more,' Elaine pointed out.

'Maybe, but you know what?' Nina said with another flare of anger. 'Last month, a Nazi tried to kill me, right here in New York!'

The psychiatrist's eyes widened. 'A . . . Nazi?'

'Yeah, an actual goddamn Nazi. You see? I can't get away from this shit! I tried to, I just wanted to stay out of trouble and write my book, but it keeps finding me!'

'Your book,' said Elaine, relieved at a chance to change the subject. 'How's that going? You told me last time that you'd been having difficulty maintaining focus . . .'

Nina huffed sarcastically. 'Oh, it's going super fine, better than ever. No, I'm now almost completely blocked. My publishers are gonna be thrilled that they've paid over half a million dollars for three and a quarter chapters. Some people I know in Hollywood want to buy the screen rights.' Macy's boyfriend, the film star Grant Thorn, had unsurprisingly withdrawn from the idea after the young woman's funeral, but his business partner had since made tentative enquiries about reopening negotiations. 'Right now, though, it'd make a really short movie.'

'Why are you blocked?'

'Why? Because every time I start trying to write about what I've discovered, it makes me think of the people who died in the process. It's . . .' She sagged, feeling emotionally drained. 'I can't move forward.'

'In what way?'

'In every way. With my life. All I keep thinking about is whether it's all been worth it, and I don't know the answer, and . . . and I'm stuck. Going nowhere.'

'But you are going somewhere,' said Elaine. 'You've made progress over just the last month – you realised you were in denial over Macy's death, and the fact that you sought help from a therapist shows that you're able to start moving on.'

'I might be *able* to start, but that doesn't mean I *have* started. On that, or anything else. The book's stalled, I can't even do something as simple as come up with baby names . . .'

'Do you know the sex?'

'Yeah. I had an ultrasound last week, and they could tell what it was. My husband, Eddie, told them not to say anything – he wants it to be a surprise – but I snuck back in and asked. It's a—'

Elaine held up her hands. 'No, no. I'm like your husband, I like surprises too. I didn't know what either of my kids was going to be until they were born.'

'I guess I prefer to plan everything in advance. He's more the make-it-up-as-you-go type.'

'So how have things been between you since you learned you were pregnant? Has he been showing any tension, or . . .'

'No, no.' Nina shook her head. '*He's* been great – he's absolutely thrilled at the prospect of having a kid, and he's been doing everything he can to help me. No, it's . . . it's me.' She sighed. 'I'm angry, I'm depressed, I'm confused – I'm a hundred and one negative things, and I'm taking all of them out on him.'

'Why?'

'Because there isn't anyone else. Since I left the IHA, it's just been me and him. I've been horrible, and I know it, but . . . but I can't help it.'

A sympathetic nod. 'Pregnancy hormones can really affect your mood. It's often a lot harder with a first pregnancy, because you don't know what to expect. It's good that he's been so supportive.'

'Maybe, but . . .' A lengthy pause as she struggled to make a terrible admission. 'I can't help thinking that he's putting up with it for the baby rather than for me.'

'But do you really believe that, Nina? Deep down, I mean?'

'I don't know. I don't know what I believe about *anything* right now.' She stared back at the marks on the carpet.

The psychiatrist made more notes before speaking again. 'I don't know your husband, but from what you've told me, it certainly seems that he loves you. He wants to help you, but you're reluctant to allow it. That's understandable – you've been through a traumatic experience, and you've put up barriers to protect yourself from further harm. The problem is that you're not letting anyone through them, even the person who cares about you the most.'

Nina managed a sarcastic grin. 'Well, duh. I didn't need a psychiatrist to figure that out. I need one to tell me how to *deal* with it.'

'I can't tell you to do anything, Nina. I can suggest, and advise, but in the end only you can come up with the answer. Although one thing I would suggest is couples therapy. If you both came in together, we could address some of these issues.'

Another mocking little smile. 'Eddie seeing a shrink? I can't imagine that ever happening. He has his own ways of dealing with things . . .'

The helicopter dived towards the Statue of Liberty. Eddie Chase gripped the controls, trying to regain height—

'Little advice, Eddie? Remember that thing I showed you called the stick? You might wanna pull it back.'

'Oh. Yeah.' Grimacing, Eddie brought the cyclic control joystick towards him. The Bell 206L LongRanger's nose came up, and the aircraft unsteadily levelled out. 'That okay?'

'You didn't crash into Lady Liberty's face, so yeah. But we oughta go back out over open water. I'm havin' some bad flashbacks to when I first met you!' Harvey Zampelli took the controls, bringing the red, white and blue helicopter around across the great expanse of New York Bay. The spires of Manhattan rolled into view as he notified air traffic control of his course.

'Well, it's only my second lesson,' said the stocky, balding Yorkshireman once the exchange in his headphones had concluded. 'And I haven't crashed it yet, so I'm not doing too bad.'

Harvey quickly touched the cross hanging from his neck on a chunky gold chain. 'Jeez, don't say things like that! It's bad luck.'

Eddie decided not to tell him how many plane crashes he'd been involved in. 'Thanks again for letting me do this,' he said instead. 'I've been meaning to learn to fly for ages.'

'Hey, no problem,' the black-haired pilot replied. 'I mean, jeez, you saved my life! That's gotta be worth the price of some avgas. I sure as hell hope so, anyway! Right? Right?' He laughed, then added, with a hint of insecurity: 'Right?'

'Right,' Eddie told him with a grin that revealed the gap between his front teeth. 'But it's not a problem for you, is it? Doing this in the middle of the day, I mean.'

'Nah, I had an empty slot, and if there ain't any paying customers, I gotta leave her sitting on the pad with the engine running anyway.' The LongRanger's flight had begun from the heliport at Manhattan's southern tip; Harvey's aircraft was one of the many offering tourist tours around New York.

'Isn't that expensive?'

'Not as expensive as having to do a full check every time I shut down and restart the engine. Quicker, too. Besides, I'm a pilot. Any chance to fly, I'm gonna take it!' He laughed again, then surveyed the surrounding airspace. 'Okay, take the controls. Remember what I told you – keep the cyclic tipped forward to maintain airspeed, but don't push it too far or we'll lose height. We wanna stay between a thousand and fifteen hundred feet. Got it?'

Eddie checked the altimeter, then closed his hands around the two control sticks. 'Yeah.'

Harvey raised his own hands. 'Okay, all yours.'

The Englishman gingerly edged the cyclic forward. He had

flown as a passenger in numerous helicopters during his military career with the elite Special Air Service, and in many more since, but his only attempts to fly an aircraft himself had been when the pilot was incapacitated, or dead. Which, he mused, had happened alarmingly often.

Today, though, nobody was trying to kill him. Operating a chopper even in peaceful conditions was still tricky, however. The Bell twitched and squirmed with every shift in the wind, and the fuselage felt as if it were swinging from the rotor hub like a hanging basket. But he held it steady, making slight adjustments to balance the airspeed indicator and altimeter.

'You're doing fine,' said Harvey. 'Okay, we're gonna follow the land.' He indicated the shores of New Jersey and Staten Island. 'Use the pedals like I showed you before, real easy.'

Eddie carefully depressed one of the anti-torque pedals, adjusting the power being fed to the tail rotor. The helicopter slowly turned. 'That okay?'

'Yeah, that's great – whoa, hold on.' A new voice came through Eddie's headphones: one of the heliport's staff, telling Harvey that he had a phone call. 'Eddie, I gotta take this. Just keep doing what you're doing.'

The Englishman gave him an okay as the call came through. 'Lena, hey hey!' said Harvey, his Bronx accent becoming even more rapid-fire. 'How you doin'? Great night last night, huh?'

Eddie tried not to be distracted by what very quickly became a personal conversation, concentrating on following the shoreline. The huge jetties of the New Jersey container terminal rolled by. He glanced down at them, only to realise with alarm when he looked back at the instruments that the altimeter was falling towards the thousand-foot mark. He moved the cyclic, but the descent continued. 'Oh bollocks.'

'Babe, I gotta call you back,' said Harvey over the headset. 'I got a slight altitude deficiency situation here.' He laughed, then ended the call. 'All right, man, I got this.' He retook the controls, bringing the LongRanger back into a climb. 'Sorry 'bout that. Women, huh? Gotta love 'em, but . . .' He briefly took one hand off the throttle to mime a duck quacking. 'Damn, that reminds me, I gotta make another call.'

There was a cellphone connected to the cabin's communication system by a cable; he thumbed through its contacts list. 'Lana, hey, it's Harv,' he said after connecting. Eddie was again an unwilling eavesdropper. 'Yeah, sorry about last night. I had to stay late at the hangar to deal with some FAA paperwork. How 'bout I make it up to you tonight, huh? Yeah, that place on Leland. Nina o'clock? Epic. See you then. Bye, babe.'

'Lena and Lana, eh?' said Eddie.

Harvey nodded. 'Yeah. I gotta be *so* careful not to get their names mixed up! That might cause problems.'

A sardonic smile. 'You're not kidding.'

'You ever been a juggler like that?'

Eddie shook his head. 'Not me. One woman's always been enough for me. More than enough sometimes.'

'You've had problems?'

'Well, my first wife wanted to kill me. And I mean she literally tried to murder me.'

Harvey made a face. 'Yow!'

'Yeah. Nina . . . well, at the moment it sometimes seems like she wants to as well.'

'You want my advice? First hint of bunny-boiling, run, run, run! Life's too short to be dealing with psychos.'

Eddie chuckled. 'It's nothing like that. It's just . . .' He became more serious. 'She's been pretty hard to get through to lately. And when I try, she . . .'

'Bites your head off?'

'Actually, yeah. She's a redhead; I'm used to a bit of mardiness, but this is different.'

34

Harvey gave him a quizzical glance. 'Mardiness? I guess that's British slang?'

'Yeah. Use it in conversation with Lana – or Lena – and she'll think you're all cultured and refined, just like me.'

'No offence, man, but your accent? Not even slightly *Downton Abbey*.' The pilot grinned, then nodded at the duplicate controls in front of Eddie. 'Okay, you're on the stick. Take us around the Narrows, then back towards the city.'

The LongRanger was now cruising parallel to the shoreline of Staten Island, the great span of the Verrazano–Narrows Bridge straddling the mouth of the bay ahead. Eddie pushed the pedal again, and the helicopter swung into a lazy turn across the water. Brooklyn spread out before them, Manhattan coming back into view beyond. 'Doin' good,' Harvey assured him, before checking his watch and making another call to air traffic control. 'Okay, gotta start heading back now. My next tour group'll be waiting.'

'Damn, and I was just starting to get the hang of this,' Eddie replied. He still felt as if he were trying to balance a carton of eggs on a fingertip, but at least now he could maintain a constant height and speed.

'Stick with me and you'll be an expert in no time. I told you I'm a licensed instructor, right?'

'Several times,' said Eddie, grinning. 'How long can I stay in control?'

'Until we get to Governors Island. I'll take over when we're in the East River VFR corridor.'

'The what?'

'Something you'll have to know about if you wanna be a proper pilot! Visual flight rules – basically, flying by eye. If you're in a 'copter, you don't need to tell ATC what you're doing in the Hudson and East River corridors, although it's kinda good sense to let 'em know. Although they'll be making the East River into controlled airspace soon for some UN summit. Pain in the ass.'

'Yeah, I know what it's like dealing with the UN,' Eddie told him with amusement.

He continued flying until the flat pear of Governors Island loomed ahead. 'I got it from here,' said Harvey as he took control once more. He reported to ATC that he was returning to the heliport, then pointed to the right, up the East River. 'You seen that?'

'It's a bit hard to miss,' said Eddie. The object of their attention was a huge Airlander airship, slowly cruising down the length of the waterway. The enormous twin-lobed craft, dwarfing even the largest airliner, was a new addition to New York's long list of tourist attractions, having arrived a month earlier to act as a mammoth advertising billboard. With the Airlander presently head-on to them, though, the commercials on its flanks were invisible. 'It looks like a massive arse from the front.'

'I always thought it looked like boobs myself. Whatever turns you on, man!' Harvey snickered. 'I'll be glad when it's gone – it's a pain in the butt. Even in VFR, you're supposed to maintain spacing with other aircraft, but that damn thing moves so slow, you've gotta go wide to keep clear of it. Airships, jeez.' He shook his head. 'What is this, the 1930s?'

'Oh, the humanity,' Eddie joked. He sat back to watch the skyscrapers of Manhattan's financial district grow larger as the helicopter descended. 'Thanks for the flight.'

'No trouble,' said Harvey, guiding the LongRanger towards the jetty where the helipads were located. 'Like I said, any time you want a lesson, I'll tell you when my next free slot is. Hopefully there won't be too many – if I'm not carrying passengers, I'm not making money! – but I owe you.'

He brought the aircraft in to land at a vacant pad. 'I'll be in touch,' Eddie told him as he removed his headphones. 'Try to remember which girlfriend's which!'

Harvey smiled and gave him a thumbs-up. A member of the

heliport's ground crew opened the cabin door, and Eddie hopped down, keeping his head low as he moved away from the chopper. Another guide waited nearby with the next passengers, who were led aboard as soon as he was clear.

The first man took him back to the terminal building. He walked through it and emerged on South Street. Heading along the waterfront, he took out his phone and found Nina's number. 'Okay, brace yourself . . .' he muttered as he made the call.

Behind him, unnoticed, a man who had been waiting outside the terminal followed at a discreet distance, making a call of his own.

2

Nina looked up as her iPhone buzzed. Her laptop was open, her notes and manuscript on the screen . . . but the cursor had remained in the same spot for twenty minutes. She checked the phone: Eddie. 'Hi.'

'Hi, love,' came the gruff reply. 'You back from the shrink's?'

'Yeah, about a half-hour ago.'

'How was it?'

'I think it helped,' she said, not even certain if she was being truthful. 'Did you do your helicopter thing?'

'Just landed. Good fun – we went around the harbour, buzzed the Statue of Liberty. I flew it for about ten minutes. Didn't crash once!'

Nina tried to inject some enthusiasm, however ersatz, into her voice. 'That's great.'

She knew at once that she had failed. 'Is everything okay?' her husband asked cautiously.

'Fine,' she said flatly. 'Where are you?'

'South Street, on my way to the subway.'

'Can you stop off at the Soupman's and get me that jambalaya soup I like?'

'What? That's all the way over by Eighth Avenue – it's a bit out of my way.'

'I'm pregnant, I get to decide what I eat and where it comes from!' She had meant it as a joke, but it came out more shrill than intended.

'Soup for you, then,' said Eddie. 'You want anything else?'

Was there a hint of sullenness? 'No, that's okay. Although, wait – you could get me my favourite sandwich.'

'The ones from Aldo's deli back across in the East Village?' *That* was definitely tinged with exasperation.

'Okay, forget the sandwich,' she sighed. 'Just the soup.'

'Just the soup. No problem.'

'Thanks, Eddie.' Silence on the line. 'Are you all right?'

'Yeah, of course,' he replied, still sounding downcast before suddenly becoming more enthusiastic – forcedly so, she couldn't help but think. 'Oh, I came up with some more baby names!'

Considering his past suggestions, that immediately put her on alert. 'Go on . . .'

'For a girl, I'm thinking Pandemonium. For a boy, Arbuthnot. Pandemonium Chase, that works, doesn't it?'

'Arbuthnot,' she repeated. 'That's not even a real name.'

'Yeah, it is! It's a good, honest Yorkshire name. You can't go into a pub where I grew up without meeting a couple of Arbuthnots.'

Nina knew that in other circumstances she would have been amused, but right now even Eddie's best efforts were failing to breach her prison of gloom. 'I think we need to keep thinking.'

'It'll be hard to top Arbuthnot.'

Something snapped. 'Stop saying Arbuthnot! That's the most stupid name I've ever heard. God! If you can't even take seriously something as simple as choosing a name, how are you going to manage being a father?'

The silence that followed was broken only by her own exasperated breathing. Finally he spoke. 'I'll figure it out when it happens. I'll get your soup, then.'

'Eddie, I—' But he had disconnected. 'God *damn* it,' she muttered, already annoyed at herself. He was, as always, just trying to help – in his own unique, occasionally infuriating way – and she had overreacted and blown her top. She glowered down at her stomach. 'This is all your fault,' she told the unseen foetus. 'You and your frickin' hormones.'

She headed to the kitchen for a drink. Along the way she passed a shelf of memories. Beside her husband's hideous pottery cigar holder in the shape of a caricatured Fidel Castro, that she had by now despairingly accepted she would never find a believable excuse to smash, was a collection of photographs. The majority were Eddie's, pictures of himself with friends now gone: his SAS mentor Jim 'Mac' McCrimmon, Belgian military comrade Hugo Castille, and others she knew only from stories.

But Nina had her memorials too. Macy in one, dressed up as Lara Croft from the *Tomb Raider* video games for a magazine photo shoot; and in another, her own parents.

Henry and Laura Wilde beamed at her from the picture, a quarter-century-younger version of herself between them. She remembered the time and place: an archaeological dig near Celsus in Turkey. It had been a hot, dry day, making their descent into the partially excavated Roman tombs both a relief and a thrill. The memory made her smile . . .

It froze on her face.

Her parents were gone, killed by their obsession, which their daughter had then taken on herself. The question she had posed at the therapist's office returned: had everything she'd achieved been worth it?

Another question from the session joined it. Was it right to bring a baby into her world? She knew herself well enough to be fully aware that her own obsession, her *need* to uncover the past, would never be sated. Was it fair to subject her own child to that same mania, to continue the cycle?

What kind of mother would she be?

Nina was forced to admit she had no idea.

She broke out of her trance, leaving her nine-year-old self behind and fetching a glass of water before returning to the study to find the cursor still blinking mockingly from its parking spot. She slumped huffily back in her chair, feeling trapped by her guilt and fear and uncertainty. She had to do something to break free, but what?

Elaine had been right, she decided. Clearing the air with her husband would be a good way to start. She reached for her phone, but then withdrew her hand. Eddie would be on the subway by now, and she knew *him* well enough to guess that he would still be pissed at her behaviour. Wait until he gets home, she decided. Until I've had my soup.

Eddie emerged from the 77th Street subway station and headed north up Lexington Avenue, holding a cardboard cup of hot soup and a bag of crusty bread. He had considered getting a cab back to the apartment, the subway journey from the soup store being a pain requiring two changes of train, but in the end he decided the longer trip might give Nina a chance to calm down about whatever had pissed her off this time.

Still, the fact that he had gone out of his way would hopefully show her that he wasn't mad about how she'd treated him. Well, not any more. His initial irritation had faded, replaced by a resigned amusement. She had endured so much in the past months, and surviving everything the world had thrown at them only to face an unexpected – though far from unwelcome – pregnancy would stress anybody out.

He still wanted the old Nina back, though. And it would take more than fancy soup to do that. He'd done everything he could to be supportive and helpful and loving, but what if that still wasn't enough?

He tried to put the depressing thought aside as he turned on to East 78th Street and headed for their building. Maybe the combination of time and food would calm her down . . .

Something triggered an alert in his mind.

It took a moment to work out what; all he initially had was a feeling of wrongness. But why? He was only a few hundred yards from home. Then he realised the cause.

A young man with dusty blond hair stood not far ahead, talking on a phone. Nothing unusual about that – except that when he had glanced in Eddie's direction, his eyes had met the Englishman's and displayed *recognition*, an involuntary split-second confirmation that somebody he was expecting had arrived. Then he looked away, but too quickly.

The mystery man wasn't a mugger. He was waiting specifically for Eddie. And he had an oddly clean-cut air that felt out of place for a street criminal, a neat, conservative haircut and casual clothes that looked brand-new.

Eddie didn't know him, but the face was somehow familiar. He had seen him before, though couldn't place when or where. He kept walking, but tensed, ready to respond to anything that might happen.

The man seemed to pick up on his wariness. He pocketed his phone and stepped to the centre of the sidewalk. There was a parked van to one side, a wall to the other. If Eddie got closer, he would be caught in a channel, the only escape routes being either to retreat the way he had come – or go through his adversary.

He chose the latter. The man was younger than him – late twenties – and taller, but the former SAS soldier was confident he could handle him.

The other man's eyes locked on to him as he reached the van – then flicked to something behind him.

Eddie spun as he heard the sudden scuff of someone breaking into a run, seeing another young man charging at him. The first ambusher rushed to catch him in a pincer—

The Englishman dropped the bag and swiped the top off the cup – then flung its contents into the running man's face. 'No soup for you!'

The jambalaya was still hot enough to hurt. The second man let out a yelp as he wiped his eyes – only for the sound to become a choked screech as Eddie's foot slammed firmly into his groin. He collapsed on the pavement.

Eddie whirled to face the blond, but a lunging fist caught the side of his face. He reeled as the blow jarred his skull, recovering just in time to intercept a second blow with his arm.

He straightened and faced his opponent, who shifted his stance. The younger man had clearly expected an easy victory, but now that he had a real fight on his hands, he was stepping up his game.

One of the man's feet lanced at Eddie's kneecap. He jinked away, an elbow barking against the van's side. Fists shot at him, left high then right low; he swatted away the first, but the second punch caught his side. He let out a grunt of pain. Satisfaction on his attacker's face, then he darted forward to deliver another blow—

Eddie caught his arm with both hands. Before the younger man could react, he forced it downwards and twisted the elbow, hard. The joint crackled. The man started to cry out – but was silenced as Eddie head-butted him in the face, mashing the cartilage in his nose with a gushing squirt of blood.

The Englishman threw him against the wall. The second man tried to stand. Eddie kicked his head, then turned to run—

Something stabbed into the back of his leg – and a searing pain tore through his body as all his muscles locked solid.

He fell, paralysed and helpless as a Taser's agonising charge burned into his thigh. Through clenched eyes he saw a third, older man emerge from the van's side door and stand over him, shouting orders to his companions. They dragged him across the sidewalk and threw him into the vehicle. The stun-gun shut off, the pain fading, but Eddie had no time to move before his attackers delivered several brutal revenge-fuelled kicks, then secured his wrists and ankles with zip-ties.

The third man slammed the door and jumped into the driver's seat. The van peeled away with a skirl of overstressed tyres.

Eddie struggled to break loose, but the plastic strips were unyielding. 'Get off me, you fuckers!'

'Shut him up,' ordered the driver, looking back. Late forties, American, narrow eyes and a small, mean mouth.

'*You* come and shut me up, you fucking shithead! I'll—' The words choked in his throat as the first man reactivated the Taser, another excruciating jolt of electricity blazing through him. A piece of rag was forced into his mouth, then a length of duct tape slapped roughly across his cheeks to hold it in place. The blond glared down at him. Eddie realised where he had seen him before – Little Italy, a month earlier, mistaking him for the Nazi who had attacked Nina. Whatever the men wanted, they had been following him for some time.

The current ceased, but all Eddie could do was scream muffled obscenities as the van disappeared into the crowded streets of New York.

The cursor continued to blink relentlessly, still fixed in place on the laptop's screen.

Nina stared at it, then sighed. Maybe she would feel more productive after lunch. Which reminded her: where *was* her lunch?

She looked at the clock on the menu bar. Even allowing for the detour to the soup store, Eddie was late. That wasn't like him; as an ex-military man, timekeeping was engrained into him at almost a cellular level, and if there had been some problem en route he would have phoned. So where was he?

A knock at the front door. 'Speak of the devil,' she said, going to answer it.

She reached for the lock – then hesitated. Why would Eddie

knock? He had keys. It was possible that his hands were full . . . but the New Yorker's innate security-consciousness prompted her to look through the peephole.

It wasn't Eddie.

Standing in the hallway were a tall, short-haired black man and a white woman with a dark bob and unflattering thick-framed glasses, both smartly dressed in light clothing. She didn't recognise either. 'Yeah?' she called. 'Who is it?'

'Dr Wilde?' said the woman. 'We need to talk to you about your husband.'

Worry filled her. 'What about my husband? Is he okay?' Were they cops? Had they come to tell her that something had happened to Eddie?

'Can we talk to you, please?'

Again, she was about to release the lock when caution returned. If they were cops, they would have identified themselves by now. She put the chain on the door and opened it a crack. 'Who are you? What's—'

Nina leapt away in fright as the door was kicked open, the chain ripping from the wood. The man advanced on her, drawing a gun. The woman followed him inside. 'Stay where you are, Dr Wilde,' she snapped. 'Shut up and you won't get hurt.'

Another two men filed into the apartment behind them. 'What the hell is this?' Nina managed to say, outrage pushing through her fear. 'What do you want?'

'Come with us,' said the man with the gun.

'I'm not going anywhere,' she replied. 'Get the fuck out of my house!'

One of the other men twitched in distaste at the obscenity. The woman ignored it, producing a tablet computer. 'You *will* come with us, or your husband suffers. Look.' She switched on the device.

Ice ran through Nina's veins as she saw the image on the

screen. It was Eddie, pinned to the floor by two men, his hands bound behind his back and tape covering his mouth.

'Hit him,' said the woman. In response, the men punched their prisoner in the stomach. There was no sound, but Nina could almost hear the impacts. Eddie writhed in pain, cheeks blowing out as he struggled to breathe behind his gag.

'No!' she cried, horrified. 'Let him go!'

'If you come with us and do what you're told, he'll be safe,' said the gunman. He gestured towards the open door. 'Let's go.'

'Not until you—'

The woman cut her off. 'Hit him again.' The screen displayed another blow, this one to Eddie's face. Blood oozed from his nostrils.

Nina stared at him, terror rising. 'Oh God! Stop!'

'Then come with us,' the man repeated. '*Now.*'

It was a command that she had to obey. The two other men went back into the hall to form an escort. She stepped out after them, the man and woman falling into place behind. The latter pulled the door shut as they left.

They took her down to the street. She thought about yelling for help, but while the man had concealed his gun between himself and the woman, he was still pointing it at her back. And even if she did get help, their comrades had Eddie at their mercy. She gave the oblivious passers-by a last despairing look before being ushered into the rear of a van.

A large box, worryingly close in form to a coffin, occupied most of the space. Its lid was open to reveal a padded interior. 'Get inside,' said the woman as her partner closed the doors.

Nina stared fearfully at the confined space. 'Are you insane? I'll suffocate! I'm not getting in there.'

'You'll be okay,' said the black man. The woman opened a small plastic case, revealing an ampoule of some colourless liquid – and a syringe. 'We're going to put you out for the journey.'

'Fuck you!' Nina spat. 'You're not injecting me with that!'

The woman's mouth tightened, and she nodded to her companions. The two other men seized Nina by her arms, the African American tugging up her sleeve. 'Clean it,' the woman told him. 'We can't risk infection.' He rubbed a sterile wipe over Nina's pale forearm.

'No, no!' she cried, panic rising. 'Don't drug me, please! I'm *pregnant*!'

Her kidnappers froze. The woman looked at Nina's belly, almost doing a double-take when she saw the small bulge. She examined it in profile, then straightened with an expression of dismay. 'Simeon, I think she really is. We can't drug her; we can't risk killing an innocent. What do we do?'

'I'll call him,' he replied, taking out a phone.

The two other men kept hold of Nina, tightly enough that she knew she couldn't break free. Instead she used the unexpected pause to try to calm herself, and assess her captors. They were appalled at the thought of harming an unborn child – yet were more than willing to torture Eddie to force her to cooperate. And as she watched the man wait for his call to be answered, she realised that there was something very odd about his clothes. The woman's, too. The style was modern, but the material was extremely coarse, as if they were made from burlap. That couldn't be remotely comfortable, but they were apparently enduring it by choice. Who the hell were they?

Simeon finally got an answer. 'Prophet,' he said, the reverence in his voice suggesting to Nina that it was more than a code name, 'we've got Dr Wilde, but there's a problem. She's pregnant. Anna thinks we can't risk drugging her for the journey. What should we do?'

A man replied, his tone both thoughtful and authoritative, but Nina couldn't make out what he was saying. 'Yes . . . yes, we will,' Simeon said when he'd finished. 'Thank you.'

'What did he say?' asked Anna.

'He agrees that harming an unborn child would be a sin, so we can't drug her. But he doesn't want her to know the Mission's location.' He gave the casket a meaningful look.

'I am *not* getting in that box,' Nina warned him.

'You're coming with us, no matter what.' He raised his gun. 'You don't need your kneecaps to give birth.'

She felt a jolt of fear. His deadly earnestness warned her that he would have no compunction about carrying out the threat. But Anna spoke before he could do so. 'We only need to blindfold her.'

Simeon nodded. He took off his tie and put it over Nina's eyes, knotting it behind her head. It was made of the same rough, scratchy material as the rest of his clothing. She fidgeted, but was unable to shift it, her vision completely blocked.

'Now what?' she demanded, trying to hide her returning fear.

She heard movement as Simeon climbed into the front of the van and started it. 'We're taking you to the Prophet,' said Anna. There was a thump as the coffin's lid was closed, then hands pushed her to sit upon it. 'Get comfortable – it's going to take a while.'

3

Anna was not lying.

The journey to their final destination took several hours. The van headed out of New York to an airport; Nina had no idea which, but guessed it was a smaller satellite terminal rather than a major hub like JFK or LaGuardia, as they drove right up to a waiting private jet. She was quickly hustled aboard, and within minutes they were airborne.

Even in flight, she was not allowed to remove the blindfold. She lost track of time, only able to estimate that four or five more hours passed before the plane eventually landed.

The first thing she felt when she was escorted from the aircraft was heat – wherever she was, it was much closer to the equator than New York. The concrete had been baked by the sun, the only relief a wind blowing in from . . . the sea? There was a salty tang to the air. She was either on the coast, or very close to it.

She was also at a commercial airport, not a private field. The whine of idling airliner engines was audible over her own plane. But any hope of attracting attention was immediately dashed as she was bundled into a car and driven a short distance to a waiting helicopter. Squeezed between Simeon and Anna during the flight, she still had no opportunity to see where she was, although this leg of the journey was much shorter, barely fifteen minutes.

At last the helicopter touched down, ending the nightmare odyssey. It was searingly hot, and the ground underfoot felt like gritty sand. She heard the low crash of waves. Definitely on the coast – but where?

Gravel gave way to paved slabs as her captors guided her from the helicopter and up a slope. She entered shade. The rattle of a door being opened, then she was pushed into a building, the coolness of the air-conditioned interior like going from an oven into a fridge. 'Wait here,' ordered Simeon. The door closed behind her.

Nina stood still, listening. As far as she could tell, she was alone. She cautiously reached up to the blindfold and, when nobody challenged her, took it off.

After the increasingly frightening scenarios her mind had conjured up, the reality was almost disappointing. Her surroundings looked like any business traveller's hotel suite, neat and comfortable but utterly characterless. The lights were off, the only illumination slits of daylight leaking through shutters outside the single window. But even this was dazzling after hours of darkness. Nina squinted as her eyes adjusted, then tried the door.

Locked.

She was unsurprised to find herself a prisoner. Going to the window, she discovered that it too was sealed. Even if she broke the glass, the metal shutter outside would keep her trapped. She turned . . .

And froze.

Hung on the rear wall was something that would definitely not have been found in a chain hotel. Instead of generic prints of landscapes and cities, she saw a tall cross, the wood raw and chipped. Crude iron nails jutted from its arms and base. The stylised symbol of an eye, six feet across, was painted on the wall behind it.

'What the hell *is* this place?' she whispered. The small relief on finding that the nails were speckled with rust and not blood did nothing to counter her unease and disorientation. Prophets, crosses, followers dressed in sackcloth – her kidnappers were clearly members of some religious sect, but what did they want from her?

She found a wall switch and turned on the lights, then checked the rest of the suite. Another door led to a bathroom, as anonymously businesslike as the main room, while a counter in one corner demarcated a small kitchen area. Cupboards contained an assortment of boxed and fresh ingredients, as well as pots and pans. Hunger pangs rose in her stomach, but she resisted the temptation to eat. First she wanted answers.

Nina went back into the main room. Two single beds, couch, armchair, desk. No television. The cross was the focus of attention – or contemplation.

A small box was mounted high in one corner. A red LED blinked as she moved: a security system with a motion sensor and camera. She was being watched. The eye behind the cross was more than merely symbolic.

Another box overlooked the kitchen. She was not surprised to discover a third surveying the bathroom. Every inch of the suite was under observation.

She returned to the first camera and put her hands on her hips as she glared up at it. 'Okay, you can see me. When do I get to see you? I know you're watching – what, are you afraid to show yourself? You're scared of a pregnant woman?'

Clack.

The noise came from the door. She went to it and tried the handle. This time, it opened. She stepped outside.

Heat rolled around her again. The sun was low, the view ahead lit by a dazzling golden glow. She was in a village, numerous small white buildings spread out before her. It had the same artificial, too-clean feeling as her room, a carefully maintained holiday resort rather than a place where people lived and worked. Or some kind of private gated community? A religious one, apparently; the tallest structure was a church rising up beyond the houses, a cross atop its spire. The symbol of the eye was affixed behind this too, an outline in wood or metal.

Nina stepped out of the shade. She was near the village's perimeter, seeing a dense swathe of palm trees beyond a chest-high wire fence with a barbed top strand. There to keep people in, or out?

Where *were* the people? Nobody was in sight, even though the weird little village looked large enough to house several dozen. But she knew *someone* was here, observing her. A high white pole nearby was topped by a grape-like cluster of glossy black spheres. CCTV cameras, pointing in every direction to give her mysterious hosts 360-degree video coverage. More such posts dotted the settlement. As she regarded the cameras, one of them rotated to stare back at her.

Not only was she being watched, but it was being made unavoidably obvious. God's eye – or that of a follower, at least – was upon her wherever she went.

She considered running into the trees, but instead advanced into the village. Right now, she needed to find out what was going on – and for all she knew, the jungle was also under surveillance.

There was still no sign of life as she moved between the pristine houses. Some had their shutters raised; she peered through a window. The interior was as neat and as impersonal as her suite, with another large cross and eye on the far wall. Increasingly unsettled, she reached the end of the street.

A path led to the helicopter landing pad, now empty, near the edge of a low, rocky cliff. Beyond it stretched the ocean. A brisk wind kicked up whitecaps as waves struck the stony shore below. She was facing away from the lowering sun, looking east – across the Atlantic, most likely. Was she on one of the Caribbean islands? Given the length of the journey, that seemed a safe bet. But which one?

She looked to her right. The church was fully visible from here, atop a little hill. Steps led up to it. If nothing else, she decided, it would give her a better view of the surrounding landscape.

She was halfway up the steps when a bell rang loudly from the steeple – and suddenly the village burst into life.

The church doors were thrown open. A throng of people poured out, hurrying towards her. All wore white clothing. Fearful, Nina tried to retreat, but they swarmed around her. There was no hostility, the group merely blocking her way, and everybody was smiling, but the silent uniformity of expression was somehow more disturbing than if they had been aggressive.

'Welcome, Dr Wilde!' a voice boomed. Nina searched for its source, seeing loudspeakers above the church door. 'Welcome to the Mission. My friends, bring her to me.' The words echoed from other speakers throughout the village.

A plump middle-aged woman gestured towards the entrance. 'This way, please.' Others moved aside to form a clear path up the steps. 'The Prophet is waiting for you.'

'The Prophet?' Nina asked, but the only response was a polite nod. Smiling faces watched her expectantly. Feeling increasingly unnerved, she went through the human corral to enter the church.

The interior was clean, white and devoid of any warmth or comfort, a place of worship that was entirely about the act rather than the feelings behind it. Even the tall, thin stained-glass windows were less inspiring than forbidding, the same eye motif topping simple grids of coloured squares.

At the far end of the central aisle was a raised pulpit, in which stood a man dressed in white robes. Simeon and Anna flanked it. The former slipped a hand into his jacket to make it clear to Nina that he could draw his gun in a moment if necessary.

She retreated, only to find that the people behind her had closed ranks to block her exit. 'Let me through!' she protested, trying to push between them. 'I've been kidnapped! Let me out!'

'The Prophet wants to see you,' said the woman amiably. Then, with a sterner undertone: 'Don't keep him waiting.'

The figure in the pulpit signalled that Nina should approach. Realising that she would not find any support from the cultists – that was the only way she could think of the smiling white-clad crowd – she reluctantly started down the aisle.

The voice resounded from more speakers inside the church. 'Dr Wilde, I'm glad you decided to see me.'

'Did I have a choice?' she called angrily.

'God granted you free will. Of course you had a choice. But making any other one might have had consequences. Something I hope you'll remember.'

Nina approached the pulpit. 'So you're Number One. Who are you? Or do I just call you Mr Prophet?'

The man appeared to be in his late forties, with dark hair that was greying at the temples. His eyes, an extremely pale blue that appeared almost glowing, fixed unblinkingly upon her. 'That's the title my followers gave me,' he said. She was now close enough to hear his unamplified voice. 'Their choice, not mine. My real name is Ezekiel Cross.'

'Appropriate,' Nina replied, indicating the symbol dominating the wall behind him.

'Yes. When I realised I'd been chosen as an agent of God's will on earth, everything about my life made sense.'

'And when was that?' she said, mocking. 'Did an angel appear before you?'

Simeon scowled, but Cross gave her a thin smile. 'As a matter of fact, yes.' He descended from the pulpit. 'Come with me.'

He led the way through a door at the rear of the church. Nina followed, Anna and Simeon falling in behind her. The robed man walked down a short passage, opening another door and ushering his guest inside.

Nina stopped in surprise. She had expected a study, but what she found was more like the control room of a television studio. The entire opposite end was a wall of monitor screens, curving around a large white leather swivel chair. The seat had touch-screens at the end of each armrest, which she guessed Cross used to operate the system.

But what had brought her to a startled halt was not the digital panopticon, but its subject.

Herself.

Every screen displayed a different picture, but all had one thing in common: they were following her. Literally, in some cases, as the camera tracked her movements. Most of the footage had been shot in the last few minutes, showing her blindfolded arrival in the Mission, her search of the suite and subsequent exploration of the settlement, right up to her entering the church.

But, she realised with increasing alarm, there was older material too, recordings of her on the streets of New York. Entering and leaving her apartment building, visiting stores, her therapist – even the medical centre where her obstetrician was based. That meant Cross's people had been watching her for some time, as her last appointment had been a month ago.

Eddie featured in some of the spy shots. The sight of her husband reignited her anger – and her fear for his safety. 'Where's Eddie?' she demanded. 'What have you done with him?'

Cross faced her. 'I've had him kidnapped to force you to do what I want.' On seeing her surprise at his blunt answer, he went on: 'I used to work in intelligence, for the CIA. For a job that was supposedly about finding facts, there was far too much hiding of the truth behind walls of lies and evasion. And then, one day, I had . . . a revelation.' A faint smile. 'Since then, I've dedicated myself to truth, to clarity. Which is why I'm not going to waste time with veiled threats.' He stepped closer, staring coldly at the redhead. 'You're going to help me find something. If you don't cooperate, your husband will be tortured. Clarity, as I said.'

It took Nina a few seconds to stammer out a reply. 'And if I do cooperate? What happens to us?'

'That's up to God's judgement.'

Fury rose inside her. 'That's not *clarity*, you son of a bitch! That's evasion—' She broke off with a gasp as Anna seized her by the hair.

Cross raised a hand. 'I'm not being evasive, Dr Wilde.' Anna let go, and Nina drew away from her with a hate-filled glare. 'You'll see what I mean when I get what I want.'

'What *do* you want?' she growled. 'Why do you need me – and why kidnap me and torture Eddie rather than just, y'know, asking nicely?'

'I have my reasons. One of which is that I had to be certain you would help me.'

'I still might not.'

His cold eyes flicked towards one particular screen. 'You will.'

Nina followed his gaze to see a slumped Eddie sitting in – no, secured to – a chair in a darkened room, apparently unconscious. Her blood froze. Somehow she knew it was a live image.

'What do you want?' she asked again, this time pleading. 'Whatever it is, just tell me, and I'll try to find it for you.'

Cross moved to survey the wall of screens. 'Do you believe in God, Dr Wilde?'

Being in a church, she should have been prepared for the question, but it still caught her off guard. 'Not . . . no, not particularly.'

'Then you're an *atheist*?' There was a venomous undercurrent behind the word.

'No.'

He frowned. 'Belief in God doesn't work on a sliding scale. You either do, or you don't. You're a believer, or you're not.'

'Then I guess I don't share your belief.'

'I thought so.' His eyes returned to the screens. 'My people have been watching you for some time. You've been to a lot of places, but not one was a church. And even a cesspool of sin like New York has churches.'

Despite her fear, Nina still felt annoyance at the slur on her home town. 'I don't have an opinion on whether or not God exists, because it's not an issue that comes up a great deal in my everyday life. God might be real, or not, but either way the subway still runs late.'

'Ah, an agnostic, then,' said Cross in a patronising tone. 'In some ways that's worse than an atheist, because at least they have conviction. You don't believe in the Lord because you can't be bothered.'

'I suppose you're going to tell me that sloth is a deadly sin?'

He shook his head. 'Nowhere in the Bible says so directly. Proverbs eighteen, verse nine comes close – "He also that is slothful in his work is brother to him that is a great waster" – but the idea of the Seven Deadly Sins is an invention of the Catholic Church.' His obvious disdain for that institution was almost as great as for atheists. 'Only what's written in the Bible itself matters. Which brings me to why you're here.'

'Which is?'

Cross came back to stand before her. 'Are you familiar with the Book of Revelation, Dr Wilde?'

'If you're asking me if I can quote chapter and verse, then no – but yeah, of course I'm *familiar* with it. The last book of the New Testament, also known as the Apocalypse of John, written in exile by John of Patmos – who may or may not be John the Apostle, depending which school of thought you follow – accepted into biblical canon at the third Council of Carthage in

AD 397 over considerable opposition . . . and argued about ever since.'

The white-robed man seemed almost impressed. 'More familiar than I expected given that you claim you can't be bothered to believe.'

'I'm an archaeologist – ancient history's kind of my thing.'

'Then you accept the Bible as a historical document?'

'I accept *some* of it as a historical document – the parts that can be corroborated with other contemporary accounts. Revelation definitely isn't one of those parts, though.'

'Why not?' His gaze became challenging. 'Have you read it?'

'When I was a student, for historical context. It reads like something you'd hear from a crazy guy living in a dumpster.' Cross and his two followers showed irritation at the criticism, but she pressed on: 'Visitations by angels, stars falling from the sky, plagues, a pregnant woman being chased by a dragon, the four horsemen of the apocalypse . . . and the end of the world. It's completely at odds with the rest of the New Testament. There were other equally crazy apocalyptic gospels that were rejected from canon – Paul, Ezra – so why this one got through is a mystery.'

Cross shook his head. 'It's not a mystery. The reason is because the Book of Revelation is *true*.' He leaned closer, a new and frightening intensity in his eyes. 'And I'll prove it to you.'

4

Cross led Nina across the control room to a vault-like metal door, using a thumbprint scanner to unlock it. Beyond was something even more incongruous within a church: a chamber that appeared to be a laboratory. Walls, floor and ceiling were all tiled in gleaming white, a stainless-steel bench standing before a glass and metal cabinet. A laptop on the countertop was the only loose item.

Nina felt a new unease. She had been in a similar lab before, part of a Russian biological warfare centre. Whatever Cross kept in here, he considered dangerous.

He went to the cabinet. 'Do you know what that is?' he asked, pointing at its contents.

She peered through the toughened glass. On top of a small pedestal sat a fragment of pottery or ceramic. It seemed to have been burned, a dark charcoal smear on the surface. 'It looks like . . . a piece of a statue?'

'It is,' said Cross, nodding. 'But it's also something else. I told you I'd seen an angel, Dr Wilde. There it is.'

'You mean you saw a *statue* of an angel?'

'Yes. But I believe – as firmly as I believe in the word of God and Jesus – that they're the same thing.' On her questioning look, he went on: 'The Book of Revelation talks of four angels, bound by God. Chapter nine, verse thirteen: "And the sixth angel sounded, and I heard a voice from the four horns of the golden altar which is before God, saying to the sixth angel which had the trumpet, 'Loose the four angels which are bound

59

in the great river Euphrates.'" And I've seen one of them with my own eyes. This was it!'

Nina held back the more scathing of her immediate thoughts. 'What do you mean?'

'I was on a mission for the CIA in Iraq, before the invasion. There's a lake between the Euphrates and the Tigris called Umm al Binni – we had a rendezvous with a group of Marsh Arabs there. Saddam had drained the marshes to drive them out, and because of that, the water level had dropped enough to reveal something in the lake. A temple. I went inside, and found the angel. The *unbroken* angel.' He held one hand about twelve inches above the other. 'It was this tall, and looked exactly as John described in Revelation – the body of a man but with the head of a lion, wrapped in six wings full of eyes.'

'If you say so,' said Nina warily.

He rounded on her. 'I don't need to *say* so!' he barked. 'I can show you!' He flipped up the laptop's lid. 'Here!'

The screen came to life, displaying a photograph of the interior of the temple. The resolution was relatively low, but still clear enough for her to realise that whatever else she thought of her captor, he had made an impressive discovery.

He had also accurately described the angel, which rested inside a gold-lined nook. It did indeed have a lion's head on a man's body, metal wing-like shapes tightly encircling it. But she found herself more intrigued by the surroundings than the centrepiece. The walls were covered in inscribed text – she recognised it as Akkadian, a long-extinct language of ancient Mesopotamia. It wasn't one she could translate, though, those words visible through the dirt and shadows remaining indecipherable.

She also recognised another language: ancient Hebrew, carved into stone tablets propped against the wall. Their lower halves were lost beneath the flooded temple's murky waters, leaving only a few lines visible. Again she couldn't read the language; Latin and Greek had been her specialities.

'This was under the lake?' she asked, intrigued. She knew she was falling prey to her own weakness, her obsession with learning more about lost treasures of the past, but couldn't help wanting to know more.

Cross nodded. 'It had been under twenty feet of water until Saddam drained the region. The Marsh Arabs avoided the area even before then; they thought it was a place of death.'

'And was it?'

'I was the only person who got out alive after the Iraqis attacked, so yes. The temple was blown up by a helicopter gunship.' He gestured at the sliver inside the cabinet. 'That was the only piece of the angel I recovered.'

Nina was still examining the photograph. 'I don't know what you expect me to do with this. I can't translate Akkadian, and I only know a small amount of ancient Hebrew. I don't have a clue what this says.'

'You don't need to. This was taken twelve years ago. I've had it translated since then. In pieces, so that no outsider would know what it all meant.' Cross brought up another picture.

Words had been overlaid upon a copy of the original image. But they were positioned almost randomly across the wall, a scattershot translation. Nina frowned. 'These are only fragments. Is there even a complete sentence there?'

'Only a few,' he replied, with clear frustration at the fact. He pointed them out. She read them: *The guidance of God led His chosen through the desert and showed them water when they thirsted*; *Three times shall it be said, seven is the number of God, and man is always lesser*; *And the Elders sent their people into the lands around*. 'They were all we could find, even after the picture was enhanced. But it told me enough.'

'Which was?'

'That this place was used by the twenty-four Elders – the ancient Hebrew leaders who sit around God's throne in His temple, just as Revelation says.' Cross indicated some of the translated text. 'You see? The Akkadian symbols for the number twenty-four – and here in the Hebrew text,' he added, pointing out one of the half-submerged slabs, 'it actually uses the word "Elders".'

Nina shook her head. 'So it was an important religious site. That doesn't prove that God personally stockpiled his angels there. The ancient Hebrews spread out over a wide area, including into Mesopotamia.'

'There's more.' Cross's finger moved to other snatches of translation. 'These Hebrew sections say that the Elders sent the other three angels away for safety, dispersing them as more tribes came into the region. And the older text, the Akkadian, describes how the angels were bound in the first place – or rather, what was bound *inside* them.'

'And what would that be?' said Nina, her cynicism muted by the fact that she now genuinely wanted to know. She had no intention of taking Cross's deductions at face value, but at the same time she couldn't deny that his find deserved proper archaeological study.

'Do you know what the Umm al Binni lake is, Dr Wilde?' Before she could speak, he provided the answer. 'It's a meteorite crater. A meteorite hit Mesopotamia around 2200 BC. The destruction it caused led to the downfall of the Sumerian civilisation – the Sumerians being replaced by the Akkadians.'

'That's conjecture,' Nina corrected. 'It's a *possible* cause for the fall of Sumeria, but there are others. And yeah, I *have* heard of Umm al Binni. It might be a meteorite crater, but considering the state of things in Iraq since the war, nobody's been in a big hurry to check it out.'

'I believe it *was* a meteorite. And you will too.' Cross went

62

back to the cabinet, gazing down at the chunk of stone within. 'Let me quote from Revelation again.'

'Oh, I doubt I'm gonna be able to stop you,' she sneered.

Anna strode right up to her. 'Don't talk back to the Prophet again. Understand? I can hurt you without hurting your baby.'

'Anna, that's enough. For now,' said Cross. 'Revelation chapter eight, verse ten: "And there fell a great star from heaven, burning as if it were a lamp." Now, what does that describe, in modern terms?'

'A meteorite,' Nina had to admit – then her mind made a connection to another ancient story. 'Wait . . . there's a section in the *Epic of Gilgamesh*, I think the eleventh tablet, that could be interpreted the same way. It describes the Anunakki – a group of Sumerian sky gods – "setting the land ablaze with their torch" and "shattering the land like a pot". That's followed by a great flood, maybe the same one from Genesis, but the timing of the Gilgamesh legend roughly coincides with a date of around 2200 BC.'

Cross exchanged glances with Anna and Simeon. 'You know your subject, Dr Wilde,' he told Nina. 'That proves you're the right person to find what I'm looking for. But I'm curious. You're willing to accept *Gilgamesh* as a source of truth. So why not the Book of Revelation?'

'Because some of the events in *Gilgamesh* can be corroborated by other sources. Revelation can't. It's a completely stand-alone piece of work, and to be frank, it reads like some sort of drug trip.'

She expected an angry response. Cross's reply, however, surprised her. 'Have you ever taken hallucinogenic drugs, Dr Wilde?'

'What? Of course not.'

'I have.' Her surprise grew at the admission. 'Part of my training with the CIA's Special Activities Division. It lets them judge if an operative's likely to give up information under truth agents. I passed the test, by the way.'

Nina gave him a thin smile. 'Congratulations.'

'But I discovered something about hallucinations, which I've since corroborated from other sources.' A glance at Simeon; had he been another CIA agent who'd undergone the same training? 'Anything you see while under the influence is taken from your own subconscious mind – it's something you've already encountered, but reflected back at you in a distorted way, like a funhouse mirror. You can't hallucinate something you've never encountered before, because there's nothing for your mind to work with. So if you've never heard of an elephant, say, it would be impossible for you to hallucinate an elephant.'

She regarded him dubiously, unsure where the sudden divergence of topic was heading. 'I'll . . . take your word for it.'

'So when I got back from Iraq and started researching – *really* researching – the Book of Revelation,' he went on, 'I realised that John's visions were very much like my experiences under drugs. The intensity, the *reality* of what you're seeing, the way your perception of time skips backwards and forwards, how all your senses are engaged – it made me think that John underwent a similar experience.'

'Wait, wait a second,' said Nina. 'One minute you're telling me you believe the Book of Revelation is true, that you take it literally – and the next you say that nope, the guy who wrote it was tripping?'

'I never said I took Revelation *literally*. I said I believe it's true – that it *contains* the truth.'

'I don't understand,' she was forced to admit.

He clasped his hands together as if about to deliver a sermon. 'I quit the CIA and went on a pilgrimage – to Patmos. There's a monastery there, the Monastery of St John, marking where John wrote the Book of Revelation.'

'The Cave of the Apocalypse.'

'You know it?'

'I know *of* it. John supposedly lived in the cave during his exile, and that's where he wrote Revelation. I've never been there, though.'

'You should.'

'Let me go, and maybe I will.'

That prompted a mocking snort from Simeon. Cross gave him a stern look, making him lower his head in penance, then continued: 'I visited the cave, and saw the crack in the ceiling through which John heard the voice of God telling him to write down his visions. I also saw that water comes down through it from above. Now, the land around the monastery is private, but that never stopped me before. And you know what I found growing in the woods? Psilocybin mushrooms. Hallucinogens. It looked like the monks had tried to clear them, but there were still patches hiding away. And if they're growing naturally there now, there's no reason to think they wouldn't have been there two thousand years ago.'

'So . . . you really *do* think that John was tripping when he wrote Revelation?'

Cross nodded. 'The water might have been contaminated. Or he could even have eaten the mushrooms, not knowing what they were. But yes, I believe that his visions were psychoactive hallucinations.' His gaze intensified. 'So I had to find out where they came from.'

'What do you mean?'

'I told you – you can't hallucinate something you haven't experienced. Yet John described mountains falling from the sky, the sea turning to blood, cities being destroyed – and he also described the twenty-four Elders, and the angels bound at the Euphrates.' He returned to the laptop and pointed at the statue in the centre of the image. 'He described this!'

She frowned. 'But he couldn't possibly have seen it.'

'No. But someone could have described all those things to him. Or, more likely, he read about them, and all the other things that came from his subconscious when he had his vision. They were described so vividly, with such detail, that his mind was able to visualise them perfectly.'

'So where did he read about them?'

'The answer's in Revelation. Chapters two and three are the letters that the Lord told John to send to the seven churches: Ephesus, Smyrna, Pergamum, Thyatira, Sardis, Philadelphia and Laodicea.'

'All in modern-day Turkey,' said Nina.

'And all places that John must have visited to know so much about them. The Ephesians hated the Nicolaitans, the Smyrnans were rich, the Thyatirans tolerated the presence of the false prophet Jezebel – and he also knew that Antipas the bishop, his friend, was martyred in Pergamum.' He watched Nina expectantly, as if waiting for her to make a connection.

One came almost immediately. 'Pergamum is another name for Pergamon,' she said. 'And Pergamon had one of the largest libraries of the ancient world.' His expression confirmed that she had guessed correctly. 'Is that what you're saying? You think John read something there that formed his visions in Patmos?'

'That's exactly what I think, Dr Wilde,' Cross replied. 'The library contained the ancient texts of the Elders – a record of the meteorite strike and the binding of the four angels at the Euphrates.'

'Well, I can tell you a big problem with your theory right away,' she said. 'Mark Antony took everything from the Library of Pergamon to give to Cleopatra as a gift. He cleared the place out, every last scroll. There's no exact date for that, but he died in 30 BC – long before Jesus was born, never mind John. And

Antipas died in AD 92, so Revelation couldn't have been written until after then.'

'The Library of Pergamon still existed for centuries after John wrote Revelation,' Cross told her dismissively. 'Either Mark Antony didn't really take its entire contents, or some were hidden from him. John was still able to visit and read what he found there.'

'That's just supposition, though,' she objected. 'You're making things up and presenting them as facts to fit your theory.'

'It's not a *theory*!' he barked, making her flinch. 'It's the truth! I know it's the truth, because God led me to it!' Another stab of his forefinger at the image of the angel on the laptop. 'I found the angel! I witnessed its power with my own eyes!'

Nina tried to control her returning fear. Cross was revealing himself as a zealot, and she knew from experience that such people were most dangerous when their beliefs were directly challenged. 'What power?' she asked, hoping to calm him by bringing him back to his pet subject.

He ignored her. 'I found the truth on Patmos. I know what caused John to write the Book of Revelation – and I know it holds something real. I came here and established the Mission away from the corruption and sin of the world, and it gave me clarity. I've seen the truth. I believe it, my followers believe it, and you'll believe it too. You won't be able to deny it when I find the other angels!'

'That's what this is about?' she said. 'Finding the rest of the angels from Revelation?'

Cross nodded. 'The Elders kept one of them at the temple in Iraq, but hid the other three for safety. I believe they wrote down where they hid them, and that this text ended up in the Library of Pergamon, where John read it.' He stared at the remains of the statue once more. 'He might not have realised its significance, at least consciously, but when he had his visions in the Cave of the Apocalypse, his mind, guided by God, brought it all back to him. He wrote down everything he saw during the vision. It was all mixed up, scrambled, surrounded by other hallucinations, but it was still based on what he'd read about the Elders and the angels.'

He whirled back to face Nina, white robes swirling. '*That's* what I believe the Book of Revelation is, Dr Wilde. It's a code. And I've spent twelve years reading it, uncovering its secrets – cracking that code. The texts I found in the temple gave me the clues I needed to decipher it.'

'This?' Nina protested, waving at the laptop's screen. 'This is gibberish!'

'You don't need to read every word in a book to understand the story. It told me enough. I know where to find the angels – at least, I know which parts of Revelation contain the clues leading to them. What I don't know yet is where these locations are in the real world.'

Realisation dawned. 'And that's why you need an archaeologist.'

'Exactly,' Cross replied. 'Someone with the knowledge and experience to join the dots, to make the connections between the places John saw in his visions and where they are today.'

'But why *me*?' objected Nina. 'Your followers have obviously given you plenty of money if you've been able to build all this. You could have just hired somebody to work it out. Why kidnap me and Eddie?'

'I didn't want to involve an archaeologist until now, because they have their own biases that would have made them deny the truth. Just like all scientists. But you don't have the *option* to deny it. And . . .' The cult leader smiled. For the first time, the sense of malevolence lurking beneath the surface came out into the open. 'You were highly recommended by an associate of mine.'

The words sent a chill through her. That suggested Cross was working with someone with a personal grudge against her – but who? She and Eddie had made a lot of enemies . . .

She didn't have time to worry further about it as Cross spoke again. 'Three locations are given special significance in the text of Revelation: "the Synagogue of Satan", "the Throne of Satan", and "the Place in the Wilderness". I think they're where the other angels are hidden.' He closed the laptop and gestured towards the door. 'Your job, Dr Wilde, is to find them.'

Nina suddenly realised that she already knew the true identity of one of the locations – but managed to hide her recognition of the fact, not wanting to give anything to her kidnapper. Instead she summoned up resistance. 'I'm not doing a damn thing until I know Eddie's okay.'

Simeon advanced on her. 'You were warned—'

'Wait, Simeon,' said Cross. 'I was always going to let you see your husband, Dr Wilde. This way. Please.' The unpleasant smile returned.

That alone made Nina feel more worried than ever, but she followed him back into the control room, Anna and Simeon again shadowing her. The screens were still cycling through clips of her at the Mission and in New York, but her eyes went straight to the single monitor showing the live feed of Eddie.

Cross went to his chair and tapped at a touchscreen. The dizzying display before him faded to black. Another command, and the curved video wall came back to life, the image of Eddie bound to the chair spread across it. The camera was offset to his right, looking down at him. 'Mr Irton,' said Cross. 'Can you hear me?'

'Yes, sir, I can hear you,' came the reply. The new voice was American, like Cross and his lieutenants, the accent suggesting that the speaker was from one of the south-western states.

'Dr Wilde is with me. Could you wake her husband, please?'

'I sure can.' Nothing happened for several seconds – then a plume of water lanced in from the bottom of the screen and hit the Englishman in the face.

Nina gasped as he thrashed and coughed. *'Eddie!'*

5

Eddie slammed painfully back to wakefulness as the frigid water hit him. He struggled to breathe, the sudden cold squeezing his chest tight – then realised he couldn't move. His arms were pinned painfully behind his back. Still straining to draw in air, he shook and writhed, trying to get loose.

No joy. Something was biting into his wrists. Handcuffs. No way to break them, but if there was enough slack in the chain, he might be able to bring his hands in front of him . . .

He couldn't. He was in a chair, a single metal pole supporting its broad back, and couldn't spread his arms far enough apart to lift them up around it. His ankles were secured too, tied to the chair's legs.

But he felt the whole seat flex slightly as he struggled. If he kept going, he might be able to crack a weld or strip a screw—

Movement nearby. He looked up, shaking icy water from his eyes, and knew he wouldn't get the chance.

Three men stared stonily back at him. The same bastards who'd attacked him on the street, shooting him with a Taser and bundling him into a van to be gagged . . . and drugged. They'd stuck him with something to knock him out. He had no idea how long he'd been unconscious, but he was both hungry and thirsty, with a groggy headache and raw, gritty eyes.

His surroundings came into focus beyond the trio. A warehouse or factory, derelict, grey daylight leaking in through grubby windows high above. Dirty crates and unidentifiable rusting machinery glinted with cobwebs. Closer by were some metal cases, their cleanliness telling him they had been brought by his kidnappers. His leather jacket lay crumpled on the floor nearby.

He also saw a video camera mounted on a tripod, connected to a laptop on a wooden bench. The red light by the lens suggested that he had an audience—

A voice cut through his fear. '*Eddie!*'

'Nina!' he yelled back. 'Nina, where are you?'

'She's not here,' said the older man mockingly. 'Prophet? He's awake.'

'Yes, I can see,' came another disembodied voice from the laptop, an American man. 'Dr Wilde, you can talk to your husband. Briefly.'

'Eddie!' Nina cried over the speakers. 'Are you okay?'

'I've been better,' he replied, blowing more dripping water off his face. 'And I'm fucking freezing. These twats just woke me up with a bucket of ice water!'

'Watch your mouth,' said the blond man, a plaster across his broken nose.

'Fuck off.'

The man's face twisted with anger. Eddie saw the punch coming, but was completely unable to resist. It hit his stomach, hard, leaving him breathless.

'No, stop!' Nina shouted. 'Leave him alone!'

'Mr Chase,' said the man with Nina, 'I'd advise you to watch your language. Go on, Dr Wilde.'

'You son of a bitch,' she muttered, before raising her voice again. 'Are you all right, Eddie?'

'Like I said,' he wheezed through gritted teeth, 'been better. Where are you?'

'I don't know – somewhere in the tropics, I think. They took me from the apartment and brought me here.'

Worry gripped him. 'Is the baby okay?'

'Yeah, as far as I can tell. They were going to drug me, but when I told them I was pregnant, they backed off.'

'Oh, so they're the *caring* kind of kidnappers. Good to know. What the hell do they want with us?'

'They're . . . they're using you to force me to cooperate. Eddie, they say they'll torture you if I don't do what they want.'

A different cold ran through him as he guessed what was in the cases. 'Why? What are they after?'

'It's about the Book of Revelation, they—'

Sudden silence as the call was muted. 'Nina?' Eddie shouted. 'Nina! Put her back on, you fucking shithead!'

The blond man punched him again as the unknown voice returned. 'You've seen that your husband is still alive, Dr Wilde. Now I want you to see what'll happen to him if you don't do as you're told. Mr Irton?'

The Taser man opened one of the cases. 'Oh, *fuck*,' Eddie gasped as Irton produced a cattle prod, a black baton two feet long with a pair of stubby electrodes protruding from one end.

'No!' cried Nina over the speakers. 'I'll do what you want; you don't have to hurt him! Please, don't!'

But Eddie knew from the look in Irton's eyes that nothing she said would stop the shock from coming. The thin-mouthed man wasn't being sadistic or taking sick joy from inflicting pain on another human being – it was just business, part of the job, the professional detachment of the slaughterhouse worker. This was something he had done before, many times. He pushed a button. The electrodes crackled.

The Englishman set his jaw. 'I'm going to kill you and all your mates,' he growled. 'That's a promise.'

'They all say that,' Irton replied dismissively – as he activated the cattle prod and shoved it against Eddie's soaked chest.

★ ★ ★

Nina's scream almost drowned out her husband's. '*No!* No, you bastard!' She threw herself at Cross, but Simeon easily intercepted her. 'Stop him, *stop*! Please! Let him go!'

She looked back at the screens as Simeon dragged her away from the cult leader. Eddie convulsed in the chair, face twisted in agony as Irton moved the sparking rod up and down his body. 'Why are you *doing* this?' she shrieked. 'You're insane!'

Cross spun to face her, a sudden anger behind his piercing gaze. 'I've never *been* more sane, Dr Wilde! God Himself has set out this path for me, for His Witnesses,' he indicated Anna and Simeon, 'for all of us. We will follow it to the end, and you're going to light the way.'

He turned back to the screens. 'Enough.'

Irton retreated, the prod's high-voltage sizzle cutting off. Eddie slumped, wisps of smoke still rising from his T-shirt. Another man, younger than Irton, checked his pulse. 'He's okay,' he announced.

'Good,' said Cross. He tapped the touch screen, and the video wall went blank. 'Dr Wilde, your husband's safety is now entirely up to you. If you locate the other angels, he'll be released.'

Nina was unable to answer at first, shaking with fear and fury. 'I don't . . . I don't know what I'm supposed to do,' she finally said, voice quavering. 'I'm not a Biblical expert, it's not my field. Why me? Why do you think I can do it?'

'Because you have a talent for finding truth where others only see myths. Atlantis, Valhalla, the Garden of Eden. You found them. And you'll find the angels of Revelation too.'

It took a moment for the full significance of his words to strike her, but when it did, it felt almost like a physical impact. 'Wait – you believe I found the Garden of Eden?'

'Yes.'

'But the way the media spun the story, it made me look like a kook. The whole thing was deliberately done to discredit me.'

It had taken her discovery of the lost Pyramid of Osiris in Egypt to restore her reputation.

'I know you found it. In Sudan. And I know it was destroyed by an American stealth bomber.' Lines of disapproval formed around his eyes; he was as angered at its obliteration as Nina had been, though she imagined for very different reasons.

'How do you know that? I never told any of that to the IHA – and I sure as hell wasn't going to put it in my book.'

'I have friends in the US government,' Cross replied. 'There are plenty who believe in the Lord and His plan as strongly as I do. And there are others whose faith is . . . weaker,' he said, with another frown, 'but who are willing to work with us. Yes, I know what you found.'

'And you also know that what I found in Eden contradicts the Book of Genesis? That humans weren't created in God's image – that we weren't even the first intelligent species on the planet?'

Nina knew that challenging his core beliefs could go badly for her – and Eddie. But while Simeon and Anna were affronted, it did not trigger Cross's anger. 'Yes, I know,' he said. 'About the Veteres – the race that walked the earth before us.'

That revelation was even more startling, as her discovery of the Veteres was something known only to a handful of people. 'And you accept it?' she asked. 'But if you know that the first book of the Bible doesn't match reality, why are you so certain about the last book?'

'I told you, the Bible isn't to be taken literally. It was written by men, and men are fallible. It has to be studied and interpreted to find God's truth. It's not easy, but it's not *supposed* to be easy. Only people who've proven themselves worthy of God's truth will get to see His plan.'

'And you think you're worthy?'

'I know I'm worthy. God has chosen me, Dr Wilde. He led

me to the angel hidden in the temple in Iraq, and it's now my job to find the others.'

'Seems like it's more *my* job,' Nina said, acerbic.

'Then you should get started. Simeon, Anna, take her back to her house. You'll have everything you need, Dr Wilde – Biblical texts, historical reference material, maps, and limited internet access. You'll be monitored at all times,' he added, raising a warning finger. 'You'll be cut off immediately if you try to contact anyone or access a site that might give away your location – such as by trying to log in to the IHA's servers.'

'I quit the IHA over six months ago,' she protested. 'Why would I have access?'

'Because you've still got friends there. I know that your UN liaison, Oswald Seretse, gave you clearance even after you left. I also have friends in the intelligence services. We weren't only observing you on the streets.'

'You've been monitoring our internet too? Oh great, now you know all Eddie's favourite websites.'

Anna's face creased as if she had just smelled a dead animal. 'Yes, and they're disgusting.' Her offence gave Nina an odd feeling of pride.

'Enough,' said Cross impatiently. 'Now, Dr Wilde, it's up to you to find where the Elders hid the other three angels. Or your husband will suffer.'

Fear returned, though this time with a sense of determination, a refusal to let Eddie's torturers win. 'If they really exist, I'll find them,' Nina told him.

'If you're as good as I've been told, I don't doubt it.' Cross turned away.

Anna and Simeon escorted Nina from the room. Her mind was already working, but not on the task she had been given. The foremost question was: told by *whom*?

★ ★ ★

An answer had not come by the time Simeon and Anna brought her back to the little house. The Mission's residents had dispersed from the church to their own homes, a few giving her friendly greetings.

Nina ignored them. However cheery the inhabitants seemed, the fact remained that she was a prisoner, and nobody was willing to help her escape. And she was being watched every step of the way, cameras pivoting to track her. Even if she broke away from her escort, the alarm would be raised in seconds. How far could she get?

Simeon ushered her inside. 'So housekeeping's visited,' she said, seeing that a number of books and a laptop computer had been placed on the desk. 'Any chance of some room service?'

Her companions were not amused. 'Get to work,' said Simeon.

'Get bent,' Nina shot back. 'I haven't eaten since breakfast. Do you know how cranky pregnant women get when they're hungry?'

The sorrowful look Anna gave Simeon made it clear to Nina that they were a couple. 'We haven't been blessed with a child,' she said.

'Maybe you don't deserve one.'

'Maybe *you* don't.' Simeon took a step closer to Nina, his glare ice-cold.

'Simeon,' Anna said. His angry scowl deepened, but he retreated. 'There's plenty of food. But if you want to cook, do it yourself. We're not your personal wait staff.'

'I'm gonna give this place *such* a bad review on TripAdvisor,' Nina snarked as they left. The door closed behind them, and as she'd expected, the lock clicked. Even so, she tried to open it, with no success. 'Shit.'

She was in no mood to cook, so made do with throwing together a salad sandwich and devouring it before moving on to a box of crackers. Munching on the dry biscuits, she looked through the cupboards again. Her captors had at least stocked her prison with a decent selection of provisions.

A small bottle amongst various packaged ingredients and condiments caught her eye. Spirit vinegar. That jogged a memory, something Eddie had once told her. She looked back through the fresh vegetables. Corn, green peppers, chilli, onions, some bulbs of garlic . . .

She glanced up at the camera silently watching her from the corner. An idea had come to her, but she would have to be extremely careful and patient to carry it out – if she even could. But if it worked, it might give her the chance she needed to run for the Mission's boundary.

For now, though, she had to at least make the pretence of working on Cross's assignment. If her watchers thought she was wasting time, Eddie would pay the price. Delaying tactics had caused Macy's death; she couldn't allow the same thing to happen again.

Another thought. Cross was insistent that she find the angels as soon as possible. Was he working to a deadline? And if so, why? The angels, if they existed, had been hidden for thousands of years. Why the rush?

She turned towards the desk. Sitting atop the stack of books was a copy of the Bible. The Old and New Testaments; Genesis to Revelation. Maybe the answer really *was* in there . . .

'Let's see what John of Patmos saw in his visions,' she said to herself as she thumbed to its final book.

6

A faint knocking woke Nina. She frowned and raised her head, eyes still half closed. 'Eddie, get the door, will you . . .'

Memory slammed back into place. She jerked upright in fear and confusion. Books and papers fell to the floor. She had fallen asleep fully clothed, her research scattered around her. How long she'd been out, she had no idea, but the daylight beyond the shutters was back; it had faded into night long before she dropped into an uneasy slumber.

Another knock at the door. 'What?' she shouted, scrambling to her feet.

'Dr Wilde?' came a female voice. 'My name's Miriam. The Prophet asked me to bring you to him.'

'He did, huh?' she said, crossing to the door. Red lights blinked on the cameras as she moved. She flipped them the bird. 'Well, he can wait until I've had a shower and some breakfast.'

A pause, then the voice hesitantly returned. 'Uh . . . he wants to see you right now.'

Nina tried the door; this time, it wasn't locked. Standing outside in the morning sun was a slim, pretty woman in her early twenties, wavy rust-brown hair dropping to her shoulders. Her clothing, a knee-length dress and a pair of sandals, was all white. 'You pregnant, Miriam?'

Her visitor was startled. 'Ah . . . no?' she said uncertainly.

Nina opened the door and pointed at her own bump. 'Well I am, and let me give you some useful advice for if you ever are: pregnant ladies always get to choose when they meet people.

Okay? Tell your Prophet I'll see him when I'm good and ready. Which might be in ten minutes, it might be ten hours. Later, tater.' She gave the freckle-cheeked woman a mocking wave, then slammed the door before going to the kitchen to search for food.

Another knock came a few minutes later. 'Yeah, what?' shouted Nina through a mouthful of cereal.

Miriam peered around the door. 'I'm sorry, I . . . I don't want to intrude, but . . . but the Prophet sent me to bring you, and – and I don't know what'll happen if I go back to him without you.'

Nina spotted the glistening line of a tear on her cheek. 'Are you crying?'

Miriam hurriedly wiped her face. 'I didn't mean to, I'm sorry . . .'

The redhead's annoyance changed to concern. Her visitor was upset, even afraid. Nina went to her. 'Are you okay? Your Prophet, Cross – will he hurt you if I don't go with you?'

She was genuinely shocked at the suggestion. 'No, no, of course not! It's just . . . I don't want to let him down.'

'Were you standing outside the door this whole time?'

Miriam nodded. 'I didn't want to make you mad, especially as you're with child.'

'Trust me, you're *way* down the list of things that have spiked my cortisol levels in the past twenty-four hours.' She glared at the nearest camera. 'So, what,' she told her watchers, 'you send this poor girl to get me as part of some emotional blackmail plan? Jesus!'

Miriam's mouth fell open in shock, this time at the blasphemy. Nina gave her an irritated look. 'I'm guessing you're not from New York if something that mild upsets you. All right, okay, I'm coming,' she told the camera with a frustrated shrug. 'First things first, though.'

'What?' asked Miriam.

'I need to pee. Maybe that's over-sharing, but I really don't care.' She disappeared into the bathroom, leaving the blushing woman staring after her.

After an unrushed break, Nina re-emerged to find her guest still waiting. She gathered her papers. 'Okay, let's go.'

Miriam led her out of the house and through the Mission. She was silent to begin with, only piping up very quietly about halfway down the street of little houses. 'Ulysses.'

'What?' said Nina.

'Ulysses, Kansas. That's where I'm from. Well, not the actual town – I grew up on a farm about ten miles away. So no, I'm not from New York.'

'Yeah, I'd guessed.'

'But I always wanted to see it. It looks amazing. Scary, though. Isn't there a lot of crime?'

Nina made a sarcastic sound. 'Sure, if you hop in your time machine and go back to the seventies. You aren't going to get stabbed in the middle of Times Square in broad daylight. Probably.'

'Okay . . .' was the uncertain reply. 'I'd still like to go one day, though.'

'What's stopping you? You're not a prisoner here, are you?'

'Of course not! I came here by my own choice, to follow the Prophet.' She smiled and gestured at their sunny surroundings. 'It's lovely here. And I'm with friends who think the same way I do. Why would I want to leave?'

'I can think of a few reasons,' said Nina, regarding the nearest set of security cameras. 'So where *is* here?'

Miriam opened her mouth to reply, then clapped it shut. 'I, uh . . . I'm sorry, but I was told not to tell you anything about the Mission.'

'But we're somewhere in the Caribbean, right?'

She clenched her hands in agitation. 'I'm sorry, really I am, but I can't tell you.'

'You do know that I *didn't* come here by my own choice? I was kidnapped, Miriam – that's a federal offence, and every country in the Caribbean, even Cuba, has an extradition treaty with the US. Anyone who's involved in keeping me a prisoner here will be counted as an accessory. That'll get you a minimum thirty years in a federal prison.' She had no idea if that were true, but could tell from Miriam's alarm that she had made her point. 'You realise that, don't you? But if you help me get out of here . . .'

Conflict was clear on the young woman's face. 'I . . . I'm sorry, but I can't, I really can't,' she said at last. 'I can't go against the Prophet. I just can't! I'm sorry.'

Nina held back her anger. Miriam was genuinely upset at not being able to help, but also unwilling – or unable – to disobey her leader. 'This Prophet,' she said instead, changing tack, 'why do you follow him? What's he offering you?'

Miriam's smile returned as if a switch had been flipped. 'He's going to lead us to the new Jerusalem! God's dwelling place will come down out of heaven to the earth, and He will live amongst us and wipe away all the tears from our eyes.'

'And there'll be no more pain or sorrow, right?' Nina recognised her words as part of Revelation, which she had read several times the previous night.

'That's right!'

'And how exactly is he going to do this?'

'I don't know. But I trust him,' she quickly added. 'Everything the Prophet says makes sense. Revelation will come to pass, and God's kingdom on earth will begin.'

'So you think your Prophet's a good man?'

'Of course he is!'

Nina's expression hardened. 'Good men don't kidnap

pregnant women, Miriam. And they don't torture people to force them to cooperate.'

She shook her head. 'He wouldn't do that.'

'He *has* done that! He made me watch my husband being electrocuted with a cattle prod!' Seeing the other woman's dismay, she pressed on: 'He's no prophet; he's an ex-CIA agent who went nuts. Whatever Cross really wants, it's not peace on earth and everyone singing "Kumbaya". You've got to help me!'

Miriam scowled. Nina realised she'd pushed too hard and put her on the defensive. 'He's not nuts,' she protested. 'You'll see. When the angels are all released and the seventh trumpet blows, you'll see!'

'What will I see?'

'The truth,' said a new voice. They had almost reached the church, and Nina looked up to see Cross at the top of the steps. 'God's truth will be revealed.' His eyes flicked towards the papers Nina was holding. 'Soon, I hope. Very soon.'

Miriam curtseyed. 'Prophet, I've brought her, like you asked.'

'Thank you, Miriam. You can go back to your studies now.'

She nodded, giving the archaeologist an uncertain look before departing. Nina glowered at her host. 'Hope you're not expecting *me* to curtsey.'

'Come inside, Dr Wilde,' he said. 'I hope we've got a lot to talk about.'

Nina followed Cross into the church. With him was a large young man she didn't recognise, hard-faced and with a distinctly military-style moustache. 'Replacement bodyguard?' she asked. 'What happened to the charmers who brought me here?'

'The Witnesses are preparing for a mission,' Cross replied. 'They flew out last night; I want them ready to move as soon as you find the location of the first angel.'

'They're the two witnesses?' Nina asked, picking up on another Revelation reference.

'Yes.'

'That explains the outfits, then.'

Cross nodded. 'Chapter eleven, verse three – "And I will give power unto my two witnesses, and they shall prophesy a thousand two hundred and threescore days, clothed in sackcloth."'

'Must be itchy for them. Especially in this heat.' Even early in the day, the temperature was already well over seventy degrees Fahrenheit.

'They can endure it. They'll endure anything to get the job done.'

They went through to the control room. It had acquired a table and chairs since her previous visit. Cross's imposing high-tech throne was at its head; he took his seat and gestured for Nina to join him. She sat at the opposite end, making a point of sliding her chair as far away from him as possible. The other man took up a somewhat intimidating position close behind her. 'Now,' said Cross, 'the Synagogue of Satan, the Throne of Satan and the Place in the Wilderness. Do you know where they are?'

'Not yet,' she lied. 'I might have some ideas – but I'm not doing anything until I see that Eddie's okay.'

The cult leader let out an irritated breath. 'All right. You can see him.' His hand went to one of the touch screens.

'And talk to him.'

His eyes narrowed. 'Don't push me, Dr Wilde. My patience isn't infinite.'

'Mine's hanging by a frickin' thread. I want to talk to Eddie before I do anything else.'

'You want to talk to him? All right.' There was a nasty undertone that immediately put her on alert, but he tapped at the pad. The wall of screens lit up, showing the same elevated angle of Eddie as before. He was either asleep or unconscious, his arms and legs still secured. 'There he is.'

'Eddie!' she called. 'Eddie, are you okay? Eddie!'

'He can't hear you,' Cross said. 'I haven't turned on the microphone yet.'

'Then do that. You want me to cooperate, you want me to find your damn angels? Then let me talk to him.'

He sneered, then ran his finger over a slider. 'Okay.'

'Eddie, can you hear me?' she said.

For a moment there was no response, then her husband raised his head. 'Nina?' he croaked.

'Oh, thank God. Are you all right?'

He tried to move, only to let out a sharp gasp. 'Ow! No, my arms are fucking killing me. These bastards left me cuffed to this fucking chair all night.' He rolled both shoulders, trying to ease the pain in his stiff muscles. 'Are you okay?'

'Yeah.'

'And the baby?'

'Fine, it's fine. They haven't done anything to hurt me – yet.'

'Wish I could say the same.'

'Me too. But I'm going to do everything I can to get you out of there. They're trying to find the angels in the Throne and Synagogue of Satan—'

Cross stabbed at the pad again, cutting her off. Only one end of the link had been muted, though. 'Nina?' said Eddie with growing anger and alarm. 'Nina, what's happening?'

'You've spoken to him,' Cross said to Nina. 'Now, this is what happens if you make another demand of me.' Another swipe at the slider. 'Mr Irton? Proceed.'

'No!' cried Nina, but he had already cut the mic. Irton stepped into frame, holding a couple of large, thick cloths.

Eddie struggled uselessly against his bonds. 'You get away from me, you fucking—'

Irton punched him in the stomach, leaving him gasping. Two more men came into view. One went behind the chair, releasing a chain that was holding it to a metal ring on the floor, while Irton wrapped both cloths tightly around the Englishman's head.

Nina realised what they were about to do. 'God, no!' she cried, jumping to her feet, but the bodyguard pushed her roughly back down. 'Don't, please!' She grabbed her notes and waved them at Cross. 'I'll tell you what I've found out!'

His response was a look of cold dismissal. 'I warned you, Dr Wilde.' He worked the volume control again. 'Do it.'

The cloths were secured. Eddie jerked in the seat, straining to draw in air through the stifling material. The two other men hauled the chair and its occupant a foot off the floor, then tipped it until the back of Eddie's head thumped against the concrete. Nina cringed, knowing that he was about to suffer even more – and that she was utterly helpless to prevent it.

Irton had moved out of sight while his companions lifted the chair; he now returned holding a bucket of water, which he held over Eddie's head . . .

And started to pour.

The water splashed on to the wrapped cloth. The weight of the sodden material pressed it down on to Eddie's face, revealing its contours – and his mouth opening wide as water filled his nostrils. He tried to cry out, but all that emerged was a gargling moan as Irton kept pouring.

Nina stood again, but was shoved back into her chair. 'Stop it! Stop! Let him go!' she screamed at Cross. 'You bastard, you're killing him!'

'He'll live,' he replied. 'British special forces, wasn't he? He'll have had SERE training; he can withstand being waterboarded. For a while, at least. Nobody can hold out for ever.' He looked back at the screens, where Eddie was squirming as the water flowed over his head. 'The CIA didn't teach us these techniques so we could resist them. They taught them so we know how to use them.'

She stared at him, appalled. 'You're insane.'

'Insanity is seeing all the evils in this world and refusing to do anything to stop them. I'm going to stop them, Dr Wilde. And you'll help me.' His intense eyes locked on to hers. 'Are we in agreement?'

'Just stop hurting him,' she said, defeated. 'Please.'

Cross was still for several seconds, then nodded. 'That's enough, Mr Irton. Bring him back up.'

Irton retreated. His companions hauled their prisoner upright, one securing the chair back to the floor while the other peeled away the soaking fabric. Eddie retched, blowing water from his nose.

'Mr Irton is an expert in enhanced interrogation techniques,' Cross told Nina. 'He can keep a man in a state where he thinks he's about to die for days at a time, if he has to. But he won't have to, will he?'

Nina's heart raced, fear and shock pumping through her. 'No. He won't.'

'Good. That'll be all for now, Mr Irton. I'll contact you if you're needed again.'

Irton looked up at the camera. 'We'll be here, Prophet.' He regarded his slumped captive. 'So will he.'

'So, Dr Wilde,' said Cross. 'Tell me what you've learned so far.'

'Give me a minute. Please.' She raised a shaking hand to her head, trying to calm herself. It wasn't only Eddie she was worried about; high stress levels in a mother could cause tremendous harm to a developing baby.

'Norvin, get her something to drink,' Cross told the other man. The bodyguard went to a cabinet, returning with a bottle of water.

Nina took it and gulped down its contents. She paused for breath, looking at the table rather than meet Cross's gaze. Her notes were spread out before her. She took them in, her pulse slowing as her mind almost involuntarily resumed work on the challenge.

One page in particular brought an answer. She looked back at the image of her husband, then engaged in a silent debate with herself as she weighed various factors: her safety, the baby's health, Eddie's life, the danger that Cross posed to all of them . . . and made a decision.

'Okay. I think I've got an idea where one of the angels is,' she announced. 'That's assuming you're absolutely one hundred per cent convinced that the three places you gave me are where they've been hidden. You don't want me to look at other possibilities, just in case?'

Cross clasped his hands together. 'I'm sure. I've been studying Revelation for twelve years. I *know* those are the places God wants me to find. The clues all point to them; the emphasis given to them in the text, the repetition of their names, makes me absolutely certain.'

'So I'm only looking for them, nowhere else?'

'Nowhere else. What have you found?'

Another glance at Eddie, still lolling in the chair. 'If I help you, you won't hurt him again?'

'If you help me, I won't need to.'

Nina took a deep breath. 'All right. I'll do what you want.'

With an expression of satisfaction, Cross shut off the screens. 'Good. Talk.'

She sorted through her papers. 'Okay. I read Revelation last night. It's not an easy read, especially since you only gave me the King James Version, but I came up with a possible link to the so-called Synagogue of Satan.'

'You know where it is?'

'I know where it might be. In Rome.'

Cross didn't seem surprised by her deduction. 'That makes

sense. There are several parts of Revelation that refer to Rome. The description of the Beast: "the seven heads are seven mountains" means the seven hills on which the city was built. The *accepted*' – there was more than a hint of cynicism behind the word – 'interpretation of Revelation is that John described Rome in riddles to hide that he was making a direct attack on the Romans who were persecuting the Christians.'

'It's not exactly the Enigma code, though,' said Nina. 'And the Romans weren't dumb. They were always watching for signs of sedition or rebellion. One of the reasons John might have been exiled to Patmos in the first place was for being critical of Emperor Domitian, but if he'd been *too* critical, he would have been executed, not exiled. Saying that Rome was a whore and the emperor a demonic beast would have put him on the fast track to a crucifixion.'

'Then the references to Rome in Revelation came from John's visions of the Elders' writings,' said Cross thoughtfully. 'They're part of the code to finding the angels.' He looked back at Nina. 'So where in Rome?'

'I'm not sure yet,' she said. 'But I think the mere fact that John made a direct association between a synagogue and Satan is significant.' She flicked back through her notes, at the same time searching her knowledge of Roman and early Christian history. 'Jewish Christians were a fairly major part of the Christian movement immediately following Jesus's death, but it didn't take long for them to be marginalised and later demonised – in John's case literally, since he flat-out accused them of being in league with Satan – by the religion's leadership. Both religions, actually; the Jewish leaders didn't want them around any more than the orthodox Christians did. By the end of the first century, they'd demanded a clear split – you were either Christian or Jewish; you couldn't be both.'

'Understandable. You have to fully accept Christ and His

teachings to be saved. There are no half-measures.'

'But before then,' she went on, not wanting to be dragged into a debate about the fate of her eternal soul, 'around the time Domitian took power in AD 81, there was still a degree of crossover. The weird thing was that Rome was actually one of the safest places for Jewish Christians. Nero scapegoated Christians following the Great Fire of Rome, and from that point on they were widely persecuted by the Romans, but Jews were tolerated in the Empire. But at some point, the Christian leaders decided enough was enough, and they declared Jewish Christianity a false church. They risked coming into Rome itself to lay down the law about which version of Christianity they had to follow.'

'The apostle Paul,' said Cross, nodding. 'He came to Rome after his third missionary journey. Acts chapter twenty-eight – he summons the chiefs of the Jews to try to convince them to follow Christ's teachings. "Be it known therefore unto you that the salvation of God is sent unto the Gentiles, and that they will hear it. And when he had said these words, the Jews departed, and had great reasoning amongst themselves." Verses twenty-eight and twenty-nine.'

Nina raised a disbelieving eyebrow. 'Have you memorised the entire Bible? Wait, don't answer that. But yeah, Paul came to Rome – or was brought to Rome, since he was there to stand trial for his alleged crimes against the empire. And it didn't go well for him, as he was executed.'

'But he was there,' Cross insisted. 'And he spoke to the leaders of the Jews.'

'*Where* did he speak to them? Does the Bible say anything?'

He thought for a moment. 'Yes. "And when they had appointed him a day, there came many to him into his lodging." Acts chapter twenty-eight, verse twenty-three.'

She was almost disappointed. 'So they went to him. Damn.

I'd thought that if Paul had wanted to speak to all the Jewish leaders, they would have chosen to meet him somewhere they had home advantage. A synagogue, in other words. They weren't specifically buildings as they are now – the word just means a meeting place.'

'The Synagogue of Satan,' said Cross, nodding slowly – then suddenly widening his eyes. 'No, wait! There was another meeting, before they came to Paul's lodging. Verse seventeen: "And it came to pass, that after three days Paul called the chief of the Jews together, and when they were come together, he said unto them . . ." They *did* assemble somewhere.'

'Where?'

'That's what you have to find out. You're the archaeologist.' Ignoring her dirty look, he addressed Norvin. 'Take her back to her room. If she needs anything, get it for her.'

'How about a plane ticket out of here?' Nina asked as she stood. She saw Cross's unamused expression. 'Jeez, you fundies have no sense of humour. I told you I'd find your angels.'

'Just remember that your husband is counting on you,' he said as Norvin escorted her to the door.

Nina regarded the monitors behind Cross with a look as dark as the empty screens. 'I hadn't forgotten.'

The laptop's browser had several tabs open, Nina flicking between them as she scribbled down more notes. The blocks Cross had put in place were frustrating, as some of the primary sources of information she would normally have used were linked to the IHA or other United Nations agencies and were therefore *verboten*.

The active tab was not displaying the website of any official organisation, however. It had taken some time to discover it: an obscure blog detailing the journeys of a Jewish traveller with an interest in her people's history. One such trip had taken her to

Rome, where she had been lucky enough to visit a site not generally accessible to the public . . .

'That could be it,' Nina whispered, scrolling through the traveller's pictures. They didn't contain the proof she was after, only an implication, a suggestion, but so far it was the best she had.

She clicked another tab. A map appeared, a twisting network of tunnels. The scale revealed that they were confined within a relatively small area, only a few hundred metres along each edge, but the numerous tiers of underground passages meant that there were several miles of them. It would take some time to explore them all.

Which was exactly what she had hoped.

She collated her notes, and was about to stand when there came a timid knock at the door. 'Saw me finish, did you?' she asked the nearest camera as she crossed the room.

Miriam was outside. 'Dr Wilde?'

'I'm guessing you've been sent to come and get me?'

She nodded. 'The Prophet wants to see you.'

'I thought he might. Okay, let's go.'

They headed through the Mission, receiving greetings from residents along the way. The sun was high overhead; Nina could feel the heat prickling her scalp. Miriam noticed her discomfort. 'Are you okay?'

'It's too hot.'

The young woman's concern was genuine. 'Oh! I'm sorry. You've got such pale skin, I should have thought . . . I could find you a hat?'

Nina felt ironic amusement that a prisoner was being treated like a VIP guest. 'That's okay, I'll survive.'

'I'm sorry,' Miriam repeated.

'For what?'

'For not being able to get you everything you want.'

Nina couldn't help but warm to the young ingénue. 'What I *want* is to get out of here.'

'I know.' Miriam gave her another look of sincere apology. 'I'd help you if I could, but the Prophet needs you.'

'Do you do everything the Prophet tells you?'

'Of course. We're his followers, he's going to lead us to—'

'To God's new kingdom, heaven on earth; yeah, I know.' Nina regarded her with sudden concern. 'He doesn't . . . take advantage of you, does he?'

Miriam flapped her hands in dismay. 'No, no! He doesn't do anything like that! Nor do any of the men here. It's written in the Book of Revelation. Chapter fourteen, verse four: "These are they who were not defiled with women."'

'No wonder they're all so uptight,' muttered Nina. 'And "defiled"? John had some serious issues.' She surveyed the village – and its inhabitants. 'There aren't any kids here, are there?'

'No.'

'So this new Jerusalem Cross says he's leading you to – what happens when you get there? "Be fruitful and multiply" was one of God's commands all the way back in Genesis, but if nobody's having children . . .'

'I don't know,' Miriam admitted. 'But the Prophet does. He's following God's plan, and when the time's right, we'll all be told what it is. It says so in Revelation.'

Nina couldn't recall reading anything that suggested that, but memorising every verse hadn't been her priority. Dismissing it as another of Cross's crackpot beliefs, she followed the younger woman up to the church. Cross was again waiting at the door, Norvin at his side. 'Dr Wilde, welcome back,' the cult leader said.

'Thrilled to be here,' she answered through a thin, sarcastic smile. 'I think I've found what you wanted.'

'I know. God is always watching here at the Mission.'

'My idea of God never had him as a peeping Tom.'

'Eternal vigilance is the price of liberty.'

Nina eyed him. '*That's* not a Bible quote.'

'No, but it's practically the motto of the CIA. The best way to protect your people is to know everything.'

'About their enemies, or about them?'

'In this case, about you.' He regarded her notes. 'You've found the Synagogue of Satan.' It was not a question.

'I *think* I've found it,' she replied. 'I'll explain everything to you inside. Assuming you haven't already read it over my shoulder.'

Cross nodded to Nina's guide. 'I'll call you if I need you again.'

'Thank you, Prophet,' Miriam replied. She curtseyed before departing, this time giving Nina a happy smile as she passed.

'So how did you persuade her to join your little cult?' Nina asked Cross as they entered the church. 'Tour the Midwest to spread the word?'

'I'm not a preacher, Dr Wilde,' he said. 'I'm just a seeker of the truth, by trade and by nature. When people seek the truth, others naturally join their quest. You should know that. You don't work alone either.'

'No, but I've never managed to get my co-workers to pay for *my* tropical retreat.'

'My followers donate to the Mission entirely of their own free will. All I ask from them is their belief in what we do, and their labour for our community. Beyond that, they're here to study Revelation and wait for its prophecies to come true.' They reached the control room. 'Which I'm hoping will happen soon.' He took his seat and gestured for her to sit at the table.

Nina noticed that her chair had been moved closer to him, and pushed it away again as she sat, to his minor but obvious annoyance. 'Okay,' she said after laying out her notes. 'Ancient

Rome, according to historical texts, had between seven and sixteen major synagogues at various times. Most of their locations have been lost; they would have been demolished and built over as the city grew. But some left archaeological traces, from their catacombs – their burial chambers.'

'How many?' asked Cross.

'Three major ones. There have been some smaller hypogea – underground chambers – discovered since the nineteenth century, but none of them are anywhere near as expansive as the ones at Monteverde, Vigna Randanini and the Villa Torlonia.'

'You think it's one of those? Which one?'

Nina had intended to explain her reasoning in full, but Cross's impatience was clear – and besides, he probably already knew to which she had devoted the most attention. 'Villa Torlonia.'

'Why?'

'Partly because of its size; it's the largest network of Jewish and early Christian catacombs in the city. The fact that it *is* both Jewish and Christian also made it look promising, because it lands right in that crossover period when the Jewish Christians of Rome were still enough of a threat to the orthodox Christian leadership that the apostle Paul went to them in person. Which made me think about that Bible verse you quoted about Paul calling the Jewish leadership together.'

She had definitely caught his attention, any lingering irritation replaced by intrigue. 'What about it?'

'Like I said, the Jewish Christians would probably choose the initial meeting place. It'd be somewhere they knew, and large enough to accommodate a lot of people, from the sound of it. So the most likely location would be at Rome's main synagogue.'

'And was that the Villa Torlonia?'

'The excavations there uncovered a large area that had once been an open-air meeting place. In other words, a synagogue. Although . . .' She hesitated. 'Nobody knows for certain.'

'What do you mean?'

'It seems *likely* to have been a synagogue, but maybe it was just a courtyard – or maybe it was nothing to do with the catacombs at all. There are even some arguments about the age of the catacombs themselves; some of the more recent surveys suggest they pre-date Christianity by a couple of centuries, but quite a few people still insist that they're from the first century AD, which would probably be far too late for these Elders of yours to have hidden anything down there.' A nervous shuffle of her papers. 'Which is why I'm warning you right now that I can't be sure I'm correct. I've given it my best shot, but I can't guarantee anything.'

Cross leaned forward, his cold eyes regarding her intently. 'Then convince me that you've done the absolute best you can.'

Nina paused, realising her mouth had gone dry. Her captor had been a CIA agent, trained in intelligence-gathering, and also in determining if that intelligence were true. That almost certainly meant he was experienced in questioning his sources . . . and interrogating them, if necessary.

If he didn't accept her assurance, or worse, thought that she was stalling, or lying . . .

'You've got my husband. You've got me. You've got my *baby*.' She pushed the chair back, rising to show him the swelling below her stomach. 'The only way we're all going to get out of this alive is if I do everything I can to help you. You've made that pretty damn clear. Well, I want to be back home and safe with my family. I want—' Sudden emotion made the words catch in her throat. 'I want to have my baby. And I want Eddie to be there with me. *That's* how you can be sure I'm doing the best I can.'

Her hands were shaking; she clenched her fists to cover it. Cross maintained his icy stare for a long moment . . . then sat back. 'I believe you, Dr Wilde. For now. So,' he said, slightly more casually, 'you think the angel is in the catacombs of the Villa Torlonia. Where? And how do we find it?'

Nina didn't answer him immediately, struggling to settle herself. 'I don't know yet,' she finally told him. 'The catacombs aren't open to the public because of the levels of radon gas. They very occasionally run tours, but only for limited periods. Anyone going down there would need specialist equipment – masks, breathing gear.'

Cross typed something on a touch screen. 'Okay, noted. How big are the tunnels?'

'There are over nine kilometres – more than five miles – of catacombs. And nothing resembling your angel has ever been found there, so it's not at the villa's museum. If it's down there, it's hidden.'

He ran his finger down the pad, then tapped at it. The video wall flicked into life, showing a somewhat pixelated copy of the catacomb map she had consulted on the laptop. 'These are the tunnels?'

'Yes.' She realised that he had called up a list of all the web pages she had checked in her research. 'The burial chambers are predominantly Jewish, although some Christian epitaphs have been found down there too. Depending on which dating scheme you accept, they were in use for between three and six centuries, so there's a lot of ground to cover.'

Cross stared at the map as if studying a battle plan. 'Nothing's been discovered that looks anything like the temple I found in Iraq?'

'No. Although I saw some photos that'll give you an idea of what it's like down there.'

He swiped back through the menu. The map disappeared, replaced by a photograph of the catacombs. Narrow, damp tunnels wound through the earth, burial niches – loculi – carved into the walls. Some of the rectangular nooks were surrounded by decorative frescoes.

These in particular caught Cross's attention. 'The paintings. Are there more like them?'

'There are more photos; see for yourself,' Nina told him. 'Most of the tunnels are plain, but some of the larger chambers are quite ornate.'

More images flashed up, the seemingly endless passages disappearing into darkness – then Cross abruptly straightened. 'What's that?'

Nina examined the new picture. It showed part of a ceiling, an image inside a circle picked out in grey and reddish-brown painted lines. 'It's a menorah. You know, a Jewish candlestick? Don't tell me they didn't have Hanukkah where you grew up.'

'I know what it is,' he snapped. 'Is that the only one down there?'

'No, there are quite a few of them. There should be pictures of a pair of menorahs on a wall – it's the most famous part of the place.'

Cross flicked impatiently through more photographs to find them. An arched wall bore two large circular paintings of the seven-branched candle holders, a wide mouth-like split in the stonework beneath them making the whole scene resemble a cartoon ghost.

'Why is that important?' asked Nina, seeing his intense interest in the scene.

'The temple in Iraq – there was the symbol of a menorah right above the angel. Wait, look.' He stabbed at the pad. The picture he had showed to Nina on her arrival filled the screens. He zoomed in on the niche. 'There.'

It was hard to make out clearly through the dirt, but there did indeed appear to be the image of a menorah inscribed on the gilded wall. 'You think it's a marker?' she asked. 'The menorah's a symbol showing the statue's location?'

Cross stared at the picture, then swiped back to the photos of the catacombs. 'It could be,' he said, almost to himself, before turning to Nina and saying more forcefully: 'It is! I'm sure of it! It tells you where to find the angel; the Elders hid it somewhere in the catacombs.'

'Where, though? There were a half-dozen menorahs just in those photos, and they were only from a small part of the whole system.'

'We'll have to search. We need to find the one with the Akkadian and Hebrew symbols for the twenty-four Elders above it. The angel's wings are made of metal – once we locate the right menorah, we can use detectors to find it.'

'Assuming someone hasn't already.'

'You said it yourself: nobody's found anything resembling it before.'

'The catacombs have been there for a long time,' Nina cautioned. 'Someone could have taken it two thousand years ago.'

Cross shook his head. 'No. It's there, somewhere. I know it. I *know*.'

Alarm rose within her. Her captor had made his decision based on nothing more than her educated guess – which with the limited time and research materials available was practically only a hunch. 'And what if it's not there? What happens to me – and to Eddie?'

He didn't respond, which unnerved her all the more. Instead he brought up a new app on one of the pads. After a few seconds, the sound of a dialling tone came over the speakers.

The call was quickly answered. 'Prophet?' came Simeon's voice.

'Where are you?' Cross asked.

'We arrived in Athens about an hour ago and met the others.'

'Is the jet still there?'

'It's ready whenever we need it.'

'You need it. Tell the pilot to arrange a flight plan for Rome, as soon as possible.'

'The angel's in Rome?' said Simeon, with clear excitement.

'In the catacombs of a place called the Villa Torlonia. I'll send you the intel. You'll need metal detectors and breath masks as well as the usual gear.'

Anna chipped in. 'I've got contacts in Europe who can arrange that.'

'Good. We need to move quickly,' Cross went on. 'What time is it there?'

'Almost twenty hundred hours,' Simeon told him.

A moment's thought. 'It'll be around midnight, local time, by the time you're on site,' said Cross. 'That should work for us – security ought to be minimal by then.'

'We won't have much time to reconnoitre.'

'You'll have to improvise. I want the angel found – tonight.'

'Yes, Prophet.' The line went silent.

'Why the rush?' Nina asked. 'If the angel's there today, it'll still be there tomorrow, or a week from now.'

Again he didn't answer. 'Norvin, take her back to her house,' he ordered. 'Dr Wilde, I want you to find out everything you can about the catacombs. My people need an efficient search pattern, and to know what to expect down there.'

'What? It's a *tomb*,' Nina replied as she stood. 'It's literally as quiet as a grave. You're making it sound like it's going to be a military operation.'

His silence this time was distinctly unnerving.

7

Nina was rinsing a plate in the kitchen when someone knocked on the door. Norvin had paid visits throughout the afternoon to check the progress of her research, but from the sound's hesitancy she guessed that this time it was Miriam. 'Come in!'

She had been right. 'Dr Wilde?' said the young woman. 'The Prophet asked me—'

'Yeah, yeah, bring me to him. I know the drill.'

Miriam lowered her head, abashed, then sniffed the air. 'Oh, that smells delicious! What is it?'

'Nothing special,' Nina told her. 'I just fried up some peppers and onions and things. I know fried food isn't something you're supposed to have while you're pregnant, but screw it – sometimes you just have to obey your cravings. And hey, at least it's not coal or something crazy like live goldfish.'

'It's making me hungry, that's for sure.' Miriam looked at the countertop. 'I'll clean all that up for you.'

Nina held up her hands. 'No, it's okay. I can take care of it.'

'Are you sure? At least let me put that in the garbage.' She indicated a wooden board on which were the finely chopped remains of several peppers.

'No, I'm going to dry them out and use them as seasoning.' Seeing Miriam's uncertainty, Nina smiled and went on: 'Really, it's okay. I'm going to be here for a while, so I at least want to be able to cook my way, y'know?'

'If you're sure . . .'

'I'm sure. Okay, let me wash my hands and we'll go see what His Prophetness wants.'

They left the little house, Miriam striking up a conversation about cookery. Nina had to bluff her way through it; she was far from a culinary expert, Eddie generally handling anything more complicated than scrambled eggs. They passed one of the poles topped by the black spheres of the security cameras, and she realised that she not only had a chance to change the subject, but that it was the only time she would be able to talk without being overheard. 'Listen, Miriam,' she said in a low voice, 'you told me before that you wanted to help me.'

The young woman nodded. 'What can I do?'

Nina chose her words carefully. Their earlier exchanges had made it clear that she would not be able to persuade Miriam to act directly against Cross, but if she could appeal to her caring nature . . . 'Miriam, I like you – you're a sweet girl, and I know that you care about what happens to me.'

She smiled. 'Thank you.'

'Then you care about my baby, too. Don't you?'

The smile became a little laugh. 'Of course I do!'

'Because the thing is, I was brought here against my will. That's put me under a lot of pressure, a lot of stress – and that's not good for the baby. It can really hurt it. Do you hear what I'm saying, Miriam?'

Miriam's expression became one of concern, but conflict was also clear on her face. 'I . . . I know that you want to go home, but I can't help you do that. I'm sorry. I really am.'

'I'm not asking you to get me on to the next flight back to New York. All I want you to do is phone my obstetrician and ask her the best way that I can keep my baby safe. I'll give you her number.' She had other numbers in mind; friends, former work colleagues, anyone who could realise the significance of the message and pass it on to the authorities . . .

But it was not to be. 'I'm sorry,' Miriam repeated unhappily. 'But I'm not allowed to make any phone calls without the Prophet's permission. I really, really want to do everything I can to help your baby,' she added, eyes wide in reassurance. 'But . . . I just can't do that. I'm sorry.'

'Then you're not really any help at all, are you?' Nina snapped. But despite the situation, she couldn't feel any anger towards the shy, sincere young woman. In a lot of ways Miriam couldn't have been any more different from Macy, but she shared the same openness of personality, her heart right there on her sleeve. 'Hey, it's okay, I didn't mean it,' she said, seeing the stricken look on her companion's face. 'You've done fine, you really have. I just wish you could have done more.'

'So do I,' Miriam replied.

They arrived at the church. Norvin was waiting at the door. 'What, I don't get a personal greeting this time?' Nina said in mock complaint.

'The Prophet's been busy. He's waiting for you,' was the big man's reply.

Nina shrugged and followed him inside. 'See you later,' she said to Miriam, receiving a smile in return.

Cross really had been busy, she saw as she entered the control room. The two touchscreens on his chair apparently weren't powerful enough for whatever he had planned, as a pair of laptops were set up on the table before him, a large printout of the catacomb map mounted on a stand nearby. The entrance to the system had been circled in red. Beside it was a smaller map of the Villa Torlonia's grounds. 'Wow,' she said. 'Looks like you're set up for a really intense session of Dungeons and Dragons.'

He gestured impatiently for her to sit as he adjusted a headset. 'Comms check,' he said into the mic. 'Come in, Simeon.'

Nina heard Simeon reply through his earphones, but couldn't

make out the words. 'Do I get to listen, or are you going to have subtitles?'

'Norvin, get her some headphones,' Cross said with annoyance. The other man gave her a wireless headset. 'Your mic is switched off, Dr Wilde. I don't need you distracting my people with chatter and' – a sidelong glare – 'snide comments.'

'As *if* I would!' she replied with paint-stripping sarcasm.

'You're trying my patience,' was his warning response before he turned his attention to the laptops. He typed commands, reading the results with satisfaction, then said: 'All team members. Camera check.'

The video wall lit up, individual screens showing different images as they had when Nina first saw it. But instead of CCTV footage of herself, this time unfamiliar faces appeared in the sickly green glow of night vision. All had small cameras mounted on their headsets, the images twitching with every slight movement.

Wait; not everyone was unfamiliar. She saw Anna on one monitor, Simeon on another, facing each other. Surnames were superimposed over the corner of each screen; theirs both read FISHER. The two Witnesses were indeed married.

Cross ran through a list, each of the ten team members responding in turn. 'Okay, we're ready,' he said at last. 'Are you clear to move in?'

Anna stood, revealing that the group was in the rear of a truck as she clambered through to the cab. A narrow street was visible through the windshield, cars parked on both sides. A taxi went past, but there were no pedestrians in sight. 'Nobody around. I think we're set.'

'Go when clear,' Cross ordered.

The screens erupted into bewildering movement, the effect almost nauseating. Nina forced herself to focus on the view from a single camera, the name at its corner TRANT. The group moved quickly out of the van's rear doors and ran to a nearby wall. It was higher than head height, but still proved little obstacle as they scrambled over it.

Beyond lay the expansive grounds of the Villa Torlonia. Nina knew from her research that the villa itself had once been Mussolini's residence, commandeered by the dictator from its owners for the far-from-princely rent of one lira a year. However, the imposing building was some distance from the team's destination: the Jewish catacombs.

The intruders dropped flat to the ground, checking their surroundings for guards. 'All clear,' Nina heard Simeon say. 'Okay, we're heading for the entrance. Stay in the trees.'

She glanced at the map. 'Where did they come in?'

'The south wall, off the Via Siracusa. Here.' Cross indicated a point.

'That's about as far as they could get from the catacombs.'

'It also has the lowest pedestrian traffic and surveillance coverage. I know what I'm doing.' He watched as his people scurried through the grounds. Lights flared in the distance, illuminating the estate's various palatial buildings; smaller ones moved between them. The torches of security guards making their rounds.

Nina found herself torn between hoping the raiders would get caught and an almost perverse involvement in the game of hide-and-seek. Simeon and Anna led the way, the others stringing out behind them as they weaved between the trees, occasionally ducking and freezing as the guards patrolled. But none of the wandering figures came close, sticking to the well-lit paths. Ever since its most famous former resident had been strung up outside a gas station, the Villa Torlonia had no longer needed high security.

'He's gone,' said Simeon as another guard disappeared behind a building. 'Move.'

Nina's seasickness returned as the cameras jolted. She fixed her gaze back on Trant's screen, seeing Anna and Simeon ahead of him. The couple came to a stop in a small stand of trees. 'I can see the entrance,' Simeon reported.

'Got it,' replied Cross. Two sets of fences surrounded a depression in the ground, a simple inner guardrail encircled by a taller chain-link barrier. 'Can you climb it?'

'Not easily, but I can see a gate.' Simeon's hand blocked the view from his camera as he peered through a set of compact binoculars. 'It's padlocked.'

'Go through it. Watch for security, though.'

'Got it.' Whispered orders, then the team ran to the outer fence. Someone produced a set of bolt-cutters and snipped the padlock's shackle. Everyone hurried through the gate, Anna closing it again behind them.

A gap in the second fence led to steps descending to the bottom of the excavation. A wrought-iron gate blocked an opening in a stone wall, but its padlock fared no better than the one above. Simeon shone a flashlight inside. A gloomy tunnel led into darkness.

'Masks on,' Cross ordered. The team members donned half-face respirators. 'Move in. Start your search patterns.'

Nina looked at the catacomb map. The ancient network of tombs was spread out over seven levels, its branching paths forming a genuine labyrinth. 'How long are you going to have them searching down there?'

'As long as it takes,' Cross replied.

The Fishers led the way, Trant and another man peeling off down a side passage behind them. The entire team quickly spread out into the maze, casting their flashlights over the loculi carved into the walls. The beams found dirt and debris, along with bone fragments. 'You're looking for symbols of menorahs,' Cross told them. 'They might be on the walls or the ceiling – maybe even the floor. If you see one, check the area around it with your metal detector.' He watched the screens as the group moved deeper. 'Whelan, slow down. You need to check the ceiling too.'

'Sorry, Prophet,' said one of the men. He shone his light back the way he had come. 'It's clear,' he said with relief.

'Good. We *have* to find the angel. We can't leave without it.'

'If it's not there, what will you do?' Nina asked.

Cross regarded her coldly. 'It's down there.' He tapped his chest, his heart. 'I *know*.'

'So long as you remember what I told you,' she muttered – just as she caught something on one of the screens. 'Wait, there!'

'I see it,' said Cross. 'Simeon, to your left.'

Simeon's camera fixed upon a painted wall. It was decorated mostly with repeating patterns of interconnected lines and circles, but within the circles themselves were more detailed friezes. Nina saw a flower, a tree, a large tent in a desert . . .

And a menorah.

She glanced at Cross, to see him regarding the image of the ceremonial candlestick with almost predatory eyes. 'Check it, now!' he snapped.

Simeon took something from his belt. He brought it up to the wall, revealing it as a metal detector, but a much more compact and sophisticated type than those used by beachcombers. He switched it on, then swept it over the picture of the menorah. Nina heard a faint warbling through her headphones, but nothing that suggested there was anything hidden behind the cracked plaster facade. He widened his search pattern, running the detector outwards in an expanding spiral, but found nothing. 'All right, it's not there,' said Cross, disappointed. 'Keep looking.'

'There's another one here,' said a man. Nina spotted a second menorah in the view of someone called Overton. This was more ornate than the first, but it soon turned out that it too concealed nothing metallic behind it.

She leaned back. 'This could take a while. Glad I ate first.'

Cross's impatience was plain, but he said nothing, alternately watching the video wall and checking the laptops. Nina realised that one of them was showing a tracker displaying his team's progress through the catacomb network. They were using extremely high-tech equipment; beyond the occasional video glitch, there hadn't been any communication dropouts, even underground. Whatever they were using, it was better than that available to civilians. Military gear? Or, considering Cross's background, intelligence-grade?

The search continued. Lights flicked over more burial chambers; the sight of a skull amongst the dirt gave Nina a brief chill. The tunnels became narrower the deeper the team progressed. Ancient artwork still adorned the walls in places; she glimpsed images of animals, fish, people standing in temples – even something that she took to be the Ark of the Covenant.

And more menorahs. Each was checked, but the only metal found was worthless detritus. Nina took another look at the tracker. The paths that Cross's team had taken were marked in red – but there were still many more passages yet to be explored. 'I told you this could take a while.'

'We've got the whole night,' Cross replied.

'And what happens when morning comes? Or if a security guard sees that the padlock's been cut and calls the cops?'

He frowned, then spoke into his headset. 'Everyone listen.' The bobbing cameras all steadied as their wearers stopped. 'We need to pick up the pace. Set your detectors to maximum gain, and sweep the tunnels as you move – if you get a reading, see if there's a menorah painted there. We've got to move faster.'

'Understood,' Simeon replied. The other team members all responded in kind.

'You'll get a hell of a lot of false alarms,' Nina pointed out.

'Better that than missing the real thing.' The metal detectors were adjusted, then everyone set off again, moving at a quicker pace.

Nina soon heard an electronic squeal. Someone called Ellison swept his flashlight around the tunnel before zeroing in on the source of the signal. It turned out to be nothing more than a rusted nail.

'Warned you,' she reminded Cross as she took off her headphones. 'You might wanna send out for snacks.'

It took all his restraint not to react to her barb. 'Keep searching,' he said instead, frustration evident.

Time trudged by. Hardly a couple of minutes passed without one of the searchers picking up a trace of metal, but each time it turned out to be junk. Nina walked around the room, under Norvin's watchful eye, to relieve the stiffness in her legs, while Cross remained fixated on the screens. She glanced into the church to see that day had turned to night outside. Returning to her seat, she saw on the laptop that barely a quarter of the tunnel network had been searched. The Fishers and their companions had been scouring the catacombs for over two hours and still come up with nothing.

'Do you actually need me here for this?' she said acerbically as she sat. 'I'm four months pregnant, remember. I need sleep, I need food – and I need to pee. Seriously, you have no idea how often I need to pee.'

Cross said something under his breath. Nina didn't catch it, but was fairly sure the second word was 'woman', and doubted the one preceding it was complimentary. 'Jerkoff,' she muttered. She was about to get up and leave whether he granted permission or not when he sat bolt upright, staring intently at one particular monitor. 'There! Anna, get closer,' he barked.

Anna's screen showed a painted menorah pinned in her flashlight beam – and from her discarded headphones, Nina heard an insistent whine. She donned them again. 'Strong reading . . . very strong,' Anna announced.

'Dr Wilde, look at this,' Cross said with urgency, and anticipation. 'Do you see it?' He tapped his touch pad, and Anna's viewpoint expanded to fill the entire video wall.

Her metal detector rose into frame. The whine became a screech each time it passed in front of the menorah. 'There's definitely something behind it,' said Nina.

'It's the angel.' Cross spoke with total conviction. 'Anna! Show me that marking above it.'

Anna moved closer, the painting swelling to fill the screens. 'Can you see it?' she asked.

'Yes. Can you, Dr Wilde?'

'Yeah, I can . . .' Nina replied quietly, almost unwilling to accept the evidence of her own eyes. Above the menorah were symbols – ones she had seen before.

The Akkadian and Hebrew that had also been present above the menorah in the sunken temple in Iraq.

She faced Cross. 'Is it the same?'

'Yes. It is.'

Nina was so astonished by the possibility that there could actually be some truth behind what she had dismissed as the insane theories of a religious crank that she didn't fully register the orders Cross was giving – until the point of a pickaxe slammed into the wall beside the painted menorah. A sharp crack of stone in her earphones made her flinch. 'No! What are you *doing*?'

'I have to see,' Cross replied. 'We've got to get it out of there.'

'But you're destroying the site!'

'I don't care.' He watched as the attack on the wall continued. 'The only thing that matters— There!' he cried. 'There it is!'

Simeon levered away a crumbling slab to reveal an opening

concealed behind the surface. Metal glinted within. 'Careful, careful!' said Cross as the niche was fully exposed. 'Let me see it!'

Anna brought her light nearer. The beam shone over a statue: a humanoid figure that Nina estimated to be a foot tall. Sheets of thin dimpled metal were wrapped around its body. But it was the head that caught her attention – not human, but animal, an ox.

'The second beast . . .' Cross announced in awe. 'The four beasts, the "living creatures" from God's temple – they're the four angels bound at the Euphrates. I knew it – I was right. I found the code hidden in Revelation, and it was *true!*'

The statue was carefully lifted from its resting place. From Simeon's muted grunt of effort, it was heavier than it looked. He blew off dust, then turned it in Anna's light. Nina got a clearer view of the effigy. She was forced to admit that it did indeed resemble the description given in Revelation. But that wasn't enough to make her imagine – to *believe*, as Cross did – that they were one and the same. 'So you've got it,' she said. 'Now what?'

'Now we get it back here. Trant,' he said, 'Simeon and Anna have found the angel. You've got the case – get to their location. Everyone else, return to the entrance. Move out as soon as the angel's secured.'

Trant began to traverse the labyrinth to meet the Fishers. In the meantime, Nina watched as Cross gave instructions to Simeon so he could view the angel by proxy. The statue was turned to show every aspect to the camera. Three sets of wings, as he had said, the dimpling in the metal giving it the impression of eyes all around . . .

Something caught *her* eye. Not on the angel, but in the empty recess behind it. 'Whoa, whoa!' she said. 'There's something in the niche – written on the wall.'

Cross saw it. 'Anna! Show me the back of the opening!'

The green haze of the night-vision camera rendered the scene flat and lacking in contrast, but it was still clear enough for Nina to make out the text carved into the stone. 'It's ancient Hebrew,' she told Cross, 'but I don't know the language well enough to translate it.'

'You don't need to,' he replied, working the touch screens. The footage on the video wall froze. A square box was superimposed over the image, which he manipulated to close in around the lettering. 'This is a translation program.'

'Yeah, I've used them before,' she said, watching as the application identified the Hebrew letters, then ran the words they formed through a database to come up with an English equivalent. It did not take long, though as she'd learned to expect from such software, the end result was awkwardly phrased. Even so, it gave her a faint chill. 'Okay, that's a little bit ominous . . .'

For the first time, Cross's expression revealed a degree of trepidation. '"It is three times spoken",' he read. '"The dragon number is of man. Have this wisdom to enter the temple of God." The dragon . . .'

'The dragon?' Nina echoed, remembering her recent research. 'You mean the Beast – Satan?' Several sections of Revelation were dedicated to the final battles between the forces of God and His enemies, led by the fallen angel.

Cross nodded, quoting another Bible verse. '"The dragon, that old serpent, which is the Devil, and Satan . . ."' He rounded on her with an air of triumph. 'This is more proof that I'm right. Don't you see? The Elders wrote that inscription when they hid the angel in the catacombs – and John read it in the Library of Pergamon. It's all in the Book of Revelation!'

She was still far from convinced, but could tell that nothing she said would dissuade him. Instead she mulled over what she had seen as Cross put his team's cameras back on the monitors. The others gathered at the entrance and removed their breath masks as Trant reached the Fishers. He was carrying a rectangular

112

case, opening it to reveal a lining of impact-cushioning foam rubber. Simeon laid the angel carefully inside and shut the lid.

'Okay,' Cross said as Trant picked up the container. 'Get back to the entrance.'

More minutes passed as the trio hurried through the passages. 'The Witnesses will bring the angel back to the Mission,' Cross told Nina. 'They have a private jet standing by.'

'Expensive,' Nina noted.

'Any price is worth paying for God's work.'

'And how are you going to get a relic like that through customs?'

'The same way we got you through. I told you, I have friends.' He returned his attention to the monitors as the trio reached the entrance. 'Anna, lead the way out. Simeon, guard Trant and the angel.'

Anna squeezed past the waiting men and opened the gate, making her way up to the top of the excavated pit. She surveyed her surroundings. 'Nobody in sight. Move out, back the way we came.' She went to the chain-link fence and swung the gate open. The first group of men ran past her and headed into the trees.

Trant left the tunnel, Simeon behind him. They reached the top of the steps—

'Back, get back!' Anna suddenly hissed. Her monitor became a blur of movement as she scrambled behind a tree outside the fence. 'Guards coming, north-east!'

'The gate – close the gate!' Cross shouted, but it was too late for her to turn back without being spotted. Trant and Simeon retreated into the pit.

Anna leaned around the tree. Two uniformed security guards were walking down a path towards the fenced-off area. Their ambling pace showed that they hadn't yet seen anything amiss, but if they caught sight of the gate . . .

Nina felt a rising tension. Unlike when the raiders had been sneaking through the Villa Torlonia's grounds, this time her concern was entirely for the unsuspecting men as they drew closer. 'Get out of there,' she whispered. 'Just turn around, don't look at the padlock . . .'

Too late. One guard stopped, his body language expressing momentary confusion before he spoke to his companion. Then the image went dark as Anna ducked behind the tree; by the time she crept around the other side, the pair had reached the gate. One saw the severed padlock, then shone a flashlight over the surrounding area.

Movement on Simeon's monitor. The breath caught in Nina's throat as she saw him draw a silenced automatic and thumb off the safety. 'No, don't,' she said to Cross, pleading. 'Don't let him kill them!'

'Their fate is in God's hands,' he replied.

'No it isn't – it's in yours! Tell Simeon to—'

She broke off as Anna's camera showed the two guards going through the gate. 'They're armed,' Cross warned as one of the uniformed men drew a pistol. 'Anna!'

She was already moving, making her way across the grass towards the gate. Simeon raised his gun. The camera on his headset made the view suddenly resemble a video game, turning into a first-person shooter as Nina found herself looking down the sights.

But it was no game. Real people were the targets. 'No, don't!' she cried, but they couldn't hear her.

The guard appeared on Simeon's monitor, flashlight flaring. He directed it down into the pit – and shouted in alarm as he saw the figures skulking in the darkness. He raised his gun—

Simeon fired first. A puff of blood exploded from the guard's chest, red turned greenish-grey by the night vision. He spun and collapsed to the ground. Simultaneously Anna rushed up behind the other man, snapping a hidden blade out from her sleeve and stabbing it deep into the side of his throat. Another gush of discoloured liquid fountained from the gaping wound as he fell.

'Jesus Christ!' Nina wailed, jumping from her seat. She had seen people die before – far, far too many times – but watching the deaths play out through the killers' eyes was appalling in a whole new way. 'You fucking psychopaths!'

Cross's jaw clenched in anger. 'Sit down! Sit down and shut up!'

'No! You're—'

Norvin shoved her forcefully down on to the chair. She gasped at a sharp pain through her lower body. Fear filled her – *the baby!* – but the stabbing sensation quickly subsided.

Breathing shakily, she looked back at Cross. 'You murdering bastard. You say you're a man of God, but you're just a killer.'

'I'm doing the Lord's work,' he replied. '"Thrust in thy sickle and reap, for the time is come for thee to reap, for the harvest of the earth is ripe." Judgement is coming, and all worshippers of the Beast will be cast into the lake of fire.'

'You don't know that they worship any beast.'

'They're Italian. They're almost certainly followers of the false prophet.'

It took her a second to get his meaning. 'The Pope? You mean because they're Catholics, they deserve to die?'

'"They were judged each man according to their works." We all will be, when the last day comes – even me. But God has chosen me to do His will, so my name is written in the Book of Life, along with all my followers.'

'You're insane,' was all she could say.

On the screens, Anna, Simeon and Trant hurried through the darkened grounds after the rest of the team. 'Simeon, you and Anna get the angel to the jet,' Cross ordered. 'I want it here at the Mission as soon as possible. Paxton will be waiting with the chopper as soon as you arrive. The rest of you, hole up and wait

115

for further instructions. As soon as the next angel is located, I want you ready to move out.' He faced Nina. 'You still have work to do, Dr Wilde. The Place in the Wilderness and the Throne of Satan . . .' He tapped at one of the pads, the monitors flicking to show Eddie still trapped in the chair. 'Your husband's life depends on your finding them.'

'I'll find them,' Nina growled, her glare at the cult leader filled with loathing. 'Not for you. For him. But I'll find them.'

8

New York City

A voice brought Eddie out of an exhausted but restless slumber. '. . . went over there earlier. Normally they have twenty or thirty people working, but there'll hardly be anyone there on those days.'

The speaker's identity came to him: Irton, his torturer, talking on a phone. A spike of fear-fuelled adrenalin instantly snapped him to full wakefulness. He was still tied to the chair, arms pinned painfully behind his back. His body cried out for him to move to ease the discomfort, but he resisted. The longer his captors thought he was still unconscious, the more he might overhear.

The respect, even deference, in Irton's voice told Eddie he was talking to his boss. 'No, I wouldn't think so,' the American went on. 'Is that still the plan? Okay, yes. No, the security's only light.'

A crunch of footsteps on the dirty floor nearby. 'Hey,' said another man. Eddie now knew that his name was Berman; the blond who had been waiting for him near the apartment. 'I think he's awake.' A hand slapped him hard across the cheek. 'Open your eyes,' said Berman. 'I know you're faking it.'

'Aw, but I was having such a shitty dream,' Eddie rasped, seeing the third man, Raddick, behind Berman. 'And *you* were there, and *you* were there . . .'

117

'Cute,' said Raddick with a mocking smirk. 'Mr Irton, sir! He's awake.'

Eddie turned his head to see Irton standing by one of the pieces of abandoned machinery. 'Chase just woke up,' he said into his phone, before moving away and resuming his discussion out of earshot. Night had arrived, only darkness visible through the skylights. Illumination inside the warehouse was limited to a lamp-lit circle around the torture chair.

'Thought you could play dead and listen in, huh?' said Berman. 'What, you think we're idiots?'

'That's one thing on a bloody long list, yeah,' Eddie replied. He had already braced himself for another blow, and sure enough it arrived a moment later. Wincing from the sting, he looked up at Berman. 'An' I just added "Slaps like a little girl" to it.'

That earned him a full-blown punch to the face. 'How was that?'

'*Fucker!*' He jerked against his bonds, making the chair rattle.

'Enough!' called the irritated Irton.

'Oh, sorry, am I interrupting your call?' shouted the Englishman. 'I'll leave if you want!'

Irton scowled, then stalked through an exterior door, closing it behind him. Eddie looked back at the other two men. 'Now he's gone, you can play with your dollies in peace.'

Berman raised a fist, but Raddick patted his comrade's shoulder. 'Hey, hey, he's just trying to yank your chain.'

'Yeah, I guess.' Berman moved reluctantly away, but gave Eddie a nasty look as he retreated. 'You and me, we're not finished.'

'Can't wait,' Eddie replied, trying not to let his concern show. He had managed to withstand everything Irton and the others had inflicted upon him so far, but it had taken all his reserves of strength and willpower, and after more than a full day in painful captivity, he honestly didn't know how much more he could take. So far he hadn't been subjected to anything that would cause permanent injury, but if his kidnappers took things up a level to force Nina to cooperate . . .

That was possibly the only thing keeping him alive. They needed him to make Nina do something for them. Without him, they would lose their hold on her. Was there any way he could turn that to his advantage?

Before he could think any more about it, Raddick checked his watch. 'I'm gonna get something to eat. You want anything?'

'Chicken wings and fries,' Berman answered.

'I'll have a burger if you're going,' Eddie piped up.

Raddick ignored him and headed for the exterior door. He had a brief exchange with the man outside, then a car started up and drove away.

Irton still seemed to be on the phone. If he kept talking . . .

'Chicken, eh?' Eddie said to Berman. 'Isn't that cannibalism? You're kind of a chickenshit yourself.'

The blond rounded on him. 'What did you say?'

'You heard me. Fucking coward. You'll slap someone who's tied to a chair, but when it comes to an actual fight, you'd shit yourself so hard your ribcage'd implode.'

Berman stepped up to him angrily. 'Screw you, Limey. I was in the United States Army. I'm no coward, I've seen action.'

Eddie snorted sarcastically. 'Yeah, right. I bet it's a non-stop adrenalin rush in the fucking typing pool.' He put on a bad, nasal American accent. 'If we don't get that toner cartridge changed in the next five minutes, there'll be hell to pay!'

'Shut up.'

'I got a paper cut, give me a Purple Heart!'

'Shut up!' Berman's hand cracked across his face.

'That the best you've got?' said Eddie, giving him a sneering grin. 'My niece could hit me harder than that. When she was six.'

The hand clenched into a fist. 'You wanna see the best I've

got?' growled the American, slamming it against Eddie's jaw.

The Englishman's head snapped back, blood squirting from a split lip – then he convulsed, mouth gaping as choking gurgles came from it. Berman stared dismissively down at him, only for his expression to change to concern as he realised his captive couldn't breathe.

'Oh, shit. Dammit, shit, *shit*!' he hissed, panic rising at the thought that he might have killed a vital prisoner. A glance at the door, but he didn't call to Irton, instead pulling the struggling man upright in a desperate effort to clear his airway.

It had no effect. Eyes wide, Eddie shuddered, tongue squirming . . . then fell limp in his seat, head lolling to one side.

'*Shit!*' Berman hesitated, then checked Eddie's neck for a pulse. He moved his fingertips across the skin, not sure of the result. Another look towards the door in fear that Irton might choose this moment to return, then he leaned closer to listen for the other man's breath—

Eddie lunged at him and sank his teeth into his throat.

Berman tried to scream, but the Englishman had clamped his jaw around his Adam's apple with the frenzied determination of a terrier, crushing his windpipe shut. He lashed and clawed at his attacker's face, but the teeth only dug in harder—

With a final growl of fury, Eddie forced his jaw shut. A horrible crunch came from Berman's neck, and he lurched backwards, a ragged, gore-spouting hole where his larynx had been. Eddie spat out a revolting hunk of torn tissue as Berman fell to the filthy floor, blood gushing down his chest.

The wounded man opened his mouth to cry out, but the only sound that emerged was a wet wheeze. He rolled on to his front, dragging himself towards Irton's torture equipment.

Eddie realised his intention. Berman wasn't trying to find a weapon, but something he could use to make a loud noise and alert his boss.

He threw himself from side to side, the chair's frame creaking in protest. His previous attempts to break loose had been halted by his captors, but with nobody to stop him, it only took seconds before metal cracked. The frame shifted beneath him, but the chair was still chained to the floor.

Eddie rocked forward to put his weight on to his feet. He strained with all his might, trying to stand. The underside of the chair's back dug into his bound arms. He felt something give, a bolt or screw breaking loose . . .

Berman reached one of the cases—

The seat back ripped away.

Eddie sprang upright. But his ankles were still tied to the chair's legs. All he could do was fall bodily on to the other man.

The landing knocked the breath from him – but Berman came off worse as his face was pounded against the dirty concrete. Eddie twisted, kicking at the broken chair as it strained against the chain. One of the ties slipped from the bottom of the tubular leg. Partially freed, the Englishman rolled and scrambled to his feet.

Berman raised his head, spitting blood. His fingers clawed at the case of torture gear—

Eddie's foot slammed against the side of his skull. Berman fell limp as a last bubbling exhalation gurgled from the gruesome rent in his throat.

Regaining his balance, Eddie slid the other restraint loose and booted the chair away. His hands remained cuffed behind his back. He had to get free, fast; if Irton had heard the scuffle . . .

He still had blood in his mouth. Hoping it was all Berman's, he brought his arms to his right side as he leaned his head back over that shoulder and spat the liquid over the cuffs. Then he pulled them as far apart as he could and bent down, straining to force them over his hips.

The metal bracelets bit savagely into his wrists. But the pain was nothing compared to what Irton had already put him through. His blood-slicked forearms slithered over his jeans as he writhed to work them lower, every millimetre of progress a battle. The handcuff chain reached his hip bone, but his arms were stretched to their limit.

He pushed harder. A burst of pain – then suddenly the chain jerked past the obstruction. He breathed hard, but knew the worst was over. His military training had taught him how to escape from numerous forms of restraint, although he found himself wishing for the flexibility of his younger self.

He dropped to a crouch, then rolled on to his back, drawing up one leg to bring his foot over the chain. The metal links rasped over the ridged sole of his boot, catching for a moment . . . then popping free. Eddie gasped in relief. Getting his other foot out was considerably easier. He jumped upright. His wrists were still cuffed, but he was almost infinitely more capable – and dangerous – now that they were no longer pinned behind his back.

Berman had stopped breathing. Eddie gave him a cursory glance that contained zero sympathy, then checked the case. The unnerving collection of CIA-approved torture implements shone in the cold lamplight. None were of any use to him right now.

But one of the rusty machines had what he needed.

He hurried to it and pulled loose a handle; a hefty corrosion-scabbed metal bar about two feet long. Wielding it like a baseball bat, he ran to the entrance and took up position to one side. A faint electrical hum reached him from outside, but he couldn't hear any voices. Had Irton finished his call?

Footsteps, frighteningly close, told him that he had.

The door opened. Irton stepped through, phone still in his hand. Shock crossed his face as he saw that the room was not as he had left it—

Eddie swung the metal bar.

Irton's reactions were good, his right arm snapping up to ward off the blow – but not good enough. The crack of the phone's screen shattering and the dull thud of the club striking first his hand and then his abdomen were almost simultaneous. He collapsed to his knees, winded.

'Ay up!' Eddie snarled as he slammed the bar down on the other man's shoulders, knocking him flat. 'Remember me, you bastard?' He kicked the fallen American hard in the side, then crouched to search his pockets.

Wallet, loose change, key ring. Eddie examined the keys. The smallest was for the handcuffs. He unlocked the bracelets and with huge relief tossed them aside, kneading the deep red grooves in his skin.

He checked the wallet. It contained a Nevada driver's licence in the name of Walter Jefferson Irton, a credit card in the same name, about two hundred dollars in banknotes and a small wad of receipts. 'So you're a torturer who claims expenses?' he asked. Irton made no reply.

A flick through the tabs showed that most of them were for convenience stores and fast-food joints in Brooklyn. There was also a parking receipt for the Brooklyn Navy Yard. Was that where he was, across the East River from Manhattan? Eddie glanced at the door, considering making a run for it before Raddick returned, but changed his mind. He might be free, but whoever these people were, they still had Nina.

He hauled Irton bodily back into the illuminated circle and slammed him against the dirty wooden bench, knocking the laptop to the floor and toppling the camera's tripod. 'Oi! Wake up!' Irton opened his pain-filled eyes. 'Where's Nina, and what do you lot want with her?'

His only response was a malevolent glare. 'Okay, so you're not going to tell me anything,' said the Yorkshireman. 'Good job there's all this stuff I can use to make you talk.' He gestured at the equipment cases.

The American's face betrayed a moment of fear, but it was immediately replaced by defiance. 'You won't break me,' he growled. 'I can withstand pain for days if I have to. I was trained by the best.'

'Funny, so was I, and I don't remember seeing you at Hereford.' He made as if to turn away – then smashed a fist into Irton's face before ramming his head down on to the table. 'How's the withstanding going?'

Irton spat out blood and a broken tooth. 'Fuck you!'

'Oh, you're using rude words now? Guess that must have hurt.' He stood behind the other man. 'Where's Nina?'

'Go to hell!'

Eddie kicked him hard behind one knee. Irton cried out as his leg buckled, hands splayed across the wooden surface to hold himself up. 'See, the thing is,' the Englishman said, 'you've been trained in all this enhanced interrogation bollocks – waterboarding, electrics, stress positions, psych stuff. Break the mind, not the body, that's the idea, right? Now me, I'm not that subtle.' He again regarded the equipment in the cases, then spotted something better amongst the debris on the floor and picked it up. 'This is more my style. Last chance: where's my wife?'

Breath hissing through his clenched and bloodied teeth, Irton glared at him over one shoulder. 'Go fuck yourself, Chase. You think you can break me? Not a—'

A grimy hammer smashed down claw-first on his left hand with such force that it dug into the wood under his palm. Irton screamed and flailed, but was pinned in place. 'I can break *that*,' Eddie said coldly. 'Tell me where Nina is, *now*.'

He twisted the hammer. Irton made a keening sound, face clenched in pain, but said nothing. Eddie frowned – then grabbed Irton's left wrist before yanking the tool free and flipping it around. The torturer tried to pull away, but the Englishman held him in place and pounded the hammer down on to each of his knuckles. Bone cracked. Irton wailed in agony.

'Where is she?' Eddie yelled, letting go. The American crumpled to the floor, clutching his mangled hand. 'Talk to me!' He stood over Irton, waving the bloodied hammer in his face. 'Tell me why you've kidnapped Nina, or I'll take your other fucking hand off!'

'All right! All right!' Irton gasped. 'Stop, stop, oh God! I'll tell you!'

Eddie gave him two seconds to compose himself. 'Come on, then.'

'God!' He strained to force out the words. 'Our leader, the Prophet – he needs her to find the angels from the Book of Revelation.'

'What do you mean, angels? The guys with wings and trumpets?'

'No, they're . . . they're statues, hidden away. The Prophet found one of them, and he's trying to find the other three. The clues are in the Book of Revelation. He knows what to look for, but he needs an archaeologist to tell him *where* to look.'

Eddie frowned. 'Why Nina? He could have just paid someone to do that. Why kidnap her?'

'I don't know. I don't!' Irton protested as the Englishman raised the hammer. 'The Prophet chose your wife for a reason, but he didn't share it with us.'

'He'll share it with *me* if I get my fucking hands on him. Where is he?'

'At the Mission.'

'And where's that?'

Irton took another breath, eyes turning defiant once more. He was willing to endure more pain rather than give up the location. Eddie hefted the hammer again—

A bang from the entrance. Eddie spun. Raddick was back, arms laden with bags of takeaway food. 'Okay, I got your—'

He froze as he took in the scene. 'Shit!' he gasped, throwing down the food and fumbling inside his coat for a gun—

Eddie hurled the hammer.

Raddick had just got the gun clear of its holster when the steel claws smacked into his forehead with a sickening crack. He fell backwards, the tool embedded in his skull.

Eddie whirled back towards Irton – as the American leapt up and shoulder-barged him, sending him stumbling into one of the lamps and falling painfully on to his side. He scrambled upright, readying himself for an attack, but instead saw Irton run into the darkness of the empty building.

'Shit!' He hurried after him. The American was limping from the kick to his knee, but after more than a day tied to a chair, Eddie was little faster, muscles stiff and aching.

But he had to catch him. With both Berman and Raddick dead, Irton was his only link to Nina.

He followed the noise of the American's footsteps. Dim light appeared ahead through grimy windows high on the walls. A new sound reached him, a frantic clatter. Irton was climbing a metal staircase. Eddie made out the structure rising diagonally across the back wall and hurried to it, vaulting up the steps two at a time.

His quarry reached the top. A door was kicked open. Eddie saw Irton briefly outlined by the stark pinkish-orange glow of industrial sodium lights before he ducked out of sight.

He got to the door a few seconds later. Would Irton attack him as he came through? A split-second judgement: no, he was fleeing – flight, not fight. He booted the door and rushed outside.

Cold wind hit him as he emerged on a rooftop. Grim industrial blocks rose ahead. Where was Irton?

Off to the left, hobbling for the roof's nearest edge. Eddie raced after him. There was an electrical substation below, the dull hum of transformers growing louder. He had to be heading for a fire escape . . .

Shock as Eddie realised that he wasn't. There was nothing but a sheer fifty-foot drop. Irton wasn't just willing to suffer to protect his boss; he would make the ultimate sacrifice.

'No you bloody don't!' gasped Eddie, fighting through his own pain to run faster. Irton was twenty feet from the edge, ten . . .

He reached it just as Eddie dived at him.

The Englishman landed hard at the very lip of the roof, grabbing at Irton, but only managing to catch his left arm as he fell towards the substation. The torturer's sleeve slithered through his fingers—

One hand locked around Irton's wrist.

The American shrieked as smashed bones ground together, crushing nerves. Eddie tried to get a hold with his other hand, but Irton's weight was dragging him over the edge. He had no choice but to use it instead to brace himself . . . and the thrashing man started to slip through his grip.

'*Where is she?*' he yelled. Irton looked back at him, fear in his eyes behind the pain. Another nauseating crunch, and Eddie felt his opponent's mutilated hand slipping further through his own. He squeezed harder, but knew it was a losing battle. 'Tell me where Nina is, and I'll help you—'

Snap!

Bone broke, skin tearing with a hot gush of blood – and Eddie found himself holding nothing but a severed finger.

Irton plunged, screaming, to be impaled on the prongs of a transformer below. Sparks exploded from it, searing electrical discharges lancing out as the high-voltage current set his body aflame. Eddie jerked back as something overloaded and blew apart with a detonation that shook the building. The substation's lights flickered, then died, along with those of all the other nearby buildings.

'He went out with a bang,' Eddie muttered, furious as much with himself for not maintaining his hold as with Irton for taking Nina's whereabouts to the grave. Still clutching the finger, he stood and turned back towards the door . . . and for the first time saw where he was.

The skyscrapers of Manhattan glittered like cubic galaxies across the dark waters of the East River. His guess that he was in Brooklyn had been right. A bridge loomed to his left behind buildings; he had lived in New York City long enough to recognise it immediately as the Manhattan Bridge. That put him somewhere in Brooklyn's Vinegar Hill district.

He looked to the right along the river. The lights of the Williamsburg Bridge spanned the waters about a mile away. A moment of surprise at an unexpected yet impressive sight closer by: the massive airship that he had seen from Harvey Zampelli's helicopter was coming in to land for the night. Its temporary home was the nearby Brooklyn Navy Yard, the decommissioned military facility that was now an industrial park and movie studio. Advertising slogans flashed across its bulbous side, their very mundanity giving him a bizarre sense of relief. Whatever was going on, he had survived it, and returned to the real world.

The feeling lasted barely a moment. He was free, but the mysterious Prophet still had Nina – and he had absolutely no idea where. *Somewhere in the tropics* was all she had been able to tell him. That didn't really narrow it down.

Another retort from the substation. He had to get away from what would very soon become a crime scene; the explosion would bring first the fire department, then the cops. Whatever Irton and the others were doing, they had given the definite impression that it was on the clock. He couldn't afford to waste time being arrested and interrogated by the NYPD.

Fortunately, he had friends in the police.

'Eddie?'

'Down here,' he said, cautiously stepping out from behind a dumpster to greet the woman. 'Hi, Amy.'

Detective Amy Martin of the New York Police Department brought up her flashlight to regard him with shock. 'Jesus, Eddie! What the hell happened to you?'

He had retrieved his leather jacket and other belongings including his phone from the abandoned warehouse, but the garment couldn't disguise that he was covered in blood. 'Don't worry, it's not mine. Most of it.'

'That's what I'm scared of!' The dark-haired young cop came down the alley for a better look at him. 'Are you okay? What's going on?'

'I'm not sure myself. But you know there was an explosion a couple of blocks from here?'

'Yeah, I heard about it over the radio just after you phoned—' She broke off in dismay. 'Oh man. Don't tell me that was you.'

'Not . . . directly.'

"Cause they found a body.'

'Yeah, and they'll find another two in the factory next to it.'

Amy shook her head and sighed. 'God. What *is* it with you? What happened?'

'Short version: I was kidnapped, but got away. But Nina was kidnapped too, and they've still got her.'

Her eyes went wide. 'Kidnapped?'

'Off the street outside our apartment. I was tied up in a warehouse being tortured until about half an hour ago.' He pulled up his shirt to reveal lurid bruises. 'I need your help, Amy.

I've got to find Nina, but I can't do that if the cops take me in for questioning. I need you to cover for me.'

'Cover for you! People have *died*, Eddie – it's kinda hard to sweep that under the rug.' She eyed him. 'Did *you* kill them?'

'Yeah, but in self-defence. And the third one, I was trying to *save* him – he jumped off the roof rather than give up where they'd taken Nina.' He saw that she was still struggling to process his first admission. 'Come on, Amy! You *know* me. And you know the kind of stuff I keep getting dragged into.'

'But you don't even work for the IHA any more!'

'I bloody know! But whoever these arseholes were, it won't be long before their boss realises his torture team isn't answering his calls any more. Soon as he knows I've escaped . . .'

'They might hurt Nina,' she finished for him.

'Yeah. She's pregnant, Amy – I'm not going to let them do anything to her or our baby.'

Her eyes widened. 'She's pregnant?'

'Yeah.'

'Congratulations! And thanks for telling me when I saw you last,' she added with considerable sarcasm.

'I was busy chasing a Nazi!' he protested. 'Anyway, look – I promise you that as soon as Nina's safe, I'll tell the NYPD everything that happened.' He glanced down the alley as an emergency vehicle swept past, lights strobing. 'But right now, I need you to run interference.'

'Interference!' she hooted. 'This is going to turn into a murder investigation. If I interfere, I could do more than lose my job – I could go to jail!'

'Amy, please!' He fixed his eyes on hers. 'You trust me, don't you?'

'Oh, please, don't pull that card, Eddie,' she cried. 'You know I do! You saved the whole damn city.' It had taken his drastic physical intervention to prevent a nuclear device from being detonated at the end of Wall Street, his arm still scarred as a result. 'Everyone in New York owes you, and . . . and I just talked myself into helping you, didn't I?' She tipped her head back and let out a groan to the sky.

He grinned. 'Thanks.'

'Don't thank me yet. There's only so much I can do, even as a detective – and,' she warned, 'only so much I'm *willing* to do. I'm not going to lie for you.'

'I'm not asking you to.' They started back down the alley towards her car. 'For now, just get me to the UN – no, wait, take me home first. I want to check the apartment. And see if there's been anything reported about Nina or me being kidnapped. If someone saw me get Tasered and dragged into a van, that should be enough to tell the cops I was the victim. And if there isn't a report on Nina's kidnapping, start one!'

They reached the car. More flashing lights were visible down the street outside the derelict building. 'Okay, get in,' Amy said unhappily. He climbed inside as she took the wheel. 'These kidnappers – do you have any idea who they are?'

'No, but you can check if their prints are on file.'

A confused look. 'How?'

Eddie held up the severed digit. 'I'll give you the finger.'

9

A trip to the Upper East Side confirmed Eddie's fears. The apartment was empty, Nina's laptop still open in her study. She always closed it if leaving the room for more than brief periods. He hurriedly washed and changed his clothes, returning to Amy's car to learn that there had indeed been reports of an incident on the street. 'What, nobody recognised me?' he complained. 'Bloody snobby neighbourhood.'

'This helps you, though,' Amy pointed out. 'One of the witness statements said that someone was Tasered and taken away. That confirms you as the victim.' She gave him a rueful look. 'I'm still not sure how it'll balance against you killing all three of them, though.'

'Worry about that when I have to,' Eddie replied. 'Okay, we need to get to the UN.' As Amy started the car, he took out his phone and dialled a number – one that he had hoped never to need again.

By the time they arrived at the United Nations, the man Eddie had called was waiting for him at the security gate, his long overcoat flapping in the cold wind. 'Eddie,' said Oswald Seretse, the Gambian official pointedly rubbing his hands together for warmth before shaking the Englishman's. 'This is quite a surprise.'

'Yeah, for me too. Thanks, Amy.' He waved her off, then went with Seretse through the checkpoint. 'Glad I caught you. I didn't know if you'd still be working this late.'

'The world's leaders are meeting at the General Assembly soon,' Seretse replied, gesturing at a stack of crowd-control barriers piled ready for deployment nearby. 'That means long hours for everybody involved. Especially long-suffering departmental liaisons like myself – all the more so when working two jobs at once.'

'You're still the IHA's acting boss?'

'After Bill Schofield was killed, the other candidate for the director's position withdrew. It has gained a reputation as a remarkably dangerous post.'

'Tell me about it.' Eddie gave him a small smile, then looked up at the glass tower of the Secretariat Building as they approached the entrance. 'God, back here again. I can't seem to bloody escape it.'

'Yes, for someone who no longer works for the United Nations, you certainly seem to visit us quite frequently.' There was amusement in the diplomat's rich Cambridge-educated tones. 'So, what can I do for you this time?'

'Nina's been kidnapped.'

Seretse halted, the humour instantly evaporating. 'I see.'

'You don't sound too shocked.'

He sighed. 'I am long past the point where I can be surprised by anything that involves you or Nina. But why come to me rather than the police?'

Eddie decided to spare him the gruesome details of his recent captivity. 'Because whatever the people who've taken Nina want her for, it's something to do with her work at the IHA.'

'But Nina left the IHA at the same time as you.'

'I don't think they care. I know what they're after, but I've got no idea what it means or why they need Nina to find it. Which is why I came to you.'

Seretse nodded. 'Come inside.'

They entered the Secretariat Building, Seretse vouching for

Eddie at another security check, and took an elevator up to the tall diplomat's office. The Englishman gazed out of the window overlooking the East River as his host sat at his desk. 'I couldn't help but notice,' said Seretse, 'that you appear to have been in the wars.'

Eddie turned towards him, showing off the cuts and bruises on his face. 'Nina wasn't the only one who was kidnapped. They took me to force her to find what they're after.'

'Which is what?'

'Angels.'

The African's eyebrows rose. 'Angels?'

'Yeah. I told you, I don't know what that means. They let Nina talk to me, and before they cut her off, she managed to tell me what they were after; turns out these angels are from the Book of Revelations.' The eyebrows went higher still. 'Some kind of statues. One of the guys who kidnapped me said that the clues to finding them are hidden in the Bible, and his boss needs an archaeologist to help decode them.'

'Why Nina? There must be other archaeologists who could do that. Why risk kidnapping her?'

'That's what I want to know.' He looked back out of the window. In the distance downriver, beyond the Williamsburg Bridge, the giant spotlit eggshell of the now-moored airship marked the Navy Yard; he had been held prisoner not far from it. 'But she's not even in the country now – she said she was in the tropics. Some place called the Mission, apparently.'

Seretse typed on his laptop, then shook his head. 'I just searched for "tropics" and "Mission", but there are almost a million results.'

'I'm pretty sure if you Google "angels" and "Book of Revelations", you'll get even more,' Eddie said glumly. 'We're not going to find these statues that way. That's why I want to get the IHA involved.'

'You want to find the *angels*?' said Seretse, surprised. 'Not Nina?'

Eddie faced him again. 'Course I bloody want to find Nina. But I've got nothing to go on, and as long as they're holding her I've got no leverage either. But if I can get these angels before they do . . .'

'It gives you bargaining power. Nina for the angels.'

'Exactly. Whoever's behind this – some nut calling himself the Prophet – seems to want to find them as soon as possible, so there's probably a deadline, something that'll make him more desperate the closer it gets. If I reach 'em first, then he'll have to let Nina go if he wants them.'

'If he truly is desperate, that might put Nina in more danger,' Seretse warned.

Eddie regarded him grimly. 'Yeah, I know. But it's all I've got right now.' He sat facing Seretse. 'So I need another archaeologist to help me. Someone who's as good as Nina, and who knows about the Bible.' A small frown. 'Bible stuff isn't even Nina's speciality. I mean, she knows way too much about pretty much bloody everything to do with archaeology, but there must be people who've spent their entire *careers* on it. Why'd they need her?'

'I can't answer that,' said Seretse, typing again, 'but I can tell you who is currently working for the IHA and their areas of expertise.' He scanned the list on his screen. 'Dr Ari Ornstein is a specialist in ancient Hebrew civilisation . . .'

'Wrong half of the Bible,' Eddie said. 'Even I know that Revelations is New Testament, not Old.'

'Indeed.' He resumed his search. 'Colette Seigner's doctoral thesis was about the conversion of the Roman Empire to Christianity. Perhaps she might be able to help?'

'I know Colette, but . . . I dunno. Christianity didn't really take off with the Romans until a few centuries after Jesus died, did it?' A huff of frustration. 'I don't know when the Book of Revelations was written, but I don't think it was that late.'

'The first century AD, I believe. And no, the Roman Empire did not adopt Christianity as its official religion until AD 380, under the Edict of Thessalonica.'

Eddie shot him a wry grin. 'Maybe you should help me.'

'The by-product of a classical education, nothing more. My speciality has always been international law. Unfortunately, I doubt that will be much help to you.' Seretse read on – then leaned forward with sudden intrigue. 'Ah . . .'

'You've found someone?'

'Perhaps. She is no longer connected with the IHA – she resigned a few years ago – but amongst her many areas of expertise is New Testament archaeology, and she even still lives here in New York.'

'Sounds good to me,' Eddie proclaimed. 'Give her a call.'

Seretse seemed faintly pained. 'There is one small issue.'

'What is it?'

'She . . . dislikes you. And she *especially* dislikes Nina.'

'Why would anyone from the IHA dislike me? Don't you bloody even . . .' he added, catching Seretse's expression. 'And who hates Nina that much?'

The diplomat turned the laptop to face him, revealing a personnel file, complete with photograph. Eddie recognised the pinched-faced elderly woman immediately. 'Oh for fuck's sake. Why'd it have to be *her*?'

'Ah, Oswald,' said Professor Maureen Rothschild, welcoming the United Nations official into her apartment. 'A pleasure to see you again. It's been, what, three years?'

'The reception at the Egyptian consulate, I believe,' Seretse replied, kissing her cheek.

'Yes, I think it was.' She moved to close the door, but her

visitor remained in front of it. With a quizzical look, she continued: 'So what brings you here this late?'

He hesitated before answering. 'It is a . . . delicate matter. We need your help.'

'We? Do you mean the United Nations, or the IHA?'

'Actually, this is more a personal request. From myself, as a friend, but also from . . . someone you know.' He moved aside – to reveal Eddie as he stepped through the door.

'Ay up, Maureen,' said the Englishman, faking a smile. 'Remember me?'

The elderly academic had long been a thorn in Nina's side, their mutual dislike dating back even before his wife's discovery of Atlantis. Rothschild had a few years earlier been appointed as director of the IHA – whereupon her first act had been to shut down Nina's work. Her disdain for Eddie was simply through association, although from the way she regarded him, he couldn't help wondering if he had just tracked something unpleasant on to her carpet. 'Yes, I remember Mr Chase,' said Rothschild dismissively. 'What does he want?'

'Your help,' Seretse told her.

'My help?' she scoffed. 'Why should I help him? He and his wife were the main reason why I had to resign from the IHA after that fiasco in Egypt. You know, being forced to leave a high-profile organisation under a cloud does *not* do wonders for your résumé. If I hadn't already had tenure, I'm sure the university would have loved to shuffle me into early retirement—'

'Nina's been kidnapped,' Eddie cut in.

That silenced her, if only for a moment. 'That's . . . terrible,' she said, with a marked lack of conviction. 'I hope she's recovered safe and well.'

'So do I. That's why I'm here. The people who've got her are religious nuts who think she can take them to something mentioned in the Book of Revelations. Ozzy' – a glance at

Seretse, who held in a weary sigh at the diminutive – 'reckons you're the best person to work out how to beat 'em to it. At short notice,' he added. 'Who lives right here in New York.'

'How wonderful to get such a glowing recommendation,' Rothschild said acidly.

'But you *are* the best,' said Seretse, smoothly moving to soothe her ego. 'There are surely few people who could match your knowledge of the Bible from both an archaeological and a mythological perspective.'

Rothschild regarded him through narrowed eyes, but his appeal to her professional vanity had worked. 'I can at least hear you out, I suppose,' she said. 'Come in.'

She led the way into a lounge. It wasn't what Eddie had pictured; his past dealings with her had led him to expect the domain of a mean-spirited Victorian schoolmistress, but the furnishings had more of a bohemian feel, with lots of plump cushions. A large black and grey dog of indeterminate breed was sprawled on the floral carpet like a shaggy rug, its tail giving the new arrivals a single lazy wag before it settled back into sleep.

'Nice dog,' said Eddie.

'Horrible, smelly old thing,' Rothschild replied, with evident affection. 'Now, what's this Biblical mystery I can apparently help you solve?' She sat in an armchair, directing the two men to a sofa.

Eddie stepped over the dog to reach it. 'It's in the Book of Revelations—'

'Revelatio*n*,' she interrupted, with heavy emphasis on the last letter. 'It's a singular revelation, not plural. Not that I would expect the uneducated or ignorant to care about the importance of a single s.'

'You're right, I don't give a hit. But whatever it's called, these nutters really believe in it. They're making Nina find the angels of Revelatio*nnnnuhhh*,' he said with mocking exaggeration.

Rothschild ignored his sarcasm, deep thought already evident on her brow. 'Revelation is full of angels. "Thousands upon thousands", to quote it, and then specifically the four standing at the corners of the earth, the seven who blow the trumpets, another four bound at the Euphrates who are sent to wipe out a third of mankind . . .'

'Those last four sound like something people might want to get hold of. The kind of people me and Nina have dealt with before, anyway.'

Her scathing tone returned. 'Yes, you two do seem to be an almost magnetic draw for megalomaniacs, murderers and terrorists.'

'But if there is potentially some kind of threat to the world,' Seretse pointed out, 'then it does become the responsibility of the IHA's experts. Even those who no longer work for the agency.'

'I suppose you're right,' she said begrudgingly. 'But what are they?'

'Some sort of statues,' Eddie told her. 'They're making Nina look for places mentioned in Revelation. The Throne and Synagogue of Satan, she said.'

Rothschild sat up. 'The Throne of Satan?'

'You have heard of it?' Seretse asked. 'You know where it is?'

'Of course I do!' She sounded almost affronted. 'It's an early Christian name for the Altar of Zeus, from Pergamon in modern-day Turkey. Every archaeologist worth their salt would figure that out in five minutes or less. I don't know what it says about Nina if she couldn't.'

'She *did* work it out,' Eddie realised. 'Of course she bloody did. She just didn't tell them – she started looking for the other ones first!'

'Why would she do that?' said the diplomat.

'To buy time. The longer she can keep these arseholes from

finding the angels, the longer she'll stay alive. I didn't believe for a minute that the guys who tortured me were going to let me go home afterwards, and I bet Nina thinks the same.'

'You were tortured?' Rothschild asked, shocked.

Eddie pointed at the cuts on his face. 'I didn't get these shaving. But this altar – is there anything on it about angels?'

She shook her head. 'No, not that I know of. It's a pre-Christian relic; all the gods on it are Greek.'

'It's definitely the same thing from Revelation, though?'

'Absolutely. Pergamon, or Pergamum, is mentioned several times in the text, and the altar itself is a major archaeological treasure. I'm actually a good friend of the man overseeing its restoration, Dr Markus Derrick.'

Eddie turned to Seretse. 'Looks like I need to get to Turkey, then.'

'Turkey?' Rothschild laughed. 'The altar isn't in Turkey any more, Mr Chase. It was taken to Berlin in the late nineteenth century. It's the centrepiece of a whole museum.'

'Berlin? Even better, it's nearer. Ozzy, can you sort me out a flight?'

'I think,' Seretse said carefully, 'it may be a good idea for you to accompany Mr Chase, Maureen.'

'Me?' she exclaimed, startled.

'After all, you know Dr Derrick, I believe you speak German . . . and as an archaeologist, you should be able to help locate this mysterious angel.'

'What, you're suggesting that I drop everything and fly to Europe first thing tomorrow morning with' – a disapproving stab of her finger at Eddie – '*him*?'

'I wasn't thinking first thing tomorrow,' said Eddie. 'I was thinking, pull strings to get on the next flight out tonight. Or a private flight, even. I know the IHA can set them up at short notice – Nina did all the time when she was running it.'

Rothschild seemed about to make a biting comment, but Seretse headed her off with slightly more diplomacy. 'Yes, the UN's accountants and I remember very well.'

The Yorkshireman glared at him. 'This is *important*, Ozzy. Nina's life depends on it. And the baby's.'

'Baby's?' the old woman echoed. 'You have a baby?'

'Nina's pregnant,' Eddie told her. 'Four months. You didn't know?'

'I haven't exactly been following her on Twitter. But no, I didn't. My God.' She appeared genuinely shaken. 'Kidnapping a pregnant woman? That's ... that's *evil*, is the only way to describe it. I'm sorry.'

Despite the expression of sympathy, Eddie still couldn't let her abrupt change of heart pass without comment. 'If she hadn't been pregnant, though, you wouldn't have been bothered?'

Rothschild straightened, regarding him down her thin nose. 'Let me be clear, Mr Chase. I don't like you, and I especially don't like your wife. In my opinion, you've cost the field of archaeology far more than you've brought to it, with all the death and destruction you've caused.'

'Oh, is that right?' Eddie replied, bristling.

'But,' she went on, 'I don't believe that a child should suffer for the sins of the parents. Especially not an ... an unborn child.' Her voice quavered for a moment, but then she recovered. 'I want to ask you a question, and I expect – no, I *demand* – an honest answer. If I help you find this angel, do you really believe you'll be able to use it to bring Nina and her child home safely?'

'Yeah, I do,' he said without hesitation. 'I'm not an archaeologist, but this kind of thing? It's what I do best.'

'Everyone has one talent, I suppose ... Very well. I'll help you.' She turned to Seretse. 'Although I would like something in return.'

The diplomat tensed at being put on the spot. 'And what would that be?'

'Nothing major. Just some consultancy work for the IHA. With a stipend, of course. I'm getting on in life, and extra income is always welcome.'

Seretse looked at Eddie, who gave him a *do it!* nod. 'I will see what I can arrange,' he said wearily.

'And what about a plane?' Eddie asked.

'It will take a few hours, but I can get a private jet to take you to Germany. Exactly how I will explain it to the accountants, I am not yet sure.'

'You're a diplomat, you can justify anything.' Eddie stood. 'We'd better get going.'

'What about my dog?' said Rothschild, waving at the animal, which sleepily got to its feet and padded to her. 'Someone needs to look after him.'

'I will take care of that too,' Seretse assured her, with an air of resignation. 'Now, you will both need your passports.'

'I'll have to go home for mine,' said Eddie. 'Where'll this jet fly out of?'

'LaGuardia.'

'Okay, I'll meet you there. Both of you.'

Rothschild finished petting the dog, then stood. 'Going on a mission with you, Mr Chase. I would never have imagined it.'

'Yeah, over eight hours on a plane together?' Eddie said sarcastically. 'Can't wait.'

Even with Seretse's best efforts to expedite the process of chartering a private flight, it was still well after two o'clock in the morning by the time all the arrangements had been made. But finally he led Eddie and Rothschild across the damp concrete of LaGuardia airport towards a Gulfstream G550 business jet. 'You will be landing at Berlin Tegel,' the official told the two travellers over the whine of its idling engines. 'With the flight duration and the time difference, it will be late afternoon by the time you arrive.'

'Hope the seats recline, then,' said Eddie. 'We'll need some kip on the way. What about when we get there?'

'I've already spoken to Markus,' Rothschild said. 'We can go from the airport directly to the museum, and he's arranged for us to stay after hours to examine the altar. I should warn you, though,' she added, 'I mentioned that we were looking for some sort of angel or Christian symbol, and he's absolutely certain there isn't any such thing on the altar itself, or on any of the pieces awaiting restoration. He's been overseeing the work for almost a decade, so if there were anything, he would already have seen it.'

'Yeah, I was afraid of that,' replied Eddie. 'Can't imagine there'd be many places to hide something in an altar.'

'Have you learned anything more about the men who kidnapped you?' asked Seretse. 'You told me your friend in the NYPD was investigating.'

Eddie shook his head. 'She ran his fingerprint, and it came up blocked. Not unknown; restricted. So did the other dead guys. That means they were all US intelligence or special forces. Past or present, it doesn't matter – spooks always cover each others' arses.'

Rothschild gave him a nervous look. 'And these are the people who've kidnapped Nina?'

A sardonic grin. 'Welcome to our world.'

They reached the plane, a uniformed attendant waving them to the cabin steps. 'This is where I leave you,' said Seretse. 'I hope you find what you are looking for. And that you recover Nina safely,' he added to Eddie.

'Thanks, Oswald,' the Yorkshireman said, offering his hand. The diplomat shook it. 'See you when we get back.'

'If I still have my job,' he answered with a sigh, followed by a faint smile. 'Good luck, Eddie. And to you, Maureen.'

Eddie hopped up the steps. 'Okay, then. Let's go.' He ducked through the entrance, Rothschild exchanging a polite kiss on the cheek with Seretse before following. The attendant pulled in the steps, then sealed the hatch.

Ten minutes later, the Gulfstream left the runway. It climbed into the sky, leaving the lights of New York behind as it headed east into the night.

10

The Mission

Nina slowly emerged from a troubled sleep. The room was already uncomfortably warm, even early in the morning. She pushed the sheet down her body, shifting to find a cooler patch on the mattress—

Someone was standing over her.

'Jesus!' Nina shrieked, sitting bolt upright. Her unexpected guest was Miriam. The young woman squealed and jumped backwards. 'What the *hell*, Miriam? Why didn't you knock?'

'I did, I did!' she replied, hands flapping. 'You didn't answer, and I was worried, so the Prophet unlocked the door.'

'I was fine, until you scared the crap out of me! God *damn* it!' Nina pulled the sheet back up to her shoulders as she got out of bed. 'Never frighten a pregnant woman, it's not good for the baby.'

'I'm sorry, really I am.' Miriam turned her back.

'Dunno why I'm bothering covering myself; your creepy voyeur boss is watching me from six different angles,' Nina muttered with a glare at the nearest camera as she found her clothes. 'What are you doing here?'

'The Prophet sent me to get you. The angel's here.'

That caught Nina's attention. She paused, half dressed. 'Already?'

'Yes. The Witnesses arrived by helicopter about thirty minutes ago.'

The archaeologist's expression hardened. 'You know that Simeon and Anna killed people to get it, don't you? They murdered two security guards in Rome.' Seeing Miriam's shock, she pushed on: 'And those two men are dead because your Prophet forced me to find this angel by torturing my husband.'

She shook her head. 'No, no, I . . . I don't believe . . .'

'This place has got nothing to do with God, or Jesus,' Nina insisted. 'The people in charge are *murderers*. You're complicit in that just by being here. But if you help me get away, or just tell the authorities where I am, I can—'

'Good morning, Dr Wilde,' came a new voice, seemingly from all around her. Cross. There were loudspeakers as well as cameras inside the house. 'Miriam, I think you should return home. Norvin is on his way to bring Dr Wilde to me.'

Miriam bobbed her head obediently and went to the door. 'Yes, Prophet.'

'How many of them know?' Nina demanded loudly as she exited. 'Huh? How many of the people here know what you're doing in their name? You murdering bastard!'

'Everyone here believes in my cause,' said Cross as the door closed. 'They believe that the prophecies in Revelation will soon be fulfilled. I am God's instrument on earth; any actions I take in His name are justified.'

'So said every despot, whack-job and psycho for the past ten thousand years. I've met people who believed they had a hotline to God before, but they were all just lunatics. What makes you so different?'

'The difference, Dr Wilde, is that I really do.'

There was unshakeable conviction behind his words. 'Jesus,' whispered Nina, shaking her head. 'You're worse than I thought.'

'You'll soon see the truth. You won't be able to deny it once you've seen the angel. Now get dressed. Norvin is here.' A sharp rap came from the door.

'*He'd* better not come in while I'm naked.' Cross did not reply, but neither did the door open, though Nina still finished dressing as quickly as she could.

Once she was ready, Norvin escorted her through the Mission. The helicopter pad was empty, she noticed, so the pilot had not stuck around after delivering the Fishers and their cargo. At the church, he took her to the control room. The vault-like door was open, Cross inside. As well as his usual pristine white robes, he also wore a pair of fine cotton gloves of the kind she had sometimes used herself to handle delicate artefacts. 'Dr Wilde,' he called. 'Good to see you.'

'The feeling's about as unmutual as it could get,' she said.

Not even insults could dampen his smug elation. 'Come in. I want you to see what you've helped bring us.'

She entered the laboratory, Norvin at her back. Within, Simeon and Anna Fisher regarded her with unfriendly eyes. Beside them on the stainless-steel bench was a metal case; the same one Trant had carried the previous night.

Cross saw her flash of recognition. 'Yes, this is it. The second angel.' He opened the case.

The angel was revealed within, cleaned and polished, its metal wings glinting under the lights. It was made from a smooth grey material, cast rather than carved: pottery or ceramic fired in a kiln.

That was consistent with how Cross had described the artefact from Iraq. She glanced at the fragment of the first angel, still sitting inside its protective glass case, then back at the new arrival. 'Is it the same as the one you found?'

'Apart from the head, yes. That was a lion; this is an ox. Or a calf, depending which translation of the Bible you use.'

'It looks more like an ox to me,' Nina noted.

'I know. The King James version seems closer so far.'

She peered more closely at the statue, spotting something inscribed into the surface. 'There's something written on it. Have you had it translated?'

'I don't need to. I already know what it says. The angel I found in Iraq had the same words.' Cross carefully lifted the statue with his gloved hands, turning it to follow the text around its body. 'Revelation chapter four, verse eight: "And they rest not day and night, saying 'Holy, holy, holy, Lord God Almighty, which was, and is, and is to come.'" It doesn't literally mean that they're talking non-stop, but that the words written upon them are an eternal statement of God's greatness. Another of John's hallucinogenic interpretations of what he'd read.'

'You should put all this stuff in a book,' said Nina, not willing to be convinced, even though she couldn't fault his logic. 'There's always a huge market for explanations of the Bible. Call it *The Revelation Code* or something, I'm sure it'll be a best-seller.'

He shook his head. 'I'm not interested in money, Dr Wilde. I'm only interested in the truth; God's truth. Which is now one step closer to being revealed.'

'Well, it *is* called Revelation,' she said, but he was distracted from her facetious comment by a noise from outside – the roar of a helicopter coming in to land. 'Expecting company?' she asked.

'A . . . friend,' he replied. 'Norvin! Go and meet him.' The big man nodded and hurried from the lab.

Cross returned the angel to the case. Nina eyed it, but the close proximity of Simeon – and his gun – deterred her from getting nearer. 'So that's two angels accounted for,' she said instead. 'What about the others?'

'That's up to you,' said Cross. 'The Throne of Satan, and the Place in the Wilderness – we still have to figure out where they are. But since you found the Synagogue of Satan so quickly, I'm sure you won't have any problems.'

Nina forced herself not to show any reaction to the first undiscovered location. She had known where it was from the moment Cross had initially mentioned it: the only possible thing it could be was the Pergamon altar in Berlin. If the former CIA man or any of his followers had possessed an archaeological background, they would have worked that out already. Fortunately, fundamentalists – of any stripe – were prone to sticking solely to their existing beliefs rather than exploring anything that might challenge them. 'To be honest, I'm amazed that actually paid off,' she told him. 'My picking the Villa Torlonia was just a guess.'

'Not just a guess,' Cross replied. 'You were *guided*.'

'By whom?'

'God, of course.'

'*God* guided me?' she exclaimed. 'I don't think so! If God were giving me a helping hand, he wouldn't have let you kidnap me and torture Eddie.'

Something about her words briefly affected the others, glances – unsettled? Concerned? – flicking between Simeon and Cross, but whatever the cause, it quickly passed. 'He's not guiding you,' said Cross. 'He's guiding *me* – but as part of that guidance, He brought you to me. Everything you've been through, everything you've survived, that was all His will.'

'Really,' Nina said flatly.

'Really! You've fallen out of airplanes, escaped sinking ships, gotten through deathtraps – and you've had so many people try to kill you that you've probably lost count. Divine intervention is the only possible explanation for your survival. Wouldn't you say?'

'No, I wouldn't,' she insisted. 'I'd put knowledge, determination, desperation and sheer dumb luck above God keeping me safe so you could use me for your crazy plan.'

'It's not just his plan,' said a new voice from behind her. 'It's mine.'

Nina spun towards the entrance – only to freeze as she saw a horribly familiar face. 'Son of a *bitch* . . .'

Victor Dalton, the disgraced former leader of the free world, regarded her mockingly. 'If you don't mind, Dr Wilde, I prefer to be called *Mr President*.'

11

'I can think of plenty of other things to call you,' said Nina, struggling to hide her shock. While in the White House, Dalton had collaborated with religious extremists to try to kill her and Eddie to suppress their discovery of the Garden of Eden. He had then been forced to resign after Eddie leaked online a graphic video of his affair with the woman who had plotted the nuclear attack on New York, only to resurface seeking revenge on both the couple and a cabal of the world's wealthiest people, whom he considered to have betrayed and abandoned him.

The last she had seen of him was on television, being arrested by the FBI. 'So you didn't end up in a supermax prison? Damn.'

'People like me don't *go* to prison,' Dalton replied, his smile becoming caustic around the edges. 'You can't jail the President of the United States, even a former holder of the office. It would be a national embarrassment.'

'You *were* a national embarrassment!'

Any trace of good humour vanished. 'I was a better president than the idiot who replaced me. But in America, anyone can be rehabilitated – and actually, I have *you* to thank for giving me my chance.'

'How?'

'I don't know what you and your psycho husband did, but the Group went chasing after you into Ethiopia . . . and never came back. You did, though, so I assume you killed them.' She didn't reply, not wanting to give him any leverage against her. 'Hey, no need to be coy – I'm happy about it! Those bastards set me up, but after they disappeared, nobody at Justice had the balls to push the charges. So everything was quietly dropped.'

'Everyone still remembers that you were busted for security violations, though.'

He shrugged. 'The American public has a *really* short memory. There's always some rock star doing drugs or an actor making an ass of himself to distract them. Once the media stops pushing a story, it becomes a footnote.'

Nina smiled a little. 'Like your political career.'

'It's not over yet!' he snapped. 'That's why I'm here. I knew Mr Cross' – a brief look at the robed man – 'from my time on the Senate Intelligence Committee; our paths had crossed, no pun intended. And I knew he shared my views about the state of America, and the state of the world.' His tone became more oratorical. 'I've joined with him to continue what I started in office . . . and soon, I'll *regain* that office. I was hounded out of the White House as a philanderer. But I'll be voted back into it as a saviour.'

Nina treated him to slow, sarcastic applause. 'Nice stump speech. Who's it aimed at – adulterers and snake-handlers?'

'It's aimed at *everyone*, Dr Wilde,' Dalton said, with a flash of anger. 'Everyone in America. And they *will* all support me.' He moved to examine the statue, brushing past her. 'So this is it?'

'That's it,' Cross told him. 'One of the angels of Revelation. The clues to finding it were in the Apocalypse of John all along, but it took me to crack the code.'

'And me to find the statue for you,' Nina said, cutting.

'For which we're both very grateful,' said Dalton, politician's smarm back at full intensity. 'But the angels will let me finish what I started in office. Once they're . . . used' – he glanced at Cross again, as if to check that he wasn't giving away some secret – 'religious conflict around the world will reach new highs. All those jihadist groups, all those terrorists, they'll be targeting America like never before – and that will create the unstoppable desire at home to unify behind a single banner. One religion: *our* religion. This won't be some fake populism backed by billionaires who want tax cuts and the EPA disbanded. This will be real, and you'll either be with it, or against it.'

'Sounds like my idea of hell,' she said with distaste.

'Then get out.' There was a sudden vehemence to his words. 'You don't like America? Leave. We don't need you, or want you.'

'I guess you don't need or want the Constitution or the Bill of Rights either. The First Amendment ring any bells?'

'We'll be taking them back to their true intent. The next election isn't far off, and by then, the world will be in chaos. America will be crying out for strong leadership, and that's what I'll give them. I'll be standing as an independent against that jackass Leo Cole, and whoever the other side puts up against him – and I'll win. Once I'm back in power, I'll secure the homeland, and kick out anyone who's a threat to it. Including your friends at the UN,' he added. 'America shouldn't kowtow to anyone else's laws. We *make* the laws. And enforce them.'

Nina could hardly contain her disbelief at his new-found megalomania. 'America has treaties with the United Nations – are you just going to ignore them?'

'The United Nations!' Both turned at Cross's outburst. 'The most corrupt and evil organisation in history. It shouldn't be kicked out of America, it should be destroyed!' He gazed reverently at the angel, then stepped away and spread his arms to make a proclamation. 'The kings of the world will witness God's judgement soon enough. Babylon will fall. And then the kingdom of God will be founded here on earth!'

Both the Fishers and Norvin watched their Prophet, enraptured, while Dalton, clearly surprised, could only stare. But

Nina was looking not at Cross, rather at the statue, exposed and unattended just a few feet away.

Her chance—

She shoved the startled Dalton aside and snatched up the figure. The others all whirled, Simeon drawing his gun, but she had already raised the statue above her head. 'Back off or I'll smash it!' she cried.

They froze – but from the fear on Dalton's face and Anna's expression of horror, they were scared of something more than the destruction of a religious artefact. 'I mean it,' Nina continued, trying to cover her anxiety.

'Don't!' said Dalton, holding up both hands. 'That would be a – a very bad idea. For all of us.'

'Why?' she demanded. 'Is it dangerous?'

'Yes. It's dangerous,' said Cross. He indicated the glass case. 'I keep that piece of the first angel in there for a reason. It shouldn't pose a threat, not any more, but I'm not willing to take chances.'

'What kind of threat?'

He gestured at the artefact above her head. 'Will you put it down?'

'Nope,' she said defiantly. 'If anyone tries anything . . .'

'If you break open the angel,' said Cross, 'we'll all die. Not just us in this room, but everyone in the Mission. Please. Put it down.'

Nina looked up at the statue. It didn't 'appear deadly, but it was unusually heavy for its size. 'Is there something inside it? Is that what you're all so scared of?'

Cross nodded. 'You remember I told you the Umm al Binni lake was a meteor crater? The meteorite that hit there wasn't just a rock. There was something more to it – something deadly. "And I saw a star fall from heaven unto the earth, and to him was given the key to the bottomless pit. And he opened the bottomless pit; and there arose a smoke out of the pit, as the smoke of a great

154

furnace. And there came out of the smoke locusts upon the earth." Revelation chapter nine, verse one. The pit was the impact crater, and I saw the smoke myself, in Iraq. When the first angel was broken.'

'Smoke came out of it?'

'Not smoke; *gas*. There was something inside the meteorite, a substance that doesn't occur naturally on earth, that reacted with the air.' He turned to Anna. 'Anna was a chemist and biochemist for the CIA – she can explain it.'

'It was a pyrophoric material,' said Anna. 'Something that ignites spontaneously when it comes into contact with oxygen. It burns at a high temperature, judging from the effect it had on the ceramic containing it' – she indicated the fragment inside the cabinet – 'until it's completely consumed. But as it burns, it gives off an extremely toxic by-product.'

'A yellow cloud, like sulphur,' said Cross solemnly. 'It kills almost instantly. I had protective gear, but the Arab rebels didn't. They all died in agony, as if they were being eaten alive by insects, after just a few seconds.'

Nina gave the statue another look, this time considerably more nervous. 'So this material, part of the meteorite . . . it's *inside* the angel?'

'Yes. The twenty-four Elders managed to contain pieces of it.'

'How? If it burns on contact with air . . .'

'Water stops the reaction,' Anna told her. 'Or at least slows it.'

'It poisons the water, though,' said Cross. 'Exactly as Revelation said in chapter eight. "The sea became blood", and then three verses later, "and many men died of the waters, because they were made bitter". The fragments must have poisoned the water supply around the crater. But the Elders figured out a way to make them safe.'

'Seal them in clay while they're still in the water, then harden the outer shell in a kiln, I'd guess. The wings were a way to reinforce it?' Nina said, lowering the statue slightly for a better look. Cross nodded in confirmation. 'And over time . . . the story of what happened turned into folklore,' she realised. 'The meteorite became a burning mountain, the locusts were the toxic gas, all inflicted on humanity by an angry God – and the statues became angels, based on existing mythology. I've seen the same four heads representing angelic beings before, in the Garden of Eden.'

Cross stepped closer, holding out his hands. 'Put the angel down, Dr Wilde,' he said. 'If you destroy it, we won't be the only ones who'll die. The cloud will spread over the entire Mission. There are almost a hundred people here – do you want to be responsible for their deaths?'

'Whatever you're planning, they're in it with you,' said Nina, but with uncertainty.

The former CIA agent picked up on it at once. 'You think Miriam's in on it? She's a sweet, innocent young girl who's following her heart. She's never hurt anyone in her life.' A firmer tone. 'Just like Macy.'

Nina's jaw clenched at her friend's name. 'You son of a bitch. Don't you talk about her.'

'I know what you think – that it's your fault she died,' he pressed on. 'And the guilt over that's been eating away at you ever since, hasn't it? That's why you went into therapy. Because of the guilt.'

Tears stung the corners of Nina's eyes. She angrily blinked them away. 'Screw you.'

Another step nearer. 'If you smash the angel, you'll murder a lot of innocent people. Including Miriam.'

She looked at the heavy steel door. 'Not if you close that. The only people who'll die will be in here.'

'Mr President?'

'Yeah?' said the sweating Dalton.

'Leave the room, please. Norvin, Anna, Simeon – you too.'

Nina hefted the statue again. 'I'm warning you!' But Dalton made a hurried exit, Cross's followers doing so more reluctantly to leave the pair alone.

'I know you won't do it,' said the cult leader. 'You can't accept more innocent people getting hurt because of you. Especially not the most innocent of all.' He looked down at the bump marking the presence of the new life inside her.

She felt a hot tear run down one cheek. 'Son of a *bitch*,' she hissed. But the statue remained in her raised hands.

'Give it to me.'

Nina drew in several angry breaths . . . then slowly lowered her arms. Cross reached out to take the statue. He had to pull it from her grip, her fingers refusing to surrender, but then it was his. 'I should have done it,' she whispered, but she knew he was right.

'I'm glad you didn't.' He placed the angel in the case and closed the lid. 'But it proves what I told you. God kept you alive as part of His plan.' The statue secure, he called out: 'Simeon! It's okay. You can come back in.'

Simeon hurried into the lab. He aimed his gun at Nina, but Cross signalled for him to lower it. The others followed, Dalton last to enter after peering nervously around the door. 'Is everything safe?' he asked.

'It's safe,' Cross replied.

Nina wiped away another tear. 'So you got your precious angel,' she said bitterly. 'Is that your plan? You're going to break it open and claim that all the victims died because it was God's will? Poison Mecca or somewhere to start a religious war?'

Dalton looked momentarily startled, but Cross shook his head. 'This isn't about war, Dr Wilde. It's about fulfilling a prophecy – and it's about *knowledge*.'

'What do you mean?'

'I was a CIA operative – a spy. It was my job to find out information about America's enemies, to discover their secrets. But when I went to Iraq, when I found the temple and the first angel, I realised there was a way to discover *the* secrets, the most important ones in all creation. The secrets of God Himself!'

Nina stared at him, unsure how to respond to his sudden messianic shift. 'God's secrets? What . . .'

'It's written in the Book of Revelation!' Cross continued, as if offended that she didn't know. 'Chapter ten, verse seven – "But in the days of the voice of the seventh angel, when he shall begin to sound, the mystery of God should be finished, as he hath declared to his servants the prophets." Do you know what that means? It means that as the seventh angel sounds his trumpet, all of God's secrets will be revealed to his prophets. And I *am* one of those prophets!'

He turned to his followers, who watched enraptured even as Dalton seemed faintly uncomfortable. 'Seven angels are given a task in turn by God. The sixth angel is ordered to loose the four angels that were bound at the Euphrates. *These* are those angels!' He stabbed one hand at the fragment behind glass, the other at the closed case. 'One has already been released, in Iraq. We've found the second angel – so there are only two more to locate.' He whirled back to face Nina, his pale eyes wide and terrifyingly intense. 'Two more for *you* to locate. When we have them, they'll be released. President Dalton will get his war, but I'll get something more important. Once all the statues have been loosed and the sixth angel's task is completed, the seventh angel will sound – and God will reveal everything to me. His plan, His secrets, the meaning of everything. I'll know it all.'

Nina was speechless for several seconds, the sheer madness of his plan almost too much to process rationally. 'So you think,' she finally said, 'that loosing the angels, releasing this gas and killing who knows how many people will persuade God to let you into his inner circle? You're *insane!*'

Both the Fishers reacted angrily, Simeon advancing with his fists balled, but Cross waved him back. The cult leader was also furious, but contained it – just. 'Unbelievers throughout history have accused God's prophets of being mad,' he growled. 'Noah, Moses, even Jesus Christ – they've all faced mockery. But you'll see the truth once all four angels are loosed. The army of the horsemen will be unleashed upon the earth, just as Revelation says – and as Babylon falls, I will know God's plan.' His voice rose to a shout. 'I *will* know!'

Appalled, Nina turned to Dalton. '*You* can't believe any of this? You're a politician – you're in this for yourself, not to fulfil some Biblical prophecy!'

'Thank you for that vote of confidence, Dr Wilde,' Dalton said sarcastically. 'But you're wrong. I *do* believe; I believe that finding and unleashing the rest of the angels will make America stronger. That's my duty to my country, as a true patriot.'

'Patriot, my ass,' Nina snarled. 'You're so crooked, you make Nixon look like Mother Teresa.'

Now it was Dalton's turn to be angered, but before he could reply, Cross, his composure now recovered, cut in. 'I'm not asking you to believe, Dr Wilde. I'm asking you to *obey*. There are still two more angels out there. The Throne of Satan, and the Place in the Wilderness – where are they?'

'I don't know. And even if I *did* know, now that you've told me what you're planning, there's no way I'm going to help you find them.'

'I didn't *only* suggest using you to find the angels out of revenge – although I have to admit, that was a bonus after everything you and Chase did to me,' said Dalton. 'I genuinely believed you were the person most likely to succeed. But if you're not going to cooperate, then you're . . . surplus to requirements.'

'No, no,' said Cross, holding up a hand. 'She *will* find them for us.'

'Did God tell you that?' Nina said with a sneer.

'No. You did.' His gaze intensified. 'I was an intelligence officer, Dr Wilde. I know people – how they think, how they'll respond to specific situations. And I know that you'll do what I ask to protect your husband.' He led the group back into the control room and went to the video wall. 'I'll demonstrate.'

A tap on the controls, and the screens blinked on – showing Eddie still secured to the chair. The camera had changed position, now staring down at him from his left side. He looked around, mouth moving as he responded to someone out of frame, but the audio was muted.

'Waterboard him,' said Cross. 'Don't hold back this time.' Irton appeared, a towel in his hands.

'God damn you,' Nina gasped as Eddie tried in vain to break loose. A silent shout at Irton, who responded by punching him in the stomach. The torturer's two assistants prepared to tip the chair backwards as their boss swaddled the Englishman's head in the thick cloth. 'Don't do it, please!'

Cross was unmoved. 'It's up to you how long this goes on. A minute, an hour . . . all day. He won't die, but he'll wish he could.' The chair was lifted and tilted back until its occupant's head hit the floor. 'All you have to do to stop it is tell me where one of the other angels is.'

'But I don't know,' she protested.

Irton brought a bucket to the chair. 'I think you do,' said Cross. 'You already know something, and you're keeping it from me. Do you think I'm an idiot? I know when someone's hiding the truth. Finding it is what I do. Irton!'

The bucket tipped, sending a gush of water over Eddie's

cocooned head. He convulsed, mouth open in a silent scream beneath the sodden material. Nina gasped in sickened, helpless fear.

'I really think you ought to do what you're told,' said Dalton, tone patronising.

'Your choice, Dr Wilde,' Cross added. 'There's only one way to stop this.'

She stared in anguish at the man she loved, the father of her child choking as more water filled his airways. She tried to resist, but felt surrender swelling inside her as his torment continued, unable to contain it—

'Berlin,' she whispered.

Cross jabbed at a control, the monitors going black. 'What?'

'Berlin,' Nina repeated. 'The Throne of Satan from Revelation – there's only one thing it can be, and that's the Altar of Zeus from Pergamon. John had obviously been there, because he knew Antipas the martyr, so he would have known about the altar as well.'

'Isn't Pergamon in Turkey?' demanded Dalton.

'The whole thing was transported to Germany in the late nineteenth century. It's a Greek relic, though – I don't know of any connection to ancient Judaism or Christianity.'

'But there must be one,' said Cross. He touched the control pad. 'Irton, let him go. For now.' He turned to Nina. 'Get back to work. Research this altar, find anything that might link it to the angel or the twenty-four Elders.'

She nodded, despondent. 'I'll do what I can.'

'What about the Place in the Wilderness?' he added. 'Are you keeping that from me too? Because if you are . . .'

'I don't know anything about that,' she insisted, truthfully.

His unsettling eyes stared into hers, then he nodded. 'Okay. Focus on the altar for now.'

'Do you want us to fly to Germany?' asked Simeon.

'No, Trant can handle it. Tell him to get the team to Berlin. You work out a plan to extract the angel once we find it.'

'*If* we find it,' said Dalton. 'If this altar's been moved, the angel might already have been discovered when it was dismantled.'

Cross shook his head. 'No. It's waiting to be found. I have faith. In God's plan . . . and in Dr Wilde's love for her husband. She won't let him suffer.'

'Go to hell,' Nina muttered, filled with shame for having capitulated. She looked at the case containing the angel. 'I should have smashed that thing when I had the chance.'

'I'm glad you didn't,' said Dalton. 'You're doing what's best for America. You'll see.'

'Anything that involves you can't be what's best for America.' But there was almost no defiance left in her, just sullen resignation.

'Norvin, take Dr Wilde back to her house,' ordered Cross. 'She has a lot of work to do.' The bodyguard escorted Nina out.

Dalton waited until she was gone before speaking again. 'Two angels found already? I knew she was good, much as I hate to admit it, but I'm surprised she located them so quickly. Mind you,' he added, gesturing towards the empty screens, 'you did give her an incentive.'

'We got lucky,' Cross said quietly.

'What do you mean?'

'I mean this.' He tapped the touchpad again. The image of the warehouse reappeared – but this time it was a freeze-framed scene of chaos.

Dalton flinched as he saw a body at the end of a smeared trail of gore. 'What the hell happened?'

'Chase happened,' came the reply.

'Chase?' The ex-politician rounded on Cross with a sudden

flash of fear, which he had to fight to keep under control. 'You mean he's *escaped*?'

'He broke out late last night. I don't know what happened after he killed Berman – this was the last image before the video link was cut off – but since I can't contact Irton or Raddick, I have to assume they're dead too. What I just showed Wilde was a recording, flipped so she wouldn't realise it was the same thing she saw before. If she hadn't caved in when she did, I would have run out of footage, and she would have realised we don't have Chase any more.'

'But – but he could bring this whole thing down!' Dalton's words rose in pitch despite his best efforts to maintain a calm front. 'If he finds this place, if he rescues Wilde, it'll all point back to me!'

'Irton's tracks are covered,' said Cross, with more than a hint of impatience. 'Chase won't find the Mission.'

'Chase once found his way into my *house*, into my goddamn *bedroom*, and that was when I still had Secret Service protection! You underestimated him, Ezekiel. That's a big mistake.'

'I know what I'm doing, *Mr President*.' Dalton was taken aback by Cross's warning tone, but the cult leader ignored his reaction. 'If Chase tries to interfere with the plan . . . we'll kill him.'

12

Berlin

'Nice day for it,' Eddie sighed, watching the rain-drenched outskirts of the German capital crawl past beyond the clogged autobahn. He and Rothschild had unluckily landed at Tegel airport just in time to catch the evening rush hour. 'Everyone's drowning in Berlin.'

His companion didn't get the reference to the old pop song; either that, or she was simply ignoring him. 'Why are we going this way?' she complained instead. 'The Saatwinkler Damm would be much more direct.'

'Calm down, the IHA's paid for the ride.' The Mercedes had picked them up at the terminal. 'It's not like the driver's trying to rip you off by taking us via Poland.'

Rothschild's pinched little mouth shrank further, but rather than make a sarcastic rejoinder, she instead spoke in German to the driver. 'There's been a car crash,' she told Eddie. 'So we're having to go a longer way around. But at least this way we'll see more of the city.'

Eddie peered at the heavy slate-grey sky and the wet tower blocks silhouetted against it. 'Terrific, I'll get my camera ready. So you know Berlin pretty well?'

'It's been a while since I was last here, but yes. I even lived here for several months after I got my masters in archaeology.'

'Yeah? Did you meet the Kaiser?'

'No, of course not, that was a long time before—' She finally got the joke and treated him to a withering glare. 'I'm no fan of Nina's, but I always thought she was at least intelligent. Her seeing *anything* in you makes me question that, though.'

Eddie shrugged, grinning. After putting up with the elderly woman's barbs on the long journey across the Atlantic, he'd been unable to resist getting in one of his own. 'Is that how you know the bloke at this museum?' he asked, changing the subject.

'Markus? Yes. We've been friends for a long time. And by that, I mean since the 1970s, not the 1910s,' she added peevishly.

The Englishman smiled again, then turned his attention back to the city. His only prior visits to Germany had been brief, and he had never been to Berlin itself. What he'd seen of it so far was what he had expected, however: lots of post-war tower blocks, though with more green space around them than similar developments in London or Paris. The car crossed over a river – or given its straightness, a canal – and continued towards the capital's heart, more unappealing concrete buildings rolling by before the visitors passed over another bridge and before long entered a large swathe of parkland.

'That's the Siegessäule,' said Rothschild, pointing ahead.

'The what?'

'The Victory Column. There.' Eddie looked past the driver and saw a tall pillar at the end of the road, a winged golden figure at its top. 'It used to be in front of the Reichstag, but Hitler and Albert Speer had it moved. A good thing, otherwise it would have been flattened by Allied bombers. This park leads all the way to the Reichstag and the Brandenburg Gate, actually.'

'Uh-huh,' said Eddie, not particularly interested. Monuments to the common soldiers who had fallen in wars meant more to him than extravagant celebrations of the politicians who claimed to have won them. But as the Mercedes negotiated the large roundabout circling the edifice, he had to admit that it was quite impressive, floodlights making the statue at its summit gleam even in the rain. 'The Brandenburg Gate's where the Berlin Wall was, right?'

'Yes, and it was the site of the signing of German reunification. So you know *some* history, then.'

'Military history I'm pretty good on. I even surprise Nina sometimes.' He looked ahead as the car turned on to a long, broad tree-lined avenue, but saw nothing through the traffic and the dull haze of rain. 'How far is it?' he asked, peering at the driver's satnav to get an idea of the city's layout. A winding river bisected the capital, its wide, snaking curves running north of their current position.

'Over a mile,' Rothschild told him.

'Glad we're driving, then. Don't fancy getting wet – I had way too much of that recently.' His expression darkened as he briefly thought back to his waterboarding ordeal. Rothschild gave him a curious look, but decided not to voice any questions.

The Mercedes continued down the long avenue. Eventually the towering triumphal arch of the Brandenburg Gate came into sight, though to Eddie's slight disappointment the road didn't go through it, traffic instead diverting around a broad pedestrianised area. Even in the bad weather, there were still plenty of tourists at the monument. 'Not far now,' said Rothschild as the gate passed out of sight behind a building.

'Great,' Eddie replied. 'This friend of yours, Dr Derrick – he's an expert on this altar, right?'

'It's been his life's work, and he's in charge of overseeing its restoration, so you could say that, yes.'

'Good. 'Cause I've been thinking—'

Flat sarcasm. 'Really.'

'A hardy har. I've been *wondering* how this angel could be

hidden in it without anyone having found it already, even if it's behind a secret panel or something.'

Rothschild smiled patronisingly. 'Do you know how big the Altar of Zeus is, Mr Chase?'

'I dunno. But an altar's basically a fancy table, so . . . ten feet long and six wide?' he guessed. 'Twelve feet?'

She could barely hide her amusement. 'A little bigger.'

The Brandenburg Gate reappeared behind them as the car turned on to a wide boulevard and headed east for roughly half a mile, then picked its way north through smaller streets before finally stopping. 'This is it?' Eddie asked. Another glance at the satnav told him that their destination was actually on an island.

'That's it,' Rothschild replied. 'The Pergamon Museum.'

A footbridge spanned a waterway in front of the imposing classical building, steps leading up to a plaza between the two long wings of the museum. A far more modern structure, a cylindrical tower, occupied most of the space. 'Big place just for an altar.'

'The Altar of Zeus isn't the only exhibit; there's also the Museum of Islamic Art, the Near East museum and the antiquity collection. But Markus can show you . . . Ah, here he comes.' A tall figure beneath a large black umbrella scuttled down the steps and crossed the bridge to meet them.

The driver opened the door for Rothschild, Eddie following her out. 'Markus, hello!' she trilled, embracing then kissing the new arrival. 'It's so good to see you again!'

'You too, after all these years,' said the square-jawed German. Eddie guessed him to be in his sixties, although his hair was a chestnut brown suspiciously rich for someone of that age. 'Ah, Maureen. *Willkommen zurück*, welcome back. Come, come inside, out of this rain.'

Rothschild took shelter under his umbrella and was about to go with him when Eddie cleared his throat. 'Oh. Yes,' she said, with faint irritation. 'Markus, this is Eddie Chase. Mr Chase, Dr Markus Derrick.'

'Nice to meet you,' said Eddie, offering his hand.

Derrick shook it with enthusiasm. 'Mr Chase.' He gave Rothschild an expectant look, awaiting a more detailed introduction, but none came. 'Okay! Please, come with me.' The group headed across the bridge, Eddie getting wet as his travelling companion stayed beneath the umbrella. 'So, you have come all this way to see the Pergamon altar, yes? It is a good thing Maureen is my friend; that wing of the museum will be closed to the public for some years as we build a new roof. But I can get you in. As the director of the altar's restoration, it is a perk of the job!' He chuckled.

They reached the glass doors leading into the cylindrical structure, which housed a lobby and visitor centre. The museum was still open, though the tourists were now mostly leaving. Derrick nodded in greeting to a security guard, who let the group through a side gate, and they headed into the building proper.

'Now, what is this about?' he asked. 'Your phone call was very mysterious, Maureen. You want to examine the altar for . . . angels? Christian symbols? You can be sure there are none. I have looked very carefully at it for over twenty years!'

'It might not be *on* it,' said Eddie. 'It might be hidden inside it, we don't know. All we do know is that these angels are something to do with the Book of Revelation – and somebody's kidnapped my wife to try to get hold of them.'

Derrick stopped in surprise. 'Kidnapped your wife?'

Rothschild anticipated his next question. 'He's married to Nina Wilde.'

'Nina Wilde? *The* Nina Wilde?'

'You know her?' Eddie asked.

'Of course I do! We have never met, but I know of her,

naturally. *Menschenskind*! Married to Nina Wilde. A remarkable career she has had, yes.'

Eddie took a moment of pleasure from Rothschild's visible jealousy – whatever her issues with Nina, Derrick didn't share them – but had more important concerns. 'They're forcing her to look for these angels. And we think they've already found one.'

'In Rome,' added Rothschild. Seretse had given them the news during the flight. 'Someone broke into the Jewish catacombs in the Villa Torlonia last night. Nobody knows what they took, but they smashed a hole in a wall to get it. And murdered two security guards as they escaped.'

Derrick was shocked. 'Murdered! Who are these people?'

'Some sort of religious cult,' said Eddie. 'Their leader reckons he's a prophet.'

'Since they seem obsessed by the Book of Revelation, it's reasonable to assume that the prophecies they're interested in are of the doomsday kind,' Rothschild said.

'Okay,' said Derrick, perturbed. They set off again. 'Then you are here because the altar – or the Throne of Satan – is mentioned in Revelation?'

'That's right,' Eddie replied. 'Soon as I told the Prof about it, she knew what it meant.'

'Mr Chase thinks Dr Wilde had already made the connection but was deliberately holding it back to buy time,' said Rothschild. 'Whether she did or not, she still apparently identified another site, possibly the Synagogue of Satan from Revelation – and because of that, two innocent people were killed.'

'Don't you bloody dare,' Eddie warned her. 'She'd have done everything she could to slow them down. If she hadn't, they might already be here.' He glanced at the museum's visitors. 'And even more people could get hurt.'

Derrick was becoming more alarmed by the moment. 'There

could be a danger to the public? I shall arrange more security.'

'If we find this angel, you might not need to,' the Englishman told him. 'Once I've got it, I'm going to use it to make them let Nina go.'

'Two points,' said Rothschild. 'First: even if we do find it, it's not yours to take – it's the property of the German government, and I doubt they'll let you simply hand it over to some murderous cult. Second: how will you let these people know you have it? You don't have any way to contact them.'

'I'll find 'em. Or they'll find me. Either way, they'll know I've got the thing. Once we figure out where it is.'

Derrick led them to a set of glass double doors with a barrier in front. He moved the obstacle aside. 'I do not know if there really is an angel hidden inside the altar, but' – he opened the doors wide – 'you are welcome to look.'

Eddie followed the avuncular German through – and stopped in astonishment.

The room was a cavernous space in its own right, but its contents were what had impressed him. The far side was occupied by what he assumed was a Greek temple, wide stairs leading up between the two arms of the inspiration for the museum's exterior. Elegant columns supported a roof bearing several statues, an opening beyond the top of the steps leading to a display room.

There was more to the temple than sheer size, though. Around its base was an elaborate frieze, larger-than-life carved figures of gods and heroes locked in combat with monstrous creatures. Sections were missing, however, pale blank stone filling the gaps.

'Okay, wasn't expecting this,' Eddie said. 'It's pretty good.' Rothschild made a faintly exasperated sound.

Derrick was apparently more used to British understatement. 'It is, yes?' He swept an arm from one side of the frieze to the other as they approached. 'That is the Gigantomachy, the battle of the gods of Olympus – Apollo, Athena, Hecate and others – against the giants. There are more panels along both the sides.'

'Lot of gaps in 'em,' Eddie observed.

'Yes, unfortunately. But there are many more pieces that we are reassembling. Some day we hope to finish the whole display.'

'So where's this altar, then?' Eddie looked up the steps, assuming it would be at the top, but saw nothing.

Derrick gave him a confused look before laughing, while Rothschild struggled to contain a mocking snigger.

'All right, what's the joke?' Eddie demanded.

'This *is* the altar,' said the German. He waved his hand again to encompass the whole of the massive structure. 'All of it! The Altar of Zeus, moved brick by brick from Turkey.'

Eddie stared up at the building in dismay. 'Buggeration. This might take longer than I thought . . .'

13

Eddie reached the end of the Gigantomachy frieze on the altar's right wing, gazing up at the final panels – displaying a warrior with his face and one arm missing beside an equally incomplete horse – before turning and retracing his steps back around the structure to the same position on the left side. A tall mirror was mounted on the back wall to create the illusion that the building continued deeper into the museum; his reflection regarded him disconsolately.

There were numerous winged figures amongst the carved combatants, which he had immediately thought were angels, but Rothschild and Derrick explained during the group's examination of the ancient temple that they were actually Greek gods such as Nike and Uranus. It was a sign of his growing concern that he hadn't made a joke about either name. The German had assured him that the sculptures were solid slabs of marble, with nothing concealed either inside or behind them, and that they long pre-dated the birth of Christ.

'So where is this bloody thing?' he asked himself. The balding mirror image had no answer. With a sigh, he went back the way he had come.

The two archaeologists were at the top of the stairs, in the display room behind the facade. Eddie ascended to find them examining another frieze set out along the walls. 'Have you found anything?'

'No, I'm sorry,' Derrick replied. 'There is nothing I know of on the altar that could possibly be any kind of Christian symbol, not even in the unrestored pieces in storage.'

'Damn. And there's no way the gods with wings might have been seen as angels?'

Rothschild shook her head. 'The early Christians explicitly rejected the Greek and Roman pantheon – they called this place the "Altar of Satan" for a reason. And the modern image of an angel, a man with wings on his back, doesn't match the Biblical descriptions of them. They generally look indistinguishable from ordinary people, but they can also be beings of fire, or lightning, or even resemble some sort of machine – "a wheel intersecting a wheel" is I think how it's worded. The angels in Revelation are just as varied, but none are described as men with wings.'

'How *are* they described?' Eddie asked. 'Anything that matches these guys?' He indicated the frieze.

'Not that I can think of.'

He turned away in frustration, trying to think of anything to help him locate the angel – and his wife. 'These arseholes found something in Italy. Nina worked out where it was . . . but *what* was it? How did they know what to look for?'

'I don't know,' said Rothschild. 'But according to Oswald, they went to a specific spot in the catacombs and smashed a wall open to reveal a cavity. Presumably they took whatever was inside.'

'The angel?' asked Derrick.

'Maybe. But nothing else appeared to have been damaged.'

'So why did they go to that spot?' wondered Eddie. 'This catacomb – is there anything on the walls? Paintings, inscriptions, that kind of thing?'

'Some paintings, yes,' said Derrick. 'I have not been there, but I have seen photographs. Most are decorative, but there are some Hebrew religious symbols . . .'

He broke off, lips pursed. 'What is it?' Eddie asked.

'Hebrew symbols,' the German replied. 'I did not think about it earlier, because you told me you were looking for *Christian* symbols.

But there is a piece in storage . . .' He searched his memory, then his eyes widened. 'Yes, I know which one. Come with me.'

He strode from the antechamber, Eddie and Rothschild hurrying down the stairs after him. 'What is it, Markus?' asked Rothschild.

'There is a panel that we have not yet managed to match to a specific location on the altar,' said Derrick, leading them into a side room. This was also closed to the public, plastic sheets covering some of the exhibits and scaffolding rising up one wall. Eddie had been married to an archaeologist long enough to recognise that the treasures in this room were Roman rather than Greek. The columned front of a pale marble structure rose almost to the high ceiling. 'The Market Gate of Miletus,' the German remarked as he headed up a ramp and through a doorway at its centre. Another barrier beyond blocked the way; he moved it.

'God, it's like I've stepped through a time portal,' Eddie exclaimed as he took in his new surroundings on the far side. Roman history had given way to Arabian, the gateway through which they had come a towering blue arch topped by elaborate castellations. 'What's this?'

'The Ishtar Gate,' Derrick told him, replacing the barrier. 'Part of the walls of Babylon. We are now in the Vorderasiatisches Museum – the Museum of the Near East.'

Eddie looked down a corridor ahead, the walls of which were lined with more relics. 'I'm almost glad Nina's not here,' he said with a grim smile. 'She'd never leave the bloody place.'

'This way.' Derrick brought them to a flight of stairs. The museum had now closed, Eddie realised; there were no other visitors. He went up the steps after the other man, who opened a side door and led them down a passage. 'This is where we are restoring the Gigantomachy frieze.'

The German showed Eddie and Rothschild into a large room. A faint smell of dust and plaster hung in the air. Lights flicked on to reveal a pair of long workbenches, upon them adjustable lamps and free-standing easels bearing photographs. Beyond the benches was a large piece of machinery that Eddie didn't recognise, though a sticker displaying the international warning symbol for a laser – a starburst at the end of a horizontal line – gave him a clue as to its function. Past that, running along both long walls, were the movable, track-mounted shelving banks of an archival storage system.

'How are the restorations going?' Rothschild asked.

'Very well. We have a new high-resolution laser scanner.' Derrick rounded the benches and stopped beside the machine, opening a large semicircular shield to reveal a steel platform within. A gleaming mirror on a rotating base was mounted behind a glazed vertical slot in the scanner's casing beside it. 'We can scan a piece over two metres long to a precision of less than half a millimetre. Once we have the scan, we can either send it to the milling machine' – he pointed out another piece of hardware at the room's far end – 'to make a copy, or we can give it to the computer to find a match with other pieces automatically. Like a jigsaw puzzle in three dimensions,' he added to the Englishman. 'The computer is much faster than a human being at putting the broken pieces together.'

Eddie regarded one of the easels, which held photos of various sculpture fragments. 'So it's worked out that these fit together, and now you're going to rebuild 'em?'

'Yes, that is right. Of course, that does not mean that they *will* fit, only that they should. That is why we make the copies, to test them, so we do not damage the original pieces.' He went to a table by the storage units, on which was a large, heavy book. 'Now, let me try to find this piece.'

Derrick leafed through the tome. Each page had a picture of a fragment of the frieze, along with a description, and there seemed to be several hundred pages. 'Hope that thing's got an index,' said Eddie.

'It could take some time,' Derrick admitted. 'There is a machine outside if you would like a drink.'

'You want something?' Eddie asked Rothschild with a shrug.

'Coffee,' she replied. 'White. Two sugars.'

'Hemlock or no hemlock?'

Her only reply was a scowl. Grinning, Eddie headed for the door.

He had not only returned with drinks, but had also finished his by the time Derrick called to his guests. 'Here, see,' he said, tapping at a picture.

Eddie and Rothschild joined him. The image showed a ragged-edged marble slab bearing the carved relief of a robed man with one hand held out from his side. A ruler beside it provided scale; the piece was about two feet tall and a foot wide.

'That's it?' asked the Yorkshireman.

'Yes,' Derrick replied. 'When I told you about the Hebrew symbols, I remembered this.' He indicated a marking beside the figure, but it was too small to make out clearly. 'Now I shall find it.' He checked a number at the bottom of the page, then went to one of the storage units.

Rothschild put on her glasses and peered at the photo. 'The sculpting is crude compared to the rest of the frieze. Where on the altar did it come from?'

'We do not know,' Derrick told her. He took hold of a wheel on the end of the rack and spun it effortlessly. The shelf unit silently rolled apart from its neighbour, revealing banks of large drawers. 'There are many pieces that we have not yet found a place for.'

'So this might not have come from the altar at all?'

'No, no,' the German insisted. 'Everything was brought from the site at Pergamon. The original excavation by Carl Humann was very thorough. Ah! This is it.'

He slid open a drawer. Inside was a bulky wooden box. He carefully lifted it out and brought it to one of the workbenches. 'Here,' he said, lifting the lid.

Eddie immediately saw that Rothschild had been right. It was obvious even to a layman like himself that the sculpture was of a far lower quality than those around the Altar of Zeus. The stone was roughly carved, even chipped in places, and the figure's face was crude and almost amateurish compared to the perfection of the Greek gods. 'Looks like someone palmed it off on their apprentice. Or their kid.'

'I can't imagine that it was made at the same time as the rest of the frieze,' agreed Rothschild. 'Where's the Hebrew symbol?'

Derrick pointed. 'There.'

The visitors leaned closer. Inscribed next to the standing figure was a coarse but recognisable representation of a menorah. Above it Eddie saw letters, barely a centimetre in height. 'What does that say?'

'Some of the characters are Akkadian – not my speciality, I'm afraid,' said Rothschild. 'But these others are Hebrew letters, *dalet* and *kaf* – although they can also represent numbers. These would mean twenty-four.'

'So this guy's the Jewish Jack Bauer?' Eddie said with a smirk.

Neither archaeologist responded to the joke, both deep in thought – and reaching the same conclusion. 'The twenty-four Elders?' said Derrick.

'It could be,' Rothschild replied, intrigued. 'We should find out if the spot that was broken open at the Villa Torlonia had the same symbols. If it does, this might also be a marker.'

'A marker for what?' asked Eddie. 'One of these angels?'

'Maybe. But if it is,' she went on, 'we still won't be able to figure out where it's hidden unless we can identify where this piece of the frieze belongs.' She turned to Derrick. 'Markus, you don't have *any* idea where it should fit?'

The German shook his head. 'No. We have not yet matched it to any part of the altar.'

'So maybe it *isn't* part of the altar,' Eddie suggested. 'Can you stand it up? Let's see the rest of it.'

'There is nothing on the other sides,' Derrick assured him.

'Humour me.'

'What are you thinking?' Rothschild asked as the German started to lift the piece. 'I know that attitude – I'd expect it from Nina.' Her own attitude was not exactly approving.

'Guess I've picked up bad habits from her. But you know what one of her other bad habits is? Usually being right. About archaeology, anyway. Kids' names, not so much.' A brief smile, which vanished in a flare of anger at the thought of her still being a prisoner.

That in turn hardened his resolve to do whatever it took to get her back. Derrick had by now stood the thick block on its end; Eddie took hold of it. 'Wait, you should not—' the archaeologist protested, but he had already pulled it around a half-turn. 'This is a valuable artefact! Only museum staff are allowed to touch it.'

'Report me to the boss. Oh, wait, that's you,' Eddie replied, switching on the bench's lamps. 'Hey, look at this.'

The back of the block appeared plain. 'Look at what?' said Rothschild.

Eddie ran a fingertip over the surface. Large parts felt rough to the touch, like a fine sandpaper – not at all like marble, even though it was the same colour as the rest of the piece. 'The front and sides are all lumpy, like the sculptor was a bit cack-handed – but this is almost flat. And it feels different.'

Derrick gave it an experimental stroke with a fingertip. 'He is right,' he told Rothschild. 'It is like . . . like a *patch*, where a flaw was repaired.' His hand moved back across the blank face. 'But this is too big to be a simple fix. I think . . .' He trailed off.

'You think there's something inside it?' Eddie finished for him. 'Like this block's hollow – they chiselled it out, stuck the angel in the hole, then filled it in again?'

'It can't be,' said Rothschild, though with some uncertainty.

Derrick bent down to scrutinise the surface. 'It is possible,' he admitted. 'Look, here – with the light at the right angle, you can see where the repairs were made.'

He withdrew, letting the woman take his place. 'Yes, I see it,' she said, almost reluctantly.

'If this angel's inside, we've got to get it out,' Eddie said.

'And how do you suggest we do that?' demanded Rothschild.

'I know a way – worked fine last time I tried it.' He hefted the lump of stone, turning as if to dash it on the floor.

Both archaeologists simultaneously shrieked, *'No!'* Derrick darted to clap his hands around it before Eddie could let go. 'You cannot do that!' he yelled.

'We've got to find the angel or they'll kill Nina!' the Englishman replied.

'There are better ways than smashing it to bits!' protested Derrick. 'We have an ultrasound scanner. I can see if there really is something hidden inside. If there is, then I will consider – *consider* – drilling into it. But this is a valuable piece!'

'The patch is at the back,' Eddie pointed out. 'Even if you open it, the bloke on the front won't be damaged. Once you work out which part of the altar it comes from, you can stick it where it belongs and nobody'll know anything happened to it. That's if it's even actually part of the altar,' he added.

'The style really doesn't match any other part of the Gigantomachy,' Rothschild reluctantly reminded Derrick.

The German scowled, but finally nodded. 'Okay. I will use the ultrasound. But we will not damage it unless we are sure this angel is there. Agreed?'

'Agreed,' said Eddie, nodding. He released his hold.

Derrick reclaimed the block with relief. He returned it to the box, then opened a cabinet and took out a piece of equipment. 'Now, this will take a few minutes to set up. But we will soon see what is inside.'

Outside, the rain continued to fall, spraying off a tram as it rumbled past the museum. Night had arrived, the darkness deepened by the thick clouds. A guard looked through the lobby's glass doors, glad he did not have to go out into the deluge.

He was not, he mused, even supposed to be on duty tonight. But there had been some sort of security scare, extra staff called in to keep watch. Being summoned on very short notice was inconvenient, but the overtime pay would make up for it.

The guard was about to continue his rounds when something drew his attention. The parking spaces immediately in front of the museum were reserved for buses, but whoever was driving the black van that had just arrived in a hurry clearly didn't care about such restrictions. The driver and passenger emerged, as did another four men from the vehicle's rear.

All wore peaked uniform caps, glimpses of dark clothing visible under rain capes. One was carrying what looked like a small suitcase. 'Hey, I think the cops are here,' the guard called to a colleague stationed at the front desk.

The older man looked up from his Sudoku puzzle. 'What do they want?'

'Don't know.' The six figures made their way across the bridge. 'Must be something to do with this security alert.'

The second guard huffed, then joined his comrade as the new arrivals reached the door. The lead cop, face hidden in shadow beneath his hat's dripping visor, rapped sharply on the glass. 'Police!' he barked.

'What's going on?' asked the first guard.

'Police!' He gestured for the door to be opened.

The pair swapped looks, then the older guard unlocked the doors. 'Come in, then,' he said sarcastically as the cops bundled into the lobby, shaking off water. 'What do you want?'

The lead cop threw back his rain cape – revealing a compact MP7 sub-machine gun, a bulky suppressor attached to its barrel. 'Sorry, I don't speak German,' said Trant as he fired.

The guard fell backwards, blood spouting from three tightly spaced bullet wounds in his chest. His companion fumbled for his holstered handgun, but another man had already brought up his own MP7. A second trio of rounds tore into the younger guard's ribcage.

Trant gave both bodies a brief glance to confirm that they were dead, then marched across the lobby. 'There'll be more guards. Spread out and find them.' He tossed away his cap, then donned the camera headset he had worn in Rome. 'We're in,' he announced.

'Good,' said Cross through the earpiece. 'Secure the building, then find the angel.'

Eddie watched as an image formed on the monitor. 'God, I thought it was hard to work out what I was looking at on *Nina's* ultrasound,' he said. All he could see was a shimmering grey fuzz.

'This will not give such a clear picture as a medical ultrasound,' Derrick told him as he edged a pencil-like probe across the rear of the carved stone block. 'Marble is hard to penetrate. But if this is hollow, we will soon know.'

Rothschild looked on, fascinated. 'This is a much more advanced model than anything I've seen before.'

'It is German, of course,' he replied, smiling. 'I am not the expert, but I have used it to look for cracks and flaws inside pieces of the frieze. And . . . there *is* a flaw.' He pointed at the monitor.

Eddie saw only a slightly different shade of grey. 'What is it?'

'That is where someone used another material to patch a hole. It is probably marble dust mixed with pitch.' He adjusted a dial. 'Now we are looking deeper inside. The patch is still there; this flaw also goes deep. But . . . yes, there!'

A dark smudge appeared amidst the electronic haze. 'Is that a hole?' asked Eddie.

'Yes, it *is* hollow,' confirmed Derrick. More movements of the probe expanded the shadowy gap in the image. He muttered in German as he tweaked the scanner's settings again, and something far brighter leapt into view. 'That is not stone,' he said. 'That is metal!'

'Metal?' echoed Rothschild. 'The Gigantomachy frieze doesn't have any metal pieces, does it?'

'No, it does not.'

'Then this isn't part of it,' Eddie concluded. 'It's like you said,' he told Rothschild, 'this sculpture was made by somebody else. Whoever they were, they did it to hide this angel – and they hid it inside the Throne of Satan. Maybe they liked the idea of giving the Greek gods a kick in the nuts by putting a symbol of their own religion right in the middle of them.'

'That is an interesting way of putting it,' said Derrick, amused, 'but yes, there may be something to it.' He turned his attention back to the monitor. 'These white areas are definitely metal, surrounding . . . I am not sure. Pottery, perhaps, but there is something else – something very dense. Lead? I cannot tell.'

'So get out the hammer and chisel,' said Eddie.

He shook his head. 'No, no. We have to study it, decide how to proceed—'

The Englishman's patience was wearing thin. 'I *know* how to proceed. Get the bloody thing out of there! The longer we piss about arguing, the more chance the bad guys'll force Nina to tell them that it's here.'

Derrick was still not convinced. 'This is a priceless historical relic! There are procedures that must be followed. I shall have to—'.

'The same people who kidnapped Nina kidnapped me too,' Eddie said. He indicated his bruised face. 'They did this to me, and more – and they killed two people in Rome. They might kill more here. Please, open it up.'

Support came from an unexpected source. 'This *is* an IHA investigation, Markus,' Rothschild said quietly. 'It's what the agency was created to do – find and protect archaeological finds that may have global security implications.'

The German put down the probe and stared at the stone block for several long seconds. 'If the IHA wants to take charge,' he said at last, his displeasure plain, 'then the IHA can take responsibility for any damage. The German government supports the agency, so I am sure it will back you. But I will not let this fall on me, Maureen. I am sorry.'

'I'll call Oswald Seretse to confirm,' Rothschild told him. She took out her phone.

'While she's doing that,' said Eddie, 'how about you get started?'

Derrick gave him a dirty look, but stood. 'I will get the tools.'

'Dr Wilde,' said Cross as Norvin brought Nina into the control room. 'My team has entered the Pergamon Museum in Berlin. Now: where is the angel?'

Nina didn't reply at once, gazing in mortified sadness at the monitor screens. Several showed live headset feeds – one looking down at a uniformed man sprawled on the floor. She had no doubt at all that he was dead. 'You bastards,' she finally said. 'You didn't need to kill anyone.' She glared at Dalton, who had an unsettled expression. 'You're just as guilty as he is.'

'If they're worthy, they'll sit with God in heaven on the day of judgement.' Cross turned back to the video wall. 'The angel. Where will it be?'

'I have absolutely no idea,' she said. 'I've never been to the Pergamon Museum, and I've never studied the Altar of Zeus, so I don't know.' Simeon, standing to Cross's right, glared at her. 'Really! I *don't know*. Just because I'm an archaeologist doesn't mean I have total knowledge of every artefact from every period of history.'

Anna was on her leader's left. 'Then what use are you, *Doctor*?' she demanded, sneering.

'Anna,' Cross warned, before addressing Nina again. 'You found the first angel. I'm sure you can find the second, if only to save your husband any more pain. Think! What do you know about the altar that we haven't already found out online?'

Nina blew out a frustrated breath. 'I don't . . . Okay, let me think. Built in the early second century BC, surrounded by a frieze showing the war between the Olympian gods and their enemies the giants . . .'

'Giants could be a reference to the giants in Genesis,' suggested Simeon. 'Or the Nephilim?'

'It's not the Nephilim,' Nina countered. 'I've met them. Okay, not "met" – they were long-dead – but . . . anyway, that doesn't matter,' she said on seeing the questioning looks aimed at her. 'The altar's been on display in Berlin for over a century. If there was anything obviously non-Greek about it, we'd already know – it would be mentioned in every piece of literature about the altar, and probably the subject of a dozen Discovery Channel specials linking it to ghosts and UFOs and Bigfoot.'

'Then what about the parts that *aren't* on display?' said Dalton.

'It's still being restored, so yeah, something might have been overlooked. But I can't tell you what, because I just. Don't. *Know*. Okay?'

Cross regarded her with cold annoyance, but nodded. 'All right. So where would they keep these other pieces?'

'I don't have a floor plan!' she cried. 'They probably have storage and archives somewhere off-limits to the public.'

He turned back to the screens. One of his men was still in the lobby, having dragged the two corpses out of sight of the main doors. 'Ellison, check the security station. See if there's a plan of the building.'

Ellison's camera darted around as he searched before locking on to a display board for the fire alarms. 'Found it,' came a voice from the speakers.

'Good. Are there any archives?'

'Second floor, there's a section marked "Archivieren". I think that means archives?'

Cross glanced at Anna, who nodded. 'Okay, that's where we'll start the search. Trant, leave two men to cover the entrances and get the rest up there.' The various monitors broke into dizzying motion. 'Dr Wilde, if you see anything, tell me immediately. Or—'

'Or you'll torture Eddie – yes, I know.' Defeated, all Nina could do was watch as Cross's men moved through the museum.

Eddie peered over Derrick's shoulder as the archaeologist worked. Breaking into the hidden cavity inside the stone block had not taken long; the substance used to seal the hole was relatively fragile, splitting after just a few taps with a small chisel. Once the first crack had appeared, Derrick's reluctance to damage the artefact quickly gave way to professional curiosity about what was hidden inside.

'Careful,' warned Rothschild as the German made his final delicate strikes.

'I know what I am doing,' he replied testily. Eddie smiled at her getting a taste of her own medicine, then watched as Derrick gently used the chisel's tip to lever the freed section upwards.

The interior was revealed beneath, light reflecting dully off copper.

'There is definitely something inside,' he announced with rising excitement. He lifted the piece away.

'So that's an angel, is it?' said Eddie, gazing at what lay within.

The figure had the body of a man but the head of an eagle, several metal wings wrapped tightly around its torso. It fitted the space inside the block almost perfectly, the gaps filled by fine dry sand to act as a cushion. Whoever had concealed it had also wanted to protect it.

Rothschild adjusted one of the lamps. 'There's some text on the body. It looks like Akkadian.'

'Will you be able to translate it?' Eddie asked.

'I can, of course,' said Derrick. 'It is hardly Linear A!' He and Rothschild shared a chuckle.

'Archaeology jokes, always hilarious,' said the Englishman, straight-faced. 'But it *is* an angel, right?'

'I think so,' Rothschild replied. 'Although by the letter of Revelation, the eagle head would actually make it one of the "living creatures" – or "beasts", depending which translation of the Bible you choose – before God's throne. They summoned and released the four horsemen.'

'What, as in the horsemen of the apocalypse?'

'Yes, although they're never called that in Revelation. Markus, can you get it out of there?'

Derrick blew sand off the figure and lifted it from its resting place. 'It is very heavy,' he noted, surprised. He set it down on the table. 'Hmm. The wings, they seem to have been pressed into the clay before it was fired. But they are only thin; I wonder how they kept them from melting? Perhaps—'

A loud bang echoed down the corridor outside. Eddie's head snapped up. 'What was that?'

'It is just the security guards,' Derrick replied. 'But they know they are not supposed to slam the doors – the vibrations can damage the exhibits.' He stood at another thump. 'I will talk to them.'

Eddie and Rothschild looked back at the statue as he crossed the room. 'I must admit,' said the elderly woman, 'I honestly didn't believe anything would come of this. Revelation is open to a great deal of interpretation, to put it mildly. But whoever kidnapped Nina was right about where to look.'

'And now they're making her tell them what to look for,' Eddie reminded her grimly. 'But we beat 'em to this. If I can persuade your friend to let me use it to get her back . . .' He glanced at Derrick as the German reached the door—

Someone outside kicked it open.

Derrick staggered back. A man dressed in black burst into the room – a sub-machine gun in his hands, laser sight dancing over its targets.

14

'Nobody move!' the intruder yelled.

Eddie's first instinct was to grab Rothschild and duck behind the workbench, but the laser spot had already locked on to his chest—

Derrick reeled back in front of the gunman. '*Was ist*—'

The man in black's finger tightened on the trigger – then, at a command through his headset loud enough for Eddie to hear, he changed his attack to a physical blow, striking the German's head with his weapon. Derrick crumpled to the floor.

Eddie shoved the fear-frozen Rothschild down, then grabbed the angel and dived after her as the man spun back towards him—

Bullets ripped into the workbench, cracking off the stone block, which exploded into pieces. Rothschild shrieked as fragments rained down on them. 'For fuck's sake!' Eddie cried. 'Just once, just fucking *once*, I'd like to find the thing and get out *before* the bad guys turn up!'

Running footsteps from outside – the attacker was not alone. Someone shouted an order as three more men rushed through the doorway. Eddie looked around. There was another exit at the room's far end, but they would never reach it before being cut down.

Trapped.

Unless—

Eddie felt the weight of the statue – and realised he had one chance of survival. 'Any closer an' I'll smash your fucking angel!' he yelled.

The sounds of movement stopped abruptly, replaced by muttered discussion. Eddie shuffled backwards to take shelter behind the laser scanner. He raised his head just enough to see that the nearest gunman had a compact camera – night-vision, from the LED illuminator beneath the lens – mounted on a headset. Somebody was observing the operation. The mysterious Prophet?

Whoever it was, he had Nina. 'All right,' said Eddie loudly, the thought of his wife strengthening his resolve, 'Everyone put down your guns. Otherwise bird-face here gets his wings clipped.'

Another brief exchange, the first gunman responding to a message over his headset; then, with his gun still in one hand, he reached into a belt pouch and pulled out a gas mask. 'Okay, not quite what I was hoping for . . .' Eddie muttered in dismay.

The other men followed suit. 'Mr Chase!' called one, voice muffled by the mask's filters. 'If you break the angel, it'll release a deadly gas. You'll die, but we'll be safe.'

'You still won't get what you're after!' Eddie shouted back.

'Yes we will! The Prophet *wants* to release the angel. He'd rather not do it here, but if it's the will of God that it happens, then it happens.'

'Bollocks! You're bluffing.'

'Then smash it, Mr Chase. You'll see. For your last few seconds on earth. Ellison, move in.'

'Shit,' Eddie hissed. His own bluff had been called – and now the first gunman was advancing again, his suppressed MP7 raised.

Nina stared at the screen, elation rapidly overcome by terror. Eddie had somehow escaped from his torturers – only to fall back into the hands of their collaborators. The lead gunman,

Ellison, moved through the room, his camera picking out Eddie hunched behind a large piece of equipment.

'They're not in full MOPP gear,' Anna warned Cross. 'If he drops the angel—'

'I know,' the cult leader replied. That told Nina that he wasn't as blasé about the angel's destruction as Trant had informed Eddie, but her husband was still in grave danger.

Ellison rounded a large workbench. Nina glimpsed someone else hiding behind it at the edge of the screen, but he continued to advance. His gun rose into frame, its laser spot a dazzling flare as it fixed on the Englishman—

'Ellison, wait,' said Cross sharply. 'I don't want the angel damaged if we can help it.' He turned towards Nina. 'Remind him that we have his wife!'

Eddie tensed, retreating further behind the open scanner as Ellison drew level with the tracked shelves. He would have a clear line of fire within seconds . . .

Ellison suddenly stopped, head tipping quizzically as he listened to another order via his headset. He looked back at the other intruders for confirmation. 'Do it,' said the leader.

'We've got your wife,' the gunman called to Eddie. 'Give up the angel and she won't get hurt.'

They weren't willing to let the statue be destroyed, then. That gave him an edge, however small. 'Let me talk to her,' he replied. 'To prove you've got her.'

Another brief exchange through the earpiece, then Ellison took off the headset and held it out as he edged closer. Eddie warily watched the other armed men as he shifted the statue to his left hand. All were alert, staring back at him, but while their guns were up, their forefingers were off the triggers. They were obeying the order to let him talk to Nina . . . but it would only take them a fraction of a second to fire.

He had to make the fullest possible use of that moment.

Impatient, Ellison twitched the headset to prompt Eddie to take it. Eddie raised his left hand to make it clear that the statue would be dropped if anything happened to him, then reached out with his right. Ellison leaned closer—

Eddie lunged – grabbing not the proffered gadget but the hand holding it, He bent the other man's fingers backwards, hard, as he yanked him nearer. Ellison's little finger snapped at its first joint.

His scream of pain jolted his comrades into life, laser sights flashing on to their target. But Eddie had already pulled Ellison to him, turning the gunman into a human shield.

His prisoner overcame his initial shock and tried to slam an elbow into Eddie's chest, but the Englishman easily absorbed the blow and savagely wrenched the broken finger around by almost ninety degrees. Ellison let out a blood-curdling shriek. 'All right, let's try this again!' Eddie shouted. 'Guns down, back off, all the rest.'

The other attackers briefly remained still, but instructions soon came over their radios. They spread out to round the first workbench, keeping their guns fixed on the whimpering Ellison, ready to shoot the man behind him the moment they had the chance . . .

'Oi! Prof!' Eddie called to Rothschild, still curled behind the second bench. 'Can you catch?'

'Wh-what?' she asked, blinking up at him.

'Can you catch this?' He waved the statue.

'I . . . I don't know. I can try.'

'Good, 'cause here it comes!' He lobbed it at her.

She gasped, flinging out both arms to catch it – more by luck than judgement, as her eyes were squeezed tightly shut.

Trant and the other masked men flinched, but when it became clear the statue had survived, they resumed their advance,

MP7s raised and locked as Eddie backed behind the scanner. They would soon reach Rothschild – and the angel.

He spotted a control panel on the machine's side. One of the illuminated buttons read SCAN. Rothschild's eyes were still closed—

He stabbed the button.

The scanner hummed – and a swathe of brilliant green light lanced from the laser.

The intruders instantly fell into disarray as the dazzling beam overpowered their optic nerves. Eddie took advantage, slamming Ellison face-first against the shelves, then shoving the stunned gunman's head into the gap between two of the storage units and spinning the nearest wheel.

The units rolled smoothly along their tracks – and a splintering crunch came from the shrinking space between them as Ellison's skull suddenly became a few inches narrower.

The laser continued its sweep, but even blinded, most of the attackers had dropped into cover. One man was still standing, though, reeling with a hand over his eyes—

Eddie grabbed Ellison's gun and felled the man with a three-round burst, then hurried to Rothschild and pulled her to her feet. 'Come on!'

He directed her past the scanner to the second exit. 'My God!' she shrilled, opening her eyes to see Ellison's limp corpse slumped between the shelves.

'Don't look at it, just get to the door. And keep hold of the angel!' He backed up behind her with his gun ready.

Nobody poked their head above the workbenches. Rothschild opened the door, Eddie following her into a corridor. 'Which way?' she cried.

He spotted a green sign, an arrow beside a running stick-man. 'There!' They ran to the emergency exit as furious orders were shouted behind them.

Eddie kicked the door open to find a narrow stairwell. He descended two at a time. 'What about Markus?' Rothschild wailed.

'They just knocked him down. He'll be okay,' Eddie replied, hoping he was right.

He reached the foot of the steps and barged through another door to find himself back in the museum proper. They were in the long hallway he had seen earlier, the walls decorated with gleaming tiles displaying paintings of stalking lions. At its far end he recognised the Ishtar Gate, but his only concern now was getting out of the building. The gunmen had made no attempt at stealth; that meant the museum's security staff were either prisoners or dead, and after what had happened in Rome, more likely the latter.

The restoration work had blocked off the nearest apparent exit, but he spotted another emergency evacuation sign. 'Down here,' he told Rothschild, going right at a run. Past the stairs they had ascended with Derrick was the marked door. 'Okay, through this,' Eddie said as he reached it—

He flinched back as if the handle were electrified, hearing noises beyond, getting closer. Not all of the Prophet's men had gone to the upper floor. 'Or not,' he amended, rushing to a smaller door across the corridor only to find it locked. The only way out was through the Ishtar Gate. 'Hurry up!'

'I'm sixty-seven years old!' gasped Rothschild. 'I can't go any faster!'

'You'll have to if you want to be sixty-eight!' He reached the great arch, throwing aside the barrier and charging through.

They emerged from the Miletus Gate on the other side. Eddie looked back as another black-clad gunman burst through the emergency exit. A moment later, Trant appeared from the stairwell, his surviving companion behind him. The Englishman fired another three-round burst to force them into cover, then caught up with Rothschild as she reached the doors to the room containing the Altar of Zeus.

Nobody was waiting for them in the cavernous space. The entrance through which Derrick had brought them was in the centre of the long wall to the left, facing the temple. He glanced at Rothschild as they ran towards it. The old woman still held the statue, and despite her heavy breathing was maintaining her pace – fear was a great driver. They might get out alive after all—

A shadow stabbed along the floor from beyond the glass doors.

'Shit!' Eddie cried, pulling back and firing a wild burst as a man appeared at the entrance. One of the doors exploded into fragments, the gunman hurriedly jerking back.

Shouts from behind. Trant and the others were in the Roman room, cutting them off, and if they tried to reach the other exit in the far wall, the man at the shattered door would have a clear shot—

'Up there!' yelled Eddie, swinging Rothschild towards the towering altar.

'There's no way out!' she protested.

'I bloody know!' They reached the broad marble steps. 'Set off the fire alarm – I'll try to hold 'em off until the cops arrive!' He turned, trying to cover both the entrances from which their enemies would come.

The man at the glass door leaned into view. Eddie loosed another burst. All three rounds went wide, smacking against the wall, but it forced the gunman to retreat. The Englishman reached the top of the stairs and darted behind a column. Rothschild still had several steps to go. 'Quick! Get—'

Trant appeared at the other entrance, firing wildly on full auto.

Bullets ripped into the marble stairs, a line of dust-spitting impacts chasing after Rothschild. Splinters hit her legs. She screamed and tripped just short of the top. The statue was jolted from her grip – and rolled back down the steps, loud clunks echoing around the room.

Trant had taken off his gas mask; his expression was a flash of pure panic as he watched the angel's clattering descent. 'Back, get back!'

Eddie also watched the stone figure with alarm. The attackers' fear confirmed that they hadn't been lying about the danger . . .

Clunk, clunk – and the angel finally reached the floor, skittering across the polished wood before coming to a halt. For a moment, all eyes were upon it, tension rising . . . then Trant spoke. 'It's safe! I'm gonna get it – cover me!'

Gun raised, Eddie whipped around the pillar – but he held his fire, conflicted. The doorway was a choke point, meaning he might be able to hold the gunmen back while he made a desperate run for the angel . . . but doing so would leave Rothschild unprotected in the open.

His indecision lasted only a split second, but that was enough for Trant to run into the great hall – and for the two men with him to aim up at the altar from the doorway.

Eddie grabbed Rothschild and dived with her over the top of the stairs as they opened fire. Chunks of pale stone exploded from the columns, ricochets twanging and screaming across the room. 'Jesus!' he gasped.

'I've got it!' Trant shouted. 'Get to the sluice channel!'

More guns blazed with suppressing fire as the others followed their leader. Eddie crawled to cover Rothschild as debris pummelled them, then raised his gun to catch anyone climbing the stairs to finish off the two fugitives . . .

Nobody came for them. The gunfire stopped. Eddie waited for a moment, then cautiously lifted his head. There was no one below – and the statue had gone. 'Shit!' he growled, standing.

'What's happening?' Rothschild asked plaintively.

'They've got the angel. Stay there.' He raced down the steps and went to the glass doors. Nobody was in sight, though he heard a door bang from the direction of the lobby.

He ran after them. They would be heading for a getaway vehicle; if he caught up, he might be able to shoot the driver or a tyre, or at the very least get its licence plate for the police.

He reached the lobby. No rearguard – the gunmen were in a hurry to escape with their prize. He went to the main doors, spotting a couple of corpses behind the security station. The rain was still streaking down outside, a large black van parked in front of the bridge.

The raiders weren't in it. They had instead gone to the bridge's side, climbing on to its wall . . . and jumping off.

Eddie barrelled into the open just as the last man dropped out of sight. The roar of engines came from the waterway below. Rather than risk being hemmed in on Berlin's roads, the raiders were making their getaway by boat along the Spree, the river bisecting the city. He ran to the wall, seeing the lead craft with Trant and two others aboard already powering away under a railway bridge to the north-west. Another picked up speed behind it, a man in the back seat sealing the angel inside a case—

The Englishman flicked the MP7 to full auto and unleashed a long burst after the trailing speedboat. The man flailed and fell over the side, but then the compact weapon's magazine ran dry. 'Fuck!' Eddie roared, watching helplessly as the two craft surged away into the darkness with their prize.

'Eddie!' He looked back to see Rothschild hurrying towards him.

'I told you to stay put!'

'I know where they're going! That man told the others to get to the sluice channel – he means the *Schleusenkanal*, along the river. We passed it on the way from the airport.'

'They must have a car waiting,' Eddie realised. Using the river would make it easy for the robbers to evade pursuit, and once they reached their rendezvous, they could quickly reach Tegel and leave the country. 'You know how to get there?'

'Yes, but—'

'Okay, come on. We might be able to catch 'em.' He ran to the street. Rothschild hesitated, then followed.

He guessed that the van belonged to the raiders, but doubted that the driver had left the keys in the ignition. Besides, the boats were doing at least forty miles per hour; he needed something much faster . . .

'And there it is,' he said as he saw the very thing approaching.

A sleek silver Porsche 911 was cruising through the rain. Eddie ran out into its path, waving his arms. The driver swerved to round him – then jammed on the brakes as Eddie pointed the gun at his car. '*Achtung!*' shouted the Englishman. 'Outta ze *Auto!*'

The middle-aged man might have been confused by the words, but he couldn't mistake the message. He scrambled out, hands up as he stared in fear at the man marching towards him.

'Here, present for you,' said Eddie, handing the weapon to the startled driver. 'Prof, get in!'

Rothschild ran to the Porsche. Its owner looked in confusion between his car and the gun, then took a couple of panicked steps backwards and pointed the MP7 at the Yorkshireman. 'You – you are not taking my car!'

'It's empty, you dozy twat,' Eddie replied. The driver gawped at him. 'I'll try not to smash your Porsche to fuck, but if anything happens, send the bill to Oswald Seretse at the United Nations in New York. Okay?'

'Oswald Seretse,' the German replied slowly. 'Okay. Yes.'

'Great. Thanks!' Eddie dropped into the bucket seat and slammed the door. Rothschild swung herself awkwardly into the passenger seat beside him. 'All right, never driven one of these before. Hope *Top Gear* was exaggerating about how hard they are to control!'

He depressed the clutch, slotted the gearstick into first, then rocketed into the night at the head of a huge trail of spray.

15

Even from a wet standing start, the speedometer needle surged past ninety in mere seconds. 'Whoa, bloody hell!' Eddie cried, struggling to hold the Porsche in a straight line as the wheel squirmed in his hands. 'Guess this one's a turbo.'

Rothschild clutched the door handle with one hand and the centre console with the other, fingernails digging into both like claws. 'Oh my God!' she screamed. 'Slow down, slow down!'

'I'm chasing them – going fast is the whole fucking point!' The one-way street became two-way at a junction. He swung to avoid the flaring headlights of an oncoming car, then slammed the power back on to whip around another vehicle ahead. The road ran along the riverbank, the long facade of another museum rising across the water to the right. 'Can you see them?'

'Not yet – and what exactly are you planning to do? They're in boats, we're in a car! And you don't have a gun any more; how are you going to stop them?'

'Not a clue. But if they get away with the angel, I've got no chance of finding Nina. So that's not going to happen, whatever I have to fucking do.' The clenched fury behind his words deterred her from asking further questions.

The channel curved, the road following it. 'There!' Eddie said, spotting churning wakes on the dark water. As the Spree widened, the boats had moved out into its centre. The Porsche was gaining rapidly, but as Rothschild had pointed out, there was no way of reaching them. 'This sluice canal – how far away is it?'

'Four or five— Ah!' She gasped in fright as the Porsche swerved to overtake another car. 'Four or five miles,' she concluded, her voice noticeably higher in pitch.

'We should be able to beat 'em there, but . . .'

'But what?'

'Exactly. They've got guns, and we don't. And the rate they're going, they'll still arrive before the cops sort themselves out, especially as we haven't even *called* the cops yet!'

'I'm sure the poor man whose car you stole will have done that by now.'

'Yeah, which means they'll be chasing *us*, not the bad guys! Shit, and Derrick needs an ambulance an' all,' he remembered. 'Why didn't you stay and help him? He's your friend!'

Rothschild bristled. 'You told me he'd be all right! And if I hadn't come with you, you wouldn't have known where they were going. They've stolen a priceless artefact – we can't let them get away with it.'

'Fuck's sake,' Eddie muttered. 'You're as bad as Nina!'

Ahead, the boats went under a bridge. 'Which way?' he demanded. 'Stay on this side or go across?'

'I don't know!' she protested. An intersection was coming up fast, a long tram trundling towards the bridge blocking their view of what lay beyond. 'I . . . This side, stay on this side!'

Eddie jammed the wheel to the left, stabbing at the brakes to send the Porsche around the tram's rear. He felt the car's heavy back end threaten to snap out on the wet road; even with decades of development and technological aids, the 911's rear-mounted engine was still a trap for the unprepared driver. A punch of adrenalin as he caught the slide, then straightened – only for the headlights to reveal that the road along the river was blocked by building work, signs warning that it was for pedestrians only. 'Shit!'

He braked hard, debating what to do. The sight of the boats

pulling away made his mind up in an instant. He accelerated again, sounding the horn as he ploughed through the signs and traffic cones.

'No, no, oh my *God!*' Rothschild wailed. Shocked Berliners dived out of the way, one man vaulting the railing and hanging above the edge of the Spree as the 911 thundered past. 'You're going to *kill* someone!'

'You bloody told me to go this way!'

'I haven't lived in Berlin for forty years! It's changed a lot!'

Eddie shot her an angry glare, then returned his full attention to negotiating the waterfront. The Porsche's left flank clipped a couple of construction barriers as he jinked to avoid a dumb-founded young couple, then its right side took a greater pounding as the Englishman was forced to grind against the metal railings along the river to dodge an oblivious headphone-wearing man. Rothschild shrieked as sparks flew past her window.

The construction zone ended just before the street passed under a large bridge, a train rumbling over the Spree above the boats. Eddie crashed through more barriers back on to the road and shot across an intersection – only to realise he was now going the wrong way down a one-way street. 'Jesus!' he gasped, flinging the car on to the kerb as a truck rushed at him. His passenger closed her eyes in terror.

He dropped back on to the street with a bang. Even with all the obstacles, they were still gaining on the boats. Eddie had no idea what he was going to do when he caught up with them, but as long as he could keep them in sight, he had a chance of recovering the angel, and bargaining for Nina's release—

He dodged an oncoming car – and saw a new problem ahead.

A road bridge crossed the Spree on the right. Ahead, the street continued along the river – but it was barricaded, steel pillars allowing pedestrians and cyclists through while blocking cars. 'Which way?' he shouted. Rothschild's eyes remained firmly squeezed shut. 'Oi! Prof! Which fucking way do we go? Do I cross the bridge?'

She risked a look. 'No, it'll take you away from the river.' With no other options, Eddie flung the Porsche into a slithering left turn. 'And don't you dare swear at me again!'

'Then bloody help me!' he snarled back. The new street was also leading him away from the Spree. 'How do we catch up with the boats?'

'If you can get on to 17th June Street, you'll be able to get back to the river.'

'Where's that?'

'The long road through the park that we came down when we arrived.' She looked at the modern apartment buildings around them. 'I don't recognise where we are. If you can find the Reichstag, I can direct you from there. Go right!'

The next road in that direction was another one-way street, two cars at traffic lights blocking it, with more bollards preventing Eddie from taking to the pavement. 'Have to try this next one,' he said, peering ahead. The Porsche rapidly closed the distance to an intersection with a broad boulevard. More traffic waited at the lights; he pulled into the wrong lane to overtake. 'Okay, hold on!'

Rothschild flinched as her memory finally caught up with the speeding car. 'No, wait!' she cried, but Eddie had already hurled the 911 into another wildly fishtailing turn – on to the broad pedestrian plaza leading to the Brandenburg Gate.

Even on a rainy night, there were still plenty of tourists milling around the Pariser Platz, forcing him to resume his symphony on the horn as he swerved to avoid knots of people and dawdling bicycle rickshaws. Making matters worse were the numerous uniformed men and women around the square's periphery; it was home to both the French and American embassies, ensuring the constant presence of the Berlin police.

'Like we weren't in enough bloody trouble already!' he complained as the cops ran to try to block him.

'They have guns!' Rothschild said in alarm. 'Perhaps we should—'

'We're not stopping,' Eddie growled. He fixed his gaze on the illuminated arch of the Brandenburg Gate at the plaza's far end and dropped down the gears, foot to the floor.

The Porsche's acceleration punched them back into the seats. Eddie's continuous shrilling of the horn finally had an effect, the tourists clearing the 911's path as it raced towards the central archway. He saw a cop beside the monument draw his gun, but was now committed. 'Duck!' he warned Rothschild.

The car blasted through the gate at over seventy miles per hour, emerging on a wide semicircular plaza. A single gunshot cracked after it, but the bullet glanced off the Porsche's sloping rear. Rothschild squealed at the impact. 'They're *shooting* at us!'

'Welcome to my bloody life!' Eddie responded as he rounded another stand of bicycle rickshaws and brought the 911 thumping back down on to asphalt. He now knew where he was, seeing the long tree-lined avenue receding ahead. 'How do we get back to the river?'

She reluctantly peered over the dashboard as the Porsche began its sprint down 17th June Street. 'Go to the Victory Column,' she said, pointing at the distant floodlit statue. 'Then back over the bridge we took this afternoon. Will we be ahead of them?'

The speedometer needle surged upwards, Eddie weaving across all three westbound lanes through the traffic. 'Damn well better be.'

Rothschild pushed herself back upright. 'Why are you so angry with me? If I wasn't helping you, you wouldn't be able to follow those boats at all. You wouldn't even have known to come to Berlin!'

'I'm mad because you dropped the bloody statue,' he said. 'I had to save you rather than get the angel – and if I don't have the angel, I've got no way of finding Nina!'

'You don't even like me! And I know Nina certainly doesn't. I'm surprised you didn't go after the angel instead.'

'Don't think I wasn't bloody tempted.'

'Then why didn't you?'

'Because . . . because I couldn't let another innocent person die for getting mixed up in our lives,' he admitted. 'Speaking of which, shut up and let me try to drive without killing anyone!' Rothschild fell silent, but her surprise at his revelation was clear.

The speeding Porsche ate up the distance to the Victory Column in well under a minute. Eddie made a last jink around a bus before flinging the car into a power slide through the roundabout. Other vehicles skidded in panic around him, but he was already clear and racing up the next avenue.

A few more lunges around slower-moving cars and he saw the bridge ahead. He braked hard, bringing the Porsche down to an almost legal speed as he reached the crossing. Railings ran along its sides, giving him a view of the river below—

Movement on the water to his right. Both boats came into sight, still holding course along the centre of the channel. He had beaten them here, but now what? 'How far to this sluice canal?' he asked.

'Still two or three miles,' Rothschild replied.

Eddie swore under his breath. He remembered the roads ahead from his journey into the city, and knew he wouldn't be able to go nearly as quickly as through the park. He needed a new plan, fast.

The boats would pass under the bridge in about twenty seconds. He stopped the car, staring at them, judging their courses . . . 'Get out! Now!'

The elderly woman opened her mouth to protest, but Eddie's expression warned her that it was in her best interests to obey. She clambered out. He waited until she was clear, then slotted the 911 into reverse and pulled hard on the wheel as he depressed the accelerator.

The Porsche swung backwards through ninety degrees to block the oncoming lane, a couple of cars skidding to a standstill. Eddie ignored the blare of horns, his eyes fixed on the approaching boats. The second, carrying two men and the angel, was still lagging behind the leader, off to one side to stay clear of its wake.

He drummed his fingers on the steering wheel, bracing himself – then put the car into gear and stamped on the accelerator.

The 911 leapt forward, all four wheels clawing for grip on the wet road. Rothschild clapped her hands to her face in shock as it sprang over the kerb, hit the railing—

And smashed through, arcing down towards the water as the first boat raced by.

Eddie was hurled forward in his seat as the car's nose hit the water – only to be brought to an equally abrupt halt as the airbag fired. The 911 floated almost vertically for the briefest moment, then the weight of the engine slammed its tail down into the river.

The airbag had already deflated. Eddie dizzily opened his eyes as water gushed into the cabin – to see the second boat racing straight at him, its shocked driver unable to change course in time—

The speedboat's keel hit the Porsche's bonnet, flinging it upwards over the windscreen and roof as if jumping a ramp. It left the water, lancing at the bridge . . .

And slammed into the arched girders beneath the crossing.

The men aboard were thrown headlong against the unyielding steel, blood raining down over the churning waters below. The boat's mangled remains dropped back into the Spree, its prow crushed like an eggshell.

The Porsche had fared little better. Its windscreen had shattered as the craft ran over it, an explosive wave rushing in. Eddie choked and gasped, pinned in his seat by the weight of water.

The torrent finally eased as the cabin was completely filled, but now the Yorkshireman faced a new threat as cold hit him like a train. The temperature of the Spree on this miserable night was barely above freezing. He fought through the initial shock and clawed for the broken windscreen's frame. The Porsche was dropping backwards into the dark depths; he kicked free of the jellyfish mass of the expended airbag and squirmed upwards through the opening. A dull boom from below told him that the car had hit bottom, bubbles surging past him. He followed them to the surface.

He breached the waves, gasping as cold air hit his wet skin, and looked around. The wrecked boat was floating beneath the bridge. Pieces of bodies bobbed around it. Someone on the bridge shouted in German. He tipped his head back painfully to see people staring down over the railings.

Eddie started swimming – not for the shore, but the boat. An echoing engine note warned that the first speedboat was slowing and coming around. A crushed and bloodied face sprang at him from the lapping waves; he shoved the corpse aside, searching in the low light for the destroyed vessel's cargo.

A case floated nearby – the one containing the angel. He grabbed it, then swam for the river's north bank, seeing a flight of concrete steps leading up from the water.

The engine noise grew louder, angrier. The first boat was racing back towards him. Onlookers above urged him on, but he ignored them, expecting gunfire at any moment.

He reached the steps and scrambled up them, cold water

streaming from his clothes. Running footsteps; he turned to see a Berliner hurrying along the footpath – and on the river, the boat arriving, Trant standing up—

'Down, get down!' he yelled, diving flat. The man on the footpath hesitated, needing a moment to translate the warning.

The tiny delay cost him his life. A sub-machine gun roared from beneath the bridge, Trant having removed the suppressor before spraying the bank with bullets. The running man took several to his chest and tumbled to the ground.

Screams came from the bridge, the onlookers fleeing. Still clutching the case, Eddie rolled clear of the river's edge, then jumped up and ran. Another burst of fire slashed through the air behind him.

He hared up a second set of steps to street level, finding himself at an intersection on the bridge's northern side. Concrete apartment blocks lined the waterfront, no shelter in sight amongst the tightly packed buildings. Instead he cut diagonally across the main road from the bridge, spotting an alley between more drab, graffiti-spattered towers.

The gunfire had cleared the streets with shocking speed, cars peeling away. A loud thump came from the river as the second speedboat bashed against the bank. More shouts, these in English. 'Get after him!'

Muscles aching from exertion and exposure, Eddie reached the alley, glancing back to see Trant and his two companions pounding up the second flight of steps. The leader saw him and whipped up his MP7, but the Englishman ran between the buildings before he could fire.

At the alley's end was a square within a complex of apartment blocks, trees standing over a little park. Bushes and hedges dotted the lawns, a brick and concrete spiral at the centre some sort of children's play area.

The nearest way out was diagonally opposite where he had

entered – too far for him to reach before his pursuers entered the square. They would have a clear shot at his back. The only visible entrance to any of the buildings was just as distant.

'Shit,' he gasped, searching desperately for a hiding place – and finding none.

16

Trant led his two remaining men, Overton and Whelan, at a
sprint down the alley. They reached the end of the passage,
guns raised – but there was no sign of their target, just rain
drenching a dimly lit garden area. The only apparent exits were a
door into one of the apartment buildings and a gap between two
blocks to the north. Trant knew his quarry couldn't have reached
either in the short time he had been out of sight. That meant . . .

'He's still here,' he warned his companions. 'Find him.'

'Careful,' said Simeon through his headset. 'This guy's a
pro.'

Sirens wailed in the distance. 'Cops coming,' said Overton.

'We've got a minute or two,' Trant replied. 'Move fast.' He
directed Overton to the left and Whelan into the centre of the
small park, then angled right towards the gap.

A line of hedges, reaching to his thighs, ran along a lawn's
edge. Trant readied his gun, then hurdled it.

Nobody there. He checked behind a nearby tree with the
same lack of result. 'Clear here,' he announced, continuing across
the grass.

Overton followed a path into the garden, checking behind
the hedges and bushes. No sign of the Englishman, or the case
containing the angel. He moved under a large tree, glad of the
brief respite from the downpour. The speedboat's driver was
cold and thoroughly damp despite his rain cape. 'Anything?'
he whispered, peering into the shadows. As he had not gone into
the museum, his headset had not needed a camera; something he

was now regretting, as those observing at the Mission could have warned him if the Brit was skulking in the darkness.

'Not yet,' Whelan reported.

'Me neither. Pick up the pace,' ordered Trant.

Overton continued under the trees. He glanced to his right to see Whelan investigating another patch of bushes, while beyond him Trant checked behind a low brick wall. Their quarry was still nowhere to be seen. He kept going, scanning ahead.

Something caught his eye, a low, blocky shape amongst some plants.

The case. He started towards it, about to alert the others – when water streamed over him from above.

Overton hesitated. He was still under a tree, so the foliage must have thinned out. Or—

The other explanation hit him at the same time as Eddie did.

The sodden Yorkshireman had climbed up on to one of the lower branches, hoping simply to stay out of sight, but when the black-clad man passed almost directly beneath him, he knew he couldn't miss the opportunity. He dropped on top of him, smashing his elbow down hard against the back of his skull and slamming him face-first to the ground.

The American went limp beneath him. Taking no chances, Eddie grabbed his hair and yanked his head up before driving a vicious knuckle-punch into his exposed throat. Cartilage crunched. The man spasmed, faint choking noises from his gaping mouth barely audible over the hiss of the rain.

Eddie rose to a crouch, searching for his pursuer's MP7 – only to realise that the man had landed on top of it. He was about to roll him away when some instinct made him check on the positions of the other raiders—

The nearest turned towards him.

★ ★ ★

Nina realised she was breathing heavily as she watched events in Germany play out on the video wall, Trant investigating the park's far end while Whelan searched its centre. The latter had just reached an open paved area containing benches, night vision turning the rainy gloom as bright as day. He turned his head, the view panning back in Overton's direction—

'Whelan, stop!' Cross shouted. The image stabilised. 'There, under the tree – there's something on the grass.'

Simeon stepped closer to the monitors, trying to make out the crumpled shape. 'Is that a man?'

'It's Overton,' said Cross grimly. 'Trant! Man down, south end of the park.' The other screens blurred as the team leader whipped around.

'What's going on?' said Dalton, agitated. 'Is he *dead*?'

'Don't screw with my husband,' Nina said quietly.

Whelan moved cautiously towards the slumped figure. 'It's definitely Overton,' he said, his camera darting from side to side as he scanned the park. Nothing moved except the falling rain.

'Whelan, look to your right,' ordered Cross. 'There's something in that flower bed – there!'

The screens revealed a blocky shape in the undergrowth. 'It's the case,' said Anna.

'It's open,' Cross growled. 'Check it out, but be careful. He's around there somewhere.'

'Cops are getting closer,' said Trant as he headed in a crouch back along the edge of the park. Sirens became audible over the background noise.

Whelan reached Overton. He nudged the motionless figure with a foot, then crossed the grass to the case and reached down to raise the half-open lid . . .

A dull thump came over the speakers.

'What was that?' said Cross, but Whelan was already turning

to find the source. The camera fixed upon something on the wet grass – an object that had not been there seconds earlier.

'It's the angel!' exclaimed Dalton.

The stone figure lay on its side, raindrops bursting against the metal and clay. 'It's intact,' Whelan said, relieved.

Sudden realisation made Cross sit bolt upright as Whelan went to retrieve the statue. 'No, wait, it's a decoy – check behind you!' he cried—

The image whipped around through a hundred and eighty degrees with a sickening snap of bone. Then the monitors filled with an extreme close-up . . . of Eddie Chase.

He released his neck-breaking hold. The camera flopped, looking down Whelan's back. Then Eddie stepped away and the dead man crumpled to the ground.

'*Definitely* don't screw with my husband,' said Nina.

Simeon and Anna both shot her angry looks, but Cross remained focused on the view from the remaining camera. Trant had reacted to his warning by dropping behind a hedge. He peered warily over it to see Eddie crouched by Whelan's corpse, collecting his MP7 before picking up the statue.

'Careful,' snapped Cross into his headset as Trant's own gun rose into the camera's field of view and lined up on the Englishman's back. 'You might hit the angel. Move in closer.'

The team leader sidestepped along the hedge to a gap, then began a cautious, measured advance. 'No, wait,' said Nina in alarm. Eddie still had his back to Trant, the angel under one arm as he cleaned mud off the weapon. 'Don't kill him!'

'Too late for that now,' snarled Simeon.

She rushed to the cult leader's side. 'If you kill him, I'll never help you find the last angel!'

'You will,' Cross replied, his cold certainty far more menacing than any of Simeon's threats.

Nina looked back in desperation at the monitors. Trant was

now directly behind Eddie, closing with each step. The MP7 was fixed on the Englishman's back.

'Aim for the head,' said Cross. The gun's muzzle rose slightly. 'Ready—'

Nina snatched the headset off him – and jammed its microphone against the earpiece. Trant flinched at a squall of nerve-scraping feedback—

Eddie heard the shriek from the other man's headphones and spun, firing a burst from his MP7 squarely into the cultist's chest.

The camera's view blurred as Trant was flung backwards, ending up pointing skywards. The image rippled as rain landed on it.

Dalton gawped at the screens. 'What just happened?'

'Eddie just happened,' said Nina with triumph, even as Simeon hauled her away from Cross.

The cult leader jumped up, facing her with an expression of rage, but before he could speak, a voice boomed from the speakers. 'Ay up. You at the other end of this camera – can you hear me?'

Eddie reappeared, pulling the headset from the dead man and peering into the lens. 'Anyone there?' he asked, tapping the microphone with a loud *whump*. 'Come on, speak up.'

'Eddie, I'm here!' Nina shouted into the headset, before Simeon snatched it from her.

The Englishman's face broke into a strained smile. 'Nina! Thank God.'

'Mr Chase!' said Cross as he put the headset back on. 'Can you hear me?'

Eddie frowned. 'Who's that? You this Prophet bloke?'

'Yes, I am. Do you have the angel, Mr Chase?'

Eddie drew the camera back and lifted the statue into view. 'Here. Say hello to everyone at home, angel. *Hello, everyone!*' he added in a squeaky voice. Nina couldn't help but smile.

'You know how dangerous it is,' said Cross. 'If you want to see your wife again, you'll—'

'No, no, no,' Eddie cut in, shaking his head sarcastically. 'Here's the deal. You tell me where you are, I turn up, you let Nina go unharmed and *then* I give you this little fella here. Otherwise, I'll put it somewhere nobody will ever, *ever* get their hands on it again. There's a lot of construction sites in Berlin – a lot of concrete being poured, if you know what I mean. Your man Irton told me you're pretty desperate to have the full set of these things. So without this, I guess your plan's fucked, right?'

Cross's jaw muscles drew tight with anger. Simeon gripped Nina harder, making her gasp in pain. 'Nobody dictates terms to us!' he told his leader. 'If we hurt her, he'll back down—'

Eddie interrupted him. 'Cops are almost here.' The sirens were now much closer. 'You want me to leave it for them?'

'Antigua,' said Cross, the word forcing its way free of his mouth. 'We're in Antigua. Bring the angel to the island, and we'll make the exchange.'

'Antigua, eh? Me and Nina'd been thinking about having a holiday there. Let me talk to her.'

Cross reluctantly returned the headset to Nina. 'Eddie!' she said. 'You're okay?'

'Bit wet. What about you? Have they hurt you?'

'Not yet.' She gave Simeon a sidelong look. 'There have been some threats, though.'

Eddie's glare through the screen seemed to be aimed directly at Cross. 'And the baby?'

'Safe, as far as I know. And Eddie . . . I've decided on a name.'

'Oh you have, have you? Don't I get a say?'

'Nope. That's what happens when you don't want to know the sex in advance.'

'Nowt wrong with Arbuthnot, for a boy *or* a girl,' he muttered, before glancing back at the alley. 'Okay, gotta go. I'll see you soon, love – trust me.'

'You know I do,' she replied. He grinned, then dropped the headset on to the grass and ran.

Dalton whirled to face Cross. 'You're giving in to him?' he asked incredulously. 'You're letting him come *here*?' A faint edge of hysteria entered his voice, before he glanced almost in embarrassment at Nina and hurriedly regained his composure.

'No, I'm not, Mr President,' Cross replied, holding in his anger. 'There's only one international airport in Antigua, so he has to come through it. We know him; he doesn't know us. We'll take the angel from him when he arrives – by force if necessary.'

'It'll be necessary,' rumbled Simeon. Anna nodded in agreement.

'He'll be ready for you,' said Nina.

'And we'll be ready for him,' Cross replied. 'Norvin, take her back to the house. Dr Wilde,' he added, as the bodyguard led her away, 'you're still going to find the last angel for me, no matter what happens with your husband. You can trust *me* on that.'

Again the threat was perfectly clear. But Nina also felt a new sense of hope. Not only had Eddie survived; right now he had the upper hand – and the angel.

And now that she knew where she was, she had options too. Without the threat of Eddie's suffering to force her cooperation, she could risk an escape attempt. She knew from her vacation research that the Caribbean island was not large, and was certain she would not have to go far to find help.

There was the problem that she was under constant surveillance, of course, both electronically as well as by guards like Norvin. She had already started preparations to deal with the latter, though. Even if she was successful, it wouldn't buy her much time – but it might be enough to let her make a run for the jungle beyond the Mission's boundary.

With the baby's well-being to consider as well as her own, though, she couldn't afford to take the chances she would have done in the past. The moment had to be right.

But she was sure it would come.

Eddie took a circuitous route back to the bridge, tossing the gun into the river along the way. He saw police cars at the intersection, and Maureen Rothschild amongst a small crowd of onlookers.

He moved up behind her. 'Ay up, Prof.'

'Oh my God, Eddie!' gasped Rothschild. 'You're alive!'

He huffed with dark humour as he ushered her away from the gawpers. 'Don't sound so horrified.'

'That – that's not what I meant. I thought they'd killed you! I heard gunshots—'

'That was me.'

'But you didn't have a gun.'

'Took one of theirs.'

She sucked in her thin lips. 'I . . . don't want to know how, do I?'

'Probably not. But,' he went on, opening his sodden leather jacket to show her what he was holding inside, 'I got the angel.'

She regarded the statue with amazement – and concern. 'Is it intact?'

'If it wasn't, I get the feeling I'd be dead already, and so would a lot of other people.' He closed his jacket again, suppressing a shiver.

'My God,' she said, this time with sympathy. 'You're freezing! You've got to get indoors and dry off.'

'I can do that back at the museum.' He took out his phone. 'Nina thought I was mad for paying so much, but I'm really glad now I shelled out for a waterproof case.'

'Who are you calling?'

'Seretse, for one; we'll need him to fix things up with the

Germans.' He looked down the street at the police cordon. 'Last thing I need is to get arrested on a murder charge. It was self-defence, but stuff like that can take days to sort out, and Nina doesn't have that long. I've got to get to her, fast.'

'You know where she is?'

Eddie nodded. 'Antigua.'

'In the Caribbean?'

'No, in Siberia.' He gave a half-hearted smile. 'Yeah, the Caribbean. I've got a mate who moved there, so that's another call I need to make. But I managed to talk to Nina, and the arsehole who kidnapped her. We're making an exchange, the angel for her.'

'Do you think you can trust this person?'

'Nope. Which is why I want to go back to the museum.'

'Oh, I hope poor Markus is all right,' Rothschild said.

'So do I. I need his help with something.' He looked across the river at the city beyond, then asked a question that left his companion puzzled. 'You know what time the shops open in Berlin?'

17

Antigua

Maps and notes covered the desk, the laptop open and displaying a chapter from the Bible, but Nina was not reading it. Instead she was in the kitchen making herself breakfast, having forced herself away from her work.

She hadn't planned to continue Cross's task, but she found herself being drawn back in, first by boredom and then by her own insatiable curiosity. She kept telling herself that she wasn't helping her captor by doing so – certainly there had been no blinding flashes of inspiration revealing the last angel's location – and that with Eddie now free and on the way to her, even if she did discover a secret hidden within Revelation, Cross would never hear it. But a small voice kept warning her that she was falling into a familiar trap . . .

'I know, damn it!' she whispered to herself, annoyed by the chidings of her own personal Jiminy Cricket. A glance at the nearest camera, then at the small glass jar beside the sink, containing a cloudy liquid in which a few of the chopped and mashed ingredients were faintly visible. While Norvin had taken over the task of escorting her, Miriam had still been acting as housekeeper; to Nina's relief, she had left her recipe untouched.

She quickly looked away, suddenly concerned that the attention would somehow alert the watchers to her plan, and took her breakfast to the desk. The Bible text was still waiting on the screen. She munched her toast, trying to ignore it, but her inquisitive side was already drawing her gaze back to the words. They were not from Revelation, but a part of the Old Testament, Exodus, which she had come to suspect was an important piece of the puzzle laid out by John of Patmos almost two millennia earlier. Exactly how, she didn't know, but the references in Revelation to specific numbers and people and places now seemed unlikely to be coincidences—

'Mommy's doing it *again*,' she told her bump as she caught herself. As irresistible as she had always found an unsolved puzzle, this time she had to fight the urge to discover the solution.

She finished her meal, battling tedium as she pretended to be working. Even then, part of her mind was still trying to fit the pieces together for real. Finally, she caved in and checked one of the reference books. A map showed the ancient Near East, Egypt to one side and the lands that were now Israel, Jordan and Syria on the other, with the possible routes of the Exodus winding across the arid desert. Landmarks mentioned in the Bible stood out: towns, mountains, oases . . .

Nina looked back through her notes, frowning as an idea gently brushed her thoughts like a passing moth. There was something important, if not on this map then in another she had seen in her research, but she couldn't quite make the connection—

The answer came to her.

It almost *did* feel like a blinding flash, so clear that she couldn't believe she had missed it before. Excited, she peered more closely at the map, about to trace one of the lines with a fingertip before remembering that she was being watched. Instead, she forced herself to follow the path with her eyes alone until it reached a particular named spot.

Could that be it? The clues were in keeping with those that had led to the angels hidden in the catacombs of Rome and the Altar of Zeus. And however insane Cross might be, the fact remained that he *had* broken the code in Revelation, lacking only the archaeological knowledge to pin down the actual locations. If he were also correct about the third clue, then she might just have identified the Place in the Wilderness . . .

The sound of the door lock snapped her back to the present. 'Dr Wilde!' said Norvin, entering before she could answer. 'The Prophet wants to see you.'

She tried to conceal her sudden nervousness. This was her chance – the only one she would get. 'Okay, let me wash these,' she said, quickly tying her hair into a ponytail before standing and collecting her plate and cup.

He folded his arms. 'Now.'

'It'll only take a second.' Nina went to the sink and ran the crockery under the faucet. 'Can you pass me that dishcloth?' She nodded over her shoulder.

Norvin grudgingly picked up the cloth. 'Here,' he said, stepping up behind her—

Nina whirled and threw the jar's contents into his face.

The big man staggered back, trying to cry out, but could only manage a strangled gasp. The recipe was something Eddie had once taught her: a makeshift chemical agent of dried chillis and garlic and vinegar, weak compared to commercial pepper sprays . . . but still more than potent enough to blind and choke an assailant.

Nina took full advantage and smashed the plate against his head. Norvin collapsed, clawing at his burning eyes. She ran for the door, hoping her observers had been frozen by the shock of the attack—

She pulled it open just as a *clack* came from the lock. The watchers had recovered and tried to seal her in, but too late.

She rushed out into the sunlight, alone in the grounds of the Mission.

Waving trees beckoned beyond the fence. She ran to it, grabbing the barbed topmost wire and pulling it upwards before forcing herself through the gap. Her clothing snagged; she tore free, pregnant belly sliding over the steel line below before she almost fell out on the other side.

Her back and one thigh were bleeding from stinging cuts, but tetanus was currently the least of her worries. She looked over the fence. The nearest CCTV camera turned to track her. Cross's voice barked from the loudspeakers: 'Dr Wilde! Come back, right now!'

She ran into the trees. The cult leader's tone became more strident as he issued orders to his followers. 'Dr Wilde has escaped! Everyone – hunt her down!'

His wording sent a chill through Nina. Another glance over her shoulder, and she saw white-clad figures pouring from the houses. They ran towards the fence after her.

'Shit!' she gasped, fear driving her on. One hand outstretched to protect the baby from low branches, she used the other to swat foliage aside as she hurried deeper into the jungle.

It took only seconds before the Mission was lost to sight amongst the greenery, but she could see nothing except plants in every direction. Which way? Following the coastline either north or south would probably bring her to somebody else's seafront property, but she might end up trapped on a promontory.

Inland. She adjusted her course, hoping she was heading due west. The country's eastern, Atlantic side was less developed than the calmer Caribbean west, but on such a small island, she couldn't imagine being more than a mile at most from any settlement.

Running a mile while pregnant presented new problems, though. At this stage, it was not a danger in itself to the baby, but nor was it actively encouraged. And she had let herself slack off in recent months, the combination of reduced exercise and occasional binge-eating now combining with the heat to sap her energy.

No choice. This was her only chance to escape.

The ground began to slope more steeply as she weaved between the trees. She angled upwards, breath starting to burn her throat. There might be a viewpoint at the top of the hill, letting her see which way to go instead of trusting to blind chance.

If she could reach it. Shouts came from behind. The cultists were spreading out through the trees after her. The dense layers of wet fallen leaves masked her footprints to an extent, but she had already been through patches of mud, leaving clear tracks. Could she risk trying to decoy them in the wrong direction?

Another shout, this time clear enough for her to make out. 'Over here!' She hadn't been seen directly, but her path had been spotted. They were on her, closing fast.

No time to decoy them – and she couldn't outrun them for much longer either, already tiring. Once they were close enough to see her, her flight was over. That would happen in a minute, less. Nowhere to run—

Hide. But where? All she could see were trees and shrubs . . .

A large rock jutted from the ground higher up the slope. She ran to it. Could she hide behind it, under it, inside it?

No – but it had a smaller neighbour, and there was a gap between them. Would she fit?

She would have to. The hunters were closing, calling to each other as they swept the hillside.

Nina crouched and backed into the hole feet-first. Stone barked against her heels even before her waist was under cover; the opening was only shallow.

She twisted to fold herself almost into a foetal position as she

ANDY MCDERMOTT

squirmed backwards, then on some desperate instinct grabbed the broken fronds of a palm from the ground and spread them like a fan, holding them up in front of her. It was a pathetic ruse, she knew. Anyone giving it more than the most casual glance would see through it.

The flat thump of footsteps warned her that her time was up. She froze, hardly daring to breathe.

A middle-aged man with a greying beard came into view past the rock, moving at a rapid jog. He cast a brief sidelong look at the stones to make sure nobody was skulking behind them . . . then continued on.

Nina felt a moment of relief – which was instantly consumed by fear as a second white-clad man rounded the other side of her hiding place. 'Anything?' he called.

The first man slowed. 'Not yet.'

'I definitely saw footprints. Try down the hill.'

'No,' said someone else. Nina recognised the voice: Simeon. 'Maintain spacing. If you spread out too far or bunch up, we could miss her.' The Witness came into view, his rough clothing instantly recognisable. He stopped to gaze into the trees ahead, his back to her.

More people passed, some of them panting. Not all Cross's followers were super-fit ex-military or CIA, it seemed. 'Are you sure she came this way?' someone gasped.

Simeon turned towards the unseen speaker. Even though he was not looking directly at Nina, merely seeing his eyes filled her with terror. The slightest movement at the edge of his vision could draw his attention . . .

'I'm sure,' he replied, glowering at the unseen man – then setting off again. 'Okay, remember she's pregnant!' he called as he ran. 'She'll get tired long before we do!'

He disappeared into the trees. More figures in white flitted between the palms, then were lost to sight deeper in the jungle.

Nina let out an exhausted breath. She waited for a minute to be sure her pursuers had moved away before hesitantly lowering the frond and emerging.

No voices, no flickers of white clothing amongst the trees. As far as she could tell, the hunters had gone.

How long before they came back, she couldn't guess. All she could do was keep going. She regained her breath, then resumed her ascent.

It did not take long to reach the summit. The trees thinned out, the sun's position high above helping her get her bearings. She finally cleared the undergrowth, looking west to see . . .

'No!' she gasped, heart sinking in despair.

She was looking at Antigua – *in the distance*. Between the mainland's coast and the jungle below was a stretch of open ocean, the Atlantic's winds kicking up churning whitecaps. The two shores were well over a mile apart, far beyond her ability to swim. She had escaped one prison only to find that it was nested within another.

Nina closed her eyes as the hopelessness of the situation rose to swallow her . . . then snapped them open again. 'No,' she said again, this time with determination. 'Not happening.' She had come this far; no way was she giving up now.

She turned, taking in the entirety of the island. It was an elongated rough triangle, about a mile in length. Its westernmost tip pointed towards the mainland; the Mission, the church spire rising above the trees, was near the south-eastern corner. Nothing was visible beyond it except the empty Atlantic. Trapped . . .

Wait, she told herself. There had to be *some* way on and off the island other than by helicopter; it would be insanely expensive to ship everything by air. That meant boats. The shoreline at the enclave itself was a wave-pounded cliff, so nobody would be able to land there. They would need somewhere more sheltered . . .

There. A small cove south-west of the Mission, almost

perfectly circular behind its narrow entrance – and visible within was what looked like a jetty. Any boats would be there.

She judged the distance. Not much more than a quarter of a mile. Even moving through the jungle it would not take long to reach – if she didn't get caught.

No sign of any pursuers below. Resolute, Nina set off downhill. Occasionally she paused on hearing calls and shouts on the wind, but none were close by. She pressed on.

The terrain flattened out. She crossed faint paths through the woods – the Mission's residents were not forced to stay within its boundaries, then – but still nobody was in sight. Crashing waves gradually became audible. She hurried through the undergrowth towards the sound, emerging at the edge of a low cliff overlooking the cove.

A pounding *whump* and *whoosh* to her right. Some quirk of geology was forcing incoming waves into the western corner of the little bay, where they hit a narrow ridge and surged upwards before erupting like a geyser. Given time, the sea would eventually gnaw entirely through the barrier to join up with the coastline on the far side, but for now the Atlantic was still dashing itself against a near-vertical wall rising ten feet above the frothing waters. Nina had read about a similar feature on the Antiguan mainland called Devil's Bridge; this was less impressive, but both had been carved by the same almost metronomic blasts of spray.

The ragged spit arced out to form one side of the cove. The curving cliff on which she stood made up the other, a stony beach at its foot. The wooden jetty extended out from it; a boat was tied to its end.

She ran along the cliff until the slope to the beach became shallow enough to traverse, then scrambled down and headed for the jetty. The boat had an outboard motor; if she could start it, she should be able to reach the mainland in minutes—

'Down there!'

Nina glanced back at the shout with renewed fear. Simeon and a couple of others were on the clifftop. They ran after her, Simeon leaping down to the shingle as his companions rounded the cove's perimeter. There was an open-walled shed near a path that she guessed led to the Mission, a couple more boats inside. The cultists could pursue her, but they would have to carry their craft to the water, giving her a head start – if she could launch before being caught.

She hurried along the jetty. The bobbing boat was secured by two ropes. She unfurled the one at the prow, then ran back to the second at the stern – seeing Simeon sprinting across the beach towards her.

She struggled with the coils of wet rope. A knot snagged on the metal cleat. She tugged at it, for a moment unable to pull it free, then it popped loose. The final loops came away, and she leapt into the boat.

Simeon reached the jetty and pounded along it. Nina grabbed the outboard's starter rope. The motor grumbled as she pulled, but didn't turn over. 'Come on!' she cried, tugging again. '*Come on!*' Another pull, Simeon's feet banging on the planks as he sprinted at her—

The motor caught, coughing out blue smoke before fully turning over. Nina twisted the throttle on the tiller as far as it would go, and the boat surged out into the little bay.

She looked back – as Simeon made a flying leap from the jetty's end, slamming down on to the stern beside the outboard.

The extra weight pitched the boat's nose upwards. Legs dragging in the water, he clawed at the hull, trying to pull himself fully aboard.

Nina hit him in the face. 'Get off my boat!'

The African American slipped backwards, dropping into the water up to his hips. He scrabbled to keep his grip as she drew back her arm to strike again—

Simeon grabbed the tiller and yanked it hard.

The sudden turn threw Nina against him. Before she could regain her balance, he clamped his left arm around her throat. 'If I go in, you go in!' he snarled. 'Slow it down.'

She struggled, but his hold tightened, cutting off her air. 'Slow down *now*,' he ordered. 'Or I'll choke you out. You don't wanna know what that might do to your baby.'

'Son of a bitch . . .' Nina croaked, but she had no choice except to comply. She reduced the throttle. The boat slowed and settled into the water.

Simeon levered himself aboard, releasing Nina, then pushing her away. 'You're lucky you're pregnant,' he told her, breathing heavily. 'If you weren't . . .'

He left the threat unspoken, but it was enough to send a chill through her. She hunched up in one of the front seats, defeated, as Simeon brought the boat back towards shore.

18

Cross was waiting when Simeon brought Nina back to the Mission: not in the control room, but in the church, glaring down at her from the pulpit. The light shining through the stained-glass windows cast a malevolent red tint over his face. 'Did you really think you could escape, Dr Wilde?' he asked. 'There are cameras all around the island, not just at the Mission – we saw you as soon as you came out into the open.'

'Yeah, I should have guessed,' was Nina's sullen reply. 'A control freak like you wouldn't stop at watching people in the bathroom.'

'So what do we do with her?' demanded Simeon.

'She should be punished,' added Anna. Norvin, the skin around his eyes a blotchy red, nodded in agreement.

Dalton, sitting in the front row of pews, spoke up. 'As much as I'd like to see her suffer, we need her. Even if we get the angel from her thug of a husband, she still has to find the last one.'

Anna gave him a cold look. 'If you hadn't insisted on getting revenge on them, we could have *paid* another archaeologist. Chase being at the museum in Berlin proves that someone else could have worked it out.'

The ex-president glowered at her, displeased that anyone would challenge him, but was interrupted by Nina before he could reply. 'The Altar of Zeus was the easiest to connect to what John wrote in Revelation,' she said. 'Finding the one in the catacombs in Rome was much harder – and there was a hell of a lot of luck involved as well.'

Simeon's unfriendly gaze turned upon her. 'I *knew* she was sandbagging us. If she'd told us about Berlin first, we would have gotten the angel without our entire team being wiped out!'

'You think the statue in Berlin would have been sitting on a desk waiting for you if Eddie hadn't gone there?' she countered. 'Someone with a great deal of knowledge of the altar found it for him, and you don't get that by waving guns around.'

Cross raised a hand to silence the argument. 'Her husband's on the way with the angel now.'

'You're sure?' asked Dalton.

'I checked with a contact of mine at Langley. He left Berlin on a United Nations flight this morning; it lands at VC Bird this afternoon.' He looked to his right-hand man. 'We'll be there to meet him – with backup.'

'If you hurt him, I'll never cooperate with you,' said Nina.

'That's up to him,' Cross replied. 'But I get the feeling Mr Chase isn't the type to give up without a fight.'

'You're goddamn right about that,' muttered Dalton.

'If he fights us, he dies,' Simeon said flatly.

Again Cross waved for silence. 'I'm not worried about the third angel. It's the fourth one that concerns me – the one hidden in the Place in the Wilderness. We need to find it, soon.'

'Why?' Nina demanded. 'Are you on a timetable?'

He gave her a patronising shake of the head. 'You've read Revelation, but you haven't taken it in. So many things in it happen according to a schedule set by God.'

'Yeah, I remember.' She indicated the Fishers. 'How long have your Witnesses been prophesying? They only get one thousand, two hundred and sixty days of walking around in sackcloth before people get fed up of their yammering and kill them.'

'And then they are reborn.' Cross lifted his head, looking up not at the ceiling but at the heavens beyond. 'After that . . . the seventh angel shall sound.'

Nina could only respond with sarcasm. 'And God lets you in on all his secrets.' She turned to Dalton. 'And you get cheered back into the White House, and Charlie Brown finally kicks that football. I know which *I* think's most likely to happen. Hint: it involves a cartoon kid with a big head.'

'There's something else you know, isn't there, Dr Wilde?' said Cross. The change in his tone made her suddenly uneasy; he sounded extremely confident. 'The location of the last angel.' His pale eyes fixed on to hers, as if drilling into her soul for the truth.

'There's nothing to find,' she replied, trying to conceal her nervousness. 'Even if you're right about it being in the Place in the Wilderness – which you might well be, considering you're two for two so far – the clues are too vague to pin down. You could be looking at practically anywhere in the Middle East, from Egypt all the way over to Iraq.'

'But your research suggests that you've narrowed it down to the route of the Exodus.'

Nina felt even more unsettled. Everything about Cross's attitude implied that he somehow knew about her own personal revelation before the escape attempt. But that was impossible. Her notes, her internet usage, even the pages of the reference books she had checked – none could have given it away. 'That was just a possibility, and it's not as if I'm the only person to have thought of it.'

Cross stared down at the redhead for a moment, then descended from the pulpit to stand in front of her. 'Then explain why, at ten thirteen this morning, you had a sudden surge of adrenalin.'

She looked back in confusion. 'I . . . what?'

'Those aren't just video cameras in your house. We monitor your heartbeat, respiration, temperature, perspiration, even involuntary eye response, all remotely. It's the same gear the CIA uses. I can track every tiny physical fluctuation of your body and know what you're feeling even before you're consciously aware of it.' An unpleasant smile, then he took a single step closer. Nina tried to back away, but Norvin moved to block her. 'Now. The response you had was exactly consistent with that of somebody who's just made a great discovery . . . and then immediately tried to hide it.'

'The CIA's been doing this for a long time,' Dalton chipped in. 'They really can tell what you're thinking.'

'It's not mind-reading,' continued Cross, 'not yet. But it's the next best thing. So, what did you find?'

'I didn't find anything,' Nina insisted.

He loomed closer, their faces just a few inches apart, then abruptly drew away to walk across the church. 'My mission in life has always been about seeking the truth, Dr Wilde. The truth of individuals, of nations, of God. So I find it almost personally offensive when someone tries to keep that truth from me. Don't insult me by trying to deny it,' he snapped as she opened her mouth to do just that. 'Even if you don't know exactly where the angel is, you know which area to search.' He turned to face her. 'And now you're going to tell me.'

'I can't tell you what I don't know.'

He came back towards her, eyes narrowing to threatening slits. 'But you *do* know. So I'm going to give you a very simple choice. Either you tell me . . .' His right hand slipped inside his robes – and drew a slim steel dagger. 'Or I'll kill your baby.'

The room closed in around Nina as he held up the knife. She looked to the others, but found no support. Only Dalton was anything other than stone-faced, the former president clearly shocked. 'You – you wouldn't,' she gasped.

'I will if I have to,' he told her, advancing slowly. She tried to flee, but Norvin grabbed her. 'I don't want to. I consider the murder of the unborn a sin against the Lord. But the mission

God has given me is more important than one innocent life. I'll make it quick and painless for the child. One stab will do it. You won't need more than minor treatment to survive.'

'You're *insane*!' Nina cried, desperately trying to pull free of Norvin's hold. 'You're out of your fucking mind! Dalton – Mr President!' she wailed. 'You can't possibly agree with this!'

Dalton stared back, for once at a loss for words. 'I – this shouldn't, but . . .' he stammered, before jumping to his feet. 'For God's sake, Nina! Tell him!'

Cross stopped in front of her. He lowered the dagger towards her belly—

'All right!' she screamed. 'Okay, I'll tell you, I'll *tell* you! Just don't hurt my baby, please!'

He blinked, almost as if emerging from a trance, then retreated and passed the knife to Simeon. 'I'm glad you did that, Dr Wilde.'

'For God's sake, Ezekiel!' said Dalton, appalled.

'I'm not proud of myself, but it had to be done,' Cross told him. He looked back at the trembling Nina. 'Now. Where is the fourth angel?'

She still wanted to resist, but knew he had no compunctions about carrying out his threat. 'The woman . . .' she croaked, mouth bone-dry. She struggled to draw saliva, then spoke again. 'From Revelation – the woman with the moon under her feet . . .'

'Chapter twelve, verse one,' said Cross, nodding. '"And there appeared a great wonder in heaven; a woman clothed with the sun, and the moon under her feet, and upon her head a crown of twelve stars."'

'I realised what the part about the moon is referring to. The Wilderness of Sin.'

'Sin?' Dalton echoed. He had returned to his seat, visibly disturbed by what had just happened. The former politician had been more than willing to order the use of violence by others, but the prospect of actually witnessing it in person had shaken him.

'A region the Israelites passed through during the Exodus,' Cross told him.

'It's nothing to do with sinfulness,' continued Nina. 'Sin was the name of a Semitic deity – one of the gods worshipped by the ancient Jews before they became monotheistic followers of Yahweh. That's God, if you didn't know.'

'Yes, I know. I'm not *completely* ignorant,' Dalton growled.

'Sin was a moon god; what was written in Revelation is sometimes interpreted as a reference to the other gods being trampled underfoot as Yahweh became dominant, but it could *literally* mean walking over the desert named after him. Now, there's also a mention of this woman – the Woman of the Apocalypse, as she's known – going to a place prepared by God.'

'"And the woman fled into the wilderness, where she hath a place prepared of God",' said Cross.

'Yeah. But I thought about what that might actually *mean*. It could be that God picked a spot and made it safe for her to stay. Or, more likely, that it was already an important religious site, which at some earlier point had been prepared, sanctified, whatever. Somewhere the Israelites had set up camp during the Exodus. I think that's what the reference to the twelve stars means – the twelve wells they found as they travelled across the desert.'

The cult leader nodded. 'That's a fairly common interpretation.'

'So the angel is in some sort of temple in this Wilderness of Sin?' asked Dalton. 'How hard will that be to find?'

Cross gave him a patronising smile. 'Quite hard, Mr President. Nobody actually knows where the Wilderness of Sin *is*.'

'It's generally considered to be the region between Elim – the location of the twelve wells – and Mount Sinai, where Moses received the tablets containing the Ten Commandments from God,' Nina explained. 'Except nobody knows which mountain that is any more. It's extremely unlikely that it's the modern-day Mount Sinai in Egypt, because that location doesn't fit any of the descriptions of the journey in Exodus or other books of the Torah or the Bible.'

'So how does that help us?' Dalton demanded.

'I think she knows something more, Mr President.' Cross turned back to Nina, awaiting an answer.

'It's only a theory,' she insisted.

'A theory you thought was important enough to hide. So tell us.'

She took a deep breath. 'Okay. There's a list in the Old Testament of the places the Israelites visited during the Exodus.'

'The Book of Numbers,' said Cross.

'Right. I think there are forty-two stations?' Another nod. 'They start out in Egypt, and after forty years in the wilderness end up on the Moab plains, in modern-day Jordan. But the part that caught my attention is the journey from the Wilderness of Sin to a place called Dophkah.'

'Numbers chapter thirty-three, verse twelve: "And they took their journey out of the Wilderness of Sin, and encamped in Dophkah."'

'Dophkah is in the Timna Valley, in southern Israel,' said Nina. 'Part of the Arabah desert. It's an archaeological site – copper's been mined there since at least the tenth century BC. That gives us a specific location to use as a starting point.'

Cross gestured towards the doors behind the pulpit. 'Show me.'

The group went into the control room. He brought up a map

on the video wall, zooming in on Israel to centre upon the Timna Valley. 'There's your starting point, Dr Wilde,' he said. 'Now where do we look?'

'That's a whole lot of nothing,' Dalton remarked. Highways ran parallel to Israel's eastern and western borders, heading to the country's southern tip at the Red Sea, but between them the map was almost empty.

Cross tapped at a touch pad. The view changed to a satellite image. Features appeared, but they were all natural: rugged desert hills and mountains, their colours a universally arid sandy-brown. 'Numbers thirty-three eleven tells us that the Israelites came from the Red Sea, so this' – he swept a hand over the area south of Timna – 'must be the Wilderness of Sin.'

'Big area to cover,' said Simeon. 'Even if we stick inside the Israeli borders, that's got to be a hundred square miles of desert.'

'But it's there somewhere,' Cross said to Nina. 'It's all in Revelation. The moon is a reference to Sin; the twelve stars tie it to the Exodus. It makes sense. And following your line of thinking about an important religious site, the "place prepared of God" is most likely somewhere that the Israelites set up the Tabernacle. Yes?'

'I hadn't thought of it like that, but yes,' she replied. The Tabernacle was a portable shrine carried by the Israelites on their journey, containing their holiest treasures, including the Ark of the Covenant. 'If they stayed at this place for some time, they could have set up a semi-permanent place of worship.'

Dalton took a closer look at the satellite view. 'Why would anyone stay in that godforsaken hellhole?'

'Because God gave them what they needed to survive,' said Cross. 'He provided water to drink, and manna to eat.'

'There's been water there in the past,' Nina added. She pointed out channels cut into the mountains. 'And that's how I know what to look for.'

All eyes turned to her. 'Well?' said Dalton impatiently. 'Tell us!'

'It's all there in Revelation,' she answered. 'Distorted as usual, coded, but John's still telling us what he learned in Pergamon. The Woman of the Apocalypse was pursued into the wilderness by a dragon – one of the guises of Satan. God protected her, helped her reach the place prepared for her—'

'"And to the woman were given two wings of a great eagle, that she might fly into the wilderness, into her place",' Cross cut in.

'But he also defended her while she was there,' Nina went on. 'She was pregnant, and the dragon wanted to devour her child right after it was born. He failed, but sent a flood to kill her in revenge. And I'm sure you're about to give me the relevant quote,' she said to Cross.

'Chapter twelve, verse fifteen,' he said. 'But I'll spare you the full text.'

'Good. Because it's the *next* verse that holds the answer. You can quote *that* to everyone if you like.'

He frowned, but recited the words. '"And the earth helped the woman, and the earth opened her mouth, and swallowed up the flood which the dragon cast out of his mouth."' A long pause, during which Cross and his followers exchanged glances, as if waiting for their own revelations. None came. 'How does that help us?' he demanded.

Nina gave him a faint but cutting smile. 'It helps a lot, if you know something about geology as well as archaeology. Remember that John is describing his hallucinogenic interpretations of the Elders' writings. They wrote about a flood – possibly a flash flood, which in the desert can happen miles from where any rain actually fell. But the earth opened up and swallowed it before it reached the Place in the Wilderness.' She paused, waiting for a response. 'Seriously? Did nobody do Geology 101? The only thing that could be is a sinkhole! A sinkhole swallowed the flood – and those things don't just disappear. It'll still be there!'

Realisation filled Cross's eyes. 'The sinkhole will mark the angel's location!'

'Finally!' said Nina. 'Yeah, that's right. *That's* what I worked out this morning. Somewhere in that desert' – she gestured at the screens – 'is a sinkhole, either near or actually in a water channel. And somewhere very close to that . . . is your last angel.'

Everyone regarded the satellite map. 'So how do we find it?' asked Dalton.

'Hell if I know,' she snorted. 'If there are any more clues in Revelation, I haven't figured them out. I don't know who the Woman of the Apocalypse is meant to represent, or what the reference to her being "clothed with the sun" means. She's pregnant – for all I know, it's a prophecy about me.' She indicated her bulge, before remembering Cross's threat and putting her arms protectively over it.

'We don't need any more clues,' Cross decided. 'We can locate all the sinkholes in the region from the satellite imagery, then find any archaeological traces near them from the air.'

'Oh, you can, can you?' Nina said scathingly. 'Maybe I should have traded my PhD for a pilot's licence.'

He ignored the comment. 'We know we're looking at waterways, so that'll cut down the area we need to check.' He turned to Dalton. 'I know people in Israel who can get us free access to their airspace, and hopefully even provide military assistance if we need it. If you can call on your diplomatic contacts to get us into the country without drawing attention . . .'

'No problem,' he replied. 'But that's the fourth angel – what about the third one?'

'We'll have it soon. Simeon? Get some people and meet Mr Chase at the airport.' He faced Nina again. 'If your husband's sensible and hands over the angel, I'll let him live.' Simeon clearly did not approve, but said nothing. 'I can be magnanimous.'

'I can't,' she replied with cold anger. 'You were going to kill my baby. That's not something I'm willing to forgive. If I ever get the chance . . . I'll kill *you*.'

She couldn't tell if the threat had affected Cross or not. 'Take her away,' was all he said.

19

Eddie emerged from the arrivals gate at VC Bird airport to see his name in crooked marker pen on a piece of cardboard. He had expected a reception committee, but at the back of his mind throughout his flight was the thought that it might not be friendly. However, he knew this one had been arranged by a friend simply because he had acquired some extra initials: *E. B. G. Chase*. 'Cheeky bastard,' he said to himself, grinning.

The man holding the card was not the one he had called, but a middle-aged Antiguan wearing a battered baseball hat and a long baggy shirt bearing patterns of shells and starfish. Eddie approached him. 'I'm Eddie Chase. Are you Nelson?'

'Thas right,' the man drawled, giving him a broad, lazy smile. 'Nelson Lightwood, at your service. At your service,' he repeated, for no reason the Englishman could determine. 'Tom ask me to take you to Jolly Harbour. Jolly Harbour.'

'That's great. That's great,' Eddie replied, unable to resist gently ribbing him.

Nelson either didn't notice or didn't care. 'You wan' me to take your luggage?'

Eddie had only a carry-on bag, and wasn't planning to relinquish it – for the moment. 'No, that's okay. You've got a cab?'

'Outside. The white Toyota.' He jabbed a thumb in the general direction of the exit. 'The Toyota.'

Eddie saw as he stepped into the humid heat outside the terminal that while Nelson was being accurate, he was not being specific; about a dozen taxis were lined up at a stand, all white

Toyota vans. He wondered why there were no American vehicles, the US being much closer, before realising the answer: the former British colony, like Japan, drove on the left. 'The one with the flower,' his driver offered.

'Tell you what, just show me.' He followed the nodding Nelson down the rank, glancing back to see if anyone was paying him undue attention.

A tall black man with a close-cropped haircut looked away just a little too quickly, while one of the three Caucasian men near him was almost giving a masterclass in how to look suspicious. All four wore similar white outfits, feebly disguised under jackets. Eddie remembered seeing the black guy lurking near the exit when he'd met Nelson. He had company, then, but he would have been surprised if he hadn't.

'This one, my friend,' said Nelson. The dented Toyota Hiace minibus looked little different from its neighbours, though Eddie was amused when he spotted its identifying feature: a fake sunflower on the dashboard. 'Step inside.' He pulled back the sliding side door.

Eddie took a place on the rear bench seat. The interior had seen a lot of use, but otherwise appeared to be a perfectly normal island taxi. Of more concern was the object beneath the driver's seat – a half-empty bottle of vodka. Hoping it was only enjoyed *after* its owner finished his shift, he waited for Nelson to amble around the vehicle and climb aboard. 'Okay, my friend,' said the Antiguan. 'Jolly Harbour.'

He pulled away. They passed the four waiting men, all of whom watched them go. Eddie looked back as the cab cleared the end of the rank to see the whole group make a beeline for a parked car.

The taxi left the airport grounds and headed south-west around the outskirts of the capital, St John's. 'How long will it take to get there?' he asked.

Nelson shrugged. 'Who can tell? This is rush hour.' The traffic didn't look to Eddie any heavier than he would expect of a quiet Sunday afternoon in England, but the squealing brakes and sudden swerves of other drivers suggested that the Antiguan attitude towards road discipline was a lot more lackadaisical.

'Well, there's no hurry.' He looked at the bag on his lap, then over his shoulder. The silver Honda his tails were driving was a few cars behind. 'You got a map of the island?'

'Sure, man.' Nelson passed him a brochure. St John's was in the island's north-west quarter; Jolly Harbour, his destination, was down on the south-western Caribbean coast. The distance between the two was only about seven miles, but he doubted that any part of the trip would be on a motorway.

Of more concern was that once past the southern fringes of St John's, there only appeared to be a few small villages dotted along the route, nothing but green between them. 'The way we're going – does it go through open countryside?'

Nelson nodded. 'Oh yeah, man,' he said, turning to peer back at him. 'We goin' along Valley Road, very pretty along there, very pretty. You get a good view of Mount Obama there, yeah.'

'You might want to get a good view *here*,' Eddie suggested, seeing a stationary bus looming in the taxi's path.

Nelson gave him another languid smile and looked ahead, slowing just in time to avoid a collision. 'No problem, man. I been driving here thirty-three years, thirty-three years. Not dead yet.'

The Honda was still holding position not far behind. 'You ever had any trouble in that time?' asked the Yorkshireman. 'I don't mean with cars, but with their drivers. Or anyone else.'

An amused grunt. 'You think we in paradise? Ha! We got some not very nice folks here, same as anywhere. I can take care of myself, my friend.'

'Good. 'Cause you might need to.'

Nelson used the mirror to meet his eyes, for the first time

showing a hint of steel behind the sleepy front. 'Tom told me why you come here. Don' worry. I don' lose a passenger yet.'

'Glad to hear it.' Eddie settled back, occasionally glancing through the rear window to check on their tail.

The taxi made its way around the periphery of St John's. The brightly painted houses became smaller and more basic as they moved away from the capital's centre, before finally petering out. 'Valley Road,' Nelson announced. 'Valley Road.'

Eddie saw lumpen tree-covered hills rising in the distance beyond a rippled plain of farmland and forests. According to the map, the road was the main route to the various villages and resorts in the south-west. It was hardly an interstate, though, the bumpy highway only two lanes wide. What little traffic there was seemed content to amble along at no more than thirty miles per hour, Nelson giving a toot of the horn to warn the driver of an old pickup doing half that speed that he was about to overtake.

The Antiguan glanced at the truck as he passed and chuckled. 'That guy, he smokin'. Say, you smoke? I get you all hooked up, man. All hooked up.'

'No thanks,' said Eddie. 'Not my thing.' Another look back. With fewer cars on the road, the Honda was running out of cover. Its driver held position behind the dawdling pickup before seeing that his quarry was pulling away and making a hasty pass. They were now in open countryside. 'How far to the next village?'

'Jennings, about two kilometres,' Nelson told him. 'Then another kilometre to Bolans. Bolans.'

Bolans was not far from their destination. If something was going to happen, it would be here, as far as possible from any witnesses. 'Stay sharp,' said Eddie. 'I think we're going to have company—'

The words had barely emerged when the Honda surged forward, catching up with the taxi in seconds. It drew alongside – and the black man in the passenger seat pointed a pistol from his open window, waving for the cab to turn down a track to the left. Nelson yelped a Creole curse. 'Better do it,' Eddie told him.

The Toyota pulled off the road, stopping a short way down the muddy track. The car halted behind it, angling to block both the view of anyone passing by and the cab's escape route. 'This all fucked up!' Nelson protested as the four men climbed from their vehicle. '*Fucked* up!'

'Just stay calm,' said Eddie. He shifted to the middle of the rear seat, putting the bag next to the sliding door, and picked up the vodka bottle. As the men advanced, he slipped it under his right arm, holding it in place by the neck.

The door was hauled open. The black man leaned in and pointed the gun at the Yorkshireman, who raised both hands to chest height. 'Toss away the keys,' he ordered Nelson. His accent was American. The wide-eyed driver obeyed, dropping the keys from his window. 'Okay, Chase. Keep your hands where I can see them. Where's the angel?'

'In the bag,' Eddie replied.

The gunman's gaze flicked to the holdall. 'Bring it out. Slowly.'

Eddie picked it up with his left hand and carefully clambered from the taxi, keeping his other arm against his side to conceal the bottle behind him. The three white guys, to his relief, didn't have guns, but the biggest held a tyre iron, repeatedly slapping it against his open palm.

'Okay, put it down.' The Englishman lowered the bag to the ground. 'Washburn, open it. Make sure the angel's inside.'

One of the other men squatted by the holdall and pulled back the zip. Inside was a thick roll of bubble wrap surrounding an object about a foot long. 'I brought your precious bloody angel,' said Eddie as the man tugged at the plastic cocoon. 'Where's Nina?'

'Safe. Until we don't need her any more,' the black man replied dismissively.

'And I suppose that now you've got the angel, you don't need me either?'

'You got that right.' He scowled. 'You killed a lot of good men in Berlin, Chase. That makes you a threat to our plan – *God's* plan.'

Eddie eyed the gun, which was fixed unwaveringly on his chest. 'What, you're just going to shoot me in the street?'

'This isn't New York. By the time the cops respond, we'll be long gone. We're leaving this island soon anyway—'

'Simeon!' said Washburn. He had peeled open one end of the thick wrapping to reveal the head of an eagle. 'It's the angel!'

Simeon glanced down to see for himself—

Eddie brought his elbow outwards, dropping the bottle – and whipped his hand down to catch it.

The gunman was transfixed by the sight of the statue for a split second too long. His eyes snapped back to Eddie – as the bottle smashed against his gun hand, shards lacerating his skin.

He screamed as the alcohol seared the wounds and reflexively pulled the trigger – but the impact had knocked the pistol away from his target, the bullet whipping past the Yorkshireman to clunk into the taxi's bodywork.

Eddie swept one leg up and kicked Simeon's bleeding hand. The gun was sent spinning into the tall bushes beside the track. The American let out another cry.

Washburn jumped up, fists balled, only to reel away with a shriek as jagged glass slashed his cheek. Holding the bloodied bottle like a knife, Eddie backed up past the taxi to give himself more room to manoeuvre.

'The angel! Get the angel!' Simeon barked, clutching his injured hand. One of the other men snatched up the bag, while his companion with the tyre iron moved past him towards the Englishman, whipping the length of metal from side to side.

Eddie retreated, watching the bar flick before him. The man

holding it was built powerfully enough to break bone if a blow landed. Behind him, the other three attackers were hurriedly returning to the Honda with the bag.

The big man lunged. Eddie jerked aside as the tyre iron stabbed past his head, glimpsing Nelson scrambling from the taxi behind his attacker. Another strike, this a savage horizontal swipe that whooshed past just inches from his nose.

He flinched back – and staggered as his heel dropped into a deep rut.

The man bared his teeth in a malevolent smile, raising the bar to smash Eddie's skull—

And screamed, one leg giving way as Nelson stabbed a long serrated knife into his thigh.

Eddie punched the hulking thug hard in the face, sending a gush of blood from his nostrils. He toppled backwards into the mud, weapon forgotten as he clutched the stab wound. The Englishman grabbed the tool, about to finish the fight permanently before deciding that a murder would not endear him to the Antiguan authorities. He settled instead for viciously kicking his opponent's crotch. The big man convulsed, every muscle in his body drawn tight, before slumping unconscious.

The Honda's engine roared. Eddie scrambled for cover, expecting his attackers to mow him down, but instead it reversed sharply before skidding back on to the main road. Within seconds it was out of sight behind the bushes, heading back towards St John's.

He turned to Nelson. 'You okay?' The Antiguan nodded, staring almost in bewilderment at the blood on his blade before hurriedly wiping it on the downed man's shirt. 'Thanks for that – I'm glad you had that knife.'

'Mos' taxi drivers do. I tell you, you only *think* this place is paradise.' He regarded the motionless figure with dismay. 'They were gonna kill you!'

'They'd have killed both of us.' Eddie spotted a glint of metal in the undergrowth and retrieved the gun. 'Come on, let's go. Somebody might have heard that shot, and I don't have time to piss around dealing with the police.'

The taxi driver didn't move. 'What we gonna do with this guy?'

Eddie snorted. 'He started it – and I bet he won't go to the cops. You didn't hit the artery, so he's not going to die. Leave the bastard there and let him limp home when he wakes up. You coming?' He went to the cab.

Nelson examined his vehicle. 'Look at this! Look at this!' he complained, poking a fingertip into the bullet hole. 'How I gon' explain that to me wife?'

'Just remind her that this place isn't paradise,' Eddie said with a grim smile.

Nelson frowned, then recovered the keys. 'I come get you as a favour to Tom. Now he better do *me* a favour!' He got back into the taxi. 'They took your bag, man,' he said, regarding the empty rear bench. 'Took your bag!'

'Yeah, I know,' said Eddie as he returned to his seat, then leaned back – with an expression almost of satisfaction. 'Real shame, that . . .'

Nelson gave him a disbelieving look, then, muttering under his breath, reversed the cab to the road and set off again for Jolly Harbour, leaving the dazed man lying in the mud.

20

'E e bah gum,' said Tom Harkaway in an exaggerated attempt at a northern accent. 'It's Eddie Chase!'

'That's Lancashire, not Yorkshire, you thick southern bastard,' Eddie replied, grinning up at the large bearded man on the deck of the motor yacht. 'We say "Ay up!" not "Ee bah gum!"' He shook his head. 'E. B. G. Chase? You daft twat.'

'Whatever, you're all bloody barbarians as far as I'm concerned.' Tom tramped down the gangway to the wooden dock, shaking his fellow Englishman's hand before clasping him in a bear hug. 'So, how's things?'

'Right now? Been better,' Eddie replied as he extricated himself. 'In the past few days I've been Tasered, waterboarded and shot at, I've driven a Porsche off a bridge, and just since I arrived on this island someone's tried to kill me. Oh, and my wife's been kidnapped by a bunch of religious nuts.'

Tom cocked his head to one side. 'Business as usual, then.'

'Yeah, more's the fucking pity. Thanks for agreeing to help me out.'

'Us SAS boys have to stick together,' replied his old squad mate. He gave Nelson a concerned look. 'Someone tried to kill him? You okay?'

'Fine, both fine,' said Nelson, sounding aggrieved. 'But my taxi got a bullet hole! Who gon' pay to fix that?'

Tom's eyes went to Eddie. 'Don't look at me,' he said. 'You're the one with the yacht.'

'Yeah, and you arrived on a private jet!' The older man sighed,

247

then told Nelson: 'I'll sort it out. Take it to Viv at the boatyard.' He gestured across the harbour at a cluster of industrial buildings. 'He'll patch it up for you. Elena doesn't have to know anything about it.'

The taxi driver looked relieved. 'Thanks, Tom.'

'Cheers for the lift,' Eddie said as Nelson departed, before turning to take in the moored yacht beside them. The name *Flirty Lady* was painted on the hull of the seventy-foot white and blue vessel; he was no nautical expert, but from its decided lack of sleekness compared to the other craft nearby, he guessed it was a good few decades old. 'Never imagined you as a navy man. Go cruising with Seaman Staines and Master Bates, do you?'

'Ha ha. Fuck off, Eddie. This is how I make a living now – tourist trips. We go out around the island, drop anchor off some of the nicer beaches and let 'em go snorkelling before partying on the way back.'

'Sounds like really hard work,' Eddie joked, surveying his surroundings. Jolly Harbour was an attractive and clearly wealthy enclave with rows of houses right on the waterline, many having their own docks. Steep little hills rose around the bay, providing a backdrop of lush tropical vegetation. 'Nice place. My mum always wanted to come here. You've got a tough life.'

'You can joke, but you try keeping up with the payments on a ship this size, even a third-hand one,' Tom told him as he ascended the gangplank. 'Then there's the insurance, fuel, berthing fees, all that crap. It's not exactly a licence to print money.'

Eddie followed him into the main cabin. 'So,' said Tom, with a penetrating look. 'You ring me last night, tell me you're coming to Antigua on some kind of urgent mission for the UN, I agree to help you . . . and now I find out that your wife's been kidnapped and someone wants you dead. Kept *that* part quiet, didn't you? What the bloody hell's going on?'

'I'm not exactly sure myself,' Eddie admitted.

'Okay. And do you know who these people are?'

'Nope.'

Tom pursed his lips. 'Riiiight. Do you even know where they're keeping your wife?'

'Nope again. Although,' he added, taking out his phone, 'if I'm lucky, I'll find that out soon . . .'

Even locked in her house with a pair of guards posted outside the door, Nina couldn't miss the clatter of a helicopter coming in to land. Soon afterwards, Cross's disembodied voice summoned her. A clack from the door lock, and two men entered to escort her through the compound.

Some of the Mission's white-clad residents were rushing about, excitedly passing on news to their neighbours. Nina saw someone familiar. 'Miriam?' she called. 'What's going on?'

The young woman hesitated, nervousness plain on her open face. The current news wasn't the only gossip; Nina's attack on Norvin had also done the rounds. But whatever had happened was so exciting, she couldn't hold it in. 'They've found the third angel!'

'It's here?' The redhead looked towards the helipad in alarm. If Cross's people had taken it from Eddie already . . .

'Yes! One of the Witnesses just delivered it to the Prophet.'

'I guess I'm going to see for myself,' said Nina as her guards directed her onwards.

'It's wonderful!' Miriam called after her. 'There's only one more angel to find, and then the seventh trumpet will sound!'

'You say that like it's a good thing,' she offered in parting. She had now studied Revelation enough to know what followed the last trumpet: war, destruction and death on a colossal scale.

She tried to hide her foreboding as she was brought to the church. The Fishers emerged in a rush as she arrived. Simeon's left hand was clamped tightly around his right, blood oozing between his fingers. Anna ushered him along, face full of concern for her husband. Both glared at Nina as they passed.

Their anger gave her a perverse feeling of hope. Even if they had taken the angel from Eddie, he had certainly put up a fight.

The cult leader was waiting inside with Dalton. The two men smiled when they saw her, though in the former president's case it was decidedly gloating. Cross, however, was almost ecstatic. 'Dr Wilde! This is one of the most important days in the history of the world – and it wouldn't have happened without you.'

'I'm absolutely *thrilled* to have helped,' she replied, in a tone acidic enough to peel paint.

Dalton's smile slid into a smirk. 'Cynicism's so unbecoming in a mother-to-be.'

'Oh, cram it up your ass, Mr President.' Nina reached them, seeing a carry-on bag on the front pew. 'Where's Eddie?'

'Still alive, unfortunately.' She wasn't sure which gave her more pleasure: the news itself, or the former politician's discomfiture at announcing it.

'It doesn't matter,' said Cross. 'What does matter is that three angels are now accounted for. The one destroyed in Iraq, the second from the catacombs in Rome, and now the third.' He indicated the bag. 'There's only one more to find – and we know where to look. We're already making preparations for the search. You'll join us, of course,' he added. 'You're right: we might still need an archaeologist on the ground.'

'Trekking around a desert while pregnant? Boy, I can't wait.'

'You won't have to wait long. We'll be leaving tonight.' Cross opened the bag. 'But first I wanted you to see this.'

He donned white gloves, then carefully lifted out an object cocooned in bubble wrap. One end had been pulled open, revealing a hint of what was inside. 'The third angel – the eagle,' he said, showing it to her.

Nina couldn't help but feel a thrill at the sight. However dangerous it might be, the angel was still an incredible find. But the feeling passed almost immediately at the thought of how Cross intended to misuse it – for devastation, not discovery. 'Is it intact?' she asked. 'After everything it went through, you were damn lucky it didn't get broken in Berlin.'

'You can blame your husband for that,' said Dalton.

'If it had broken, it would have been God's will,' Cross said as he started to peel away the wrapping. 'It doesn't matter *where* the angels are released, just that they *are*.'

'Although some locations are better than others, obviously.' The ex-president seemed to be enjoying some private joke.

Cross paid no attention, fixated on freeing the statue. 'Here,' he said with reverence as the last wrapping came away. 'At last.'

Dalton came to see for himself. 'Three down, one to go.' He turned to Nina. 'What do you think, Dr Wilde?'

Nina didn't answer, her attention fixed on the statue. Something was *wrong*, she realised. Compared to the second angel, it was different – the way it caught the light, the tint of the ceramic, the arrangement of the metal wings surrounding the body . . .

Cross caught her confusion. 'What are—' he began, before looking sharply back at the relic. He ran his gloved fingertips over its surface, then turned it to examine the inscribed text, almost squinting as he tried to make out details.

'What's the matter?' Dalton demanded.

'It's . . . it's not real,' whispered Cross. He gave Nina a frenzied glare, as if it were her fault. 'It's a fake! Look at the lettering! It's *stepped* – like a low-resolution copy!' He tugged off one glove to scratch the statue with his fingernail. Tiny flecks of the surface broke away.

Nina almost laughed. 'I think you've been scammed. Or *scanned*, rather. Eddie must have put the real angel into that laser

251

scanner at the museum and 3D-printed an exact copy. It's nice work, though. Somebody's even gilded the wings to make them look like real metal.'

'But . . . but why?' asked Dalton. 'He must have known we'd realise it was fake, so he couldn't have exchanged it for you.'

'He wasn't going to exchange it,' said Cross. He turned the statue upside down, examining its base. A small length of metal was set into the flat surface – something that had not been present on the angel taken from Rome. 'It's an *antenna*!' Fury filled his voice. 'It's a tracker, a GPS beacon. He *wanted* Simeon to take it from him. Now he knows where we are!'

He raised the statue as if about to smash it on the marble floor, then forced back his anger, regarding the replica for a moment before lowering it again. 'We need to move up our schedule,' he said more quietly, calculating.

'Wait – where's the real angel?' said Dalton.

'Chase must still have it, or has gotten someone to bring it to Antigua for him. He needs it to get his wife back.' Cross looked at Nina. 'He'll be coming here. But we'll be ready for him.'

Eddie zoomed in on the map on his phone to a small island off Antigua's eastern coast. 'That's where they are – where Nina is.' He had bought the GPS tracker and its phone app from a spy shop in Berlin that morning, getting the bruised but otherwise unharmed Derrick to conceal it inside the replica. 'You know it?'

Tom nodded. 'Elliot Island. Never landed there, though – it's private property. You get too close, and the residents turn up and wave you away. Not a big deal; its beaches aren't great, so it's not a prime tourist spot.'

'Know anything about the people who own it?'

'Some religious commune, I think. There's a church. Apart from that . . .' He shrugged.

'I need to get out there, without them seeing me. It won't take 'em long to realise that wasn't the real statue – oh, and there we go.' The tracker's dot vanished, a message popping up to announce that the signal had been lost. 'Still, it told me what I needed.'

'When you say you need to get out there,' said Tom warily, 'I'm assuming you want me to take you?'

Eddie smiled. 'That'd be helpful, yeah.'

'I told you, they'll see us coming. The *Flirty*'s not exactly a stealth boat.'

'That's why it's perfect. How quick can it get out there?'

'At full pelt? An hour and a half, maybe.' He looked through a porthole at a call from the dock. 'Who's this?'

'That's for me,' said Eddie. He went out on to the deck to find Maureen Rothschild at the bottom of the gangway. 'Hi, Prof! You made it, then.'

'Yes, I did,' she replied, with a distinct lack of enthusiasm. 'I waited in the plane for ten minutes before going through customs, as you asked, and by that time, a jumbo jet full of tourists had arrived! I had to wait in line behind three hundred people. And when I finally got out, it took an age to find a cab. Why couldn't I have come with you?'

'Trust me, you wouldn't have wanted to be in my taxi,' he told her, marching down the walkway to pick up her travel case. 'I had a reception committee. And they weren't there to give me cocktails in a hollowed-out pineapple.'

Rothschild's eyes went wide. 'You were ambushed? Are you all right?'

'I didn't know you cared.' He ascended the gangway.

'I'm displaying simple human decency, Mr Chase,' she replied tartly as she followed. 'Something in which you apparently still need lessons. What about the statue? Did they take it?'

'Yeah, just like I'd hoped. So now I know where they are.' He helped her on to the yacht. 'You've got the real one?'

Rothschild huffed. 'No, I left it on the plane. Of course I brought it!'

'Sarcastic, snappy . . . you're more like Nina than either of you'd want to admit.' Eddie put down the case. 'Tom, this is Maureen Rothschild. Prof, this is Tom Harkaway, an old mate of mine.'

'Nice to meet you,' said Tom, extending his hand.

She shook it dubiously, eyeing a pouting pin-up girl painted on a bulkhead beside the vessel's name. 'Thank you. This is a . . . nice boat.'

He chuckled. 'It's seen a fair few parties.'

'Speaking of which,' said Eddie, 'how fast can you drum up some passengers? A party boat without partiers'll look a bit suspicious.'

Tom pointed beyond the houses along the harbour's western edge. 'There are two big resort hotels just over there, the Tranquility Bay and the Jolly Beach. It shouldn't be too hard to find some people who want a cruise.' He paused. 'You want me to give them a *free* cruise, don't you?'

'Quickest way to fill up the boat, innit?'

'And who's going to pay for all this?'

'There's a bloke at the United Nations called Oswald Seretse . . .'

Rothschild shook her head. 'Poor Oswald. He's in for a shock.'

'Not as much as the arseholes who took Nina.' Eddie took the gun from inside his jacket and checked the magazine.

'Jesus, put it away!' cried Tom, eyes wide. 'You don't want to get caught with that. The Antiguans had a big crackdown on guns after some tourists were murdered a few years ago. Shoot someone and you'll get anything from twenty-five years to the death penalty.'

'Didn't seem to worry the bloke who took the statue,' Eddie

replied, slipping it back out of sight. 'You know any local cops?'

Tom nodded. 'I've got some friends.'

'Could be worth bringing 'em in. Pretty sure I'll need backup.'

'But the police won't land on a private island without a good reason.'

'They've kidnapped Nina, for fuck's sake!'

'They don't have proof that she's there,' Rothschild pointed out.

'She's right,' said Tom. 'They'd need a warrant or probable cause to go and look.'

'All right, then they can fucking come and arrest me for trespassing!' The Yorkshireman frowned, then an idea came to him. 'You've got distress flares, haven't you?' His friend nodded. 'Okay, if I fire off a flare, that means either I've found Nina, in which case they can come ashore and arrest 'em for kidnapping, or I'm being shot at, in which case they can come ashore and kill the bastards! How does that sound?'

Rothschild and Tom exchanged looks. 'I've heard better,' the latter admitted.

'This is how you come up with all your plans?' exclaimed the elderly woman, incredulous. 'Random improvisation? It's amazing that you're still alive!'

'I'm not hearing anything better, and the clock's ticking.' Eddie regarded the case. 'All right, Prof, I need the angel. Tom, we need to set things up.'

'I'm going to regret this, aren't I?' muttered the older man, but he nevertheless went back into the cabin to search for a flare.

'You're really going to do this?' asked Rothschild as she opened the case. 'You're going to give them the statue, even though they want it for something dangerous?'

'Yep.' Eddie took out another bubble-wrapped item; this time, it was the real angel.

'You are insane, you know.'

'You're not the first person to say that. But I'm not planning on letting them keep it. Why do you think I want to get the cops involved? I'll talk to Ozzy too, see if we can bring Interpol and the State Department into it. Pretty sure a US citizen being kidnapped should get their attention, especially when it's someone famous like Nina.'

'Nina,' she echoed, with a wistful nod. 'You really do love her, don't you?'

'Course I bloody do,' said Eddie, surprised by the question. 'I'm married to her, she still puts up with me even after all the crap we've been through – and she's having our baby. Why would you even have to ask?'

Her eyes couldn't quite meet his. 'No reason.'

He was sure there *was* one, but he had neither the time nor the inclination to discover it. 'Right,' he said, removing the angel from its padding. 'Let's get this party started.'

21

The journey around the island showed Eddie two very different sides of Antigua. The waters of the western shore, facing the Caribbean, were a calm and incredibly clear turquoise. By the time the *Flirty Lady* had made her way along the southern coast and turned north into the Atlantic, however, things had become considerably more choppy.

The dancers on the main deck were coping with the swaying floor with surprising ease. Tom had rounded up a group of young, mostly German holidaymakers. The promise of unlimited alcohol magically ended any questions about why the free cruise was being offered, and after one of the revellers connected an iPhone to the yacht's speaker system to pump out an endless succession of Euro dance tracks, further conversation became impossible anyway.

The bridge provided only a modest amount of soundproofing. 'I must be getting old,' Eddie complained loudly after closing the door, deciding that Rothschild had made a very sensible decision by staying ashore. 'Modern music all sounds the bloody same!'

Tom, at the wheel, grinned in agreement. 'If they'd just stuck one track on repeat, I doubt I'd know the difference.' He pointed ahead. 'There it is.'

'That's Elliot Island?' From this distance, only trees were visible above the rocky shoreline. 'Where's this place with the church?'

'Eastern side. You can't see it from here.' He turned the wheel to the left. 'We'll go up its west coast and around to the north, then head back south past the village. That should bring them out to keep an eye on us, and give you your distraction.'

'Did you talk to the police?'

'Had a word with one of my mates. He says they'll be ready for us, but they won't come out unless something actually happens. I asked him about the people who own the island; apparently they keep well in with one of the local politicians, so he's a bit cagey about going on to private property without a damn good reason.' Tom nodded at a ship-to-shore radio. 'Once you fire a flare, I'll call them in, but it could take them a while to get here from Nelson's Dockyard.'

'Hope they've got something faster than a pedalo. All right, I'd better get changed.'

A few minutes later, Eddie had stripped down to a pair of swimming shorts. Tom gave him a wolf whistle. 'Fuck off,' said the Yorkshireman with a grin as he donned a scuba tank, then put everything he was taking with him in a bag that he clipped to the cylinder. 'Okay, where's the best place to drop me?'

The *Flirty Lady* was now circling the island's north-western shoreline. Tom indicated a small bay. 'That should put you about three quarters of a mile from the village. I'll time it so we go past when you get there.'

Eddie surveyed the coast. 'What're the waters like?'

'This side of the island's shielded from the really big waves coming in from the Atlantic. Shouldn't be any trouble to swim.'

'Sharks?'

'Sometimes.'

'Yeah, that's helpful.'

'They don't work to a timetable. But you're more likely to see stingrays than sharks. They're generally friendly – don't bother them and they won't bother you.'

'Me, bother anyone?'

They both chuckled, then Tom opened the bridge door and

called to a white-shirted crewman keeping an eye on the partygoers. 'Melvin! Take the wheel for a minute.' The Antiguan hurried up to the bridge. 'Right, let's get you into the water.'

He helped Eddie down the stairs. 'Hey, are we going swimming?' asked a cheerfully drunk blond German.

'Just me,' Eddie replied. 'Lost a contact lens overboard.'

'Ah.' The young man regarded him with owlish curiosity before smiling. 'Ah! That is English humour, yes? Monty Python, Mr Bean? I get it!'

'That's the one,' Eddie replied, impatient. 'You know there's free beer over there, right?'

The youth danced unsteadily away between his friends. Eddie shook his head. 'Kids. Who'd have 'em? Oh, wait. Me.' He sat on the boat's port side and put on a pair of flippers.

Tom stood in front of him to block the view of anybody on shore. 'Looks clear to go.'

Eddie peered past him. There was no sign of any human activity on this side of the island, but that didn't mean it was deserted. He tested the scuba regulator, then pulled a diving mask over his eyes. 'I'm ready.'

His friend nodded. 'Melvin! Reduce to eight knots!' He waited until the chug of the diesel engine slowed, then turned back to Eddie. 'Good luck.'

'See you soon.' He put the regulator into his mouth, gave Tom a thumbs-up, then rolled backwards into the ocean.

Even in the subtropical warmth, the water briefly felt like ice. He flinched, then the initial shock passed and he kicked to move away from the yacht. Its swirling wake briefly pounded him, fading as the *Flirty Lady* continued on its way.

He turned on to his front and started swimming. Small fish glided past, paying little attention to the intruder in their realm, but to his relief nothing larger – friendly or not – appeared in the crystalline depths.

It took only a few minutes before the seabed became visible, gradually rising to meet him. The currents became stronger as the water shallowed. He ploughed on, waves buffeting him, until his fins brushed the ground.

If anyone was watching, they would be able to see him by now. Eddie breached the surface and stood, water streaming down his mask before clearing to give him a view of the little bay.

Nobody in sight.

He waded ashore, kicking off his fins. The stony beach was deserted. He looked along the tree line, but saw nothing. A glance back out to sea: the *Flirty Lady* was out of sight, though he could still hear the faint rumble of its engine and the pulse of Europop.

He removed the scuba tank and opened the bag, taking out a baggy shirt and a pair of deck shoes with thick rubber soles. Both were soaked but would dry out quickly enough in the heat. The distress flare and gun went into his pockets.

The final item was the angel. He picked it up, then hurried across the beach into the trees beyond.

Fifty yards away, a camera mounted on the trunk of a palm tracked him until he was lost to sight amidst the greenery.

'This is getting tiresome,' said Nina as her two guards escorted her into the control room. 'Bring me here, send me back, bring me again . . . you might as well set me up a bed in the corner.'

'I wanted you to see this,' Cross replied from his chair. 'And you too, Mr President,' he added as Dalton entered, looking as annoyed as Nina at the summons.

'See what?' Dalton demanded.

The cult leader activated the video wall. 'This was filmed a few minutes ago.'

Nina took in the surveillance footage. The camera overlooked a small beach, the Antiguan mainland visible on the horizon. It slowly panned across the vista – then abruptly zoomed in on something in the water.

A figure emerged from the ocean, plodding through the breaking waves and discarding a pair of flippers. She recognised him instantly.

'Your husband's here,' said Cross.

Nina's delight was mirrored by Dalton's alarm. 'Chase is *here*?' he squawked. Learning that the Englishman had escaped from his kidnappers in New York had unsettled the former politician; his being only a short walk away brought outright horror. 'Here on the island? Oh my God!'

'Hope you've got space in your baggage for your ass, because he's about to hand it to you,' said Nina, unable to contain a smirk.

Dalton went to Cross, grabbing the swivel chair and pulling its occupant around to face him. 'You've got to stop him! That man's a maniac, a psycho! You have no idea how many people he's killed – and now he's coming for *me*!'

'He's not coming for *us*,' Cross corrected, his annoyance clear. 'He's coming for her. Look.' He paused the playback, zooming in on Eddie as he took something from a bag. 'He's brought the angel. The real one.'

'You're sure it's real?'

'Of course I'm sure. The fake was a decoy so he could locate the Mission, but now that he's bargaining for the lives of his wife and child, he'll have to use the actual angel.'

Dalton withdrew, still agitated. 'So where is he? Why aren't you tracking him?'

'The cameras only cover the shoreline. Don't worry, though,' he added as the ex-president shot him a look of dismay. 'Once he gets close to the Mission's perimeter, we'll pick him up again.' He tapped another control. 'Paxton? Get the chopper ready. We move out as soon as the angel's secured.' He waited for an acknowledgement, then made another announcement. Nina heard it echo over the public address speakers outside. 'This is Ezekiel. A visitor is about to bring us the third angel. Everyone be ready for him.'

He stood, turning to Nina. 'Come on, Dr Wilde. Let's meet your husband.'

The sound of a voice over loudspeakers in the distance made Eddie crouch behind a tree and draw the gun, checking the vegetation for threats. Nobody was there, but he was now on full alert.

Cautious, he continued through the jungle. Before long he saw faint paths. Rather than follow them, he moved parallel to one, keeping in the undergrowth as he advanced.

Something man-made ahead, a straight line standing out amongst the curves of nature: a wooden post about fifteen feet tall at the intersection of two paths. He looked at its top. A black sphere was mounted upon it. A camera. Had it seen him?

'Mr Chase!' The voice he had heard earlier, now perfectly clear and audible. 'My name is Ezekiel Cross. Welcome to the Mission.'

'Oh, *bollocks*,' Eddie muttered. That answered his question.

'We saw you the moment you set foot on the beach,' the unseen man continued. 'And we know you've brought the angel – the *real* angel. Your wife is here with me.'

'Let me talk to her!' he yelled at the camera.

He didn't expect a response, but after a moment he heard a new voice: Nina's. 'Eddie! It's me, I'm okay. They're—'

She was cut off, Cross speaking again. 'Follow the path if you want to see her.'

Eddie glared at the camera, then continued onwards. Before long, he saw a wire fence ahead. 'Keep going, Mr Chase,' said the voice. 'Head to your right. There's a gate.'

He reached the fence. Through it he saw the village spread out before him. Small wooden houses led his eye to the Mission's centrepiece: a church, its spire rising high above its surroundings.

Also visible were three men dressed in white, coming up the slope towards him. The sight of more cameras overseeing the entire village explained how they knew his position. 'All right, I get it – you've got the whole Big Brother thing going on,' he shouted at the nearest. 'You can see me, but I can't see Nina. Where is she?'

'She's outside the church, with me,' said Cross. 'You have my word that you won't be harmed as long as you bring me the angel.'

Eddie eyed the approaching men. None appeared armed, though he didn't accept his mysterious host's assurances for a moment. Keeping the gun trained on them, he went along the barrier until he reached the gate and entered the compound.

The men came closer. 'Back off,' he warned them, waving the gun.

'Let him through,' said the amplified voice. The white-clad reception committee moved back. Eddie started towards the church, the men following at a discreet distance.

The houses he passed were all pristine and tidy, almost to the point of sterility. 'I'm in fucking Toytown,' he muttered, wondering where the residents were. Apart from the men behind him, there was no sign of anyone.

That changed as the church came into full view ahead. A crowd waited outside – he guessed eighty or ninety people. All were dressed in white.

Except one.

'Nina!' he yelled, seeing his wife at the front of the congregation.

'Eddie!' she cried back, joy in her voice as well as tension.

Two men, Simeon one of them, stopped her from running to him. 'I'm okay, the baby's okay!'

'You can see she's alive and well,' said the voice. For the first time, Eddie laid eyes on the man responsible for everything that had happened; the robed Cross stood close to Nina, speaking into a small headset microphone. A black case was at his feet. 'You came to make a trade.'

'Yeah,' Eddie replied. 'But first . . .' Holding the statue under one arm, he took out the flare and popped off the plastic cap. Pointing it upwards, he used his thumb to hook the pull-tab on its base. The projectile rocketed from the tube with a flat bang and a trail of smoke, arcing into the sky. Its parachute deployed after a few seconds, the bright white star drifting out to sea.

People in the crowd exchanged anxious looks. 'That was to tell the Antiguan police that you're holding a kidnap victim!' Eddie called as he resumed his march towards the church, aiming his gun at Cross. Simeon angrily drew a pistol in his bandaged hand. 'They know I'm here too, dickhead. So killing me'd be a really bad idea. I'm told Antigua has the death penalty for gun crimes.'

Cross waved for his henchman to lower the weapon. 'Only God will take any lives here.'

There was a commotion at the church doors. Eddie looked towards them – and was shocked to see Victor Dalton pushing through the crowd to reach Cross. 'He's called the *cops*?' the former politician said. 'We've got to get out of here! If I'm still here when they arrive, I'll be linked to a federal crime!'

The Yorkshireman neared the group. 'You!' he barked at Dalton, who flinched. '*You're* behind all this? I should have fucking killed you when I had the chance!'

'Paxton's ready with the chopper,' Cross told his partner, unconcerned.

Eddie looked around at the whine of a turbine engine starting up, seeing a helicopter on a pad near the cliffs. Beyond it he spotted the *Flirty Lady* cruising southwards past the village, its passengers waving to those on shore. 'Going somewhere?'

'We have a plane to catch,' replied Cross. 'But first, Mr Chase, we had a deal. The angel for your wife.'

'Eddie, you can't let them take it,' protested Nina. 'They'll use it to kill hundreds, maybe even thousands of people!'

Simeon raised his gun again. 'We're doing God's will. Now, hand it over.'

Eddie kept his own weapon and gaze fixed on Cross. 'You're right, we made a deal. I'll honour my side, if you honour yours.' Dalton's gaze flicked nervously between the two men.

Cross was silent for a long moment, then he nodded. 'Let her go.'

'*What?*' barked Simeon. Anna was equally shocked.

The cult leader turned his cold gaze upon them. 'Do you trust me?' he asked.

The question caught them both off guard. 'Yes, of course,' said Anna. 'But—'

'Then don't question me. We can find the last angel without her.'

She nodded. Simeon was more reluctant, but lowered his gun. Cross looked back at Eddie. 'The angel?'

The Englishman put the statue on the ground, then warily stepped closer to Nina, holding out his free hand. She reached for it, then stopped. 'Don't give it to them, Eddie,' she pleaded.

'You trust *me*, don't you?' he asked.

'Yes, but . . .' Another moment's hesitation, then she took a firm hold of him. 'There *aren't* any buts.'

'That'll upset Sir Mix-a-lot. Okay, let's do this.' The couple backed away, Eddie keeping the gun raised. 'There's your statue.'

'Hold it,' said Simeon. 'How do we know this isn't another fake?'

Cross picked up the figure. He turned it over in his hands, holding it up to the sunlight to examine the fine details. 'It's real,' he announced. 'It's real!' He faced his congregation, holding the figure above his head. 'The third angel of the apocalypse is ours!' Joyous awe spread through the crowd, some of his followers bursting into tears.

Eddie was less enthused. 'The angel of what?'

'I *told* you not to give it to him!' said Nina. 'They've got some insane plan to bring about the apocalypse so Dalton can get back into power.'

'Wouldn't the end of the world kind of screw up his political career?' he asked as they retreated further. 'Hard to get out and vote if it's raining fire and brimstone.'

'They didn't let me in on their endgame. But I know it involves loosing the angels – breaking open the statues to let out what's inside, something that reacts with air and turns into toxic gas.'

'That'd explain the gas masks they had in Berlin, then.' Eddie flicked the gun at the three men who had followed him to the church; they let him and Nina pass. 'But don't worry, they'll never get a chance to do it. Like I said, the cops are on the way. Even if they leave in the chopper, they'll still get stopped at Antigua airport, or whichever other island they try to fly out from.' He winked at her. 'See? Trust me. I know what I'm doing. More or less.'

Cross returned to the black case and reverently placed the statue inside next to its fellow from Rome, then closed it. 'My friends,' he said, his voice still coming from the loudspeakers, 'my faithful followers, I must leave you now. Three of the angels bound at the Euphrates have now been found, and I know where the last one is hidden. I'll find it, I promise, and I *will* fulfil the prophecy of the Book of Revelation. When the angels have been released, the seventh trumpet will sound – and then Babylon will fall and Satan will be cast down into the lake of fire. When that is done, nothing can stop God's kingdom on earth from becoming a reality.'

Eddie looked askance at Nina. 'Is this bloke for real?'

'Unfortunately, yes,' she replied. 'He believes every word he's saying.'

He twirled a forefinger at his temple. 'Wibble.'

'The problem is, he's been *right*.' At Eddie's look of surprise, she went on: 'About some of it, at least. The clues hidden in Revelation really did lead to the angels. And now he knows how to find the last one. I told him where to look.'

'You did?'

'I didn't have a choice. Eddie, he . . . he threatened to kill the baby.'

He stopped abruptly, his face turning utterly cold and blank. Nina had seen the frightening look before, after the murder of his friend 'Mac' McCrimmon, and knew what it meant: he had targeted someone for death, and would be both relentless and merciless in carrying out that mission. 'Then I'll kill *him*,' he said simply.

'No, wait,' Nina gasped. But he was already taking aim. She grabbed his arm, trying to force him off-target—

Simeon whipped up his own weapon – but before either man could fire, screams and cries came from the crowd as they too realised the danger. Several people rushed to put themselves between Cross and the Yorkshireman.

Nina recognised one of them. 'Miriam!' The young woman was terrified, but she held her position, arms spread wide in a desperate attempt to shield her prophet. 'Eddie, don't shoot!'

'Nobody shoot,' said Cross. 'Simeon, stand down. That's an order!' Simeon bared his teeth in frustration, but obeyed.

Eddie jerked his wrist from Nina's grip, his chilling mask replaced by anger. 'What're you *doing*?'

'You called in the cops! If you kill him in front of all these people, it'll be cold-blooded murder – and you said Antigua has the death penalty. I'm not going to let you throw your life away.'

He glowered at her, but then a shout caught everyone's attention. 'Boats!' called a man on a small parapet at the base of the church spire. 'Boats are coming!' He pointed south. 'The police and the coast guard!'

'Thank you, Tom,' Eddie muttered. For the cops to have arrived so quickly, his friend must have decided *what the hell* and radioed them long before the flare was launched.

'See?' said Nina, pulling her husband's gun hand firmly downwards. 'They can handle everything from here.' The pair of them resumed their retreat up the hill.

'It's time to go,' Cross said, still speaking over the PA system. He picked up the case. 'Mr President, if you'll come to the helicopter?'

Eddie and Nina were now out of Dalton's earshot, but his agitated body language told them he was still worried. 'It doesn't matter,' Cross's amplified voice assured the politician as he, Dalton and their entourage, including the human shields, started towards the helipad. 'We won't be stopped at the airport.'

Eddie watched them with growing suspicion. 'Why's he so fucking confident?'

'I don't know,' Nina replied, her own unease growing. 'But I think we should get out of here.'

'We need to tell the cops what's going on.'

'The only place they can land is over there.' She pointed towards the cove to the south-west. 'If we meet them, they can contact the airport and stop Cross from leaving, can't they?'

'Yeah, that was the plan. But . . .' Eddie stared after the cult leader as his group reached the helipad. 'Something's not right.'

Norvin opened the helicopter's doors. Dalton was first to scramble aboard, Anna and Simeon following. But Cross remained, signalling for his white-clad guardians to face him. 'My followers,' he said, 'my friends: you have all had faith in me, faith in the word of the Lord and in the prophecy of the Book of Revelation. I *will* find the fourth angel, I *will* see that Babylon falls. But another prophecy must be fulfilled, here, today, right now. Revelation chapter six, verse ten: "And they cried with a loud voice, saying, How long, O Lord, holy and true, dost thou not judge and avenge our blood on them that dwell on the earth?"'

'Doesn't he ever shut up?' complained Eddie.

Nina waved for him to be quiet, trying to remember what followed. 'I don't like this . . .'

Cross continued his recital. '"And it was said unto them, that they should rest yet for a little season, until their fellow servants also and their brethren, that should be killed as they were, should be fulfilled."' He opened the case. 'Miriam. Will you take the second angel?'

Nina watched with rising concern. 'What's he doing? Why's he giving it to Miriam?'

'Who's she?' Eddie asked.

'One of his followers – she's just a kid, an innocent. Why is he . . .' A horrible possibility occurred. 'Oh my God.'

'What?'

She looked at him in alarm. 'The angels – Cross thinks that for him to learn God's secrets, all four angels have to be released. But one was *already* released, in Iraq, so they don't have to be broken at the same time.' Possibility became certainty, and as her gaze snapped back to the helicopter, it seemed that Cross was looking past Miriam directly at her, almost taunting. 'He's going to do it *here*! Miriam, don't!'

She was drowned out by Cross's amplified voice. 'Miriam has taken the angel,' he announced, kissing her on both cheeks before entering the helicopter. Norvin was last aboard, closing the door. Some of the other villagers were filing towards the helipad with a clear mix of emotions from worry to near-rapture. 'Now may God's will be done!' The aircraft took off, rising vertically at full power before heading west.

'Miriam!' Nina cried again, as futilely as before. The young woman, tears glistening on her cheeks, raised the statue high above her head. The other cultists cleared a space around her.

'And God shall wipe away all tears from their eyes,' boomed Cross. The helicopter was rapidly disappearing, but his voice remained. 'And there shall be no more death, neither sorrow, nor crying . . .'

He paused. Nina used the moment of silence to scream Miriam's name again, begging her to stop—

'Neither shall there be any more pain.'

Miriam's mouth opened in a silent cry . . . then she threw the statue to the ground.

22

'*N*o!' shrieked Nina. But it was too late.

The angel shattered against a rock – and a sickly yellow gas erupted from the meteorite fragments exposed at its core. Miriam screamed as the glutinous vapour swallowed her, the cloud expanding with frightening speed.

Some of the cultists at the helipad stood their ground, while the nerve of others broke and they fled. It made no difference. The gas consumed them in moments, people flailing in agony before vanishing into the opaque mass.

Eddie and Nina broke through their shock and ran. Behind them, panic spread through the congregation at the church, faith wavering and breaking at the sight of death rolling towards them.

The cloud reached the houses, swirling and slithering around them like a liquid snake. An elderly woman tried to run but tripped and fell; her husband hesitated, then went back to help her, only for both to succumb to the toxic gas as it swept over them. Some followers ran into the church in the desperate hope that its walls would provide sanctuary. Seconds later, all were dead. Others raced for the jungle, but anguished screams cut through the air as they were caught one by one.

'What the fuck *is* that stuff?' Eddie gasped.

'Something you don't wanna get near!' Nina replied. 'Through that gate, there!'

They sprinted for the opening. One final choked wail reached them, then the Mission fell silent.

Eddie threw open the gate, letting Nina through. She was

already short of breath, clutching at her abdomen. 'Are you okay?' he asked as he caught up.

'No!' she snapped. 'I'm pregnant and running from a huge poisonous cloud! I am *not* okay!'

'Love you too,' he said, managing a brief grin, which vanished as he looked back. The looming mustard-yellow miasma was still rising behind them. 'How far's this dock?'

'Just down here!' Nina saw water between the palms ahead.

'And there *is* a boat, right?'

'Yes, there's a boat! What, did you think I was planning to *swim* out of here?'

'Five more months of this, just five more months . . .' Eddie told the jungle. She glared at him, but forgot her anger as they cleared the trees and saw the jetty. The boat was still there. 'I'll get it started!' He ran ahead to the jetty, quickly unknotting the mooring rope and jumping aboard.

Nina reached the dock. 'Eddie, look!' She pointed at the bay's entrance. Two boats were carving through the sea towards it. 'It's the police!'

Eddie spotted them – then with alarm saw something closer. The death cloud had broken through the trees and was roiling along the edge of the bay, towards its mouth. 'Shit! It's going to cut us off!' He looked around, finding that the cove had no other exits to the ocean.

Nina clambered into the boat as Eddie tugged at the starter cord. The engine clattered, then roared. He shoved the prow away from the jetty, then revved to full power, swinging out into open water.

The police boats were almost at the cove's mouth – but so was the gas. Oozing across the shore, it rolled the last few dozen yards over the rocks and dropped lazily down to the incoming waves. 'The water!' Nina exclaimed, seeing a change in its movement. The thick, oily mass appeared to be reacting on contact with the sea, becoming thinner. 'Cross said water stopped the reaction – it might absorb the gas too!'

'Not quick enough,' Eddie realised. He had already judged how long it would take their boat to clear the bay, and unless the cloud completely vanished, they wouldn't make it.

The two police vessels reached the opening. 'No, get back!' Nina shouted, waving her arms to warn them off; the cops probably thought it was nothing more dangerous than smoke. 'Turn around!'

Too late. The cloud drifted across their path, blocking them from view . . .

Both boats burst from the dense fog, yellow vortices streaming out behind them. The men aboard thrashed and screamed. One vessel veered sharply away as its pilot hit the steering wheel in his blind panic. It rolled in a tight turn, engine still at full throttle, then flipped over, hurling its dying occupants into the water.

The other craft charged onwards, holding course—

Straight at Eddie and Nina.

'Whoa, *fuck*!' Eddie yelped. He jammed the tiller to its limit, leaning into the turn to keep from capsizing. The coast guard powerboat surged past barely a foot behind them, bounding over their wake before smacking back into the water. It kept going, heading for the jetty.

'Turn, *turn*!' Nina cried after it, but there was nobody alive on board to hear. The boat rammed into one of the jetty's pilings, wood and fibreglass disintegrating in a huge shower of smashed fragments. Its ruptured fuel tanks exploded, sending a black mushroom cloud boiling into the sky.

But a different cloud dominated the couple's thoughts. Even though the water seemed to be affecting it, the sulphurous mass had still engulfed the bay's entrance, and was now spreading across its interior after them. 'We'll have to get back on shore,' Eddie said, 'and hope it doesn't cover the whole fucking island!'

He turned the boat towards land, beyond the burning jetty.

'Eddie, wait!' Nina pointed at the rock spit. 'There's a blowhole or something where the waves hit the rocks.' Right on cue, a great burst of spray erupted from the corner of the cove. 'The cliff's only narrow, and the sea's right on the other side – we might be able to ride a wave over it!'

He shot her a disbelieving look. 'Those pregnancy hormones must've screwed up your brain. It's *me* who's supposed to come up with the insane plans, not you!'

'It's the only way out!'

Eddie grimaced, but knew she was right. The deadly cloud would soon cover the entire bay. 'Let's hope I time it right,' he said, revving the engine.

The boom of water striking the rocks grew louder as they approached. Spray was being flung high into the air over the barrier, but most of the frothing waves stopped a couple of feet short of its top. Some managed to clear it, but there was no way to predict which ones.

Eddie slowed, watching the waves roll in – then twisted the throttle to full. A large breaker had already passed beneath them, and they rapidly caught up with it. 'Come on, come on – *shit!*'

He had mistimed it, the crest smashing against the wall and reaching almost to its top, then falling just as they angled up its rising shoulder. He turned away hard, but momentum carried them onwards—

The backwash as the wave retreated saved them from a catastrophic crash, but the boat's side still slammed against the rocks, throwing its passengers sideways, before being pulled clear. Water sluiced into the hull as the craft lurched upright and careered back into the cove.

The Yorkshireman shook foam off his face. 'Jesus!' he gasped, regaining control. 'Are you okay?'

Nina sat up, clutching a bruised arm. 'Yeah. I think.' She flicked wet strands of red hair from her eyes, then flinched as she saw what lay ahead. 'Oh, crap!'

The cloud now covered more than half the bay, consuming the jetty, and was still advancing on them. If they had made landfall, they would never have been able to outrun the vaporous juggernaut.

Eddie hurriedly turned away, but the boat was rapidly running out of space to manoeuvre. He looked back at the cliff. 'We'll have to go for it,' he said reluctantly, 'but we'll only get one more chance. You ready?'

Nina braced herself. 'No, but do it anyway!'

He half smiled, then turned his attention back to the water. He had no choice but to follow the first large wave that came along, and hope it would propel them over the ridge.

None were coming. The sickly cloud roiled ever closer.

A deeper trough – then a new wave broke through the deadly fog.

Eddie didn't know if it would be strong enough, but he had to use it. He waited for it to pass beneath the boat, then – as the first yellow tendrils stretched out towards him – jammed the throttle to full power.

The boat leapt forward, following the wave. One last tweak of the tiller, aiming for the spot where the impacts were focused, then he gripped Nina with his free arm and held on for dear life—

The wave struck, surging upwards before exploding against the cliff and sending a broad spout of water and spray skywards . . .

Carrying the boat with it.

It tipped back almost vertically, riding up the wave to be flung off its top into a blinding mass of spume. The keel hit the rock with a hideous raw crunch, the boat teetering atop the ridge like a seesaw for a nerve-shredding moment, then the weight of the water falling back into the hull pulled the prow downwards. It rasped over the summit and dropped into the sea on the far side with a pounding smack.

The landing flung Nina and Eddie from their seats. The Englishman spat out seawater, then scrambled back to the motor. He looked up – to see the deadly cloud spill over the clifftop and drop towards them like a slow-motion avalanche.

'For fuck's *sake*!' he yelled, grabbing the throttle. The propeller clashed against rock, making the tiller jar painfully in his grip, then finally bit into clear water. The boat surged away as the malevolent mass silently fell down behind it.

He swung away from the shore, only looking back once he was sure they were at a safe distance. 'Christ . . .'

Nina was just as shocked. The cloud was draped over the island's eastern side like a monstrous jellyfish, still swallowing up the jungle tree by tree. Its advance did appear to have been slowed over the water, but at a price: the azure sea around it had turned a bloody red. 'My God. I can't believe how big it is!'

'All of that from one little statue? What the bloody hell was in it?'

'Part of a meteor, according to Cross. Something that fell to earth in ancient history and became part of apocalyptic mythology.'

'Yeah, I can see why.' He glanced towards Antigua. 'Shit, we've got to warn somebody! If that stuff reaches the mainland . . .'

Nina looked more intently at Elliot Island. 'I don't think it will. Look, over by the Mission. It doesn't seem to be pumping out any more gas, and the wind's starting to push the cloud out to sea. Cross told me that whatever creates it gets burned up when it reacts with air; maybe it's all been consumed.'

'Along with everyone in the village,' Eddie reminded her.

'Oh God, yes . . .' She nodded sadly. 'I don't think most of them were bad, just . . . just misguided. Cross found people who could be persuaded to follow his beliefs, used them to build his organisation, then left them to die once they'd served their purpose. Poor Miriam . . .'

Eddie was less sympathetic, but kept his opinions to himself. 'Over there,' he said instead, pointing. The *Flirty Lady* was visible in the distance, having moved well clear of the island. 'That's my mate's ship. We can radio the mainland from it and tell 'em what's happened. Hopefully we'll be able to stop Cross and Dalton from taking off.'

'Hopefully,' said Nina, though with little confidence. The damaged propeller was slowing them; it would take a while to reach the ship. She looked back towards the Mission. The gas cloud was indeed dispersing in places, the church spire now visible through the yellow haze, but a good third of the island was covered. 'Because they've got another angel. If they release it in a city . . .'

She didn't need to say more. Eddie shared her grim look, then guided their vessel towards the yacht.

23

'So they got *away*?' Eddie barked at the speakerphone.

'I am afraid so, yes,' came the voice of Oswald Seretse. It was now dusk; Tom Harkaway had brought the *Flirty Lady* into the nearer port of Nelson's Dockyard rather than returning to Jolly Harbour. He had alerted the authorities about the events on Elliot Island by radio after Eddie and Nina boarded, but by the time word reached the airport, a private jet had already taken off. 'The aircraft filed a flight plan to Geneva, but it now seems unlikely it is actually going there.'

Eddie shook his head. 'Black flights. Fucking CIA.' He turned to Nina. 'That must be how they got you out of the States without anyone asking questions. The CIA's got a whole fleet of planes they use to whip people around the world, as passengers – or prisoners. Cross and Dalton must still have mates there.'

'But we know where they're going,' she replied. 'Israel. It'll take them at least twelve hours to arrive, so that gives us plenty of time to alert the Israelis and get them to arrest them when they land.'

Even over the phone, Seretse was clearly uncomfortable. 'There are two problems, Nina. The first is that we have no proof of Victor Dalton's involvement other than your word. He was not seen by customs officials at Antigua airport, and there is so far no evidence to suggest that he was even on the island. Without such proof, making direct accusations against him would be . . . unwise. He may have been forced out of office, but he still has supporters.'

'I didn't *imagine* seeing him, Oswald,' she snapped.

'I am sure you did not. But the second is that when he was president, Dalton was a great supporter of the Israeli government; the US representative on the United Nations Security Council while he was in office had a one hundred per cent record of voting in favour of Israel or vetoing resolutions that were against its interests. If he really is going there, he will have many friends in high places.'

The couple had been brought by helicopter to Government House in St John's; in the room with them were the island's Governor General, and the Prime Minister, James Jefferson, the latter responding with a burst of indignation. 'Whether President Dalton was here or not, the man who owned Elliot Island, this Ezekiel Cross, has committed an act of terrorism against my country!' he snapped. 'He released a chemical weapon! We don't know how long it will be before the island is safe to visit, and even though the gas cloud has gone, the sea has been poisoned – we have already had reports of dead fish and birds.' He glared at his companion. 'You have to do something, Calvin. You're the Queen's representative here. Even if the British government is too afraid of the Americans to act, we must still issue a formal protest to the United States, and tell them to find this CIA plane!'

The Governor General, an elderly Antiguan named Sir Calvin Woodman, had the expression of someone who had expected a relaxing day in paradise only to find the beach littered with landmines. 'We cannot do anything until we know exactly what has happened,' he protested. 'The Americans are sending experts to check the island.'

'And when will they be here?' Nina demanded.

Seretse gave her the answer. 'Both USAMRICD and the CDC have been alerted about the release of a possible chemical agent. Specialists will be arriving overnight.'

'Yeah, but they won't be able to do anything until morning,' said Eddie. 'And the people who caused it'll be halfway around the world!'

'I have done all I can,' Woodman offered feebly. 'The experts are on their way, and we must wait to see what they find. As for this allegation about President Dalton, I find it extremely hard to believe.' Ignoring Nina's angry look, he went on: 'We must wait for absolute proof of his involvement before demanding further action.'

'So fuck-all's going to get done, then,' said Eddie. It was now the Governor General's turn to look indignant.

There was a quiet rap on the door. An Antiguan woman entered at the Prime Minister's response to announce that the chief of the country's defence forces had arrived. 'I'll see him in my office,' the politician told her. Woodman left with him.

'Mr Chase?' the woman added. 'Professor Rothschild is here.'

Eddie nodded. 'Show her in, thanks.'

Nina gave her husband an unhappy look. 'Professor Rothschild?'

'Yeah.'

'As in Professor *Maureen* Rothschild?'

'Uh-huh.'

'The bane of my professional existence? The woman who spent years undermining my career? The miserable old bag I *absolutely cannot stand*?'

'That's the one. Unless there's another Professor Maureen Rothschild who decided to drop in for no particular reason.'

'God *damn* it, Eddie!' cried Nina, jumping up – then whirling as the door opened again. 'Maureen,' she said, with a fixed, icy smile of greeting. 'What an unexpected surprise.'

'Surprises usually are, Nina,' Rothschild replied as she entered.

'Hey, Prof,' said Eddie, standing. 'No trouble getting here, then?'

'Your friend Tom arranged a cab for me. I'm glad you made it back in one piece, Eddie.'

Nina eyed him. 'You two are on first-name terms now, huh?'

'He saved my life,' Rothschild told her. 'That *is* usually something of an ice-breaker. Although unlike you, I don't intend to marry him.'

Eddie clapped a hand to his chest. 'Ow! I'm heartbroken.'

'We needed someone with extensive archaeological knowledge to find the angel statue in Berlin,' Seretse said over the speakerphone. 'Maureen kindly agreed to help us.'

Rothschild smiled. 'In return for some IHA consultancy work.'

'*What?*' demanded Nina.

'Now, love,' Eddie said, putting his hands on her shoulders, 'you remember that you don't even work for the IHA any more, right?'

'That's not the . . . Oh, shut up.' She huffed and pouted.

'I did overhear what you said just before I arrived,' revealed the elderly woman, to Nina's slight mortification, 'and while I would never be so rude as to voice my own feelings about you in public, I have to admit it's not exactly a dream reunion. But I'm honestly relieved that you're still here to be as charming as ever. And,' she added, 'I understand congratulations are in order. Do you know if it's a boy or a girl?'

'Uh . . . no, no, not yet,' Nina mumbled, caught off guard. Eddie gave her a curious look.

'Well, I'm happy for you both. But anyway, what happened to you?'

It took several minutes to describe everything that had transpired, and by the time Nina and Eddie finished, Rothschild's face was pale. 'My God,' she said quietly. 'Nearly a hundred people dead? That's . . . that's appalling.'

'There'll be a lot more joining them if these arseholes get what they're after,' Eddie reminded her.

'Victor Dalton, though? I've met the man; I can't believe he's involved in this.'

'He'll do whatever it takes to get back into power,' said Nina. 'And I was dragged into this specifically because he wanted revenge on me and Eddie. He made it personal – and so did Cross when he threatened my baby.'

Seretse broke the uncomfortable silence. 'Nina, you said Cross will be going to Israel to search for the angel near a sinkhole. Do you know exactly where?'

'Somewhere in the southern desert,' she replied. 'The clues in Revelation point to the route of the Exodus.'

'Which clues?' asked Rothschild.

'The ones relating to the Woman of the Apocalypse. The reference to "the moon under her feet" I think meant the Wilderness of Sin, because Sin was—'

'A Semitic moon god, yes,' Rothschild interrupted. She went to the door and called to the aide. 'Excuse me? Do you have a bible?'

A copy was quickly procured. 'Thank you,' she said as the woman left. 'Most Caribbean nations are extremely Christian, so I thought there would be one to hand. Now, let's have a look at Revelation.' She opened the book to its final section. 'Chapter twelve, let's see . . . "a woman clothed with the sun, with the moon under her feet and a crown of twelve stars upon her head".'

Nina nodded. 'The twelve stars are probably the wells of—'

'The wells of Elim, yes. Nobody has identified the precise location yet, but the most likely possibilities are in the Sinai peninsula, which fits in perfectly with the following station of the Exodus on the coast of the Red Sea, most likely at the tip of the Gulf of Aqaba.'

'And then,' Nina pressed on, irritated, 'they headed north towards the next station, Dophkah, which is—'

'Timna, of course.'

'Will you *stop* doing that?'

Rothschild looked down her nose at the younger woman. 'I'm only trying to help, Nina. I thought my experience might be useful to you.'

'She did work out that the statue was in that temple in Berlin,' Eddie pointed out to his wife.

'Anyone could have figured that out,' she replied.

'Cross didn't.'

'Anyone who isn't an insane religious nut, then! But . . .' her expression softened slightly as she looked back at Rothschild, 'if you hadn't done it, Cross would have gotten the third angel – and Eddie wouldn't have found me. I'd be on my way to Israel at gunpoint by now. So . . . thank you, Maureen.'

Rothschild was surprised, but pleased. 'Perhaps if your baby's a girl, you might consider naming her after me?'

'All right,' said Eddie, seeing Nina's eye twitch even at the humorous suggestion, 'let's get back to stopping this psycho, eh? The last angel's somewhere in Israel – but where?'

'There must be more of a clue to the location than simply being near a sinkhole,' said Rothschild, checking the Bible passages again. 'They're not uncommon.'

'I know,' Nina said. 'I'm sure there's something more to the symbolism, but I don't know what.'

The elderly woman tapped the page. 'The whole section with the Woman of the Apocalypse is cloaked in symbolism. The moon under her feet, the twelve stars . . . so what about the sun? "Clothed with the sun" – what could that mean?' She read on. 'And then there's verse fourteen: "The woman was given the two wings of a great eagle, so that she might fly to the place prepared for her in the wilderness."'

Nina remembered the verse. 'Cross told me the repetition of the reference to a location is what made him think the woman is the key to finding the angel. It appears in verse six as well as fourteen.'

'So the whole thing is a clue . . .' Rothschild put down the book, she and Nina both staring intently at the text. 'The wings of an eagle. That has to be relevant . . . the wings of a eagle.'

'What about 'em?' Eddie asked.

'She's given wings to reach the place prepared for her . . . Nina, which version of the Bible was he using?'

'The King James,' Nina told her.

'This one's the New International, so there are differences in the translation. If I remember, the King James says that she goes into "her place" rather than "the place prepared for her".'

Eddie cocked his head. 'Is there a difference?'

'There's a *huge* difference,' Rothschild replied. 'The location is hidden behind symbolism, remember. It's the same place as in verse six, but this time it's referred to specifically as *her* place, the woman's place. But where is that?'

He smirked. 'I'd say the kitchen, but I know Nina'd hit me.'

'So hard you'd wish you felt as good as the last time you got shot,' his wife confirmed. 'But yes, that has to be symbolic. What would be a woman's place that could also represent a physical location?'

The two women were briefly silent, deep in thought – then, to Eddie's surprise, Nina's cheeks flushed. 'What's up?' he asked.

Her expression was one of distinct embarrassment. 'Well, it could be something a woman has that, ah, a man doesn't. A kind of, um, sacred passage.' Her face became even rosier.

Rothschild arched her eyebrows. 'Really, Nina, you're such a prude. She means a vagina,' she explained for Eddie and Seretse.

Eddie laughed. 'Yeah, I know. But thanks for saying it out loud!'

'Indeed,' Seretse added.

'Yes, okay, we've all had our little joke,' Nina snapped, not amused. 'But that could be what the symbolism represents. The angel is in a place prepared by God, somewhere holy, sacred, that's reached through the so-called woman's place. A passage leading to somewhere safe from where her child emerges, but also where the dragon is forced to wait outside.'

Rothschild read from the Bible. '"The dragon stood in front of the woman who was about to give birth, so that it might devour her child the moment he was born."'

'Yeah. You can interpret the dragon however you like – Satan, the armies facing the Israelites, whoever – but for whatever reason, he can't get into this place. Why not?'

'The wings of an eagle,' said Rothschild. 'The wings are symbolic too. This passage or canyon, whatever it is; it might seem that it can only be *reached* by an eagle. It's high up.'

'Easy to defend,' Eddie added. 'If you've got an army after you – or a dragon – you want to be above them and make them come through somewhere narrow. If you've got a good defensive position, you can hold off a much bigger force for ages.'

'If it's high up,' said Nina with sudden excitement, 'then Cross'll be looking in the wrong place!'

'How so?' Seretse asked.

'Because he's looking for sinkholes, based on the verse about the dragon releasing a river and the earth swallowing it. He thought – *I* thought – that meant the Place in the Wilderness must be in a river valley. But if Maureen's right, it would be higher up. Possibly much higher, if you need wings to reach it.'

'So how did the Israelites reach it?' said Eddie.

'It's only symbolic. The Castle of the Eagles in your favourite movie isn't literally full of eagles, is it?' Ignoring his amusement at how the plot of *Where Eagles Dare* would change if that were the case, she addressed the phone. 'Oswald, Eddie told me he came over here on a UN-chartered jet – can you get one to take us to southern Israel?'

What sounded suspiciously like a resigned sigh came over the speaker. 'I thought you might ask. I had already arranged for it to be refuelled for you.'

'Thank you, Oswald. And we'll need access to the IHA's databases en route – maps, terrain, all the archaeological and historical files we have.'

'We?' echoed Rothschild. 'I thought you'd resigned from the IHA, Nina.'

'I just keep getting dragged back there, don't I?'

'I shall arrange for whatever you need,' said the United Nations official.

'You might not be able to get *everything* we need,' said Eddie. 'But I've got a mate in Israel who can sort out the rest.'

'If by "the rest" you mean weapons, I would rather not know,' Seretse said with another sigh.

'I appreciate it, Oswald,' Nina told him. 'I don't know if we'll be able to find the place, though. There's still an awful lot of ground to cover.'

'I might be able to narrow it down,' said Rothschild, looking up from the Bible.

Nina went to her. 'What have you found?'

'The line describing the Woman of the Apocalypse as being "clothed by the sun". I just had an idea about what that might mean.'

'What is it?' Eddie asked.

'Dophkah – Timna, as it's now known – has been a source of copper for millennia. In some places, the copper veins were so rich, they were even visible on the surface.'

'Like the old silver mines we saw in Egypt on the way to the Pyramid of Osiris,' Nina said to Eddie, remembering a similar find.

'Accessibility is also an issue with mining, though,' Rothschild went on. 'There are places high up where the copper can be seen in the rock but it would be almost impossible to mine, so it's still there. I've seen examples myself, and they're quite spectacular in the right lighting. Such as at sunrise,' she concluded, with meaning. 'The copper seams reflect the dawn light, and the rock seems to glow like the sun itself.'

'"Clothed with the sun",' Nina said quietly. 'You think that could be what Revelation means?'

'I personally wouldn't want to commit an expedition merely on a possibility, but,' she gave Nina a look of grudging admiration, 'your career has been built on wild, crazy gambles, and I have to admit that it's more than paid off for you.'

'Why *thank* you, Maureen,' replied Nina thinly. 'But if you *were* to take a wild, crazy gamble, would you suggest looking for sites facing either due east or due west to catch the sun?'

'Due east is more likely,' said Rothschild. 'The dawn has far more symbolic importance to ancient religions than sunset. But I'm sure you knew that already.'

'Yes. I did.'

The two archaeologists exchanged frosty smiles, then Rothschild nodded. 'But . . . good luck anyway, Nina.'

'Thanks,' she replied, before giving the older woman a quizzical look. 'Can I ask you something, Maureen?'

'What?'

'You still don't like me. So why *did* you agree to help Eddie find me?'

Rothschild seemed reluctant to answer, so Eddie stepped in. 'For the baby,' he told Nina. 'A baby shouldn't suffer because of its parents. That's what you said, right, Maureen? Especially an unborn one.'

His wife was taken by surprise. 'That's . . . Maureen, thank you so much,' she said, this time with genuine gratitude.

Rothschild hesitated again before speaking. 'There was a little more to it, actually,' she admitted. 'You're having a child. It's a great gift, maybe the greatest. I, ah . . .' Her voice lowered. 'I was going to have one, once. But . . . he never came to term.'

'My God,' said Nina. 'I'm sorry. I had no idea.'

'It was a long time ago. But I still think about what might have been . . .' A moment of sad reflection, then she looked back at the couple. 'I wish you all the best with the baby – and with what you're about to do. I hope you find the last angel.'

'So do I,' said Nina. 'Because I've seen what'll happen if we don't.'

24

Israel

'Colonel Brik,' said Cross with a smile, shaking hands with the Israeli officer. 'Meshulam, my old friend.'

'Ezekiel,' Brik replied. 'It is good to see you again.' He looked up as a second passenger emerged from the jet – another man he recognised, though in this case not from any personal encounters. 'Wait, that is—'

'President Dalton is not officially here,' the former CIA operative told him. 'This visit is . . . off the record.'

The Israeli nodded. 'Our mutual friend in Tel Aviv said you were travelling with someone important. But this I did not expect!'

Dalton stepped down on to the concrete, already looking uncomfortable. The temperature at Ovda airport – a small civilian terminal that shared runways with the sprawling military base to the east – was not excessively hot at this time of year, but the morning air was extremely dry and dusty, stinging his eyes.

'Mr President, this is Colonel Meshulam Brik,' Cross told him. 'Colonel, it's my honour to introduce President Victor Dalton.'

Brik offered his hand. 'Pleasure to meet you, Colonel,' said Dalton, giving him a firm but brief shake. He surveyed his surroundings. The airbase was located on a long plain, crumpled mountains rising to the east and west. 'Kind of an isolated facility you have here.'

'We do not mind,' Brik replied. 'When your country has enemies on all sides, it is best to keep your defences far from their eyes.'

'I guess so,' said Dalton, nodding politely. 'Although Egypt,' he waved to the west, 'and Jordan,' another flick of the hand in the opposite direction, 'aren't your enemies right now.'

The Israeli gave him a somewhat patronising smile. 'Mr President, Israel has only one true friend in the world – the United States. Everyone else either is or could be our enemy. We are prepared for all possibilities.'

'Well, we're glad to be Israel's friend. And I promise you I'll do everything in my power to make our relationship even stronger.'

'Thank you, Mr President,' said Brik. He glanced at the plane as more people emerged, Simeon and Anna leading the group. Cross had already sent a team to Antigua's airport before evacuating the Mission; the expedition now numbered ten in total. 'There is a helicopter ready for you, as requested. The facilities of my base are at your disposal – if you need food or sleep, we can give you whatever you need.'

Dalton looked about to take him up on the offer of sleep, but Cross spoke first. 'Thanks, but we're ready to go. We've got a lot of ground to cover.'

'Of course.' Brik nodded. 'Still dedicated to duty and secrets, Ezekiel? You have not changed.' He raised his voice to be heard over the roar of a helicopter gunship taking off from the base. 'You will have free access to Israeli airspace in this region, along with complete discretion from myself and all my men. You also have my personal assurance that you will receive whatever help you need.'

'That's much appreciated, Colonel,' said Dalton.

Cross shook Brik's hand again. 'Thanks for this, Meshulam.'

Brik shrugged. 'I owe you a favour, my friend. All I ask is that one day, you tell me what all this is about.'

The American smiled. 'Don't worry. I guarantee you'll know soon.'

A few hours later, and some twenty miles to the south, another business jet landed in Israel, this one at the commercial airport of Eilat at the northernmost tip of the Gulf of Aqaba. Its occupants were as tired following the lengthy transatlantic flight as Dalton had been, but their journey had been more productive.

'So we know where to look,' Nina said with a yawn as the flight attendant opened the hatch and lowered the stairs. 'We've got four possible locations for the Place in the Wilderness.' She had used the IHA's extensive databases en route to search for places where the terrain matched her theory: an area of high, inaccessible land featuring both a narrow passage and a sinkhole, with current or exhausted copper deposits. Even with the assistance of a computer program, it had been a tiring task.

'Assuming you and Rothschild were right,' Eddie said, donning his battered black leather jacket.

'I found the other two angels, didn't I?'

'*Cross* found 'em,' he reminded her. 'He did all the groundwork, anyway. But that doesn't mean he got the last one right too.'

'We can't take that chance. Not after seeing what that gas does to people.'

They descended the steps, harsh sunlight striking them. 'Ay up,' said Eddie on seeing the tall, lean young man waiting for them. 'Hope Mossad sent you to take care of us and not *take care of us*, if you know what I mean.'

Jared Zane gave the Englishman a mocking smile. 'If I was going to kill you, you wouldn't even have known I was here.' He was an agent of the Mossad, the Israeli intelligence agency, who had worked with Eddie and Nina to hunt down a group of escaped Nazi war criminals – the last survivor of whom had sought revenge on the couple only a month earlier.

'Ah, but you might be saying that to lull us into a false sense of security!'

'Oh, shut up, *alter kocker*.' The Yiddish insult roughly translated as *old fart*.

'Cheeky little bastard.' Both men grinned.

'Ah, boys,' said Nina with an exaggerated sigh. 'Have you finished shaking your peacock feathers at each other?'

Jared smiled. 'Hi, Nina. Good to see you again.'

'You too! And thank you.'

It was more heartfelt than simply meeting them at the airport warranted. Jared regarded her curiously. 'What for?'

'For saving my life – again. If you hadn't warned Eddie that one of the Nazis from Argentina had survived and was out for revenge . . .'

He dipped his head modestly. 'You and Eddie saved *my* life, so it was the least I could do.' He glanced down at her baby bump. 'I'd heard you were pregnant. Congratulations!'

'Don't remember telling you,' said Eddie.

'I'm from the Mossad. We know everything.' Another grin, then he became more businesslike. 'Although in this case, we *don't* know everything – or at least, I don't. It seems I don't have a high enough security clearance. After you phoned,' he said to Eddie, 'I tried to find out if this Ezekiel Cross and ex-President Dalton were coming to Israel. It wasn't long before I was called into my superior's office and told to stop asking questions.'

'So someone's covering it up?' Nina asked.

The young man nodded. 'It must be somebody high up. Whether in the Mossad, or the government, I don't know. Dalton was very popular here in Israel.'

'Surprised Mossad let you help us,' said Eddie.

A small grimace. 'Actually, I'm not technically on duty right now. My superior let me take a leave of absence on short notice – *very* short notice – so I could show some visiting friends around the country.'

'Very generous of him,' Nina remarked knowingly.

'Even bosses get called into *their* boss's office sometimes. And they don't like it either.'

Eddie smiled. 'Good to know spooks have office politics too.'

'It's not all hanging from cliffs and car chases. Anyway, I've got a jeep waiting, and all the gear you'll need. Including something for you, Eddie. I know you need to compensate for your inadequacies with big guns, so I brought you a fifty-calibre Desert Eagle.'

Eddie pulled a sarcastic face. 'So what did you bring for yourself, a bazooka?'

Jared laughed. 'Don't worry about the customs check; I've dealt with it,' he said as the attendant brought out the couple's luggage. 'Nina, let me take that.' He picked up Nina's travel bag.

'You can take mine an' all if you want,' Eddie suggested.

'Carry it yourself,' Jared replied cheekily. 'You're an old man, but not *that* old.'

'Fucking kids!' Eddie mock-grumbled, picking up his bag. He and Nina followed the curly-haired Israeli to the terminal.

'So,' said Jared, 'since you didn't want to tell me the details over the phone, what's this all about?'

Twenty minutes later, Nina and Eddie finally finished their explanation. 'Okay,' Jared said unhappily as he drove a Land Rover Discovery north into the Israeli desert, 'what *is* it with you two? Everyone else's archaeology involves carefully digging junk out of the dirt, but with you it's always maniacs trying to destroy the world!'

'You think I *want* that?' Nina hooted. 'I'd love nothing more than to spend three months excavating a site with only a trowel and a sieve.'

'Me, not so much,' said Eddie from the seat behind her. 'I'll be on the beach with the kid while you're doing that.'

'No you won't, you'll both be with me. And enjoying it.'

'You need to do more research on what kids actually like.'

'I liked it when I was a kid!' she protested.

'Yeah, but you're weird.'

Nina glared over her shoulder at him. 'You're lucky I needed the space up front, or you would *so* be slapped right now.'

Jared smiled. 'Okay, so: crazy ex-CIA guy with chemical weapons, here in my country to look for more. How do we make sure he doesn't get them?'

Nina took out a map of southern Israel. 'I found four places where the last angel might be. If Cross is still working from the theory that it's near a sinkhole in a river valley, then he shouldn't go near them.'

Jared glanced at the map. 'If he's searching in this area, he'll never be far away. Israel is only about twenty kilometres east to west at the Timna Valley, and it gets narrower the farther south you go.' He gestured to the right. 'The border with Jordan is only a kilometre away.'

'He'll still have almost a hundred square miles to cover,' Nina insisted. 'And he'll be looking at the valleys when he should be searching the highlands. We can beat him.'

'Assuming *your* theory is right.'

Her face became rueful. 'If it's not, then a lot of people could die. So I have to hope that it is.'

They drove on. The highway stretched north through a sandy plain, small settlements and sparse patches of irrigated farmland soon surrendering to the desolation of the desert. Barren mountains rose on the horizon to each side. Eventually they neared a turn-off, a side road heading west towards a small village. 'Okay, that's . . . Be'er Ora,' said Nina, struggling with the pronunciation. 'We go past it and head up into the mountains. The first site is about three miles, five kilometres, from here.'

Jared made the turn. 'How accessible is it?'

'We should be able to see it from the ground. We may need to climb to check it, though. You brought climbing gear, didn't you?'

'Everything you need.' The Israeli indicated the equipment in the 4x4's cargo bed. 'You shouldn't climb when you're pregnant, though.'

'I shouldn't be kidnapped or chased or jump over cliffs in speedboats when I'm pregnant either,' she snapped.

'But it could be—'

Eddie leaned forward and put a hand on Jared's shoulder. 'When you hear that tone of voice, trust me, mate, that's when you shut up.' He added in a stage whisper: 'Then you do what you were going to do anyway without telling her – Ow!'

Nina swatted the side of his head. 'Warned you.' He withdrew, amused.

Jared drew in a breath. 'My mother keeps pushing for me to get married. I think I might wait a while longer . . .'

The Discovery headed through the little village, the road rising into the parched peaks beyond. Asphalt quickly gave way to a stony track. Jared switched the 4x4's terrain mode to maintain grip. 'This could be rough,' he said. 'How far do we follow the road?'

'Until it runs out,' said Nina, examining the map. 'It'll take us over this range and into a valley – we go south down it and then turn west again.'

'I don't think this first one'll be it,' Eddie said dubiously. 'It's too close to that village. Somebody would have found it already – I mean, this whole area's a national park, isn't it?' Jared nodded.

'We still have to check, though,' said Nina.

The Land Rover picked its way between the peaks, scrabbling up a steep pass before dropping back into a flat, sandy valley. Had Nina stuck with her original theory of the angel's location, this would have been one of the places to search: it was bone dry at the moment, but alluvial channels carved into the ground proved that when water did flow through this part of the desert, it did so with force.

They headed south. 'There should be a smaller valley about half a mile away,' she told Jared. 'It leads into a canyon; the place we're looking for is another half-mile along it.'

'Let me see the map,' said Eddie. Nina passed it to him. 'Still don't think this can be it. It's too easy to get to. If we turn off and follow this ridge here,' he pointed to it, 'we could *drive* to the bloody place. There's probably a falafel stand there for tourists.'

'Soon find out,' she replied. But he had already convinced her that they were unlikely to find anything on their first try.

That turned out to be the case. Jared took Eddie's advice and, rather than continue along the canyon floor, ascended a steep rise to the top of one of its sides. From there they had a clear view of their intended destination. Nina was the first to look through a pair of powerful binoculars. 'You were right, Eddie,' she admitted. 'There are no signs of any copper deposits. I can see a sinkhole in the canyon, but it's not very deep, and the passage in the rock above it is too wide and too shallow to look like, ah . . .' Her cheeks flushed as she glanced at the young man beside her. 'Like what we think it should look like,' she concluded lamely.

'She means a woman's bits,' Eddie informed him, failing completely to hide a smirk.

Now it was Jared's turn to look faintly embarrassed. 'You mean like, uh . . . breasts?'

'No, kid,' said the Englishman, trying not to crack up. 'The *other* bits.' Even Nina couldn't help but laugh.

'Okay, okay,' huffed the Israeli.

'You do know what I mean, right?'

'Yes, I do! *Tahat*.'

'Don't worry about it, Jared,' said Nina, unable to resist a little teasing of her own. 'I think it's sweet.'

'I should leave you two here,' he muttered. 'But this isn't the place, is it?'

She shook her head. 'It doesn't match the clues hidden in Revelation. We should move on to the next one.'

'I've got an idea,' said Eddie. 'How about we go straight to the one that's the furthest from anywhere, and work backwards? Like I said, if this place was too easy to find, somebody would have done it by now.'

Nina opened the map. 'We're here,' she tapped one of the marked spots, 'and the one deepest into the desert is . . . here. About five miles north-west.'

Eddie examined the contour lines around it. 'Steep cliffs. Looks like that mountain from *Close Encounters*.'

'It's joined to the rest of this higher range to the north, so it might be reachable that way.' She looked at the two men. 'Shall we do it back-to-front, then?'

'If we'd done that four months ago, you wouldn't be pregnant,' said Eddie. It took her a moment to figure it out, and when she did, he hurriedly ducked away from another swat of her hand. 'But yeah, I'm up for it.'

'It'll take us a few hours to get there,' Jared warned. 'There isn't a direct route – we'll have to follow these valleys and cut through this pass.' He traced the path with his fingertip.

'So long as we *can* get there, that's the important thing.' Nina folded the chart back up. 'Okay, let's get started.'

She looked towards the distant peaks, catching a glint of light in the cloudless sky. A helicopter, crossing the desert. She watched it for a moment, wondering if her enemies might be aboard conducting their own search, before deciding it didn't matter. If it *was* Cross and Dalton, they were some distance from any of her potential sites.

Victor Dalton shifted in his seat, uncomfortable and annoyed. The Bell 430 helicopter was large enough to accommodate all the members of Cross's expedition, but the window seats were occupied by those scouring the ground below through binoculars. With Paxton piloting and Cross in the co-pilot's seat beside him, the ex-president had ended up sandwiched between two of the cult leader's men, without much of a view. 'It's too damn hot back here,' he growled into his headset's mic. 'Can you turn on the air con?'

'It's already on, Victor,' Cross told him dismissively. 'This isn't Marine One; you'll have to manage.'

'There's a big fan right above us,' added Simeon, with a mocking glance up at the main rotor. Anna chuckled.

'Damn right it isn't Marine One,' Dalton muttered. He tried to look over the pilot's shoulder at the desert below. 'Any sign of what we're after?'

'Not yet,' Cross told him. 'But we've only checked three sites so far. We'll find it, though. Have faith.'

'Right now, I'd rather have legroom.'

'I see a sinkhole,' Simeon reported. 'Ten o'clock, thirty degrees down.' Other binoculars turned to locate it. Paxton slowed the chopper and began to circle.

'Well?' Dalton demanded impatiently after a couple of minutes. 'Is that it?'

'We're still checking,' said Cross. 'But there's nothing nearby that might be ruins, or a cave system, and the sinkhole itself is empty, so . . . I don't think so,' he decided, crossing off another marker from the map. 'Okay, Paxton, take us to the next site. Four down.'

'Too damn many to go,' Dalton grumbled as the helicopter wheeled about to begin the next leg of its laborious search.

The other group of explorers were enduring an equally laborious, and considerably less comfortable, journey. Even for a vehicle of the Discovery's off-road prowess it was hard going, with no roads to follow, nor even tracks.

Eddie had taken over navigation duties from Nina, having much more experience from his military career. Despite this, the map's lack of fine detail meant they were sometimes forced to backtrack from terrain beyond the Land Rover's abilities. 'Shit,' he exclaimed as he looked ahead, seeing that what on the chart was an open, if narrow, valley was in reality blocked by a near-vertical ridge of rock taller than a man. 'Okay, Jared, turn us around. We'll have to head back to that big boulder and try to get up the hill.'

'It might be too steep,' the Israeli said as he reversed.

'If we don't try, we'll need to go all the way back around this fucking mountain.' Eddie glared out of the side window at the offending peak.

Jared retraced their tracks to a large sand-weathered rock, then turned north to face a steep incline. 'I don't know if we'll be able to get up this.'

Eddie assessed it. 'So long as you put it in low range and keep moving, you'll make it. And for Christ's sake don't go at an angle, or we'll roll over.'

'We will? Wow! I'd never know these things without you to tell me. All that time the Mossad spent teaching me how to drive off-road . . .'

'All right, don't be a cheeky twat,' said the Yorkshireman. 'Just go for it.'

Jared aligned the Discovery with the shallowest route up the incline, then started his ascent. The big 4x4 managed a reasonable pace at first, before its wheels began to slip and scrabble. 'There's more grip over there,' Eddie suggested, pointing to where the rock had less of a covering of sand.

'I know, I've seen it!' the younger man replied testily as he turned the wheel. 'Did the SAS give you training in stating the obvious?'

'No, just in taking the piss out of kids who think they know everything.'

Nina was more interested in something to one side. 'Look, over there,' she said. Jared kept his eyes on the climb, but Eddie followed her gaze. A cluster of loose stones had built up in a dip: stones of a very distinctive tint. 'Those rocks – you see the greenish colour on them? That's copper, oxidised copper. There must be deposits higher up.'

Eddie peered up the hillside. 'Can't see anything. They might have rolled half a mile to end up here, though.'

'It's still a promising sign. Let me see the map again.' Eddie handed it to her; she perused it, so deep in thought that she was oblivious to the Land Rover's lurches as it clawed its way up the hill.

The slope finally eased. 'I wouldn't relax yet,' Jared told Nina as she looked up from the map. 'We still have to get back down.'

'But we've found it,' she said. 'This is the valley!'

Spread out before them was a winding gorge. Its walls grew higher in the distance, the pale sandstone cliffs almost vertical as they passed out of sight around a bend. 'If my theory's right, that the line "clothed with the sun" from Revelation refers to somewhere with copper deposits facing east, then it should be at the top of a cliff down there,' said Nina. 'Come on, let's go.'

The Discovery set off again. They headed along the canyon, before long rounding the bend to see . . .

'There!' exclaimed Nina. 'It's up there!'

The valley opened out before them, creating a broad natural amphitheatre several hundred feet long. It forked at the far end, one leg turning north-east and the other almost due south, closing off the western end of the great open space with a towering cliff. A couple of taller peaks rose beyond it, forming a massif surrounded by ravines.

Jared stopped the 4x4. Its occupants got out, Nina scanning the barrier through binoculars. A vertical cleft in the rock was obvious even to the naked eye, and under magnification she glimpsed beyond it a narrow, twisting passage cutting deep into the sandstone, blue sky visible at its top. The channel was about sixty feet deep, the base of its entrance almost two hundred feet above the canyon's floor.

But it was not the shape that had caught her attention; it was the *colour*. Patches of shimmering turquoise-green stood out clearly on the surrounding rock where veins of copper had been exposed to the elements. There were also streaks and spots of a darker golden hue. The soft stone was being relentlessly scoured by the desert winds, gradually revealing new deposits of raw, unoxidised copper as the surface layers fell away. Even with the sun high in the sky they shone with a warm light; at dawn, Nina imagined, the reflected glow would be quite spectacular.

'Is that what we're after?' Eddie asked.

'Looks like it,' she said. 'A narrow passage – the, ah, woman's place – high up where someone would need wings to reach it, surrounded by copper that would catch the dawn light. It fits what John of Patmos wrote in Revelation, after being filtered through his hallucinogenic visions.'

Jared squinted up at the opening. 'Where does it go?'

'There was definitely a sinkhole on its far side in the satellite photos,' said Nina. 'Let's get a closer look.'

They drove the rest of the way down the valley. Reaching the cliff, they found that a steep pile of scree had built up along its foot, reducing the distance to the bottom of the crevice by some forty feet. 'Still a fair old climb,' said Eddie.

'Fifty metres? No worse than that cliff we climbed in Italy,' Jared said.

'The one you almost got killed on when you slipped and fell?'

'I caught myself.'

'*I* caught you.'

The young man frowned, then reluctantly admitted: 'Huh. Yeah. You did.' Eddie gave him a smug look.

'But you can get up there?' asked Nina.

'Looks straightforward enough,' her husband assured her. 'Although we'll need to use ropes if the rock's that crumbly.' He looked at Jared. 'You up for it?'

'Any time, old man,' the Mossad agent replied. He opened the Discovery's tailgate and began to take out the climbing gear.

25

'Nothing here either,' reported Cross, marking another site off his map. 'Okay, Paxton, let's move on.'

Behind him, Dalton had by now abandoned any attempt to disguise his irritation. 'All this time, and nothing down there but sand and potholes. I should have gotten out when we went back to Ovda to refuel. How long before we have to gas up again?'

Paxton checked the gauges. 'Another two hours, sir.'

'Two hours! Christ.' The exclamation brought disapproving glances from Simeon and Anna. 'How about we refuel early so I can get out?'

'We're not going to disrupt the search because you're uncomfortable, Victor,' said Cross. 'We have work to do – God's work.'

He spoke politely, but it was perfectly clear to all that a challenge had been issued. 'Now wait one damn minute, Cross,' Dalton rumbled. 'I don't intend to be jolted around in this sweatbox for another two hours just because it interferes with your schedule. And my title is still "Mr President", thank you very much.'

'Of course . . . Mr President.' Cross managed to keep all but a tinge of disdain from his voice. 'But it's your schedule too. And considering how the timing has worked out perfectly for us, we need to stick to it.' He looked back at the former politician. 'It's in both our best interests. Don't you agree, Mr President?'

Dalton became acutely aware that he was surrounded by his partner's most loyal disciples, and that all of them were armed. 'I suppose so, yes,' he said, trying to salvage some decorum. 'But if I can't even look out of a window, I'm not contributing much.'

'That you're not, Mr President. That you're not.' Dalton glared at him, but the cult leader had already turned away.

With a loud grunt, Eddie pulled himself up into the cleft in the rock face. He caught his breath, then stood. The passage was narrow, about six feet wide at its entrance and barely half that deeper within.

Huffs and scrapes from behind. He turned to see Jared's head appear over the edge. 'Need a hand?' the Englishman asked.

'No, I'm fine.' The Mossad agent hauled himself on to level ground and shrugged off the long coil of rope he was carrying before detaching his climbing harness from the line. 'That wasn't hard.'

'I believe you. Thousands wouldn't,' Eddie replied as he removed his own gear, then took a walkie-talkie from his belt. 'Nina? We're both up here and safe.'

Nina's voice crackled from the radio. 'What can you see?'

'So far, nothing. The passage twists too much.'

'According to the satellite, it should go back a couple of hundred feet before opening out at the sinkhole.' A mix of eagerness and anxiety entered her voice. 'You *will* be able to get me up there, won't you?'

'Oh, I dunno, might be too risky,' Eddie told her, knowing full well that he and Jared would be able to bring her up the cliff with no risk to the baby. He smiled at the yelp of complaint that was audible from below even without the radio, then went on: 'Yeah, we'll be able to. We'll see what's back there first, though. No point hauling you all the way up here for nothing.'

'Okay,' she said reluctantly. 'Tell me what you see the whole way, though.'

'Rock, rock, rock, rock . . .'

'You're a funny man, Eddie.'

'Yeah, that's why you love me. Don't worry. If we find anything, I'll tell you.' He lowered the radio. 'Jared, you ready?'

'Always,' the Israeli replied.

'Good. Let's go.'

The two men started down the passage, boots crunching over the gritty sand. They rounded the first turn, losing sight of the entrance but seeing something new ahead. 'That's tight,' said Jared. The walls narrowed still further to a point where they were less than two feet apart. He had to turn slightly sideways to pass through. 'Hey, will you even be able to fit?'

'You calling me fat?' Eddie replied. 'Just 'cause you're built like a fucking beanpole . . .' But the obstruction presented no difficulty, the crevice widening out again after a short distance. 'Okay, there's a narrow section, but you'll be able to get through,' he said into the walkie-talkie. 'Good job you're only four months pregnant and not eight.'

Nina was already becoming impatient. 'Have you reached the sinkhole yet?'

'No, I'll tell you when we do. It's nice in here, though.' Beneath the snaking line of blue sky directly overhead, the rock walls were banded in different shades of brown, glinting seams of copper running through them. 'Like being in a tiramisu mine.'

'Great, now I've got a craving for some. Thanks, hon!'

Eddie smiled, then followed Jared up the passage. It occasionally narrowed, but was still navigable. Presenting more of a problem were fallen rocks, some almost blocking the way. The Israeli looked up after climbing over one, seeing a ragged gap high above from where the stone had fallen. 'I don't think these cliffs are safe.'

'Well, we don't have to climb 'em,' Eddie replied as he traversed the blockage. 'But if you hear a big cracking noise from above, don't look up to see what it is – just leg it!'

Jared chuckled, then looked ahead. 'Hey, it's opening out.'

'Nina, we're almost at the end,' Eddie reported. 'I'll tell you what we see.' The pair continued on, the passage gradually widening – until they emerged in the open.

'What is it?' Nina demanded. 'Have you found the sinkhole?'

'Yeah – and more besides.'

He and Jared stepped out into a roughly egg-shaped depression in the mountain, the far wall of the bowl rising up to flatter ground about fifty feet above. The sinkhole Nina had seen on the satellite imagery was indeed here, an almost perfectly circular opening near the hollow's centre. Eddie peered down into it. Blue-green water rippled gently around ten feet below him. Small pieces of debris floated on its surface. He couldn't see the bottom.

Just above the pool, a cave was cut into the shaft's wall, forming a ledge. He didn't need a doctorate in archaeology to know instantly that it was not a natural feature. Beneath the shelter of the overhang were several small archways, tunnels leading into the mountain. Inscribed around each were blocks of text.

The Englishman didn't recognise the language, but his companion did. 'It's Hebrew,' said Jared, eyes widening.

They hurried around the sinkhole and climbed down for a closer look. 'Can you read it?' Eddie asked.

The Israeli examined one of the carved sections. 'Some of it,' he replied. 'It's ancient Hebrew, not modern. There are a lot of differences.'

'But you know what this is?'

Jared perused some of the other writings. 'I think it's a temple. This word here,' he pointed it out, 'is definitely *Yahweh* – God.'

Nina was almost at bursting point with her radioed demands for an update. Eddie told her what they had seen, then added:

'I'm assuming you want to come up here and look for yourself?'

'No, no, I'll just stand around in the baking sun while you two poke around,' came the sarcastic reply. 'Of *course* I want to come up there!'

Jared pretended to wince. 'So that's what being married is like? I think I'll have to disappoint my mom for a few more years.'

'Nah,' said Eddie with a grin, 'I'm sure you'll go on disappointing her for the rest of your life.'

The younger man now winced for real at having left himself wide open for the joke. '*Hamor*,' he muttered, before looking back at the tunnels. 'Should we check what's inside before we bring her up?'

'Only if you want her to kill you,' Eddie replied breezily. 'Come on, let's go back and rig up a belay.'

Less than thirty minutes later, Nina had been brought up to the passage. 'That was only about half as terrifying as I'd expected,' she said as Eddie helped unclip her harness from the rope. 'Are you sure the baby will be okay?'

'Little Arbuthnot'll be fine,' he assured her.

'More like Arbuth-*not*.' She turned to Jared. 'I'm glad you waited for me rather than rushing in. Exploring those tunnels on your own probably isn't a good idea.'

'You think it might be dangerous?' he asked. 'Booby-trapped, like the Spring of Immortality?'

'It's possible. If the last angel is here, it could be protected.'

'The other angels weren't,' Eddie pointed out.

'No, but this site's different – Revelation suggested it was a place of great religious importance, some kind of redoubt for the Israelites. The angel might not be the only thing here.'

'Let's see, then.' Eddie led the way through the twisting cleft, helping Nina over the fallen rocks.

'Oh, wow,' she gasped as they emerged in the bowl beyond. 'Definitely a place prepared in the wilderness. I want to go down to that cave.'

'What's the magic word?' Eddie asked with a smirk.

She glowered at him. '*Now.*'

He laughed. 'Near enough. We'll set up a rope to make it easier for you.'

Nina overcame her impatience long enough to wait for the two men to put down the climbing equipment, then tie a line around a boulder and hang it over the edge. Eddie went first, supporting her from below as Jared helped her descend. She found her footing on the ledge, taking in the ancient inscriptions before her, then looked back at the pool. 'What are those things in the water?'

Eddie scooped up the nearest floating piece of detritus as Jared swung down. 'Fungus, it looks like. Some sort of mushrooms.'

'Probably best not to drink the water, then, or we might end up having our own hallucinogenic visions. Let's take a look inside.'

'Which tunnel?' asked the Israeli. There were four entrances before them.

'You tell us,' said Eddie. 'You can read the language.'

'I can only read *parts* of it,' he protested. 'I'm a Mossad agent, not a rabbi.'

'This one,' said Nina, indicating the left-most.

'How do you know?'

'Because I can't read ancient Hebrew, but I *can* read symbols. I've seen this one before.' She went to the archway, pointing at something carved above it: a menorah, accompanied by the characters that she and Cross had identified as representing the twenty-four Elders. 'It was in the temple in Iraq and the catacombs in Rome. I'm also guessing it was on the piece of the Altar of Zeus where you found the angel in Berlin.'

Eddie nodded. 'So it's the way to the last angel?'

'Most likely.' She went to the neighbouring opening, taking a flashlight from her backpack and shining it inside. A short tunnel opened out into a chamber, but it appeared empty. 'This was an important religious site, but it was also a shelter where the Israelites could hold out against their enemies. They supposedly wandered in the wilderness for forty years, but the desert's not *that* big. The Old Testament books concerning the Exodus are very vague about the timescale. They probably established settlements at various points along the way – or fortifications, in this case. There was a water supply here, so they took advantage of it.'

Jared checked another archway. 'This one's empty too,' he announced, disappointed.

'It's a big find, though. Even if there isn't anything else here, I think this is definitely one of the stations of the Exodus. That'll keep the archaeologists busy – and the theologians arguing.' Nina returned to the left-hand tunnel and cautiously entered it, taking off her sunglasses and shining her light around the walls and ceiling. Faded paintings were revealed on the stone, images of people and animals framed by elaborate patterns. 'These are a lot like the ones in the catacombs.'

'No traps?' Eddie asked, joining her.

'Not yet. But look, the tunnel slants upwards.' The beam fell upon a steeply sloping floor.

'Great,' said Jared gloomily. 'It really *is* like the Spring of Immortality.'

'I don't think there'll be any killer statues or giant crabs,' said Nina as she started up the passage. 'But let's be careful, huh?'

They proceeded deeper into the mountain. The tunnel's walls had been smoothed by both hand and time, giving the undulating passage an unsettlingly organic feeling. Its colour changed as they climbed through different strata. Stubs of side passages occasionally branched off, copper deposits having been grubbed from the rock, though more often than not the valuable metal had been left *in situ*. Eddie paused to rub one of the seams. 'Wonder why they stopped mining it?'

'Out of reverence, I'd imagine,' said Nina, examining a wall painting. Unlike those at the entrance, which showed general scenes of the Israelites' lives, this was clearly religious in nature: robed figures standing with their heads bowed before a tent in the desert. 'This tunnel seems to be going somewhere important – maybe a temple. Once it was established, mining was probably considered disrespectful.'

Jared peered at the image as Nina moved away. 'What is it?' Eddie asked.

'The tent . . . I think it's the Tabernacle. The shrine to God that the Israelites carried with them,' he explained, seeing the Yorkshireman's quizzical look.

'The Tabernacle of the Covenant,' said Nina. 'Where they kept the Ark.'

'What, like the *lost* Ark?' Eddie asked. 'As in, Raiders of the?'

'That's right. The actual one.'

'Wow. If you found that, it might finally make you more famous than Indiana Jones.'

'I've had more than enough of being famous, thanks!' she said firmly.

They continued upwards. 'It's getting damp,' Nina observed before long. In places, the walls had a faint sheen, some of the painted scenes smeared by water and mould.

Eddie sniffed. 'Something smells a bit dodgy.'

'It might be these.' She played her light over something low on the wall. A small patch of bulbous white mushrooms was growing on the glistening stone. 'Fungi.'

'Yeah, I know I am.'

'What? Oh God,' she added with rolled eyes as she got the pun. Eddie chuckled. 'There are more up ahead.'

The walls were indeed home to other colonies of the fungal growths. They were so pale in colour that they almost seemed to glow in the reflected light. But Jared was already looking past them. 'Hey, I can see something.' He moved to investigate.

Eddie and Nina followed. 'Okay, we found where the smell's coming from,' the Englishman announced, wrinkling his nose.

A vertical shaft thirty feet in diameter opened out before them, dropping into darkness below. The walls were home to more mushrooms, the largest bigger than a clenched fist. A faint light came from what Nina at first thought were small holes in the ragged ceiling high above, before closer inspection revealed that the milky glow was actually being refracted through veins of some type of translucent crystal.

But the most arresting feature was man-made.

A narrow bridge of blackened wood led across the chasm to an archway flush with the wall on the far side, the opening barricaded by a heavy door. A now-familiar symbol was marked upon it: the menorah of the twenty-four Elders. Beside the entrance, a large nook had been carved from the rock, numerous small objects sitting within. 'Careful,' Nina warned. 'That doesn't look safe.'

Eddie moved to get a look at the crossing's supports. 'No kidding.'

He retreated so Nina could see. The near end of the rickety bridge was supported by what she could only think of as a hinge; the whole thing seemed designed to plunge intruders into the pit below.

She dropped a loose stone over the edge. A faint splash echoed back up the shaft after a couple of seconds. 'It must be a cenote,' she mused. 'There's a reservoir at the bottom; it might even join up with the sinkhole outside. And this' – she waved her hand at the bridge – 'is a trap to tip people into it.'

'I'll go back and get some rope,' said Eddie.

'No, wait a minute. Look at that.' She shone her flashlight at the nook. Set into its back was a piece of glinting metal: a bronze slab almost a foot wide and several inches deep. There was a slit in the rock beneath it, through which a rod protruded to support the shelf. 'We've seen something like that before, in the Atlantean temple in Brazil. It's a weighing scale.'

'To weigh what?' asked Jared.

'Those.' She shifted the beam to pick out the objects below the scale: stones of various sizes. 'There's more text by the door. It's some sort of test; a puzzle. It probably tells you what you have to do to get in.'

'Which you've got to cross the bridge to read,' Eddie said dubiously.

'Yeah, that's kinda worrying. But I don't think it automatically throws everybody who tries to cross down the shaft. It's more likely that it only catches people who fail the test. The people who knew the answer, the ones who built this place, could come and go as they wanted.'

Jared conducted his own examination of the bridge. 'That may have been true when they built it. But look at it! It's falling apart. If it really was made by the Israelites, then it's over three thousand years old.'

'It might not be as old as you think,' Nina countered. 'The people who hid the angels, the Elders, did so a long time after the Exodus. John of Patmos discovered their writings in the Library of Pergamon, and that wasn't founded until around 350 BC.'

Eddie made a sarcastic sound. 'Oh, so it's only over *two* thousand years old. That makes it *completely* safe.'

'The site may have still been used for a long time after that, though.'

'Or it might not. Seriously, don't even think about crossing it until we get some ropes.'

'I'll go back for them,' said Jared. 'Wait here for me.'

'Don't bloody worry, we're not going anywhere!' the Englishman told him. Jared smiled and headed back down the tunnel.

Nina watched him go, then moved to the bridge. 'Oi,' said Eddie.

'What?'

'You're thinking about putting a foot on it, aren't you? Just to test your theory.'

'No I wasn't,' she said, not entirely convincingly.

He shook his head. 'I dunno. You say you're done with all this stuff, but give you half a chance and you're back climbing cliffs to reach ancient temples. Even when you're pregnant.'

The words had been spoken with humour, but Nina's expression revealed that she had taken them very seriously indeed. 'What is it?' he asked.

'I'm worried that . . . that I'm going to be a bad mom,' she admitted in a quiet voice.

Eddie was surprised. 'Why would you think that?'

'Isn't it obvious?' She held out both hands to encompass their surroundings. 'I'm four months pregnant, and I'm in a cave halfway up a mountain in the middle of a desert looking for an ancient relic with the power to kill thousands of people! I should be going to Lamaze classes or pigging out with a big tub of chocolate fudge ice cream.'

'Just because you're having a baby doesn't make you an invalid. And it doesn't mean you have to give up everything else, either.'

'That's the thing, though,' she said. 'I don't *want* to give this up. Not now; not at all. And that's why I'm worried about becoming a mother – because I'll *have* to give it up. Which makes me . . . selfish. We're having a child, but I just keep thinking about how that'll stop me from . . . from doing what I *do*.'

She turned away from him, looking down into the darkness

of the cenote. 'You know what's weird? We were both dragged into this in the worst way possible, but now that we're free . . . I'm almost glad I'm here. I could have told Oswald to hand this over to someone at the IHA, but I wanted to do it. I *wanted* to do it,' she repeated, with emphasis. 'I deliberately chose to do something that could be dangerous, even though I'm pregnant. What the hell kind of mother does that?'

'But . . . you do still want a child?' Eddie asked hesitantly.

'Yes, I do – of course I do!' She looked down at the slight swell of her abdomen. 'I want us to have a baby together. But it's kind of scary, and I hadn't realised just how scary because I had other issues going on. First I was in denial about how much Macy's death had affected me, and because of that I was hyper-obsessed with working on the book – and then I was blocked because I was depressed and not sure if everything I'd done in my life was actually worth it.'

'You were?' he asked, surprised.

'I wasn't seeing a shrink to get over my fear of public speaking. And I know I should have told you exactly why I was having therapy, but I couldn't. I didn't want to burden you with my psychological problems.'

'Yeah, you should have done,' he said, though with sympathy rather than in remonstration. 'We're married. Being burdened with your problems is sort of my job! But just because we're having a kid doesn't mean you have to give up everything important to you. It just means you need to change how you do it. You can still write your book, for a start.' He moved up behind her. 'And since you're not at the IHA any more, maybe you can do some of that "proper" archaeology you go on about, and dig little bits of junk out of the dirt instead of being surrounded by gunfire and explosions.'

'I could definitely live with that,' she said, managing a small smile, albeit brief.

Eddie wrapped his arms around her waist. 'You can do anything you put your mind to; I know you, you're too bloody stubborn to give up! Trust me, you'll be a great mum.'

'I don't know,' said Nina glumly. 'I really don't know if I will . . .'

Echoing footsteps signalled Jared's return. 'I brought the rope and some gear,' the Israeli called as he reappeared.

'Good lad,' said Eddie. 'Okay, let's set this up.'

Nina watched as they pounded a pair of pitons into the rock wall, then fixed the rope to them. 'You do realise that if the bridge collapses when you cross it, you'll swing back and slam into the wall, right?'

'Course I do,' her husband replied. 'That's why I'm sending the kid!'

Jared gave him a startled look, which quickly became one of smug superiority. 'Actually, I was going to volunteer anyway. You can't leave something like this to an unsteady old man.'

'You keep thinking that,' said Eddie. He secured the rope to the younger man's harness. 'You sure you want to do this?' he asked, more concerned.

Jared looked down into the pit's inky depths. 'No . . . but somebody has to, and my mom really *would* be disappointed in me if I let a pregnant woman risk it!'

'Thank you, Jared,' said Nina, with an appreciative nod.

'I'll play out the rope to you,' said Eddie, picking up the coil of nylon line. 'If the bridge looks like it's going to give way, run right back. If you fall, I'll catch you.'

Now the Israeli was the appreciative one, although he couldn't resist making a crack. 'Hope your withered arms can take the weight, *alter kocker*.'

'Or I could fucking *kick* you over there . . . Ready?'

Jared steeled himself. 'Yeah.'

'Okay. Watch yourself.'

The Israeli cautiously put one foot on the narrow bridge. The old wooden beams had been dried out over flames to harden them; even so, they creaked. He edged forward. 'Seems solid so far.'

'Your weight's still being taken by that hinge,' Nina reminded him, her nervousness growing. 'Please be careful.'

'Don't worry, I will!' He aimed his flashlight down at the bridge, then advanced until he was clear of the support. The creaks grew in volume as he shuffled along . . . then eased.

Nina let out a relieved breath. 'Thank God.'

'You're doing fine,' Eddie called, carefully letting out more rope. 'Just take it easy. You're about a third of the way there.'

Jared moved on – then abruptly stopped. 'Some of the planks are missing.'

'Then don't step on the holes!'

The advice drew a glare, but he adjusted his step to traverse the gap. The next intact board held, though with a raspy protest. A second space, wider, but this too he successfully crossed. 'It's holding.'

'Great,' said Eddie, trying not to let his concern show. He knew that a loss of confidence could be as dangerous as any broken plank. 'You're almost halfway across. Just keep going, nice and steady.'

Jared used his torch to check the remainder of the bridge. 'There aren't any more gaps,' he said as he took another careful step. 'I should be able—'

Crack!

Nina shrieked as the gunshot snap of breaking wood echoed around the cenote. Jared staggered, trying to regain his balance . . .

He failed. Arms flailing, he toppled towards the abyss.

26

Eddie yanked the rope, pulling Jared on to his back just before he plunged. The whole bridge shook. The Israeli's flashlight spun away into the darkness below as he grabbed at the crossing. 'Jared!' yelled the Yorkshireman, reeling in the line. 'Hold on, I've got you!'

Jared secured himself. 'It's okay, it's okay!'

Eddie held the line taut. 'You sure?'

The younger man waited until the bridge stopped shuddering, then very slowly sat up. More moans came from the supports, but the structure held. 'Yes! Let it out again so I can get up.'

Reluctantly, Eddie did so. Jared cautiously rose to a crouch. Nina aimed her flashlight to illuminate the bridge ahead of him. He surveyed the dusty wood, then continued onwards with great care. Eddie played the rope out in his wake.

The Mossad agent passed the three-quarters mark – then froze, as did Nina and Eddie, as a pole cracked beneath him. The structure swayed . . . then steadied. Nina shone her light at the supports. 'I think it's okay,' she said.

'How does the bridge feel?' Eddie asked Jared.

The Israeli glanced back. 'About two thousand years old! Nina, can you give me more light?'

She brought the beam to the top side of the crossing. Jared composed himself, then set off again. Five feet to go, three . . . 'There,' he said with a gasp of relief. 'Okay, I'm going to secure the rope.'

It did not take long to hammer another two pitons into place and fasten the line to them. Eddie tested that it was firmly secured by hanging beneath it. 'All right,' he said, 'we can get across without worrying about falling into the lair of the white worm.'

Nina raised an eyebrow. 'Okay, your movie references keep getting more obscure.'

'Now we need to get that door open. I'm guessing the dynamite method isn't going to be approved.'

'Nope,' she told him. 'Jared, come back over so I can look at the scale. We shouldn't risk having two people on the bridge at once.'

'Or even one person,' Eddie said.

Jared remained in place, examining the alcove beside the door. 'No, you'll need my help. There's more ancient Hebrew here.'

'Okay,' Nina decided reluctantly. 'Translate as much of it as you can and tell me what it says.'

He nodded. 'I need a light.'

Eddie held up his own torch. 'Hope you can catch better than you can walk across bridges.'

'Yeah, yeah, old man. Just throw it to me.'

Eddie tossed the torch across the gap; Jared caught it with one hand. 'Show-off.'

The Israeli grinned, then directed the light at the alcove. 'What do you see?' Nina asked.

'There are about thirty stones, all different sizes,' he reported. 'Each one has a letter carved into it . . . No, wait, they must be numbers. I can read parts of the text. It says that God's number is seven, and then something about . . . wisdom, needing wisdom?' He was silent for a long moment, scanning the ancient words. 'Okay, I think it says that you have to prove your wisdom, I guess, to get through the door. You were right about it being a test. You have to know the . . . the number of a man?'

An idea had already formed in Nina's mind at the mention of

the word *wisdom*, and now it came to her in a flash of – appropriately enough – revelation. 'That's right!' she called, excited. 'It *is* the number of a man. I don't remember the exact chapter and verse from Revelation, but I know what it says: "Let him that hath understanding" – or wisdom in some translations – "count the number of the beast: for it is the number of a man."'

'That sounds familiar,' said Eddie. 'You're about to quote some Iron Maiden lyrics, aren't you?'

'Not quite. The King James Version isn't as catchy. But according to John of Patmos, the number of the Beast is "six hundred threescore and six".'

'Six! Hundred threescore! And six! The number of the Beast!' he sang tunelessly. 'Yeah, definitely not as catchy.'

'What was that noise?' demanded Jared.

'Tchah! Kids today don't appreciate the classics. So are you supposed to put three stones with sixes on them on to the scale?'

'Seems like it,' Nina told him . . . though with a hint of doubt.

'I can do that right now,' Jared called out. 'It's using the Hebrew system, so the symbols we need are *tav resh*, six hundred . . .' He plucked a pebble from the group, then located a second. '*Samekh* for sixty, and then . . . here – *vav*, six. Six hundred plus sixty plus six. So I put these on the scale and the door should open, yes?' He picked them up, about to deposit them on the bronze slab—

'No, no!' Nina suddenly yelled. 'Don't do anything!'

'What's wrong?' Eddie asked, alarmed – though not nearly as much as Jared, who froze with one hand above the scale.

'Give me a second. I need to think.' She closed her eyes for a moment. 'The number might not *be* six-six-six. That's the generally accepted version today, but there are several ancient copies of Revelation where it's written as six-*one*-six. The Codex Ephraemi Rescriptus, Papyrus 115 from the Oxyrhynchus excavation in Egypt . . . they pre-date the King James Bible by over a thousand years.'

'Both versions can't be right,' said Eddie.

'No, they can't. One of them is a transcription error . . . but there's no way to know which.'

Jared put the stones back in the niche. 'So should I change the second number to *yud*, ten?'

'I don't know,' admitted Nina.

'It's a fifty-fifty chance,' Eddie pointed out.

'I don't want to risk Jared's life on a coin-toss.'

'What should I do?' asked Jared. 'Shall I come back over?'

'Hold on.' Nina stared at the alcove, then redirected her flashlight. 'Jared, can you move sideways so I can see the door?'

The Israeli reluctantly leaned aside, holding the rope for support. 'What is it?' asked Eddie. 'You found something?'

'Maybe.' The light shone upon the symbol of the menorah. 'That's the sign of the twenty-four Elders – the people who contained the meteorite fragments in the angels, then dispersed them for safe keeping. Cross showed me a photo he took inside the ruins – the same symbol was there too.' She frowned, trying to tease out a memory. 'There was some writing with it, something about numbers . . . Jared, what exactly does it say there about the number of God?'

Jared checked the text upon the door. 'As near as I can tell, it reads, "The number that is Yahweh is seven."'

'That's what it said in the temple Cross found,' Nina said thoughtfully. 'Seven is the number of God . . . and man is always less than God.'

'So the number of a man would be six?' suggested Eddie.

The truth came to her as she finally remembered the rest of the translation the cult leader had shown her at the Mission. 'Yes – but the Elders said more than that. "Three times shall it be said" was how they put it. And in the catacomb in Rome, they said it again: "It is three times spoken, the dragon's number is that of man." It's not just the number six on its own, and it's not six hundred sixty-six – it's six, repeated three times for emphasis. Just like in your song,' she added with a smile. 'Six! Six! Six! *That's* the number of man – and that's the answer to the test.'

She called out across the cenote. 'Jared! The stone that represents the number six – put it on the scale three times.'

'You mean, put it on, take it off, then put it back again twice more?' he asked, puzzled.

'That's it exactly. But for God's sake, keep hold of the rope in case I'm wrong!'

Jared took a firm hold of the line as he used his other hand to pick up one particular stone. With a nervous look back at Nina, he placed it on the scale.

The metal shelf dropped slightly under its weight. Everyone held their breath . . .

The bridge remained intact. 'Well, that's a start,' said Eddie, exhaling.

'It made a noise,' the Israeli reported. 'There was a clank from behind it, like two pieces of metal hitting each other.'

'Do it again,' Nina said.

Jared picked up the stone. The scale rose back to its original position. He repeated the process. Another faint sound came from whatever mechanism was hidden behind the wall. A third time; a much louder bang resounded through the shaft. Jared grabbed the rope with both hands – but the bridge stayed in place.

'Look!' cried Nina. 'It's opening!' The door swung slowly inwards. It stopped after moving only a foot, but that was enough for Jared to step on to a solid floor. He pushed it wider. 'What can you see?'

'Another tunnel,' he replied.

'Wait for me. I'm coming over.'

'*We're* coming over,' Eddie corrected. 'And you're not taking any risks, either. Hold on.' He hooked Nina's climbing harness to the rope. 'Right, now you can go. But take it easy.'

'Okay, *Dad*,' she huffed.

'Hey, I actually *am* going to be a dad, so I'm allowed to be overprotective.'

'Point taken.' They smiled at each other, then Nina set off, sidestepping across the bridge with both hands on the rope. A moment of worry as she reached the broken plank, but she picked her way over without incident. Once clear, she hurried to the doorway, standing on the step before detaching the harness.

'You okay?' Jared asked as he helped her through.

'Fine, thanks.' She panned her light around the new passage. It had the same rounded cross-section as on the other side of the shaft, but its decorations were far more elaborate, gold leaf and precious stones set around the paintings of religious scenes. The door was not merely a barrier; it also marked the boundary of an inner sanctum, a place of great importance to the ancient Israelites.

Eddie made his way across behind them. 'All right, so what have we got?'

'This must be the entrance to their temple,' Nina said, pointing the flashlight along the tunnel. The ornate walls curved away out of sight. There was no sign here of the mushrooms growing around the cenote; the door had apparently acted as a seal, keeping the air inside dry. 'Come on.'

'Will there be any more traps?' asked Jared, eyeing the paintings with suspicion as they started down the tunnel.

'I don't think so. This place was protected by a combination of obscurity and inaccessibility, and probably had people defending it too. Revelation said it had been "prepared", so somebody had to be here to do that. That door was the final barrier, to make sure that only people who knew the true meaning of the Elders' texts would be able to get in.'

'All the same,' said Eddie to Jared, 'keep an eye out, will you? Just in case anything pops out of the walls.' The younger man hurriedly redirected his flashlight beam to the sides of the passage.

No booby-traps interrupted their progress, however. Before long, something came into view ahead. 'Ay up,' said Eddie, surprised. 'There's a light in there.' The tunnel opened out into a larger chamber, where they could clearly see the gleam of gold even without their torches.

'It's not daylight,' Nina noted. There was an almost rainbow-like iridescence to the illumination. She entered the room – and stopped in astonishment. 'Oh . . .'

Eddie moved up beside her, equally amazed. 'Christ, that's impressive. What *is* this place?'

She surveyed the wonders before her, almost unable to believe what she was seeing. 'Based on the description in the Book of Revelation . . . I think we've just found God's temple.'

The chamber was an expansive oval, an existing cave made much bigger by years, even decades of patient excavation. The walls were largely covered by drape-like hanging tapestries bearing Hebrew symbols. The dominant feature was a massive opal over two feet across embedded in the rock of the high ceiling. There was evidently a fissure in the mountain above that reached to the surface, letting in sunlight, which was then refracted by the great gemstone into a brilliant prismatic display.

The brightest spot was directly beneath the opal, a dazzling beam shining downwards like a laser. It landed upon a large golden throne, which stood on a patch of highly polished quartz set into the floor. More thrones, similar in design but somewhat smaller, encircled it. Nina started counting them, but already knew how many there would be. 'Twenty-four,' she said, confirming her belief. 'These are the thrones of the twenty-four Elders.'

Eddie glanced at the central seat. 'So whose is number twenty-five?'

'God's. He sits in the middle of everything, with his followers around him.' Nina moved hesitantly into the ring. She was not religious by nature, but couldn't help feeling a reverential awe. 'Everything matches John's description. The circle of thrones around God's seat, the rainbow surrounding it . . .' She indicated where the opal was casting a spectrum of light on the floor, catching the swathe of quartz. 'Even this; John described it as a "sea of glass", which considering that he was having a vision based on something he'd only read is pretty accurate. And then there's the altar, the seven lamps . . .' A large menorah stood before the throne, near a golden dais with a horn-like protrusion at each corner.

Jared nervously followed Nina and Eddie into the circle, having to force himself not to avert his eyes from the throne beneath the opal. 'It feels like this is something I shouldn't be allowed to see.'

Nina noticed something at the chamber's far end. 'If you're worried about being struck down by God, then you really shouldn't get any closer to that.'

Beyond the golden circle was something extremely incongruous in the splendour of their surroundings: a simple tent made from animal skins. It was rectangular, around fifteen feet wide and three times as long. Time had dried and decayed the hides in the stillness of the chamber, but they had clearly been exposed to the harsh elements of the desert beforehand. The entrance was draped in woven curtains, the faded remnants of once-vibrant colours still showing after uncounted centuries.

'Okay, that doesn't really go with the other furniture,' Eddie said.

'You don't know what it is?' she replied. 'Oh, right; you always skipped Sunday school when you were a kid, didn't you?'

'I had better places to be. Like literally anywhere.'

'I know what it is,' gasped Jared. 'It's . . . it's the Tabernacle, the communion tent!'

Eddie couldn't hold back a smile. 'So the Ark of the Covenant is actually *here*? In your face, Indiana Jones!'

Nina started towards the tent. 'Wait, wait,' said Jared, suddenly worried. 'Should we go in there?'

She gave him an incredulous look. 'Are you going to tell me that because we're not Levites, we'll be killed if we get too close?'

'No, but . . . it's a holy place. The *most* holy place.'

'And this is why I didn't go to Sunday school,' said Eddie, joining his wife. 'So this kind of thing doesn't scare me off. If the angel's here at all, it must be in there or we would have seen it by now. We've got to find it.'

The younger man nodded reluctantly. 'Okay. But be careful. I don't want to be the one who destroys the Tabernacle!'

'You think *I* do?' Nina hooted.

They approached the entrance. Nina shone her flashlight over the curtains, then removed her backpack before hesitantly moving them aside and slipping through. The two men followed.

The animal-skin walls were thick enough to block the glow from the crystal. Jared added his light to Nina's. The space they had entered occupied two thirds of the tent's total length, but was only sparsely furnished. A wooden table stood to one side, whatever offerings had been placed upon it long since turned to dust. Near it was a seven-branched menorah on a tall stand, dark smears of old oil upon the metal lamps. Beyond them, before a white curtain, was a golden altar, glinting in the torch beams.

'Is that the Ark?' Eddie asked.

Nina shook her head. 'That must be the Altar of Incense. If the Ark's in here, it'll be beyond the veil.' She indicated the curtain.

'That's where that saying comes from, is it? Huh. Learn something every day.'

'Stick with me, kiddo,' she told him with a smile, leading the way through the room. 'On the other side of the veil is—'

'The Holy of Holies,' said Jared. '*I* learned all this at school,' he added to Eddie, who grinned.

'That's right,' said Nina. She examined the altar, then turned her attention to the curtain. 'Okay. If God *is* going to strike us dead, he'll do it about . . . now.'

She parted the veil. Swathes of the material disintegrated like gossamer as her hand brushed it. She cringed in dismay at the damage, but pressed on through.

The last room was square. The only thing in it was a large box, coated in gold.

All three recognised it instantly.

They had found the Ark of the Covenant.

27

'G od,' whispered Nina, adding: 'Literally.'
      Jared stared open-mouthed. 'It . . . it's the Ark,' he
managed to say. 'It really is the Ark of the Covenant!'

Eddie whistled a few bars of 'The Raiders March'. 'We need
our own cool theme tune,' he said. 'This is it? The real thing?'
Nina nodded. 'Bloody hell! This is a massive find – and you
weren't even looking for it!'

'No, but here it is.' Awed, Nina circled the relic. It did not
quite match the popular image from classical paintings and a
certain Steven Spielberg movie, the smaller details differing, but
it perfectly fitted the description given in the Biblical Book of
Exodus. The main body of the gold-covered chest was a little
under four feet long, finely detailed patterns similar to those in
the Jewish catacombs and the tunnel outside inscribed into the
plating. Rings of the precious metal supported two long poles on
each side, covered in gold leaf.

Atop the Ark was the mercy seat. Despite what the name
suggested, it was not a place of rest, rather an elaborate lid. A
pair of cherubim stood upon it. Two of each of their four
wings extended backwards, meeting above the centre of the
chest. She peered at one of the cherubim, feeling a thrill of
recognition as she saw the face of the angel – rather, the *faces*,
plural. Both creatures had four positioned around their heads,
each looking in a different direction: a lion, an ox, an eagle and a
man. She had seen the same arrangement on the mechanical
guardians of the Garden of Eden. The image had been

remembered and passed down over many millennia as a symbol of fearsome, godly power.

She stepped back, almost overcome by excitement at the magnificence of the find – before remembering that it was not why she was there. She reluctantly turned away to cast her light around the rest of the room. 'There's nothing else in here?'

'It doesn't look like it,' Jared confirmed.

'Then the angel must be in the Ark.' She produced a camera and took several photos for the record, then returned to the chest, suppressing her professional disquiet at what she was about to do. 'Can you lift the lid?'

Now it was Eddie's turn to hesitate. 'You sure? You know what's supposed to happen if you open this thing. Lightning, firestorms, melting Nazis . . .'

'And I thought you weren't superstitious.'

'No, but I'm movie-stitious.'

'We don't have a choice – the clues to the angel's location in Revelation pointed here. Cross is already in Israel, and sooner or later he'll realise he needs to widen his search, so we've got to get it out of here before that happens. We can't leave it and hope that *he* gets melted when he opens it.'

'Maybe I should close my eyes,' Eddie grumbled, but he moved to one end of the chest. Jared gave Nina an uncertain look, but went to the other. The Englishman warily tapped one of the poles before risking touching the lid itself. 'Not struck dead on the spot. That's a start.'

'Okay,' said Nina, 'now very carefully, lift it up.'

The two men strained to raise the mercy seat. 'It's heavy,' grunted Jared. 'The statues must be solid gold.' They pulled harder.

With a scrape of metal, the Ark of the Covenant began to open.

★ ★ ★

The Bell 430 continued its monotonous search of the empty desert. Dalton made a show of checking his watch for the third time in as many minutes. 'How much fuel has this damn thing got left?' he complained.

'We'll go back to Ovda after we check the next valley,' Cross replied. 'Then you can get out. I'm sure that'll be a relief.' *For everyone*, he didn't need to add.

'Just remember that you wouldn't even be here without my help,' Dalton snapped. 'I was the one who told you Nina Wilde was the best person to find the angels, I got you into Israel without—'

'There's someone down there!' Simeon barked. The ex-politician was instantly forgotten as all eyes went to the windows. 'I can see a truck.' He raised his binoculars as Paxton slowed the helicopter. 'No sign of anybody with it.'

Cross brought up his own field glasses. Sunlight flashed off the windows of a 4x4 parked near the foot of a cliff. He looked up the sheer rock face, spotting the faint line of a rope. It led to a narrow yet tall cleft in the massif, a very thin pass snaking away to . . .

'A sinkhole,' he said, seeing what lay at its end. 'There's a sinkhole on that mountain.'

Dalton craned his neck to peer at the landscape below. 'It can't be the one we're looking for. I thought we were checking the valleys, not the hills.'

'We were,' said Cross with growing realisation. 'And we were wrong!' He snapped the binoculars back to the cliff. Faint sparkles in the rock marked where the intense sunlight glanced off copper deposits. 'It reflects the sun. "Clothed with the sun" – that's what John meant! And you'd need the wings of eagles to get up there . . .'

'Wilde lied to us?' said Anna.

'Maybe – or she hadn't figured it out when she told us

where to look. But she has now. She's down there!'

'Wilde's *here*?' said Dalton, disbelieving. 'Are you sure?'

'It's her. I'm certain.' He turned to the pilot. 'Paxton, bring us down as close to the sinkhole as possible.'

Dalton became even more unhappy. 'We're not going back to refuel?'

'We won't need to. The angel's down there.'

'And so are Wilde and Chase,' Simeon reminded him.

'Not for long,' said Cross as the helicopter began its descent.

Nina watched with nervous anticipation as the mercy seat was inched upwards.

'Almost there,' Eddie told Jared. 'Move it over on three.'

Jared nodded. The Yorkshireman counted down, then with loud grunts they shuffled sideways to set it down on the stone floor with a heavy *clunk*.

Nina leaned over the chest to see what was inside. Her flashlight beam found the very items named by legend. A scroll, supposedly the first part of the Torah, written by Moses himself; a wooden staff, which she took to be the rod of Aaron, brother of Moses; an earthenware jar, which had contained some of the manna sent by God to feed the Israelites in the desert . . . and two flat slabs of stone, inscribed with ancient Hebrew text.

Her heart quickened. She was looking at the tablets holding the original Ten Commandments.

But she forced herself to ignore them for now. There was one more relic inside the Ark.

The fourth angel.

It was of the same design as the other two she had seen, a dense ceramic body shrouded by metallic wings. The head of this figure was that of a man, his brow creased in stern warning. She carefully lifted it out, feeling the weight of the deadly meteoric material trapped in its core. 'That's what you're looking for?' Jared asked.

Nina nodded. 'The last angel – the last harbinger of the apocalypse, if you believe Cross. But we've beaten him to it. Whatever he had planned, he can't go ahead with it without this.'

'Unless he decides, "You know what? Bollocks to it, I'm going to do it anyway",' Eddie said grimly. 'He's still got one angel he can release somewhere.'

'I know.' She held up the statue. 'But at least we can secure this—'

She broke off as she saw dust motes falling through the flashlight beams, the first few specks quickly joined by more, and more, drifting from the tent's roof. 'What's doing that?' Eddie demanded. He glanced at the Ark. 'We haven't bloody brought down the fury of God and the wrath of sixty special-effects people, have we?'

'It's outside,' said Jared. A deep rumbling sound gradually rose in intensity.

Still holding the statue, Nina hurried back through the veil. More dust was falling in the tent's outer room, scraps of rotted fabric dropping to the floor. She pushed through the curtain into the throne chamber. The noise grew louder—

The light coming through the giant opal in the ceiling suddenly flickered. A moment later, a shadow passing over the crack above briefly plunged the room into darkness. Then the illumination returned to its spectacular norm, but the bass rumble continued.

'It's a chopper!' Eddie said. The aircraft had gone right overhead, coming in to land on the mountain above them.

'Cross,' said Nina. 'It's Cross!'

'How do you know?' asked Jared.

'Because who *else* would it be? This always frickin' happens to us!'

Eddie drew the Desert Eagle. 'Looks like I'll find out if this thing's as good as my Wildey.'

Jared produced his own, smaller gun. 'We need to get out of here.'

'We'll never get clear,' Nina realised. 'There's no way we'll be able to climb down the cliff and back to the jeep in time. And even if we could, they've got a helicopter! We can't outrun them.'

'So what do we do?'

'Chuck that thing in the sinkhole,' Eddie suggested, nodding at the angel. 'They won't have brought scuba gear. It'll take 'em ages to find it, if they ever do.'

'Yes, but we'll probably be dead!' the Israeli objected.

'And they might still find it,' added Nina. 'We don't know how deep the sinkhole is – if it's only ten feet, it won't take them long to search the bottom.'

'Then drop it off the bridge down the big shaft,' Eddie persisted.

'But if it breaks, then as far as Cross is concerned the angel has been released, and he wins.'

'What, then?' he demanded, exasperated. 'We can't run, there's nowhere to hide the thing, and if we smash it, that's the same as letting him get it? What the bloody hell are we supposed to do?'

'I don't know!' She turned her eyes to the refracted daylight coming through the ceiling as the noise of the helicopter settled . . . then began to die down. It had landed, the pilot shutting off the engines. 'You're SAS,' she told Eddie, turning back to the two men, 'and Jared, you're Mossad – what would *you* do?'

The question galvanised the younger man. 'They'll have seen our truck – it's probably what made them land – so they know we're here. They'll expect an ambush.'

Eddie nodded in agreement. 'We'll have to decoy them.'

'Yeah. But how?'

The Englishman looked back at the tent. 'If Cross is such a Bible-basher, he'll know what that is, and what's inside. We need to keep his attention on it.' A moment's thought, then: 'There's an app for that.'

Simeon swung down from the lip of the sinkhole into the sheltered cave beneath, whipping up his MP5 sub-machine gun and sweeping it across the entrances. Nobody moved within them. He brought his left forefinger to the trigger of the M203 grenade launcher mounted under the weapon's barrel, ready to fire a shrapnel-filled high-explosive round at any hint of activity.

Still nothing stirred. He took cover beside the right-most opening as more of his men dropped down and spread out to check the other archways. 'Clear,' one soon reported. The others gave the same message.

Simeon cast a wary eye into the underground chamber before moving to look up to the surface. 'Nobody here.'

Cross, Anna and Dalton gazed back down at him. 'Good,' said the cult leader. He lowered himself to the cave, Anna following. 'What have we got?'

'Four entrances. I don't know which they took.'

Cross surveyed the arches, then pointed at the left-most. 'That one, with the symbol of the twenty-four Elders. Prepare to move in.'

'Hey!' came an aggrieved shout from above. 'You going to leave me up here?'

'Simeon, Norvin, help Mr Dalton down,' said Cross, the upward flick of his eyes as much a disparaging roll as an indication of the disgraced politician's location. Simeon let out a sound of contempt, then he and the bodyguard took up positions to catch Dalton as he clumsily clambered over the edge.

Even with their support, the ex-president touched down with

a thump. He shook himself free of them. 'All right, I'm here,' he announced. 'Now, what's the situation?'

'They're down there,' Cross told him, going to the entrance. One of his men, a jut-jawed blond named Hatch, crouched to examine the floor; faint footsteps in the dust confirmed his leader's statement.

'And what else is down there?'

'The angel, is all I can say for sure. Other than that . . .' He regarded the symbol above the opening with intense curiosity, then signalled for his team to advance.

Simeon took point, Norvin behind him. The others followed in single file. They cautiously made their way up the sloping passage, listening for sounds of activity. But they heard none. It wasn't until they reached the growths of mushrooms that Cross broke the silence. 'Manna?' he wondered in a whisper, pausing for a closer look.

'Sir!' Simeon hissed. 'I heard voices – and there's something up ahead.'

The mushrooms forgotten, Cross made his way to the front of the group, joining Simeon at the edge of the cenote. The cult leader aimed his flashlight into the depths, revealing water a long way below. His right-hand man, meanwhile, used his own light to track the rope across the rickety bridge. 'Through there,' he said, seeing the open doorway.

'I hear them,' Cross murmured. Two people were speaking; the words were indistinct, but one voice was male . . . and the other female. 'It's Wilde.'

Simeon raised his MP5, aiming the grenade launcher at the doorway, but Cross pushed it down. 'No! You might damage the angel. We need it intact.'

Anna listened to the voices. The discussion seemed casual, unworried. 'They don't know we're here.'

'It could still be an ambush,' her husband warned. 'And I

don't like the look of this bridge.'

'They got across it; so can we,' said Cross. He tested the rope. It held.

Dalton squeezed past the other team members. 'What's going on?'

'Keep your voice down,' Simeon growled. Dalton twitched in anger, but the African-American went on: 'They're on the other side of this shaft. We've got to get across without letting them know we're here.'

'Norvin, you go over first,' Cross told his bodyguard. 'If the tunnel on the far side is clear, cover it while the rest of us follow.'

Norvin nodded, slinging his MP5 and taking hold of the rope. He sidestepped across the bridge. His companions watched with growing anxiety, a few stifled gasps escaping when the structure swayed under his weight, but after steadying himself he was able to continue on to firm ground. He quickly readied his gun and checked the tunnel, then signalled that the way was clear.

'Maybe you should wait here,' Cross suggested to Dalton.

'Like hell,' Dalton replied. 'I want to see the look on Wilde and Chase's faces when we take the angel from them.'

'As you wish.' The white-clad man turned his back on him, waiting for Simeon to cross before starting his own journey. 'Come over after Anna. Hatch, watch out for him.'

One by one the group traversed the cenote. By the time the last man made it, Cross had already instructed Simeon and Norvin to advance. They crept along the decorated passage, guns raised. The voices became louder as they neared its end. 'I see lights,' Simeon whispered.

'Careful,' said Cross, but he was already almost unconsciously increasing his pace, glimpsing wonders waiting ahead. Gold glinted under a strange rainbow glow. He forced himself to slow and listen. 'It's definitely them.'

Nina's voice reached him. '. . . way beyond what I'd expected to find. I mean, we came looking for the angel, but to discover this as well? It's incredible.'

'Yeah.' The other speaker was Eddie Chase. Simeon's hands tightened on his weapon, while Dalton gulped faintly, his mouth suddenly dry.

'This will change Biblical archaeology for ever,' Nina went on. 'It's quite possibly the biggest thing I've ever discovered. The actual Ark of the Covenant, intact, and in God's temple as described in the Book of Revelation? Amazing!'

'Uh-huh,' came the reply.

Simeon reached the entrance, silently panning his gun across the chamber. The voices were coming from a tent at the far end, lights glinting through thin patches in its ancient coverings. 'They're in that,' he said, his own voice barely above the volume of a breath. 'Room's clear.'

'The Tabernacle . . .' Cross whispered, astounded. The cult leader entered the room, then stepped aside to let his armed followers past as Dalton stood beside him. He knew where he was, almost overcome by religious awe at the sight of God's throne beneath the shaft of spectral light, but managed to restrain his wonderment. His first priority was securing the angel.

Which would be easy. The archaeologist was still talking, her husband muttering the occasional reply. Cross issued an order: 'Take them.'

Simeon took command, using hand signals to direct the others towards the tent. The men spread out to surround it, while Anna hung back inside the circle of thrones to cover a wider area. The African-American silently made his way to the entrance, reaching out to pull back the curtains . . .

'Ay up.'

The voice came not from the tent – but from behind Cross and Dalton.

336

28

Both men whirled – to see Eddie and Jared emerge from behind the tapestries, guns raised. 'Chase!' Dalton cried.

Simeon and the others spun, but the two ambushers had already moved to use Dalton and Cross as human shields. 'Drop your guns!' Eddie commanded, grabbing the politician and spinning him around to shove the Desert Eagle's blocky muzzle hard into his back. Jared simultaneously jammed his own gun into Cross's face. 'Do it, or they die!'

'Drop them!' shrieked Dalton. 'He's a psycho!'

Cross was more restrained, but his face still creased with anger as Jared pulled him around. 'Do what he says.'

The team lowered their weapons to the floor – with the exception of Simeon, who brought up his MP5 and took careful aim at what he could see of Jared. 'Let them go,' he growled.

Cross raised a hand. 'Put it down, Simeon. That's an order.'

Confusion crossed Simeon's face. 'But—'

'We're in God's temple. I won't allow it to be desecrated. Only God has the right to take a life in here.' When Simeon did not respond at once, he shouted, not in fear but anger: '*Do it!*'

With deep reluctance, Simeon placed his sub-machine gun on the floor. 'Okay, hands up and kick 'em away,' said Eddie. Guns skittered across the floor, Simeon's ending up between two of the thrones. 'Nina? You can come out now.'

Nina emerged from the tabernacle, even with Eddie's assurance nervous at the sight of Anna, Simeon and five other men watching her. She gingerly slipped past them and crossed the chamber. In one hand she held the angel; in the other, Eddie's phone, its voice memo app playing a recording. 'Right,' said Eddie's voice from the speaker. She thumbed the screen to silence it, then pocketed the device.

'Clever,' said Cross, almost approving. He looked at the tent. 'So you found the angel, but . . . is the Ark of the Covenant *really* in there?'

'It is,' said Nina, joining Eddie. She gave Dalton a scathing glare. 'Oh, hey, Mr President. You're a long way from the campaign trail, aren't you?'

'What are you going to do with us?' Dalton demanded. He had outwardly regained his composure after his near-panic at finding himself face to face with the Englishman, but there was still fear in his eyes.

'We're gonna leave you in here,' Eddie told him. 'The Israelis can pick you up once we've taken that statue somewhere safe.'

'And how exactly are you planning on holding us?' asked Anna, sidling closer.

'Stay where you are,' Jared warned. 'Keep your hands up. All of you.' The biochemist's hands were already half raised; she scowled, but brought them higher.

'We'll take out that bridge,' said Eddie, answering her. He addressed Cross. 'So you'll have plenty of time to spend with the Ark.'

'What's inside the Ark?' Cross asked Nina. 'Is it what the Bible described?'

There was no sense that he was trying to buy time to regain the advantage; he was genuinely desperate to know the truth. 'It is,' she replied. 'The angel was in there, but so were Aaron's staff, a scroll of the Torah – and the Ten Commandments.'

'I have to see them.' He tried to move towards the Tabernacle. Jared yanked him back. 'Don't move!'

'Let him go!' Anna darted closer, halting only when the Israeli pushed his gun into the cult leader's cheek.

'It's okay,' Cross told her. 'Stay where you are.'

'And you, back off,' Eddie warned Simeon, seeing that he had used the moment of confusion to move closer to his gun. The black man scowled, but retreated. Jared lowered his weapon, pressing the muzzle into his prisoner's back.

'Consider it a trade,' Nina said to Cross. 'The Ark for the angel. Whatever you wanted the statue for, after what happened at the Mission there's no way we're going to let you take it.'

Dalton shook his head in aggravation. 'You got something to say?' asked Eddie.

'Only that you two have already caused great harm to America by refusing to see the big picture, and now you're going to do it again,' he complained. 'Yes, what's inside the statue is extremely dangerous, and yes, regrettably lives have been lost. But what I'm doing will strengthen the security of the entire nation, whether or not you're willing to realise that. That's what being president is all about: knowing when force *has* to be applied, and making hard decisions for the greater good.'

'Nice speech,' Nina said. 'Just one minor point – you're not the president. And the reason you're not is that you proved you can't be trusted.'

'The reason I'm not is because Travis Warden and those other cocksuckers in the Group threw me to the wolves rather than getting their media outlets to spin things my way!' Dalton exploded. Cross gave him a disapproving glare. 'Oh, don't get up on your damn moral high horse, Ezekiel. Not with what you're going to do. A bit of bad language is nothing compared to—' He stopped abruptly.

'Compared to what?' Eddie prompted. 'Come on, don't make this the one time in your life when you don't want to hear the sound of your own voice.'

Nina stood before Dalton, holding up the angel. 'You thought you'd have two angels, so I imagine you also had two targets for them. What are they?'

'Damned if I'm going to tell you,' the former president growled.

'Damned if you don't.'

'*Dead* if you don't,' added Eddie.

Nina shook her head. 'Face it, *Victor*, you're finished. You'll be directly linked to what happened in Antigua; the place was full of security cameras, so there'll be plenty of proof that you were there when Cross killed almost a hundred people.' A flash of fear in the politician's eyes told her that was something he had either not considered, or been fervently hoping nobody else had. 'The best you can hope for is to plea-bargain your way into a minimum jail term, but there's no way you'll ever get so much as a sniff of power again.'

For a moment Dalton seemed about to break . . . but then he summoned up a reserve of haughty defiance. 'I'm not telling you a goddamn thing. And you, Chase,' he snapped, looking back at Eddie, 'get that damn gun off of me, you Limey son of a bitch!'

He tried to pull out of the Englishman's hold. Eddie responded by driving a knee into the back of his leg, making him cry out and stumble.

Jared instinctively glanced towards the scuffle to see if his friend needed help—

A sharp metallic *snick*, and Anna charged at him, brandishing a glinting switchblade that she had pulled from her sleeve.

Jared caught the movement, but his line of fire was blocked by Cross. He hesitated for an instant, not wanting to shoot a prisoner in the back – then shoved Cross aside—

His shot caught Anna's left arm, blowing a chunk of flesh from her bicep. She screamed – but had already dived at him, the blade held out before her like a lance.

It stabbed into Jared's thigh.

He yelled, leg buckling as she crashed against him. Eddie hauled Dalton around as he tried to aim at the wounded woman, but she was shielded behind the fallen Mossad agent.

'*Anna!*' cried Simeon. He hurled himself behind the circle of thrones and snatched up his fallen MP5. Eddie spun to face the new threat—

'Nobody shoot!' boomed Cross. 'No one shoot!' He raised both hands, turning to address both Eddie and his own followers. 'There won't be any killing in God's house.'

'Don't bet on it,' Eddie snarled, pulling Dalton closer as he kept the Desert Eagle locked on Simeon's cover. The metal of the throne was thick, but a .50-calibre round was more than capable of punching a hole right through it, and the man behind.

'He shot Anna!' Simeon shouted.

Cross glanced at her wound. 'She'll live.'

'You won't,' gasped Jared, bringing up his gun—

Anna wrenched her blade around, tearing it deeper into his muscle. His cry this time was a full-blown scream of agony. But despite the pain, he swung the gun towards her . . .

She swiped it from his hand. The pistol clattered across the stone floor to end up near a tapestry.

'Nina, get the gun!' Eddie shouted.

She started forward, only for Cross to block her way. 'Dr Wilde,' he said. 'It seems we have a stand-off.'

'Like buggery we do,' said Eddie.

Cross glanced towards his men, some of whom had recovered their weapons in the chaos. Washburn, his slashed cheek now home to a line of stitches, glared at Eddie. 'We outgun you, over two to one,' the cult leader said. 'But I'm not willing to see a bloodbath in this holy place. Unless,' he added, 'you leave us with no choice.'

Nina regarded him coldly. 'Yeah, I was wondering how long

it would take before you gave yourself a get-out clause.'

'I don't want to do it. But I'm being completely honest; I'm willing to offer a deal. Let us leave with the angel, and I give you my word before God that as long as you remain in this temple, we won't kill you.'

'Prophet!' protested Simeon. 'Anna needs medical attention. We can't let these—'

Cross raised an angry hand, silencing him. 'Those are my terms, Dr Wilde,' he continued. 'They're non-negotiable. If you want to stay alive, hand over the angel.'

Eddie drew Dalton closer, tapping the gun against the grey-haired man's head. 'Aren't you forgetting something? You want me to go all Lee Harvey on your mate here?'

Cross gave his prisoner a dismissive look. 'You can keep him. I don't need him any more.'

'What?' said Nina, shocked.

'*What?*' echoed Dalton, with considerably more anger.

'His political connections were useful, and he did suggest that you were the best person to find the angels,' Cross explained. 'But right now, the office of the President of the United States is a symbol, if not the embodiment, of the utter corruption of the so-called elites of this world. Do what you like with him.'

Dalton shook with fury. 'You slimy little son of a bitch!'

Eddie was barely more pleased. 'We don't want him either!'

'Time to make a decision, Dr Wilde,' said Cross, ignoring him. 'You can have a shootout that will leave you, your husband and your friend dead—'

'And you too,' Eddie warned, keeping behind Dalton as he shifted his aim to the cult leader.

'But we'll still have the angel. My followers will carry out the plan. Babylon *will* fall, even if I'm not there to witness it. Or you can give us the angel and we'll leave you to give this man first aid.' He glanced at Jared, then nodded to Anna. 'Which he'll need.' The young Israeli screamed again as Anna ground the knife deeper into his thigh.

'God damn it!' Nina cried. 'You said we wouldn't be hurt!'

'I said you wouldn't be *killed*. Your choice, Dr Wilde. The only way for all three of you to stay alive – all four of you,' he added, gaze flicking to the apoplectic Dalton – 'is to give me the angel.'

Nina regarded the statue in her hand, then looked helplessly at her husband. 'Eddie . . .'

'They're going to kill us anyway,' he rumbled.

Cross shook his head. 'No. I gave my word before God. I won't break it, and my followers won't either.' He gestured to his men. They hesitated, then lowered their guns. Simeon held out, but a second, more forceful signal finally prompted him to obey.

Eddie rapidly reassessed the odds. If he was accurate with the Desert Eagle, he would kill or incapacitate anyone he hit, but he doubted he would get off more than two shots before being cut down. He was also certain that Dalton's presence wouldn't deter the gunmen in the slightest, the ex-president now nothing more than a meaty bullet sponge.

But he still wasn't willing to give Cross what he wanted. 'If they take the angel, they'll kill a lot of people,' he reminded Nina. 'I don't want to say this, but the best thing to do is smash the fucking thing right now. Better twelve people die than twelve thousand.'

'I know, but . . .' The numbers made sense in terms of cold logic, a small sacrifice to save countless lives . . . but there were more than twelve lives in the chamber. She brought her palm to the small swelling below her waist. 'I can't,' she whispered. 'I can't do it. It's just . . . I can't,' she repeated.

'Shit,' said Eddie under his breath, though with full under-standing and sympathy.

Nina looked back at Cross. 'I absolutely have your word, before God, that you won't kill us?'

'We'll take the angel and leave,' he replied. 'As long as you stay in this throne room, we won't harm you. I've made you a promise, and my followers will keep it too.' He locked eyes with each of his people in turn. All nodded, even Anna and Simeon. 'Anna, let him go.'

Anna tugged the blade out of Jared's leg. The Israeli let out a cry, clapping a hand over the wound as she stood painfully.

Cross held out a hand. 'The angel?'

'Nina . . .' said Eddie.

'I have to,' she told him, conflict clear in her voice. She placed the statue on the floor, then stepped back.

Cross crouched to examine it with reverence before picking it up. He turned it over in his hands, paying close attention to the fine details, before announcing: 'It's real. It's the last angel. And,' he said as he stood, 'it's mine.'

'You're really going to let them live?' demanded Simeon.

'Yes, we are. I gave my word to God.' He bowed his head to the central throne, then started towards the exit. 'Everyone move out.'

Keeping his gun aimed in Eddie's direction, Simeon scurried to Anna, giving Jared a poisonous glare as he checked her wound. The other men went to the exit. Eddie stayed behind Dalton, Desert Eagle at the ready. 'Nina, get behind me.' She retreated, using one of the thrones as cover.

'You're letting them *go*?' Dalton asked Eddie with angry disbelief.

'You want me to start shooting?' he fired back. ''Cause you'll be my bulletproof vest!'

'Nobody needs to shoot anyone,' said Cross, holding the statue up to the iridescent light coming through the opal. 'Not in here. But if you leave the throne room before we're gone . . .'

'Knew there'd be a fucking catch,' Eddie muttered.

Cross and Simeon exchanged whispered words, then the latter spoke to his troops. 'Norvin, get the Prophet and the angel out of here. I'll take Anna; the rest of you, cover us.' He glanced at Cross, then went on, trying to suppress his frustration: 'Don't fire unless fired upon.'

Hatch and the other men took up positions at the entrance as first Cross and Norvin, then Simeon and Anna left the room, the cult leader looking longingly at the Tabernacle before departing. 'If there is a God, he'll make that fucking bridge collapse under them,' said Eddie as the remaining gunmen retreated.

Dalton watched them go with dismay. '*Now* what do we do?'

'Oh, so when everything goes up shit creek, you ask *us* for advice? You fucking idiot.' The Yorkshireman shoved Dalton away and moved to look down the tunnel, spotting Hatch backing away, gun raised. 'That Bible-thumper promised God that we wouldn't be harmed in here, but I bet that promise ends the second we set foot outside the door.'

Nina retrieved her backpack, then hurried to Jared. 'Eddie, I'm sorry, but I couldn't do it,' she said as she took out a first-aid kit. 'I couldn't do that to our baby. I'm sorry.'

'It's okay,' he told her. 'We'll figure something else out.' Hatch disappeared from view; Eddie went to the tunnel entrance. 'Jared, you okay?'

'I never realised being stabbed would hurt this bad,' the Israeli replied through clenched teeth.

'Just wait until you try to walk on that leg.'

'Thanks a lot, *alter kocker*.' He gasped as Nina cut away the torn material to reveal the bloodied wound beneath. 'How does it look?'

'I'm not an expert, but . . . not great.' Blood was still pumping from the gash.

'Just do what you can to stop the bleeding,' said Eddie. 'I'll come and help you in a minute.'

'Where are you going?' asked Nina.

'To stop that lot from leaving.' There was no sign of anyone in the tunnel, though he could still hear activity in the cenote. Raising the Desert Eagle, he crept down the passage.

He soon saw the doorway ahead. The raiders had not left a rearguard – at least not on this side of the bridge. He moved closer.

The rope was still in place, pulled taut above the crossing. But he saw as he neared the door that it was moving, jiggling up and down—

He realised what was happening just as the person hacking away at the line with a combat knife finally severed the last few strands. The far end of the rope fell away to hang limply down into the cenote. Eddie held in an obscenity, hearing movement from the other side of the bridge.

He leaned around the edge of the opening . . .

And his eyes widened in fear as he saw Simeon aiming his grenade launcher.

Eddie sprinted back into the darkness as a shotgun-like *bam!* propelled a forty-millimetre grenade across the chasm.

It struck – but he wasn't the target.

Instead, it hit the end of the bridge. The explosion as the ancient wood was blasted into splinters blew Eddie off his feet. The shattered structure toppled into the abyss with a noise like the clattering of dried bones.

On the far side of the cenote, Simeon and Hatch, holding a flashlight, scrambled backwards as the detonation sent broken stones flying at them. A deep crunching reverberated around the passage – then a great chunk of the cenote's wall sheared off and smashed down on to the end of the tunnel, almost completely blocking it.

Simeon regained his composure. 'Don't think they'll get out

of there,' he said, as Hatch shone his light over the boulder. The two men shared a triumphant smile, then hurried to catch up with their leader.

Nina had just finished cleaning Jared's wound when the explosion ripped through the passageway. 'Eddie!' she yelled, running down the tunnel to find him.

A choking cloud hit her, reducing her flashlight's beam to a haze. She buried her nose and mouth in the crook of her arm. 'Eddie, can you hear me?' she called, voice muffled.

Coughing answered her. 'Yeah, I'm okay,' her husband rasped. 'Just got knocked over. My ears are still ringing, though. Not that that's anything new.'

She groped in the darkness, her hand finally touching leather. 'Can you stand?'

He took her arm. 'More or less.' Another bout of coughing, then they headed back to the throne room. 'Bastards took out the bridge with a grenade. They cut the rope, too.'

'So how are we going to get out of here?' They cleared the wafting smoke, the sparking light of the temple beckoning them ahead.

'Dunno, but we'll have to— Oh, for fuck's sake.'

Dalton stood inside the entrance, pointing Jared's pistol at them. 'Stay where you are! Drop the gun, Chase.'

'Sorry, Eddie,' said the Israeli from the floor, one hand covering his wound. 'I wasn't fast enough to stop him.'

'No problem,' Eddie replied, eyes fixed contemptuously on the older man's trembling hand. 'The dozy twat's left the safety on.'

Dalton frowned, but with a flicker of uncertainty. Eddie shrugged and advanced on him. The politician twisted his wrist to bring the safety lever into view, tipping the weapon away from its target – and the Englishman instantly snapped up the Desert Eagle and aimed it unwaveringly at his head. 'Drop it.'

Dalton flinched, then with a muted moan of defeat let the pistol fall to the floor. 'Now that's what I call an executive decision,' said Nina.

'Dickhead,' said Eddie as he collected the weapon. 'If someone you're pointing a gun at tells you the safety's on, you know how you test that? By pulling the fucking trigger!'

'Pardon me for not being a psychotic killer,' Dalton replied, fuming.

'Oh, you're a killer,' Nina told him as she returned to Jared. 'Just not the kind who gets his hands dirty. Until now, at least. How does it feel to be out in the field, and on the wrong end of some blowback?'

The ex-president struggled to get his temper back under control. 'Never mind that,' he said. 'If the bridge is gone, we're trapped in here! What are we going to do?'

'Shoot you if you don't stop whingeing,' said Eddie. 'Nina, you got my phone?' She passed it to him. He checked the screen. 'No network. Can't say I'm surprised, but it was worth a try.'

Nina bandaged the Mossad agent's leg. 'You said they cut the rope. From this side?'

'No, the other side,' Eddie replied.

'So we might be able to use it to get across the cenote?'

'Maybe, if that explosion didn't shred it or knock the pitons out of the wall.'

'We need to check.' She secured the bandage. 'How does that feel?'

Jared sat up slowly, face drawn tight with pain. 'Like I got stabbed in the leg.'

Nina helped him up. 'Can you walk?'

He took a couple of experimental steps. 'Just about,' he gasped.

'Guess you won't be winning this month's Mossad fun run,' said Eddie.

Jared gave him a strained grin. 'At least I'll be trying, old man.'

'Yeah, you're bloody trying all right. Come on, let's see what's left of the bridge.' He waved the Desert Eagle at Dalton. 'Oi! Commander-in-Chief, lead from the front. Let's go.'

The group made their way back down the decorated passage. Some of the paintings near the doorway had been damaged by flying debris, but to Nina's relief the majority were intact; even given their grim situation, part of her was still overjoyed that the temple and its contents had not been destroyed.

Whether she would ever tell anyone about her find was another matter. 'That's . . . not ideal,' she said, shining her light at the empty space where the bridge had been.

Eddie had reclaimed his own torch from Jared. 'Nor's that.' He illuminated the rock blocking the tunnel across the shaft. 'Looks pretty unstable, but I don't fancy trying to pull it loose from that hole.'

'We could send Dalton over,' suggested Nina jokingly. The politician was not amused.

Eddie redirected his torch at the rope. As he had feared, it had been damaged by the blast – the outer layers of strands closest to the grenade's point of impact were torn and ragged – but it was still in one piece. He pulled on it, testing both that the pitons were still fixed to the rock and that it would not snap under stress. 'It'll hold. I think.'

'What are you going to do?' Jared asked. 'Run it around the shaft and try to pull that rock out of the way?'

'It won't reach.' The length of line was just enough to span the shaft's diameter, but the smooth, curved walls forming the cenote's circumference were much longer.

'Then we're trapped here?' exclaimed Dalton.

'At least we'll have something to eat,' said Nina, staring at him for just long enough to make him uncomfortable before indicating a clump of mushrooms that had survived the explosion.

'Actually, we'd probably find some of these inside the jar in the Ark. It's supposed to contain manna, the food God sent to the Israelites, and the description of manna was like a kind of mushroom or fungus.'

'These are in a cave, not out in the desert, though,' Jared pointed out.

'Yes, but we saw them in—' An electric thought hit her. 'The pool outside, the sinkhole. There were some floating in the water!'

'So?' asked Dalton. 'They probably grow all over this place.'

'But we've only seen them in the tunnels. So,' she pressed on, 'there's water at the bottom of this shaft, and we came up a slope for some distance to get here. What if it's the same water in both, at the same level, and they're connected? The mushrooms we saw outside might have come from here!'

Eddie looked down the shaft, seeing a glimmer of a reflection from his torch. 'It's a long drop – seventy feet, easy.'

'But the rope's about thirty feet long. If someone hung from the end before letting go, that would cut the drop to not much more than thirty feet. And they'd be landing in water.'

'We don't know how deep it is,' said Jared. 'If it's only shallow, they'd break their legs.'

Eddie picked up a hunk of broken stone and lobbed it over the edge. The sound of a loud splash rolled up the shaft. 'It's more than a foot deep,' he said, 'or we would've heard it hit the bottom. But that doesn't mean it'll be a soft landing for whoever tries it. Who, let's face it, will be me.'

Jared hobbled to the edge. 'No, I can do it.'

Eddie snorted. 'Stabbed,' he told the Israeli. 'Pregnant,' he said to his wife. 'Wanker,' he concluded, jabbing a thumb at the affronted Dalton. 'I'm the only one who *can* do it.'

Nina was already having second thoughts. 'If there isn't a way through to the sinkhole, or it's too narrow to fit through, you'll be trapped down there.'

Jared looked back towards the throne room. 'I'll probably be struck dead for suggesting this, but we could tear up the tapestries to make a longer rope. Or maybe take down the Tabernacle—'

'And how long'll that take?' Eddie cut in. 'Cross'll be on the way back to his helicopter by now. Once he's gone, we've lost him – and the angel.' He tested the hanging rope again. 'Buggeration and fuckery. I'm actually going to have to do it, aren't I?'

Nina tried desperately to think of an alternative, but came up with nothing. 'Eddie, just . . . don't die. Please. In fact,' she continued, pleading giving way to determination, 'you're not *allowed* to die. Your daughter needs you.'

The torches weren't pointing at his face, but his smile still lit up the shaft. 'We're having a little girl?' he exclaimed, delighted.

Nina beamed at him. 'Yeah. I know you wanted it to be a surprise, but if there was ever a time when you should know . . .'

'We're having a girl!' he cried, embracing her. 'Holy shit, we're having a daughter. That's amazing!' He kissed her.

'Well, it was that or a boy, a fifty-fifty chance,' she reminded him with a grin.

Jared clapped him on the back. 'Well done, old man.'

'Congratulations,' said Dalton, with considerable sarcasm. 'Now maybe we can try to get out of here?'

Eddie released Nina. 'Okay, you're right,' he told her. 'No fucking way am I going to die before I see her. And preferably not for a long time after that.' He pocketed his gun and flashlight, then took a firm hold of the rope and moved to the edge. 'We're getting out of here. I mean, I've got to be there to take her ice-skating at Rockefeller Center, intimidate her first boyfriend . . .'

'Be nice,' Nina told him. 'And be careful!'

'Always am. Usually. See you soon.' He blew her a kiss, then stepped backwards to begin his descent.

The damaged rope was rough to the touch, scraping his palms. He could feel the fibres straining under his weight. But he was now committed to the climb – either it would hold, or his drop would be even longer than expected.

He had made many such descents before, and this one was no more challenging than any other. The only complication was the sheer smoothness of the cenote's wall, forcing him to bring his feet up higher than he liked to maintain grip with his soles. But he made quick and steady progress, until . . .

'I'm out of rope!' he shouted. He took all his weight with his left hand as he wound the line's severed end around his right, then held himself in place as he took out the torch and directed it downwards.

A black pool shimmered below. It filled the entire shaft. No protruding rocks broke the surface, or even debris from the destroyed bridge, but he couldn't tell how deep it was. He could judge the distance to the surface, though: it was still a thirty-foot drop, about as far as an Olympic high-dive. A simple landing if the water was deep enough. If it wasn't, or he hit wreckage, his bones would shatter.

'Can you make it?' Nina called from above.

'Going to have to!' Eddie brought his feet up until he was almost perpendicular to the wall. Landing on his back would hurt, but it would bring him to a stop at a shallower depth than if he dropped vertically.

Assuming he didn't hit something first.

But it was either that or climb back up and remain trapped in the tunnels. 'Okay,' he said, taking a deep breath as he psyched himself up. 'One, two—'

The rope snapped – and he fell.

29

A brief sickening feeling of free-fall and fear—
    Impact.

Pain flared through Eddie's back – then the water crashed over his face, causing a moment of panic before he regained his senses. He thrashed his limbs. No sharp agony from broken bones. Relieved, he tipped himself upright and breached the surface to draw breath, probing with his feet. They touched an uneven floor about five feet below, strewn with debris. Landing flat had saved his life; if he had dropped straight down, he would have hit solid rock and broken both ankles.

'Eddie! Are you okay?' cried Nina.

'I'm fine!' he shouted, straightening to his full height and bringing the waterproof flashlight above the rippling surface. The water was littered with splintered wood and mushrooms stripped from the walls by the explosion.

The latter reminded him what he was looking for. He surveyed the walls. The cenote widened out at its base to form a bulbous, lopsided cavern, but there were no exits above water level. He lowered the torch under the surface and submerged again.

Nothing was visible. The falling wreckage had churned up the pool, disturbing long-settled sediment. He resurfaced, swearing under his breath. He would have to search blind . . .

Or would he? 'Nina! Switch off your light!' he called, clicking off his own torch.

'You sure?' she asked.

'If there's a way through to the sinkhole, I might be able to see daylight.'

'Okay!' Her light went out. Eddie closed his eyes, letting them adjust to the darkness, then opened them again.

At first he saw only blackness. But then a vague cyan haze took on form to one side. He waded closer. The ghostly sheen gradually became more distinct. Dropping below the water, he saw a rough rectangle of dim light lower in the wall. 'I think I've found a way out,' he told the others after surfacing.

'Big enough to get through?' asked Jared.

'I'll find out in a minute!' He swam across the pool, then submerged again.

There *was* a passage through the rock, around five feet wide – but far shallower, two feet high at most. That he could see daylight on the far side suggested the tunnel was not long, but if he got caught on a jutting rock . . .

He resurfaced. 'Okay, I'm going to try to reach the sinkhole. If I get through—'

'*When* you get through,' Nina corrected. 'Daughter waiting, remember?'

'*When* I get through, I'll fetch the rest of our gear, then try to push that rock out of the way so I can throw another rope across to you.'

'See you soon,' she said. He switched his torch back on and waved it at her, then took several deep breaths and plunged back under the water.

The passage took on form, a pale blue void in the surrounding darkness. He swam into it, finding the highest point. Even that was uncomfortably claustrophobic, and it quickly became even tighter as he advanced. Stone scraped his head. He angled downwards, but within seconds felt rock brush his chest.

He switched tack, using his hands as much to pull himself forward as to swim. The light ahead grew brighter, but the ceiling and floor continued to close in. His heels struck the stone above, forcing him to slow and switch to a more frog-like kick.

The end of the underwater tunnel was now in sight, though. He kept kicking, dragging himself along—

An overhanging protrusion caught his shoulder. He tried to drop under it – only to find he had no more room to manoeuvre, his chest flat against the floor. He shoved himself sideways, but found his way blocked in that direction as well.

He backtracked, heart starting to race as the remaining oxygen in his lungs was consumed. A crab-like crawl across the passage, then he started forward again. This time the floor rose up to meet him, pushing him against the ceiling. Rock nudged his body from above and below.

He was running out of air! Clawing at the floor, he hauled himself through the fissure. The slabs of stone squeezed more tightly against him, his clothing catching on rough edges—

His other shoulder became wedged.

No time to back up and try another route. It was either onwards – or nowhere. A fist clenched around his lungs. He dug his fingernails against the rough surface and pulled, writhing as he tried to break loose . . .

His pinned shoulder shifted slightly, jacket slipping against the rock – then with a jerk he pulled free. He squirmed past the obstacle and kicked out of the passage.

The sinkhole waited above, a near-perfect circle of blue. He swam to it, breaking the surface with a gasp—

And immediately clamped his mouth shut as he heard voices.

Heart thudding, breathing heavily through his nostrils, he eased himself to the pool's side. He had emerged near the cave dug out below ground level – and somebody was inside it.

Eddie brought his breath under control, then carefully moved along the pool's edge until he could see into the cavern. Two of Cross's men, armed with MP5s, stood within. Both thankfully

355

had their backs to him, watching the tunnel leading to the cenote. A rearguard.

He looked up at the lip of the sinkhole. Nobody else was there, as far as he could see. But he couldn't hear any engine noises either. For a moment he was worried that Cross had already left, but decided, based on the time between the helicopter's arrival and the bad guys entering the temple, that they had not yet made it back to their aircraft.

As much as he wanted to help Nina, she and the others would be safe where they were for now. If there was a chance to prevent Cross from leaving, he had to take it. But he would have to deal with the sentries first.

He held on to the ledge with his left hand, then quietly drew the Desert Eagle and brought it above the surface, tipping it to drain the water from its barrel and receiver. He knew he ought to eject the magazine and rack the slide to make sure the mechanism was fully cleared, but doing so would make a noise that the guards couldn't possibly miss.

He would just have to take his first shot – and hope the second didn't jam.

The two men were halfway between the pool and the tunnel entrance, both facing away from him, though the man on the left had turned his head towards his companion as they talked. He would be the quickest to react – which made him the first target.

The Englishman raised himself higher in the water, then aligned the Desert Eagle's sights on the man's back. A .50-cal shot would go right through him at this range, but it was the second guard who concerned Eddie. If the guy was quick, he might be able to spin around and retaliate before the Englishman could recover from the recoil of firing the huge gun one-handed . . .

Eddie steeled himself – and pulled the trigger.

The gun's boom was near-deafening, resounding like the striking of a massive bell. Even with his arm tensed, the recoil kicked it backwards. But the impact on the first guard was far greater. A great burst of gore exploded from the exit wound, blood and viscera splashing over the walls. Already dead, he crumpled to the floor.

The second man jumped in shock, but recovered almost instantly, whirling to face the threat—

The Yorkshireman hauled the gun back down and unleashed a second ear-pounding gunshot. The bullet shattered the man's shoulder, almost severing his left arm. He was flung backwards, sending a wild spray of fire against the cavern's ceiling.

Eddie pulled himself from the water. His opponent was down, but not out. The MP5 flailed towards him—

A third thunderous shot – and the man's head burst apart as if a bomb had detonated inside his skull, only his lower jaw and tongue remaining intact amidst the carnage.

'Don't think I'll be telling my kid about this bit,' Eddie said as he lowered the smoking Desert Eagle. He glanced at the tunnel leading back to Nina, then reluctantly collected the first dead man's MP5, slinging it over his shoulder before jumping to grab the lip of the cavern's overhanging roof. Water dripping from his clothes, he pulled himself up and looked around, spotting boot prints in the dust. He started uphill after them.

He had barely gone twenty yards before hearing the distant whine of an engine. Cross and the others had reached the helicopter. 'No you fucking don't,' he muttered, checking that the MP5 was ready for action as he ran.

The climb was steep and rocky, but he saw flatter ground some way above. He hurried up the slope, hearing the chop of rotor blades picking up speed. It would be at take-off revolutions soon; once it left the ground, it would be out of his weapon's range very quickly.

Dust billowed over the edge of the rise as the noise reached a crescendo. A moment later, the red and white aircraft rose into view, already tipping into flight away from him . . .

Eddie whipped up the MP5 and fired on full auto.

A stream of bullets arced into the air after the chopper. He was at the limit of the weapon's effective range, but sheer firepower was enough to score several hits. Sparks spat from the fuselage as rounds struck home, punching through the thin aluminium to strike more vital components beneath. A puff of smoke came from one of the exhausts. 'Yeah!' he yelled as the helicopter lurched. 'Get back down here!'

Cross grabbed his seat for support as the Bell jerked violently. Paxton wrestled with the controls, an alarm shrilling urgently in time with flashing warning lights. 'I'm losing oil pressure in number two engine!' the pilot shouted. 'I'll have to shut it down!'

'Can we still fly on one engine?' demanded Simeon, holding Anna in place.

'Yeah, but it'll be tricky. We should make it back to Ovda, though.'

The landscape swung past the windshield as the helicopter slewed around. Cross spotted something on the hillside below – a figure in dark clothing. 'It's Chase!'

'I *told* you I should have killed him!' Simeon snarled.

Cross shot him an angry look, but he had bigger concerns than insubordination. The Englishman fired another brief burst. Norvin flinched, but no more bullets came. 'He's out of ammo!'

'Take us back around,' said Simeon, grabbing his MP5. 'I'll deal with that son of a bitch!'

'No, we need to get out of here!' Paxton countered, knuckles white as both hands gripped the shuddering controls.

'Take us back to the airbase,' Cross ordered, to Simeon's disappointment. He looked back at his right-hand man as the aircraft gained height. 'Don't worry, they won't get out of there.' He reached for the radio. 'Time to call in a favour.'

Eddie glared after the chopper as it stabilised and headed into the distance. 'Bollocking fuck-nuts!' he said, discarding the empty MP5 and squishing back down the mountain. He didn't know where the helicopter was going, but Israel was only a small country; Cross and his remaining people would probably be on a jet with the angel within the hour.

He dropped back down into the cavern, retrieving the climbing gear before returning to the cenote. The rock blocking the mouth of the passage proved to be as precariously balanced as he had thought; it only took a couple of minutes to force it over the edge. It fell to the foot of the shaft with a booming splash. 'Eddie!' said Nina with relief from across the gap. 'Are you okay?'

'Yeah, but Cross got away,' he said glumly. 'What about you?'

'I'm fine. Jared's stable, but from the way he's been acting, you'd think he was fit and ready to run a marathon.' The Israeli, sitting against the open door, grinned. 'And Dalton's been a moaning prick, but that's nothing new.'

The politician was hunched against the tunnel wall. 'You know, I'm getting really tired of your attitude.'

'And I'm getting really tired of your continued existence. Now, Mr President, kindly shut the fuck up.' She put both hands to her bump. 'Mommy doesn't normally use rude words, hon – that's Daddy's department – but sometimes they're justified. Don't you use them, though, okay?'

Dalton rolled his eyes. 'Nauseating.'

'Yeah, I bet you were a fun dad,' Eddie snarked. 'Okay, Jared? We'll rig up a Tyrolean traverse and use the harness to bring you over.'

He pounded new pitons into the rock and fixed ropes to them, then threw the rest of the coils across the chasm. Jared and

Nina caught them and pulled them in. The Englishman then lobbed over the hammer and more steel pegs. Once one rope was secured on both sides, the other was tied to Nina's climbing harness so it could be pulled back across, then she, Jared and finally Dalton made their way over. 'Thank God!' the latter gasped as his feet made contact with the floor.

'Thank Nina,' said the Englishman. 'I would've left you over there.' He set about retrieving the climbing equipment. 'We'll need this to get back down to the Landie.'

'Great,' grumbled Dalton. It'll take us hours to drive out of this desert.'

'If only we'd had access to the CIA's black funds for a helicopter,' said Nina sarcastically. 'You know, Mr President, they really should have revoked your access to all that stuff when you resigned from office.'

'And you don't work for the IHA any more, yet they seem happy to fund your whims at the drop of a hat. It's high time the United Nations had its funding brought into check—'

Eddie jabbed a finger at his face. 'Oi! Mr Pussy-dent!' Nina let out an involuntary guffaw at the sheer childishness of the insult, and Dalton's outraged reaction to it. 'You know how she told you to shut the fuck up? Shut the fuck up.' Dalton seethed, but bit his lip at the Yorkshireman's menacing stare.

'The only thing we want to hear from you is what Cross intends to do with the angels,' said Nina as Eddie finished gathering the gear. They started down the tunnel. 'Where's he planning to release them?'

'I've got nothing to say,' Dalton replied stiffly.

Nina blew out an incredulous breath. 'Seriously? You don't get it, do you? Cross *betrayed* you! He got everything he needed from you and then left you here to die. You've got nothing to gain by protecting him.' The ex-president stayed silent. 'Maybe you think you're maintaining plausible deniability, and that somehow you'll be able to worm your way out of responsibility for what happened at the Mission. But trust me: you won't be celebrating your political comeback when you return to the States. You'll be in a federal prison on charges of conspiracy to kidnap and murder, if not outright terrorism.'

'I told you: people like me don't go to jail,' he retorted.

'Then maybe it's time for a bit of vigilante justice,' said Eddie, making a show of checking the Desert Eagle. Dalton fell silent.

They emerged in the cavern. Eddie helped Nina out of the sinkhole, then Jared, before climbing out himself. The two men then pulled Dalton up. 'Are you okay?' Nina asked Jared, seeing him grimace.

'Yeah, yeah,' he replied, not with full conviction. 'But you're right, I won't be doing much on this leg for a while.'

'Hopefully you won't have to.'

'Still got to climb down,' Eddie reminded them. He started towards the passage through the cliffs, the others following. 'How long'll it take before we can tell anyone what's happened?'

'I think going west rather than back the way we came will be the quickest route to a highway,' Jared replied. 'There's one running parallel to the Egyptian border. We should get cell reception there.' They clambered over the fallen rocks and continued along the narrow, winding ravine.

'So what about it?' Nina asked Dalton. 'Your only chance of staying out of prison is to tell us where Cross plans to release the angels. If you help stop the attacks, you might just save your sorry ass.'

'If I'm going to say anything,' he replied with disdain, 'it'll be through my lawyer to the Attorney General. It sure as hell won't be to the likes of you.'

She shook her head. 'You really *do* think you'll still be able to get back into the White House, don't you? Jeez. I know politicians have an inflated sense of self-belief, but you're outright delusional!'

'We'll see,' was his reply.

'Twat,' said Eddie, turning sideways to pass through the tight clench. 'All right, we're almost at the cliff.' The light ahead grew brighter as they neared the last twist in the chasm. 'I'll rig the rope, and . . .'

He trailed off as he rounded the last corner – and heard a rising noise. The others stopped behind him. 'What's that?' Nina asked.

The answer came a moment later as an Apache helicopter gunship rose into view, its cannon swinging towards them.

30

Dalton pushed forward, waving at the helicopter's pilot – Colonel Brik. 'Hey! It's me! Help me! I'm—'

Eddie seized him. 'Back!' he yelled, driving the others into cover around the corner—

The gunship opened fire, its thirty-millimetre chain gun blazing. Shells tore into the chasm's walls, ripping out chunks of rock.

Eddie shoved Dalton away and grabbed Nina, shielding her with his body. Jared stumbled against a wall as he tried to run, while the politician fled before tripping in his panic.

Brik jinked the aircraft sideways to give his gunner a better angle down the narrow cleft. The curve of the walls still blocked their targets from view, but that didn't ease the trigger finger of the man in the forward seat. More shells screamed against the cliffs, fractured stone spalling in all directions.

'Move, move!' Eddie screamed, barely audible over the gun's thunder. A lump of rock smacked against his head as he pushed Nina onwards. Just ahead of them, Jared managed to hobble around the next bend before his leg gave way.

The cannon fire stopped, a few last pieces of debris ricocheting past. Then the only movement was the dust blown through the ravine by the rotor downwash. 'What the hell was *that*?' Nina demanded.

'That was one of our Petens!' Jared replied, shocked. The Apache – Peten, meaning 'adder', was the Hebrew name for the American aircraft – was painted in the brown and grey camouflage pattern of the Israeli Air Force. 'Why's it attacking *us*?'

'I bet *he* knows,' Eddie growled, going to Dalton. He dragged him upright. 'Hey! Where did that fucking chopper come from?'

The politician was wide-eyed with fear. 'It's some old contact of Cross,' he panted. 'Colonel Brik, base commander at Ovda. Cross must have called him.'

'Still think he's on your side?' said Nina angrily. 'He just tried to kill us!'

'He hasn't stopped,' Eddie warned. The Apache's engine note changed, the gunship pulling back from the cliff and descending. 'Get in further – go, go!'

They squeezed through the narrow clench, but Eddie knew they were still not safe. 'Cover your ears!' he cried.

'Why, what's happ—' Dalton began, but the sight of the others pressing their palms firmly to their heads rapidly prompted him to do the same. Eddie hunched down, bracing himself against the wall as he again shielded Nina—

A sharp hiss – then the entire cliff shook with the impact of a rocket. Another *whoosh*, and a second missile struck just inside the cleft. A gritty shock wave blasted pulverised fragments of stone down the passage, the blast knocking those within to the ground.

The echoes faded. Eddie coughed, spitting out dust. 'Is everyone okay?'

'I . . . I think so,' said Nina, wincing. Despite Eddie's efforts to protect her, pain coursed through her hip where a flying rock had struck her. 'We were lucky.'

'They haven't given up,' Eddie said ominously. He stood, listening. Even with the ravine's strange acoustics, it was easy to tell that the gunship was on the move. Seconds later, a hot wind stinking of burnt aviation fuel tore through their shelter as the gunship thundered directly overhead.

Dalton pushed himself back against the wall. 'Oh God! They're going to shoot us from above!'

'They can't lower the gun that far,' Eddie told him. 'And this place is too twisty for them to get a clear shot . . . Shit!' Realisation hit him. 'They're going to the other end to seal us in!'

Nina looked after the aircraft with alarm. 'How many rockets do they have?'

'Too fucking many.' He had seen rocket pods beneath the Apache's stub wings; each could hold nineteen Hydra or CRV7 seventy-millimetre unguided missiles.

'*Do* something, Chase!' cried Dalton.

'Like what?' he snapped, drawing the Desert Eagle. 'Shoot it down with this?'

'Why not? It's huge! I know those helicopters are armoured, but—'

'The cockpit can take a hit from a fifty-cal round. I *might* get through the armour somewhere else, but I've only got a few bullets left. I fired an entire mag at Cross's chopper and didn't cause enough damage to bring it down – shit, incoming!' He heard the Apache's engine note change again and hurriedly put down the handgun to cover his ears. The others did the same—

More rockets pounded the far end of the cleft. This time Brik ordered his gunner to keep firing, missile after missile exploding against the cliffs. The ground shook with the man-made earthquake, then a deeper, more fearsome vibration flung everyone to the floor again as rock gave way under the onslaught.

An entire section of the massif collapsed into the hollow, hundreds of tons of debris plunging down the sinkhole, and more blocking the narrow passage through the cliffs. Another blinding, choking wave of dust rolled over the fugitives.

Eddie checked that Nina had not suffered any more injuries, then looked through the haze to find Jared and Dalton. 'Are you okay?'

'Yeah, but we're trapped in here!' the Israeli replied.

The dust swirled in the Apache's downdraught as the gunship passed back overhead. Dalton watched it in dismay. 'So . . . so what are they going to do? Hover at the end of the ravine and pick us off if we show our faces?'

'Pretty much,' Eddie told him, helping Nina up.

'There must be *something* you can do!'

'Oh, so now I'm the answer to all your problems? We can't get back to the temple, and if we try to climb down the cliff, they'll shoot us.' The Englishman tipped his head, looking up between the sheer walls. 'I could chimney-climb to the top, but there's no cover, so they'd only have to gain a bit of height to take a shot—'

He broke off. He had still been in the SAS when the Apache entered British military service, and had taken the opportunity to get a close look at the new machine that would be providing his fellow servicemen with air support. Now a memory returned from when he had actually sat inside one. The gunship's cockpit was indeed designed to resist bullets, but not from every angle. One part had been left unarmoured to save weight, on the grounds that it would never normally be exposed to an enemy . . .

Nina realised that he was forming a plan. 'What is it?' she asked.

'*I* might be able to take a shot,' he said, ejecting the Desert Eagle's magazine to count the remaining rounds. Four, including the one already chambered. 'If the Israeli Apache is like the British one, then the window right over the pilot's head is regular Perspex rather than bulletproof. I can shoot the bastard – if I can get to the right angle.' He slapped the mag back into place, then gave his companions a grim look. 'Problem is, to get to that angle, someone'll have to keep 'em busy.' He quickly explained his idea.

'That's suicide!' Dalton objected.

'Then you'll be glad to know I wasn't expecting you to volunteer.' He turned to Jared. 'Sorry, but you're the best bet.'

The young man straightened, wincing as he put weight on his injured leg. 'I'll get it done.'

'Eddie, he can't,' Nina protested. 'He won't be able to move fast enough!'

'I can't get *him* to do it,' said Eddie, with a contemptuous jerk of his thumb at Dalton, 'and I'm not bloody letting you try. Not with our baby on board.'

'I can do it, Nina,' Jared assured her.

'And we need to do it now.' The helicopter had moved back over the valley to watch the open end of the cleft. 'Okay, Jared, wait until I'm almost at the top and then show yourself. Hopefully that'll keep 'em occupied long enough for me to get into position.'

'And if it doesn't?' asked Dalton.

'Then I'll chuck you off the cliff into their rotors!' Ignoring the grey-haired man's outrage, he went to Nina. 'Okay, love, I'll get going now. Whatever you do, stay safe.' He kissed her, then gently placed one hand against the swell of her lower body. 'Both of you.'

He hurried back to the narrowest part of the passage and began his ascent, arms and legs spread to give himself support on each side of the fissure. The climb was quick at first, but before long the strain of holding his full weight started to slow him. He twisted to brace one shoulder against a wall, taking some of the pressure off his arms, and looked up. About thirty feet to go; halfway there.

He resumed his climb. Each step crunched against the limestone, dust and grit falling away from his feet. His breathing became heavier as he shuffled upwards. A chimney climb would normally be made in a crack in the face of a cliff, giving him three walls where he could find handholds and support, but here there was nothing but air on two sides.

And the cleft was gradually widening the higher he went. He could no longer use his shoulders for support, instead having to push his palms against the wall behind him. If his arms weakened, or his feet slipped on the crumbling surface, he would plunge straight back down.

To his death, from this height.

Fifty feet. Just ten to go. He glanced down, seeing the others watching. 'Jared, get ready!' he called.

Five feet. The rock, now fully exposed to the elements, became rougher. More grip, but it was also more fragile.

He looked towards the valley. A dark shape was visible through the rippling heat haze, the Apache drifting lazily sideways as its crew watched the entrance to the crevice. Shit! It was too high; they would spot him the moment he reached the clifftop. 'Go now, *now*!'

Jared heard the call. 'Okay, wish me luck,' he said, starting down the passage.

Nina watched his limp grow more pronounced with each step. 'Jared, you can't,' she said, hurrying after him.

'I can't let you do it,' he replied.

'I can't let *you* do it! You can hardly walk, never mind run. You're about to deliberately put yourself in front of a machine gun – if you can't move fast enough, it'll kill you!'

'Nina, you're pregnant—'

'Yeah, I'm pregnant. But as Eddie reminded me, I'm not an invalid, and even with a baby inside me I'm still quicker than you.' To prove her point, she darted past him. He tried to block her, but the mere effort of pivoting on his wounded leg caused him to gasp and stagger. 'I'm not going to let you kill yourself just because you want to prove how tough you are.'

'No, don't!' he cried, hobbling after her, only to clutch at the rock for support as he almost fell again. 'I promised Eddie—'

'I promised him *more*, when I married him,' Nina replied, glancing back up at her husband. 'But I never promised that I'd always do exactly what he told me. Seriously, what's that all about?' She composed herself. 'Now get back and watch Dalton. I've got a feeling I'll need as much room to run as I can get.'

Before Jared could object, she scurried on, a curve in the confined channel taking him – and Eddie – out of sight. The gunship's engines became louder as she crept to the final corner and peered around it.

The opening was no longer a vertical crack, a ragged chunk of rock having been blasted from one side as if a giant had taken a bite from the cliff. The helicopter was out of sight, but getting closer. From what Eddie had said, the gunner would have his sights fixed upon the cleft. She would only have a few seconds between making herself visible and the first shells landing – if she was lucky. If the man in the chopper had razor-sharp reactions, she might not even get *one* second.

The brutal aircraft drifted into view against the empty sky. It was higher than her position, the cannon under its nose pointed down at its target. She needed it to descend for Eddie's plan to work.

There was only one way to make that happen.

Nina steeled herself . . . then stepped into view.

Eddie was still straining to hold himself just below the top of the crevasse, his eyes locked on the gunship. He couldn't risk climbing out into the open, but nor could he stay where he was for ever. 'Come on, Jared,' he whispered. 'Give me my shot . . .'

The Apache continued its lazy motion – then suddenly the engine note changed.

★ ★ ★

369

Nina stared up at the helicopter for what felt like an eternity, the insectile machine's silhouette burning itself into her vision. Then movement from its gun turret snapped her back into the moment.

The chain gun's muzzle flashed with fire as she turned and ran back down the passage. The first shell hit the ground where she had been standing, the anti-armour round ripping deep into the limestone before exploding and showering her with fragments. She shrieked, but could no longer hear her own voice over the pounding of thirty-millimetre fire.

The gunner tracked her. Even though she was out of his direct line of sight, the shrapnel from the shells bursting on the walls was as dangerous as a direct hit. Terrified, she sprinted for the next bend—

Red-hot agony seared into her thigh as a metal shard tore through skin. She screamed, falling.

More shells blasted the walls, the detonations closing in—

The cannon fell silent.

'Cease fire, cease fire!' Brik ordered. He had slipped the Apache sideways to maintain a firing angle down the tight ravine, but the person he had briefly glimpsed had made it back into cover.

From gunfire, at least.

'Switch to rockets,' he told the gunner. 'I'll bring us to firing position.' The gunship's missile pods were fixed, requiring the whole aircraft to be brought into line with their target.

'Two degrees to port,' the gunner told him. Brik applied pressure to a rudder pedal, turning the aircraft. A vertical line superimposed down the centre of the gunsight bisected the entrance. 'Okay. Bring us closer, descend ten metres.'

The colonel began the manoeuvre, the cross hairs slipping down towards the base of the cleft.

★ ★ ★

The moment the Apache fired, Eddie pulled himself on to the clifftop. If his plan had worked, Jared, acting as his decoy to draw the aircrew's attention, would have already retreated beyond the chain gun's line of fire, forcing the gunner to switch to rockets – and requiring the helicopter to come lower to line up its fixed weapons. That would put him out of sight for the precious seconds he needed.

If the plan hadn't worked, his friend would already be dead.

The firing stopped. The gunship hung in the air . . . then descended.

Eddie ran for the cliff's edge. The Apache came back into sight. It was about a hundred metres away, but drawing closer, still gradually losing height.

He could see the weak spot – the top window of the upper canopy, right in front of the main rotor head. But to his dismay he realised he didn't have a clear shot. The gunship was now too *low*, the spinning rotor in the way. A bullet might pass cleanly through and hit its target . . . or strike a carbon-fibre blade and be deflected away.

No matter what, he had to take the shot before the gunship fired its rockets. He lined up the Desert Eagle's sights – and pulled the trigger.

Sparks and paint flakes spat from behind the cockpit. His aim wasn't at fault; as he'd feared, the bullet had glanced off the rotor and been thrown off target. Now he only had three bullets left.

And the Apache's crew knew he was there.

Colonel Brik hadn't heard the gunshot, the Apache's roar and the insulation of his helmet blotting out most external sounds, but he couldn't miss the sharp *clank* of a large-calibre bullet impact less than a metre behind his head. He swore, looking up to see a figure on the cliff. 'Hostile, above! Take him out!'

The gunner searched for the new threat. The chain gun,

slaved to his head movements, followed his gaze – only to clunk to a stop with a warning buzz as it reached the limits of its travel. 'Can't traverse!'

Brik was already increasing power. The Apache rose towards its prey.

Eddie took aim again as the gunship climbed. The chain gun was at maximum elevation; it would be able to target him in moments—

He fired. The second shot did no better than the first, the bullet twanging off the rotors. So did the third. Only one round left. The cockpit's upper canopy came into clear view beneath the whirling blades, but he was out of time.

The cannon strained against its restraints, then finally found its target—

The Englishman unleashed his last shot.

It struck home, punching through the acrylic window into the cockpit to hit Brik in the head.

His composite flight helmet was built to resist normal small-arms fire, but the Desert Eagle's half-inch-wide bullet was considerably more powerful. It shattered as it tore through the protective layers, but the individual fragments still carried enough momentum to rip into the top of the Israeli's skull. Bone splintered, hot metal churning through brain matter like mixer blades.

The gunner fired the chain gun – as Brik's spasming limbs sent the Apache lurching violently sideways. Eddie dived backwards as the first few shells hit the cliff, but the rest of the shots went wide.

The helicopter spun towards the ground. The gunner screamed, hauling frantically at his duplicate flight controls, but Brik still had a death grip on his own sticks—

The main rotor smashed against the sheer cliff below the

cleft. The blades disintegrated, and the airframe plunged as gravity eagerly reclaimed its hold. The Apache hit the ground hard, the stumps of the rotors digging into the earth and flipping it over before fuel and munitions ignited, blasting the tumbling wreck into a billion blazing fragments.

The rumble of the explosion faded. Eddie shook off grit and crawled to the edge. The gunship's burning remains were strewn below – along with those of the Land Rover, which had been parked beneath the passage. 'Bollocks,' he said as he recovered his breath. 'Looks like we're in for a long walk.'

He stood and went to the top of the ravine, looking into it with trepidation as he searched for Jared – only for his heart to freeze in fear. There was a figure lying unmoving below, but it wasn't the Israeli.

It was his wife.

31

Eddie ran back to the chasm's narrowest point and made a rapid descent. He dropped the last ten feet and shoved past Dalton, ignoring the politician's questions as he ran down the passage. The limping Jared was ahead; he quickly caught up. 'What the fuck have you *done*?' he roared at the younger man.

'I tried to stop her!' Jared protested.

'Not fucking hard enough!'

'She got past me and ran off! I tried to catch up, but . . .' He regarded his wounded leg. More blood had soaked the bandage. 'Then the chopper started shooting.'

Eddie held in another curse and ran on, rounding a corner to see broken rocks strewn over the floor – and a dust-covered figure lying amongst them. He hurried to her. 'Nina! Nina, are you okay? Can you hear me?'

No movement for agonising seconds as he checked for a pulse . . . then she painfully turned her head, squinting up at him. 'Did you get it?'

'Yeah, I got it.'

'Hooray for us . . .' She tried to sit up, but cried out as she moved her leg. 'Oh! Damn, that hurts!'

He saw blood on her thigh and examined the injury. 'Looks like shrapnel. Jared!' he said as the Israeli hobbled into view. 'The first aid kit's in the bag – get that useless shithead Dalton to bring it.'

'Is she okay?' Jared asked, worried.

'No,' he snarled, ''cause you let her do your job! Go!'

'Don't be angry at him,' Nina told her husband as the shamefaced young man turned away. 'He wanted to do it, but I stopped him.' She gestured towards the entrance, the passage now pockmarked with ragged holes. 'And I'm glad I did, because if I hadn't, he would have been killed.'

'You're glad you got a piece of shrap in your leg?'

'Okay, maybe not *glad* exactly . . .' She shifted position as carefully as she could to look down at her stomach. 'God, I hope she's all right.'

'Me too. I'll get that bit of metal out, then check if she's okay.'

'How? I don't think we brought an ultrasound scanner.'

The corners of his mouth creased upwards, just a little. 'Getting sarky? You can't be that badly hurt, then.'

'Yeah, you just keep telling me that and maybe I'll start to believe it.' Nina too managed a small, pained smile.

Jared soon returned, Dalton following with the backpack. Eddie took out the first-aid kit and cleaned Nina's wound, then used tweezers to grip the protruding end of the metal shard. 'Okay, this'll hurt,' he warned.

Her sarcasm was now more overt. 'Yeah, I'm *so* glad you told me that in advance.'

'Well, I could've just yanked it out without warning while I was in the middle of talking to keep you distracted, but—' He yanked it out without warning.

She shrieked. 'Aah! Son of a—Bastard—*Shit!*'

Dalton winced at the spurt of blood, but still found the time to be patronising. 'The world's most famous archaeologist, eloquent and classy as always.'

'Shut the fuck up,' the couple told him in unison. Dalton huffed.

While Eddie dressed the wound, Jared limped to the end of the passage and peered at the wreckage below. 'They took out the truck!' he said as he returned.

Dalton went in alarm to see for himself. 'We're *stranded*?'

'Someone'll be along soon,' Eddie replied, unworried.

'We're in the middle of a desert! How can you possibly know that?'

'Because when a twenty-million-dollar helicopter gunship crashes and explodes, the people who own it usually want to find out what happened pretty sharpish. And I doubt shooting at a pregnant archaeologist, a Mossad agent and an ex-president was an officially sanctioned mission.' He looked at Jared. 'How far away's its base?'

'Ovda? About thirty kilometres,' the Israeli replied.

'So I bet you there'll be another chopper here in the next ten minutes.'

'Hopefully not another gunship,' said Nina. She drew in a sharp breath as Eddie finished working on her wound, then carefully sat up and regarded Dalton. 'So while we're waiting, *Mr President*, I think we should talk about Cross. Now that he's tried to kill you, it's safe to assume you aren't best buddies any more?'

'You've got that right,' Dalton growled. 'That son of a bitch! He *used* me!'

'Matthew chapter seven, verse fifteen: "Beware of false prophets",' said Nina, to his annoyance. 'He doesn't care about your political rehabilitation, and he never did. He just saw you as a means to an end, a way to bring about the apocalypse. So maybe now you should stop thinking about how to protect him and start thinking about how to save your own ass.'

'Not much point getting back into power if the world ends five minutes later,' Eddie pointed out.

'If you tell us where Cross plans to release the angels, I'll do everything I can with the UN, Interpol and the US and Antiguan governments to explain that you helped us try to stop him,' Nina said. 'If you don't, and Cross succeeds . . .' Her expression hardened. 'I'll let you twist in the wind by your balls as you're brought up on charges of terrorism and mass murder. Good luck with your immunity deal, Mr President.'

Worry was clear in Dalton's eyes, but he still jutted his jaw in defiance. 'I'm not going to be intimidated into making deals. I was the President of the United States, not some two-bit police informant!'

Eddie advanced upon him. 'If I chucked him off the cliff, do you think anyone'd really care?'

Dalton took a worried step backwards, but before he could respond, Jared looked around sharply. 'Quiet,' said the Israeli. 'I can hear something.'

Nina picked it up a moment later. 'Sounds like a helicopter.' In the distance, she heard the thrum of rotor blades.

Eddie gave Dalton a last threatening glare, then started towards the entrance. 'Be careful,' Nina called. 'They might shoot first and ask questions later.'

'I'll be ready to run, just in case!' He looked down the valley. The burning Apache had left an unmissable marker of its position: a column of dirty black smoke. He leaned out of the ravaged chasm to scan the sky, quickly spotting the dark dot of an approaching helicopter. To his relief, it had the rounded profile of a transport aircraft rather than the narrow, angular shape of a gunship.

It took the chopper a few minutes to reach the crash site, circling overhead before descending into the valley. It was military, an Israeli Black Hawk in pale desert camouflage. It appeared unarmed, but all branches of Israel's military were ready for combat at a moment's notice, so Eddie decided to play things with care. He moved to the centre of the opening, waving both arms above his head.

The Black Hawk slowed to a hover, one of its side doors sliding open. A man inside stared at him through binoculars. Eddie changed his signal, spreading both arms and holding them up in a Y-shape to indicate that he needed help – and also to make it plain that he was not holding a weapon. The helicopter's passenger looked back down at the wreckage, but it was obvious there was nobody alive in the flaming tangle of metal. Brief discussion with the pilot over his headset, then the man made an exaggerated thumbs-up gesture and the aircraft came about to head for the clifftop above.

The Englishman returned to the others. 'They're landing,' he announced. 'Jared, you do the talking. It'll be better to have a Mossad agent tell 'em what's happened rather than the bloke who just shot down one of their Apaches with a handgun . . .'

Members of the Black Hawk's crew descended into the ravine on ropes to be given Jared's account of events; unsure how to take it, and especially confused by the presence of a former world leader, they settled for lifting the injured out on stretchers before taking them back to their base at Ovda. Even without knowing any Hebrew, Nina and Eddie could tell that the crew were deeply suspicious of their passengers and their involvement in the loss of their commander's aircraft, but it was also clear that the relatively junior military officers and men aboard did not want to tangle with the Mossad. One of Jared's first requests – or demands – was for a field telephone, which he used to contact his superior in Tel Aviv.

That same superior arrived at the base by helicopter as the sun set two hours later, meeting its new acting commander before both men strode into the hospital ward where the rescuees were being kept under guard. 'Sir!' said Jared as they entered, jumping to his feet even with his injury and snapping to attention.

Eli Shalit was a small, thin man with prominent cheekbones and a bristling moustache. He waved a hand for the agent to sit back down, then cast his intense gaze over the room's other occupants. 'Dr Nina Wilde and Edward Chase,' he said. 'Welcome to Israel. And you too, Mr President,' he added, with a distinctly dismissive nod at Dalton.

'You know who we are?' Nina asked.

'Jared told me on the telephone, but I had also read his report on the events of four months ago, when he was seconded to the Criminal Sanctions Unit. Israel is very grateful to you both for helping to eliminate that nest of Nazis.'

'Our pleasure,' said Eddie, a little sarcastically.

Shalit gave him a cynical smile. 'I know that you are not a great fan of the Mossad. But that does not lessen our gratitude. Now.' He put his hands behind his back. 'We have a situation, I believe.'

'You could say that,' Nina told him. 'There's a religious maniac about to unleash chemical weapons because he thinks that bringing about the apocalypse will let him learn all of God's secrets. That's definitely situation-y.'

'Indeed it is.' The Mossad official's gaze went to Dalton. 'Mr President, your presence here is causing some . . . trouble, shall we say, in our government. You had important friends here – I mean, *have* friends, of course,' he corrected, in a way that suggested the slip was by no means accidental – 'who saw to it that you were able to enter our country incognito, who provided you with help, resources . . . only now, I am told by one of my best men,' a nod at Jared, 'it seems that you are connected to an act of terrorism in the Caribbean, and to the madman who intends to carry out more of these acts. What do you have to say, Mr President?'

The colour had visibly leached from Dalton's face; nevertheless, he drew himself up to stand tall and arrogant before the Israeli. 'First, I would point out that I am in no way responsible for any of the acts carried out by an individual with whom I had the misfortune of being acquainted before I realised his true intentions—'

He paused at Nina's disbelieving cry of '*What?*', then continued: 'Second, I would also point out that as soon as I realised these intentions, I disassociated myself with this individual and have done everything in my power to help track him down and prevent further loss of life.'

Nina almost laughed at his sheer gall. 'You are so full of shit! If it wasn't for you, none of this would ever have happened.'

'We made an agreement, if you recall,' Dalton pointed out. 'I give you information about Cross's plans, and in return you make it unequivocally clear to all the relevant authorities that I helped you try to stop him. You were the one who offered that deal, Dr Wilde. I agreed to it, so I expect you to honour it. And your husband too,' he added, with a warning look at Eddie.

The Englishman glowered back at him, folding his arms. 'Don't remember shaking on it.'

'Eddie,' said Nina reluctantly. 'He's right, we need him. And we can't afford to waste time – Cross and the Fishers might be halfway to their targets already.'

'Don't I even get to punch him in the face?' Eddie asked, clenching one hand into a fist. Dalton twitched.

'As much as I'd like that, no. Not this time.'

'Next time, then,' he muttered, before nodding to the politician. 'Okay, we'll put in a word for you. Won't be the one I'm thinking of right now, though.'

'ou've got your deal,' Nina told Dalton. 'Now it's your turn. ..'s Cross's plan?'

Dalton took a couple of heavy breaths before answering, aware that whatever agreements were in place, he was still linking himself to the cult leader's plot. 'All right,' he said at last. 'Simeon and Anna Fisher are going to take the statues to Mecca, and to the Vatican in Rome.'

'As opposed to the Vatican in Hogfoot, Arkansas?' Nina said scathingly. 'Yeah, I know where it is.'

'Mecca. And Rome.' Shalit turned from side to side as if looking towards each of the two cities. 'I would not describe either as a close friend to Israel – though one is far less friendly than the other. I am sure you can guess which. But it is not in Israel's current interests that it is destroyed. We have enough enemies without arousing a billion and a half angry Muslims against us. And they *would* rise against us, even if we had nothing to do with it.' Another edged smile at Eddie. 'Those with no reason to hate us will still take any reason to fight us.'

'They're going to release the gas there?' Nina asked.

'Obviously,' Dalton snapped. 'On the flight over, Cross kept saying how the timing was perfect. The Hajj is on in Mecca right now, so there are Christ knows how many Muslims there on pilgrimage, and the Pope has an audience in St Peter's Square tomorrow, which will also have thousands, tens of thousands of people watching. That was what he wanted: maximum victims, maximum impact.'

'It's also what *you* wanted,' Eddie said, disgusted. 'Typical fucking politician. You're already trying to distance yourself from it!'

'So that was how the two of you planned to set off a religious war?' asked Nina. 'Attack Mecca and the Vatican, let it come out that American evangelical Christians were responsible, and watch the fireworks while you set up Fortress America?'

Eddie shook his head, speaking before the politician could issue another denial of his direct involvement. 'That's what I get for missing Sunday school. I never read the bit of the Bible where Jesus says that mass murder is brilliant. Oh, wait, that's because it *doesn't fucking exist*!'

'You're not Christians any more than Jim Jones and his crazies were,' Nina told Dalton.

'Don't lump me in with those loons,' he replied. 'I had nothing to do with Cross's followers. They joined him because they wanted him to bring about the end of the world.'

'Which he did, for them.'

'Yes, he did. And don't forget that you're a part of it too,' Dalton went on, jabbing an accusatory finger at her. 'You found the angels for him.'

Nina gawped in sheer disbelief at his attempt to swing the blame back on to her. 'Only because Eddie and I were kidnapped, *on your orders*! Jesus!'

Shalit held up a placatory hand. 'Dr Wilde, we have the information. The question now is: how shall we act upon it?'

'We've got to stop 'em, obviously,' said Eddie.

'Yeah,' agreed Nina, turning to Shalit. 'You need to contact the authorities in Rome and Mecca, tell them to watch for Simeon and Anna.'

The Israeli spymaster smiled mockingly. 'I am sure the Saudis will be happy to obey the Mossad.' Even Dalton smirked.

'Okay, then contact the UN and get *them* to talk to the Saudis!' she pressed on, annoyed. 'Call Oswald Seretse in New York.'

'You've probably got his number,' said Eddie, with a sly glance at Jared. 'Someone once told me Mossad has *everyone's* number.' The younger man grinned.

'I am sure we have,' replied Shalit. 'I shall make the call.'

'What about the find?' Nina asked. 'The Temple of God, and the Ark of the Covenant – they need to be secured.'

'They will be,' he assured her. 'I have already arranged for troops to guard the site until our archaeologists can reach it. And I shall also notify the IHA, of course. Such a discovery is of global importance, after all. Now, Dr Wilde, Mr Chase, if you will come with me?'

The couple followed him to the door. Dalton started after them, but Shalit held up a hand. 'Mr President, stay here, please.'

Dalton was affronted. 'This is a diplomatic matter; I should be involved—'

'I am *being* diplomatic when I say that you should stay here. For your own safety.' There was an unmistakable hint of threat behind his politeness. 'I have already spoken to officials from your State Department. They have requested that you be returned to the United States as soon as possible, on the orders of the White House.'

'What?' said the politician, startled.

'I guess President Cole wants to discuss your immunity deal,' Nina suggested, smiling coldly.

'Best of luck with that,' added Eddie. 'Jared, will you be okay?'

The young Israeli glanced dismissively at his injury. 'It'll take more than this to keep me down, *alter kocker*. I'll be back.'

The Englishman grinned. 'Glad to hear it. See you later, kid. And you, Mr President.' The Israeli gave the couple a cheery wave as they departed with Shalit, leaving the sputtering Dalton behind.

Shalit commandeered what had been Colonel Brik's office to call Seretse in New York. Once through, Nina explained what they had found in the desert, and what had happened afterwards. 'I see,' said the Gambian diplomat, speaking slowly and carefully, as if trying to process what he had just heard. 'I shall of course immediately contact the Saudi and Italian ambassadors to the UN, and the Vatican's permanent observer. But the Fishers could be in Italy and Saudi Arabia already – a private flight there from Israel would not take long.'

'I know, I know,' Nina replied wearily. 'Have the investigators in Antigua got any CCTV footage of Anna or Simeon they could send to the police and security forces?'

'Not yet, I am afraid,' said Seretse. 'Teams from the CDC and USAMRICD have entered the Mission to check the contamination levels, but their most recent report said the computers have been either wiped or encrypted.'

'Might have known,' Eddie complained. 'Bloody spooks, they're all paranoid. We'll give you descriptions so you can put together e-fits, then.'

'Digital facial reconstructions are not as useful as photographs,' said Shalit with a small shake of the head. 'The Mossad has run tests; even top agents failed forty per cent of the time to recognise a suspect when trying to identify them from an e-fit alone. That number is much higher with ordinary law enforcement personnel.'

'So what do you suggest?' Nina said with exasperation. 'We've got to *try* to stop them!'

'There is something you can do,' said Seretse. 'If you go to the Vatican and Mecca in person, you will be able to confirm any possible sightings of the Fishers. I know it is a long shot, but we must try. Will you go?'

Eddie and Nina exchanged tired looks. 'We don't have much bloody choice, do we?' said the Yorkshireman.

'No, we don't,' she agreed with a marked lack of enthusiasm. 'Everyone does remember that I'm four months pregnant, right? I'm supposed to be eating crazy food and being waited on hand and foot, not rushing around the world and being shot at!' She took a long, deep breath. 'Okay, rant over, I'm done.'

'In that case, I will tell the ambassadors that you will assist with the search in person,' said Seretse. 'Nina, you should go to Rome; Eddie to Mecca. I am sure you understand why I did not suggest sending you to Saudi Arabia, Nina,' he added.

'Countries that oppress women, flog bloggers and behead people for sorcery aren't exactly high on my list of vacation destinations,' she said scathingly. 'I'll take Rome any day. But St Peter's Square is huge! There'll be thousands of people there if the Pope's giving an address. And I can't even begin to imagine how many people there'll be in Mecca during the Hajj.'

'Yeah, I know,' said Eddie. 'Just have to hope the cops are on the ball – and that we get lucky.'

'I shall make the arrangements,' Seretse told them. 'It may take some time, but I will call you back as soon as everything is confirmed.'

'Great,' Nina muttered as he disconnected. She turned to her husband. 'Oh God. How do we keep ending up in these situations? I tell you, after this is over, we're taking a three-year vacation.'

He grinned. 'You'd be bored out of your mind after a month.'

'Probably. But we've got the baby to look forward to, so who knows? Motherhood might be the best thing ever to happen in my life. Apart from meeting you,' she added.

'It will be, I'm sure of it,' he said. 'So you're feeling more confident about being a mum now, are you?'

It was her turn to grin. 'I'm probably tempting fate by saying this, but after everything else I've been through since I met you, I should be able to handle a baby.' They both looked around at a chuckle from Shalit. 'Something to say?'

'Only that whether you are a soldier, a scientist or a spy, nothing can prepare you,' the Israeli replied, humour in his eyes.

'That's reassuring,' Eddie said.

'I'm ready for it,' Nina insisted. 'Whatever it brings.'

'Yeah?'

'Yeah.'

'Good.' He kissed her. "Cause so am I.' A glance back at the phone. 'Just a pain in the arse that we've got to save the world first.'

'I know,' she said with a sigh. 'But we need to make sure our daughter's got a world to be born into, so . . . let's finish this.'

32

Saudi Arabia

Even with his United Nations diplomatic status temporarily restored, Eddie still faced bureaucratic obstacles on his arrival at the King Abdulaziz international airport outside the city of Jeddah the following morning. The first came when a customs officer checked his passport and declared with a scowl that he had recently visited Israel; the fact that the jet chartered by the UN had *come* from Israel escaped the man's notice. Not even Eddie's diplomatic papers dissuaded the surly apparatchik from insisting he was not allowed to enter the country, and only the appearance of more senior figures silenced him.

However, this brought other problems. The newcomers, clad in traditional robes and ghutra headgear, were from the Mabahith, the Saudi domestic security agency: the country's secret police. This in itself made Eddie wary of them, as the Mabahith was infamous for human rights violations and its brutal treatment of anyone who spoke out against the repressive Saudi regime – and the first words from the younger of the two, a skinny, broad-nosed man in his twenties, suggested they were not going to be helpful. 'You have wasted your time coming here, Mr Chase.'

'Nice to meet you too,' the Englishman replied sarcastically.

The second man, a craggy fifty-something, was more polite.

'Welcome to Saudi Arabia, Mr Chase. I am Abdul Rajhi of the General Investigation Directorate. This is my associate, Prince Saleh al Farhan.'

'Prince?' said Eddie in surprise.

Rajhi did not respond, instead continuing: 'We are grateful for your help in discovering a terrorist threat, but I am afraid that you will not be able to help us search for this man Fisher in person.'

'Why not?'

His expression became patronising. 'Because you are not a Muslim, of course. Unbelievers are not permitted to enter the holy city of Mecca. We have the picture you provided; it is already being distributed to police, hotel staff and officials at the Kaaba. We will find him without you.'

'You still might not recognise him,' Eddie objected. 'There's a big difference between looking at a photofit and a real person. And he could be in disguise. I'm the only person who's actually seen the guy before – you need me there.'

'We will easily be able to find a black American,' said al Farhan haughtily. 'We have records of everyone who has entered our country, and who is staying at every hotel.'

'What, you think he'll be using his real name? He'll have a passport from Sudan or somewhere and be calling himself Muhammad.'

'That may be so,' al Farhan said, drawing himself to his full height, 'but you will not be allowed into Mecca!'

Eddie was about to remind him of his diplomatic status, but one look at the brick wall of the Saudi's face told him it would be pointless; even with the threat of murder on a massive scale, rules and dogma still counted above all else. Instead he turned to the older man. 'You've been in your job for a while, yes?' he asked.

Rajhi was surprised by the question. 'Yes. Over twenty years.'

'And you're pretty high up in the Mabahith?'

He nodded. 'I am, yes.'

'Then you must remember what happened two years ago. In Mecca. At the Kaaba.' Rajhi frowned, not sure where he was heading. 'With Pramesh Khoil?'

Now realisation dawned, the official's eyes widening. 'So how's the Black Stone these days?' Eddie pushed on.

'The Black Stone,' Rajhi echoed, to his companion's puzzlement. 'You are *that* Eddie Chase?'

'No, there's seventeen of us, we work different days. Of course it's bloody me!'

Al Farhan asked a question in Arabic, but his superior hurriedly shushed him. The older man thought for a moment, then said to Eddie: 'May I speak with you in private?'

'Go ahead.'

To al Farhan's consternation, Rajhi took Eddie aside for a whispered conversation. 'The theft of the Black Stone is one of my country's most closely guarded secrets! If it was ever revealed to the masses that one of our holiest relics had been stolen – by infidels! – and replaced by a replica, there would be . . .' He didn't need to finish; his horrified shake of the head was enough to paint a picture of chaos.

'Yeah, but me and Nina got it back for you,' Eddie reminded him. 'Now, she's not likely to include that bit in her memoirs, and I won't be shouting about it on Twitter, but it'd be *really appreciated* if you'd let me help you.'

Rajhi considered that, then waved al Farhan over. 'Under exceptional circumstances, non-Muslims are allowed to enter Mecca,' he announced. Now it was his companion's turn to be shocked. 'I consider this threat to the Hajj to be one of those times. Mr Chase will help us find this terrorist.' The younger man began a strenuous objection, but Rajhi made a firm gesture to silence him before turning back to the Yorkshireman. 'As a representative of the United Nations, you will be expected to follow the highest standards of behaviour.'

'I'm always on my best,' Eddie replied with a broad grin.

Rajhi did not seem convinced, clearly knowing Eddie's reputation, but had no choice but to accept his word. 'Very well. I will have a helicopter take us to Mecca.'

'Cool. I can play some bingo while I'm there.' Both Saudis regarded him with vaguely offended bewilderment. 'British humour,' he told them. 'Come on, let's find this guy.'

The flight from Jeddah to Mecca took Eddie across the desert into the climbing sun. There was little between the two cities except sand and mountain ranges, but even from a distance of twenty miles he could pick out the grey sprawl of Islam's most holy settlement – and its most grandiose landmark.

'Is that the clock?' he asked, pointing at a dark, angular shape rising from the city's heart.

'The Abraj Al Bait tower,' al Farhan told him via his headphones, with distinct pride. 'The tallest building in Saudi Arabia – and one of the tallest in the world.'

'Your mates in Dubai have still beaten you, though,' said Eddie, taking a small amount of pleasure in the Saudi's annoyance at having his bubble pricked.

'The Kingdom Tower in Jeddah will soon be taller,' al Farhan insisted. 'But the clock tower is still bigger than anything in America. Or England.'

'Size isn't everything.'

Rajhi made a muted sound of amusement. 'I can tell you do not know our country.'

The helicopter passed over the rocky hills west of the city, heading for its centre. The Grand Mosque, to which millions of Muslims made a pilgrimage each year, was clearly visible as a roughly circular complex of buildings surrounding the Kaaba, the cube-shaped structure that was home to the Black Stone. But it was overshadowed – at certain times of day, literally – by a mammoth piece of twenty-first-century engineering.

The Abraj Al Bait was a megastructure in every sense of the word. Over six hundred metres high, it dwarfed the likes of the Empire State Building and even One World Trade Center in New York not only in height but by sheer bulk, its broad base sprouting several smaller – though still skyscraper-tall – towers. The complex was topped by the world's largest clock, four vast gold-slathered faces displaying the time to all points of the compass. Even from miles away, Eddie could read it clearly; London's Big Ben was a wristwatch in comparison. The whole structure was a combination of five-star hotels and vast shopping malls, a monument not so much to Allah as Mammon. Only the wealthiest pilgrims could afford to look down upon the Grand Mosque from their suites over a quarter of a mile above.

And it was the helicopter's destination. Rajhi concluded a brisk discussion over the radio, then addressed Eddie. 'They think Fisher is at the Fairmont Hotel, in the clock tower,' he said. 'They have a copy of the passport he was using, and will have CCTV waiting so that you can identify him.'

'If you think it's him, why don't you just arrest him?' Eddie asked.

The security official sucked in air through his teeth. 'The Abraj Al Bait is owned by the government – by the royal family.' He glanced surreptitiously at his partner. 'The police do not want to cause a disturbance unless they are absolutely sure there is a threat.'

'Nobody wants to kick up a stink, right?' Eddie shook his head. 'If it's Fisher and he releases the gas, there really *will* be a stink.' He gazed at the approaching colossus, then down to the Grand Mosque. The great courtyard was already filled with pilgrims, slowly circling the Kaaba. 'If he's here, why hasn't he already done it? There are loads of people there – lots of targets. What's he waiting for?' He looked back at his companions. 'What times are your prayers today?'

'The next *salat* is at nine minutes past noon,' said al Farhan.

'I'd ask what time it is now, but, well . . .' He grinned and indicated the clock face, which told him it was ten past eleven, then became more serious. 'That's what he's waiting for. These guys really, *really* don't like Islam, so killing a load of Muslims in the middle of praying on their pilgrimage to Mecca would be pretty big for them symbolically.'

'That only gives us an hour to find him,' said Rajhi. 'But what if he has set the gas to be released on a timer?'

'When we catch him, we will make him tell us where it is,' al Farhan said ominously.

'Simeon Fisher is ex-special forces,' Eddie told him. 'You won't break him – not in time. But he'll probably have the angel with him.'

'How can you be sure?' asked Rajhi.

'He thinks he's one of the Witnesses from the Book of Revelation. They were killed before the seventh trumpet sounded – and since their boss wants that to happen, they're probably going to make it a suicide attack. They'll go out surrounded by their enemies . . . and take them with them.'

The clock loomed ever larger as the helicopter swung towards a helipad atop one of the lower towers. Up close, the domineering structure was revealed as gaudy, even ugly, traditional Arabian design elements like arched windows simply enlarged and stretched to fit the enormous slab-like walls without any consideration of human scale. Eddie admitted – and had also been told on numerous occasions by his wife – that he lacked taste in matters aesthetic, but even he considered this as tacky and vulgar as the worst excesses of Las Vegas. But he decided to keep his views on architecture from his hosts.

Dust blew from the pad as the chopper touched down – even almost fifty storeys up, the desert still constantly reminded everyone of its presence – and several men ran to meet it, heads low. Al Farhan gripped Eddie's arm before he could leave his seat. 'You are an unbeliever in our most holy city,' he said, eyes narrowed. 'Do not disrespect it, or us. Remember that.'

'How about remembering that I'm trying to stop a nutter killing thousands of people?' Eddie shot back, pulling free.

He stepped on to the helipad, feeling brief vertigo. The clock tower's summit was well over a thousand feet above him, more than the tallest building in London, but the sight of the surrounding horizon reminded him that he was already several hundred feet up. The disorientation passed, but all the same he fixed his eyes on the new arrivals: officers in the beige uniform and beret of the Saudi police, and two men in Western-style suits who engaged al Farhan in rapid conversation as the group headed for the building's entrance.

'This is Mr Essa, the hotel manager,' Rajhi told Eddie as they filed into an elevator. Essa was the older of the two suited men, a slim, elegant figure with a neatly trimmed grey beard. 'And Mr Nadhar, chief of security.'

Eddie greeted them. 'Have you found Simeon Fisher?'

'That was not the name he was using,' said Essa. Although he was of Middle Eastern ancestry, he had a distinct French accent. 'But he appears to be the man you are looking for. He checked in late last night. Mr Nadhar has pictures.' The elevator started its descent.

The other well-dressed man, somewhat bulkier than his boss, handed out sheets of paper to the visitors. Eddie took a close look. One was a colour photocopy of a passport. The country of origin was Mozambique, the name Samora Costo, but even with the addition of a moustache and beard, Simeon's face was unmistakable.

Another picture was a still from a lobby security camera. The figure at the reception desk was only small in the frame, but again Eddie recognised the Witness, the identification made easier by the bandage on his hand. 'That's him,' he said.

'Which room is he in?' asked al Farhan.

Nadhar checked a list. 'Room 1416.'

'Is he still there?'

'I checked the computer just before you arrived. He last used his keycard at around eight thirty this morning. But I do not know if he is still in his room.'

Rajhi issued orders in Arabic, one of the cops relaying them by radio. 'We will use a SWAT team,' he told Eddie.

'Risky,' replied the Englishman. 'You need to evacuate all the rooms around it – better yet, the whole floor. I've seen how fast this gas spreads; it's not like anything normal.'

'We know what we are doing,' sniffed al Farhan.

The elevator stopped at a lower floor. Essa briskly led the way through the hotel's corridors. Eddie took the opportunity to make a phone call to Nina. 'Hey. Where are you?' he asked.

'Just coming in to land,' she replied. 'What's happening there?'

'I'm at Simeon's hotel, but we haven't found him yet. The Saudis are going to raid his room.'

'Did you persuade them to evacuate the Grand Mosque?'

'I can't even get them to evacuate the hotel,' he sighed. 'What about you?'

'Well, I managed to speak to the Pope—'

'You know, I love that our conversations have "I spoke to the Pope" casually dropped into them.'

She laughed, putting a smile on his face. 'Yeah. I spoke to him by phone with Seretse, and tried to persuade him to call off today's audience. But he said no.'

'Seriously?'

'He said that if it's cancelled at such short notice, Anna will know we're on to her, and she might change her attack to an unpredictable time and place. In effect, he's acting as live bait to draw her out. I understand his reasoning, but I don't like it.'

'Not even you get to tell the Pope what to do, eh?'

'Sadly, no. And I've got so many good ideas!' Another laugh. 'But the authorities in Rome and at the Vatican have agreed full cooperation to track her down.'

'What time's his speech?'

'It's due to start at ten o'clock – that's noon, your time.'

'Just before prayers here,' Eddie noted grimly. 'They're either doing a simultaneous attack, or close to.' Ahead, he saw more uniformed cops waving away curious guests as a group in tactical gear hurried into the hotel. 'Okay, I've got to go. Call me when you get to the Vatican.'

'Will do. Love you.'

'I love you,' he replied. 'See you soon.' Hoping with all his heart that he would, he ended the call and followed the rest of his group into a conference room. The SWAT team were already prepping their weapons. 'What, you're just going to run up there and kick the door down?' he said. 'No recon?'

'There is no time,' al Farhan told him. 'If this gas is as deadly as you say, then we have to stop him before he can use it. Essa?'

The hotel manager gave the cops a hurried briefing in Arabic, using a laptop and projector to show a plan of the hotel's fourteenth floor. Room 1416 was on the building's southern side, overlooking the city, not the Grand Mosque. 'He won't be attacking from there, then,' Eddie mused, as much to himself as to Rajhi beside him.

'Why not?' asked the Saudi.

'Not enough targets. There's only a big empty construction site behind the hotel – I saw it when we landed. If his room faced the mosque, he could just smash a window and let the gas blow out over the crowd.'

'So where will he attack from?'

'Good question. Worst-case scenario is that he's already inside the mosque.'

'There is security at all entrances. They have been given his picture.'

'Yeah, but how many thousands of people go through every minute? Could you pick out one face from all that lot? You need to evacuate the place.'

Rajhi shook his head. 'I am afraid that is not possible,' he said, his resignation showing that the decision had already been made by someone above him.

Eddie muttered an obscenity, then looked back at al Farhan as he finished giving instructions to the SWAT team. They rapidly donned one-piece coveralls, then put on full-face respirator masks and secured the hoods tightly around them. Al Farhan put on a headset as the masked force marched out of the room. 'They know what to do,' he told Rajhi.

'I hope so,' said Eddie. 'What's the plan?'

The younger official gave him a scornful look. 'They are going to storm his room and capture or kill him, then secure the weapon. What else?'

'I dunno, maybe check if he's in there first? Fibre-optic camera, thermal scope, drone looking in through the window – hell, just knock on the door! And what about evacuating the other guests?'

'We do not have time to waste,' al Farhan sniffed. 'Now, be silent. I need to listen.' He turned away, pressing his headphones to his ears for emphasis.

'I will tell you what is happening,' Rajhi told Eddie as he found a headset of his own.

'Aren't you his boss?' Eddie asked. 'He's putting lives at risk by rushing into this.'

'I am his boss, yes,' said Rajhi, with a heavy nod. 'But he is a member of the House of Saud – the royal family.'

Eddie raised an eyebrow. 'So he really is a prince?'

'From one of the cadet branches, yes.' He lowered his voice as al Farhan spoke to the SWAT commander. 'There are thousands of princes. He is not in the line of succession, but he has the attention of those who are. It is . . . not in my best interest, shall we say, to get in his way. If he is successful today, it will be of great benefit to him politically.'

'And if he fucks up, a lot of people'll die,' Eddie countered. Rajhi's only response was a tired shrug. 'Great. Maybe I should've stayed at the airport after all.'

Al Farhan listened intently to the reports over the radio, then issued an instruction. 'They are on the fourteenth floor,' Rajhi reported to Eddie. 'Moving to the room . . . taking up positions.'

The other official glanced at him, for a moment almost seeming to be seeking approval – then he turned sharply away, his expression becoming determined. '*Hejwem!*'

The loud bang that followed was audible to Eddie even from Rajhi's headphones, as was a hubbub of shouting voices. 'They are in the room, searching, searching . . .' said the older man, holding his breath, then exhaling in a mix of disappointment and relief. 'He is not there.'

'What about the statue?' Eddie demanded.

Al Farhan relayed the question. Seconds passed . . . then the answer came. 'No. They cannot see it.'

'That means he's got it with him – he's definitely going to attack. Look, you've *got* to evacuate the mosque.'

The prince scowled at him. 'You do not tell me what to do!'

'If he releases the gas in the middle of a crowd, it'll kill everyone. I've seen it!'

Al Farhan stormed over to him, his nose just inches from the Englishman's. 'This is the Hajj – the holy pilgrimage! Two million people make it each year, and there are tens of thousands of them down there right now. Some have waited their whole lives to be here, spent everything they have to make the journey. We cannot turn them away. There would be a riot!'

He spoke to Rajhi. 'Get more men to the Grand Mosque. Guards at all entrances, and cameras and snipers on the roofs. We have Fisher's photograph – check all black men against it. We must find him!' A brief pause, remembering that he was technically addressing his superior. 'That is my recommendation.'

Rajhi nodded. 'It is a good one. Carry it out.'

The younger man departed, issuing more commands. 'You seriously think you'll be able to pick out one man in that crowd?' Eddie asked Rajhi, making his disapproval clear. 'You've only got just over half an hour to find him.'

'We will call in soldiers to help the search,' he replied. 'You may not think so, but we do know what we are doing. We have dealt with threats to the Hajj before. Now that we know what he looks like, we have very good spotters, facial recognition systems . . . If he is in the Grand Mosque, we will find him, I promise you.'

'Let's hope.' The Saudi seemed confident in his security forces, which improved the Englishman's mood slightly – and then prompted a thought. 'The security at the mosque – is it visible? Are the guards out in the open?'

'At the entrances, yes. We want visitors to feel safe, and it also helps us control the crowds. There are other guards inside, though they are more discreet. And there are undercover men also, but we do not tell that to the public,' he added with a sly smile.

'Simeon would know about them, though,' said Eddie, 'because Cross would know. He was in the CIA; intel's his business. So it's got high security?'

'As high as any place that is open to the public, yes.' The

security official recognised the growing concern on the other man's face. 'What is it, Mr Chase?'

'Something's wrong, but I'm not sure what . . .' He slowly paced across the room, trying to collate his thoughts. 'Even if he thinks that me and Nina are dead, Cross would still know that after what happened in Antigua, people would be looking for him – and his Witnesses. So if the security at the Grand Mosque is as good as you reckon, Simeon would be taking a big risk by going in there. He might get caught before he can release the gas, and that'd wreck Cross's plan.'

'So you think he might attack a different target?'

'What else is there, though? Where else could he . . .' Eddie stopped as an answer came. He tipped his head to look upwards – not at the ceiling itself, but to take in the hulking structure beyond. 'The clock tower's got an observation deck, hasn't it?'

'Yes . . .'

'Open-air?' Their eyes widened simultaneously. 'Shit! He's not going to release the gas from the ground – he's going to drop it from the roof!'

'He may be up there already,' Rajhi said in alarm.

They hurried for the exit, as did the two hotel representatives. There were still some uniformed police officers nearby; Rajhi summoned them, and the group ran through the corridors, eventually descending into the mall at the clock tower's base to reach the elevators serving the observation deck. There was a long line of tourists waiting; the arrival of the cops aroused consternation.

There was no sign of Simeon amongst the waiting visitors, though. 'Give security down here his picture, just in case he hasn't turned up yet,' Eddie told Essa and Nadhar. The hotel manager scurried away to the ticket booth.

An elevator disgorged returning tourists, who were startled to find several armed policemen waiting for them. A quick check that none was their target, then they boarded. Nadhar gave Eddie a dubious look as the elevator set off. 'It is not safe for civilians to come with us.'

'Trust me, I know what I'm doing,' the Yorkshireman replied. 'And I've seen the guy in person, not just photos.'

'He has seen you too,' Rajhi pointed out.

'Yeah, I know. And he's not a fan!'

The ascent in the high-speed elevator did not take long. 'Where will he be?' asked Nadhar as the doors opened.

'He'll be on the side facing the mosque to make the attack,' Eddie said, 'but he might stay out of the way until it's time. Does the deck go all the way around the clock?' The answer was in the affirmative. 'We'll need to spread out.'

He made his way through a doorway into a covered gallery, to be met first by a rush of wind, then the glare of the desert sun.

But no desert. It was not until he passed through one of a line of arches and into the open air that the horizon came into view beyond the edge of the observation deck. All that stood between him and a very long drop was an ornate balustrade, a covering of netting supported by large metal hoops along the balcony's length preventing anyone from climbing over it.

The holes in the net were easily large enough to fit a hand through, however. And as Eddie squeezed between the tourists for a closer look, he saw that it was made from a nylon mesh. The lines were thick enough to resist being torn by hand, but would offer almost no resistance to a blade. It would only take Simeon seconds to cut a larger hole through which he could throw the statue.

If he was here. He turned away from the dizzying view of Mecca to the people staring down at it. The vast majority were of Arab descent, but with other ethnicities among them – Persian, African, South East Asian, Caucasian. He focused on the black faces. None were Simeon. 'I don't see him here,' he told Rajhi as he rejoined him.

'The men are moving around the balcony,' the Saudi replied. 'I have told one to watch the elevators, in case he tries to escape.'

Eddie glanced up, seeing one of the colossal clock faces, a hundred and fifty feet across, looming above the balcony. Its massive hands now read 11.36. There was still time to stop Simeon before the call to prayer. 'We should go around too,' he said. 'I'll go that way.' He pointed clockwise around the balcony. 'You go the other, and we'll meet on the far side.'

'Mr Chase,' said Rajhi as Eddie turned away.

'Yeah?'

A faint smile. 'Please do not cause a diplomatic incident.'

Eddie grinned. 'Who, me?'

He set off through the crowd. Most people were jostling for the best view, though quite a few visitors had been struck by vertigo and retreated back under cover through the archways. That meant the searchers would have to check more than just the balcony; Simeon could be lurking inside. Eddie looked back for Rajhi to make the suggestion, but the security official was already lost amongst the throng.

Hoping the idea had also occurred to his guide, he continued along the walkway. The clock tower was rectangular rather than square, its northern and southern sides considerably longer than the east and west. It took him a couple of minutes to reach the first corner, surreptitiously checking every dark-skinned face he passed.

Still no sign of the American. Was he even here? Maybe he was in the Grand Mosque after all . . .

He went through a covered section topped by a golden minaret at the observation deck's corner, then started along the eastern balcony. The crowd here was thinner – the view across

Mecca's hotels and residential areas was far less impressive than the mosque.

Ahead, he saw one of the cops. The man was only giving the visitors the most cursory checks, Eddie realised. 'Slow down, you daft sod,' he muttered. Shalit, the Mossad spymaster, had been right: for most people, identifying someone in the flesh from only a photograph was surprisingly hard – and that was assuming the subject hadn't changed their appearance. If Simeon had disguised himself, the cop might have walked right past him . . .

The thought brought him to a sudden halt. What if the cop *had* missed Simeon? He looked more closely at every potential suspect nearby. Still no sign of him. Maybe he was just being paranoid—

An internal warning bell sounded.

A black man dressed in a colourful striped robe and matching hat was crouched near the outer wall. He appeared to be changing a camera's battery or memory card . . . but it was not what he was doing, rather the way he was doing it, that caught the former SAS soldier's attention. He had served in Afghanistan, and seen first-hand the various ways that insurgents attempted to camouflage their preparations for an ambush or placing an IED by pretending to do something innocuous. But however hard they tried, it was almost impossible for them to conceal their tension, their rising adrenalin . . .

The robed man had betrayed that tension. Only for an instant, a twitch of the head to check that the policeman had gone by – but that was enough to tell Eddie he had something to hide.

He couldn't tell if it was Simeon, though, the man facing away from him. It was possible he was a criminal rather than a terrorist; a pickpocket relieving wealthy tourists of their valuables. But he had to check, and do so without alerting the suspect.

Eddie moved to the balustrade, positioning himself beside an Arab family gawping at the scenery. He leaned outwards, head almost touching the taut netting as he tried to peer past them. He still couldn't see the black man's face clearly, his features obscured by short dreadlocks protruding from beneath the hat. But he *could* see that his free hand was fiddling with something made of glossy white plastic inside a satchel. Whatever it was, it was no memory card.

The man gave the retreating cop another wary glance, then bent lower, putting down the camera to lift the white object out into the open—

Eddie's view was suddenly blocked by the face of a small boy as his father lifted him up to see the vista below. He frowned and tried to look past him, only to draw first surprised, then offended looks from both parents. 'Sorry,' he told them, retreating. The father eyed him with suspicion, then raised his child higher.

The Englishman sidestepped to peer behind them – and saw a bandage on the man's hand.

It *was* Simeon. He took the object out of the bag. Eddie felt a chill as he identified it.

A drone.

The satchel contained a compact quadcopter. And beneath it, he glimpsed a familiar stone shape. The angel.

Simeon's plan became clear. A drone that small would not have enough power to maintain flight with the statue hanging from it but it would still be able to slow its fall. If he released it from the observation deck, the little aircraft could carry the angel far enough to reach the Grand Mosque.

And then detonate. There was a pale yellow strip taped to the figure. Plastic explosive. Enough to shatter the angel and disperse its deadly contents across the crowded courtyard.

If that happened during the call to prayer, tens of thousands of worshippers would be killed – and far more outside the mosque and in the city beyond. Eddie fought a surge of fear. The cop was now too far away to call back without alerting Simeon, and he couldn't see any of the other officers nearby. But with the American about to make his attack, he couldn't risk letting him out of his sight to find backup. If he had been armed, he could have simply shot the cultist and ended the threat right there, but the Saudis had not allowed him to bring weapons into the country.

He would have to take him down with brute force.

Eddie moved out from behind the tourists. Simeon was twenty feet away, still concentrating on preparing the drone. The Yorkshireman closed on him. He needed to score a solid, brutal kick to the back of his head to knock him down, then put him in a choke hold and drag him away from the statue before he could set off the explosive—

Laughing, the father lifted his son higher, pretending to throw him. The little boy screamed in fear.

Simeon's head snapped around at the noise – and he saw Eddie.

33

The two men were still ten feet apart. Eddie started to charge – but Simeon snatched a gun from the satchel. The Englishman instantly changed direction, diving through an arch. A bullet cracked off the pillar behind him.

Tourists scattered in blind panic, people being knocked down and trampled. The policeman tried to fight through the crush, yelling for them to move as he drew his gun—

Simeon fired again. The bullet hit the cop's throat, blood splattering over the polished marble floor. He fell backwards into the crowd, their screams growing louder.

Eddie glanced around the pillar. Simeon grabbed the satchel, leaving the little drone behind as he raced through an arch into the covered gallery. Another shot came from an entrance to the clock tower's interior.

The Englishman sprinted to the dead cop and grabbed his gun – a revolver rather than an automatic – then followed the American. Chaos met him inside, trapped visitors trying to flee and a second policeman down in a puddle of blood. 'Where did he go?' he yelled.

'Down there!' shrilled a woman, pointing. 'He went down there!' Eddie pushed through the crowd towards one side of the lobby.

A gunshot somewhere ahead. He ducked, but it had not been aimed at him. Two more retorts followed. He forced his way into an open space, seeing one of the tower's security staff dead on the floor. Where was Simeon?

'Chase!' Rajhi battled his way through the throng, gun drawn. One of the cops was with him. 'Did you see him? Where did he go?'

'There!' Eddie replied. A door near the dead guard was ajar; from the way it was painted to match the walls, he guessed it was only meant for maintenance and emergency use. He hurried to it, the cop and Rajhi meeting him. The lock plate had a pair of bullet holes in it. 'Cover me.'

He readied his gun, then kicked the door wide. Nobody there. A metal staircase spiralled upwards. The clank of hurried footsteps echoed down from above. Eddie aimed up the stairs, but all he could see of Simeon was his shadow against the railings.

'He's got the angel, and it's rigged with a bomb,' he told Rajhi as Nadhar and another policeman arrived. 'Come on!' He led the way after the American, the Saudis following. 'He was going to use a drone to blow it up over the mosque. He can't do that now, so he's gone to Plan B.'

'What is that?' Rajhi asked.

'I dunno – and maybe neither does he. Where do these stairs go?'

'To the machine floor for the clocks,' Nadhar told him.

'Can he get outside from there?'

'Only through a hatch, and it can only be reached from a special lift.'

'So either he's trapped – or he actually does have a Plan B.' A door banged above. 'He's off the stairs.'

'The clock room,' Nadhar confirmed, grim-faced.

Eddie reached the next landing, knowing Simeon would have had enough time to prepare an ambush. 'Okay, Mr Nadhar,' he said. 'You know what's in there – where's the nearest cover?'

Nadhar briefly closed his eyes to picture the room. 'We will be in the north-eastern corner,' he said. 'There is a display for

VIP tourists to the left, and on the right there is some machinery.'

'Which will give the most cover?'

'The machinery.'

'That's probably where he'll be.'

Rajhi issued orders to his men. 'We are ready,' he told the Englishman.

Eddie took hold of the door's handle. 'Okay, on three. One, two, three – *go!*' He yanked the door open.

The first cop rushed through – and took three bullets to the chest. He crashed to the floor, lifeless limbs flailing. The second man was right behind him; he tried to retreat, but another two rounds caught him in the upper arm and shoulder. He fell back on the landing, a bullet splintering the door frame behind him.

'Shit!' Eddie gasped, helping Rajhi pull the wounded man into cover. 'Did you see him?'

Rajhi repeated the question in Arabic, getting a strained reply. 'By the machine,' he translated, glancing through the doorway. 'It is about ten metres away.'

Eddie looked for himself, spotting a large generator or transformer. 'He's got a Glock 25,' he said, remembering the glimpse of Simeon's gun as he took it from the satchel. 'Nine mil, these wounds look like. And he's fired twelve shots, so he's got three left. If we can make him use 'em, that'll give us a chance to get into the room while he reloads.'

'Unless he has reloaded already,' warned Rajhi.

'Find out in a second,' Eddie replied as he crouched beside the door. 'Okay, I'll draw his fire; you run after the third shot.'

'What if there is a fourth shot?'

'Then we're fucked!' He steeled himself, then leaned out, gun raised.

Simeon was lurking behind the machinery, watching the entrance. He saw the movement and instinctively fired – but he had been aiming higher, expecting someone to run through it. The bullet hit the door frame just above the Yorkshireman's head. He adjusted his aim, but Eddie returned fire, his shot ricocheting off the transformer's side. Simeon flinched, his next attack going wide and blasting plaster from the wall.

One bullet left. Eddie sent a second round in his enemy's general direction, then sprang out into the open.

The tourist display Nadhar had mentioned was off to the left, closer than Simeon's cover. He raced for it, some sixth sense prompting him to dive as the American tracked him and fired again. The bullet seared over him, blowing out one of the display's flat screens.

The third shot – and there was no fourth. The Glock's slide was locked back. The weapon was out of ammo . . . but Simeon was already ejecting the spent magazine.

'Now! Run, *run!*' Eddie yelled as he scrambled behind the display. Rajhi and Nadhar erupted from the doorway. The Saudi official followed Eddie, but the hotel's security chief headed straight for Simeon's position. 'No, he's reloading—'

Too late. Simeon whipped his gun back up and fired. The bullet hit the running man squarely in the heart. Nadhar fell as the American drew back behind the humming machine.

Rajhi cursed. 'What do we do now?'

'I don't know, but whatever we do, it's got to be fast.' Eddie surveyed the machine room. It was a large, high-ceilinged space, dominated by the four giant clock mechanisms in the middle of each wall. Massive electric motors turned the hands outside, great brass gears slowly rotating to keep the time. Grey metal panels mostly covered the back of each clock, but around each hub was an opening to allow access to the mechanism. Beyond them were visible the complex webs of wiring feeding the millions of LEDs that illuminated the clock faces at night. More banks of machinery provided power, and additional cover was offered by a replica mechanism at the room's centre, as well as further displays for visitors.

He looked back at Simeon's position. The American couldn't defend both sides of the large machine at once, but there was no cover along the most direct approach from either direction. 'We'll have to get around him, use this stuff for protection,' he said, indicating the chamber's contents. 'If you get a shot, take it.'

Rajhi nodded, then cocked his head at a sound. 'What is he doing?'

Eddie strained to listen, hearing a faint tearing above the background noise. 'Shit! The bomb taped to the statue – he's taking it off.'

'Why?'

'So he can blow up something else. Maybe us . . .' His eyes went back to the exposed section of the northern clock face. 'Or he might be trying to make a hole so he can chuck the statue out.'

Rajhi looked dubious. 'He will not reach the Grand Mosque from here.'

'He doesn't need to – the gas'll still kill everyone outside the hotel.' He moved around the rear of the display. 'I'll get behind that model,' he said, pointing at a scale replica of the clock tower in a glass case. 'Cover me.'

He brought up his gun – and ran.

Simeon broke off his task to swing out from behind the machine and fire. Eddie simultaneously unleashed a suppressing shot back at him. The Englishman felt a whipcrack of displaced air on the back of his neck as the round seared past, but his own bullet forced his attacker to retreat. He dropped down behind the model clock, then looked around its plinth – to see the American lean out from the other side of his hiding place.

Another exchange of fire, and broken glass showered Eddie as a round punched through the case. His own retaliatory shot hit the machine Simeon was using for shelter. This time it did not simply glance off; something sparked, its electrical hum turning into a menacing growl. A warning buzzer rasped on a control panel.

Simeon looked up at it in alarm before pulling back into cover. Eddie moved to the other side of the plinth. If he could force him into the open . . .

A yellow cover on the machine's side bore a warning symbol. He locked on to it and fired again. The plastic shield flew off, some component beneath shattering. There was a sharp *crack* of electricity and more sparks spewed out, followed by a spurt of smoke as the growl grew louder—

Simeon broke from hiding as flames spat from the transformer, running for the north clock with the statue held in his outstretched left hand. Eddie hesitated, not wanting to risk breaking the angel.

Rajhi opened fire, sending several shots after the running man. Simeon dived to the floor, his hat and the fake dreadlocks flying off. Eddie tracked him, but now his target was shielded behind a display of gleaming giant cogs.

The Saudi moved into the open and took aim—

Simeon was faster, unleashing a trio of shots. Only one hit, but that was enough. Rajhi fell with a cry of pain, blood staining his robes.

Eddie instinctively glanced to check if he was alive or dead. The former, for now, but in the split second his eyes were off Simeon, the American had burst back into motion. He recovered his aim and zeroed in—

The former Marine had the same combat sixth sense as the Englishman, ducking and jinking just as Eddie fired. The bullet hit him, but only a graze, ripping the shoulder of his colourful robe. He gasped, but kept running, disappearing behind the clock's hulking mechanism.

And now Eddie was out of ammunition, the revolver's six rounds gone. He looked back at Rajhi, but the security official's automatic was nowhere in sight. Searching for it would make him an easy target. 'Maybe I can throw this at him,' he muttered, glaring at his useless weapon.

There was another tourist display near the north clock's motor, more screens flashing up images of the tower. From there, he might be able to round the mechanism and tackle his opponent.

Might. Even at a sprint, it would still take him a few seconds to cover the distance, more than enough time for Simeon to put a bullet in him.

But he had to try. Sounds of activity reached him; he couldn't see what Simeon was doing, but knew it couldn't be anything good. Keeping the gun raised, he readied himself . . . and ran.

The crunch of glass underfoot gave him away the instant he moved. Simeon whipped into view. With a yell, Eddie pointed the revolver at him. The sight of the gun caused the American to flinch – but then he realised the bluff and opened fire.

The distraction had given Eddie the tiny advantage he needed, though. The shots passed behind him. Before Simeon could refine his aim, he flung himself headlong behind the display stand.

But he was not safe even there. More bullets tore across the room, revealing the display's backing as nothing more than painted plywood. Splinters stabbed at Eddie as he scrambled along on his hands and knees. One of the screens above him exploded as a round ripped through it, falling glass hitting his head.

The gunfire stopped. Eddie peered around the display. Simeon had moved back behind the mechanism. A shadow on the panels backing the clock revealed that he was placing the explosive beside the hub. Once he used the bomb to blow open the clock face, he would be able to hurl the angel into the crowds below . . .

The bomb. Simeon would have to move away from it or be caught in the blast. If Eddie could get close enough, he might be able to catch the American before he could throw the statue.

He stood – then sprinted for the clock.

Simeon lunged back into view, his gun coming up—

Eddie threw himself into a dive. Two shots tore past him as he hit the floor and rolled behind the clock's drive. Simeon ran towards him.

He jumped up – and hurled the empty gun at the cultist's head.

Simeon jerked back, snapping up both arms to deflect the spinning hunk of metal away from his face. A grunt of pain, then he recovered, advancing once more as Eddie ducked behind the giant motor.

A *bleep* from the hub. The gunman looked back in alarm, then dropped—

The bomb detonated.

The explosion was more powerful than either man expected. Metal panels blew from their supports as a ragged hole ripped open in the clock's face. Shrapnel flew across the machine room. A supporting beam tore loose, scything away more panels and crashing down on top of the hub. A fierce wind shrieked in through the rent.

Simeon, caught in the open, had been knocked over by the blast. Eddie saw his chance and rushed at him.

The gun came up again—

Eddie kicked it from his hand. The pistol glanced off the motor and disappeared through the opening into the emptiness beyond. Simeon cried out. His opponent drove another kick at his head.

The blow made contact, blood spurting from Simeon's burst

lip, but the American still managed to grab Eddie's leg – and now he was off balance as Simeon tried to drag him down.

He staggered – and his hand slapped one of the giant cogs. He jerked it away just before it was crushed in the gears, but he was now past the point of no return and fell heavily to the floor.

Simeon clawed at him. Eddie lashed out with his other foot. A sharp *smack* – and the African American lurched back as the Yorkshireman's boot heel struck his eye socket.

Eddie dragged himself upright and pressed his attack, kicking the dazed man hard in the stomach before grabbing him and throwing him against the exposed gears.

Simeon's robe caught in the cogs. He tried to fight back, but was abruptly restrained as the material pulled tight around his neck, the mechanism slowly but remorselessly drawing his clothing between its teeth. Eddie hit him again, then looked around. Where was the angel?

Outside, he could see the clock's long hand, pointing towards the eight. It had been damaged by the explosion and flying debris, a long, jagged split along its length surrounded by shards of carbon fibre. Closer to him, the motor was making a deep, ominous buzzing noise. The broken girder had wedged against the shaft bearing the clock's massive hands, jamming the mechanism. It was at risk of overheating and catching fire, or even exploding as the electrical system overloaded.

But there was a greater threat. The statue lay under the hub, just inches from the gaping hole in the clock face.

And it was *moving*, creeping towards the precipice.

For a moment Eddie thought the wind was blowing it, until a vibration through his feet told him the true cause. The fallen beam had jammed the clock – but the motor was still trying to turn the gears. The entire mechanism was shuddering, transmitting the movement through the floor.

Ripping cloth. He looked back to see Simeon tear free from

his robes. The American's eye was almost shut where Eddie had kicked it, but his other was open and blazing with rage.

Simeon was still a danger – but if the angel fell, the gas would kill thousands. He had to save it—

Eddie rushed to the hub. The shaft was not far above the floor, forcing him to crouch to reach the statue. The vibration became more pronounced as the overload built up. He ignored it, groping for the sculpture and pulling it from its hiding place.

Running footsteps behind him—

He jumped up, turning to face his opponent – as Simeon delivered a flying kick squarely to his chest.

Eddie spun backwards . . . and toppled through the hole.

34

Mecca rolled far below the Englishman, the wind screaming in his ears as he fell—

He hit the clock's long hand and grabbed at it in terrified desperation. He jolted to a halt, the fifty-six-foot pointer digging hard against his armpits as he dangled from its upper edge.

But he was far from safe. The clock's hands were as elaborately decorated as the rest of the enormous timepiece, but the curli-cued gold details were simply applied to the surface, offering no grip. And he could feel the whole thing shaking from both the impact of his landing and the vibrations of the overloading motor. He kicked backwards, trying to brace himself against the clock, but managed only to break off LEDs set into the sheer face.

Still clutching the angel, Eddie strained to raise himself higher. If he could secure the statue inside his jacket, he might be able to climb back to the hole—

The clock hand jolted, almost shaking him loose. He squeezed both arms against it to pin himself in place. But he still began to slide sideways . . . and downwards.

The minute hand was moving – and at a much faster rate than sixty seconds per minute. Loud cracks came from the gear mechanism at the hub's end as teeth were stripped from an overstressed cog—

An explosive *bang* of shearing metal, and the long hand swung freely from its axle, six tons of steel and composites sweeping down towards the vertical. Eddie slithered along its edge – until it dropped out from under him.

He plunged, both raised arms scrabbling helplessly for a hold—

His feet hit a jagged slab of carbon fibre. It snapped under his weight, but slowed him for the fraction of a second he needed to thrust his left arm into the crack down the clock hand's damaged rear.

Broken shards tore through his jacket and slashed his skin, making him scream, yet he still managed to grab a thick skein of wiring. Some of the LEDs embedded in the front of the huge pointer tore out, but more held. He jerked to a stop as the minute hand swung pendulously back and forth over the six o'clock position.

Eddie gasped for breath. Directly below him was the observation deck. He saw the curved supports of the protective netting, and considered letting go and dropping on to it, before realising that would be suicide. The net was pulled drum-tight; falling on to it from this height would be like landing on a trampoline, catapulting him over the edge.

But the hand's tip was less than fifteen feet above the netting. If he climbed down further, he might make it . . .

A fierce jolt cancelled all thought beyond holding on. He looked up. The entire axle assembly was visibly shaking, more fragments of the ruptured clock face falling past him. The wind drew a streamer of smoke out through the hole; it became darker and thicker as he watched, swirling away into the sky. The overloading motor was catching fire.

Simeon appeared at the opening. He looked down, expression changing to an almost offended anger as he saw Eddie still alive below. He ducked back inside with a barely suppressed obscenity, returning holding a broken metal spar – which he threw at the Englishman.

Eddie whipped his right arm above his head just fast enough to take the painful blow. If it had struck his skull, it would have knocked him senseless. The steel bar fell away, bouncing off the netting to be flung into the void.

Another violent shudder. He managed to jam the statue inside his jacket before taking hold of a carbon-fibre spearhead with his right hand, forcing himself to ignore the pain as it cut his palm.

Above him, the hour hand was now rocking violently against the axle like a ruler twanged on the edge of a desk. More panels in the clock face buckled outwards. The smoke grew more dense, and even over the wind he could hear a fearsome electrical growl. It wasn't just the clock's motor: the overload was feeding back into the transformers powering it, and he knew from experience that could have explosive results.

The same thought occurred to Simeon. A concerned glance back into the room, then he leaned out and gripped both edges of the minute hand. 'You might as well let go!' he called down to Eddie as he held himself in place, then pressed the insteps of his boots hard against the pointer's sides. 'Because it'll hurt a lot more if I have to come down there!'

'And I thought suicide was a sin!' Eddie shot back.

'Don't worry – you were always going to Hell!' The American started a controlled descent towards him.

Eddie looked back at the netting. It now offered his only chance of survival, but he had to get to the bottom of the clock's hand before Simeon caught up. He shifted position, easing his grip on the wires – only to clamp his fingers tight again as the pointed carbon shard in his right hand creaked menacingly under his weight. Blood oozed as the sharp edges sliced his skin.

Simeon came closer, muscles visibly straining with the effort of holding on, but he showed no signs of slipping. He was now only six feet above the Englishman. Above him, the escaping smoke turned black. 'Hey, how you hanging?' he said with a malevolent grin.

Eddie searched for a better handhold, but the only possibilities were either too fragile to support him, or even more razor-edged. And now Simeon was upon him—

One foot swiped down, grazing the back of his left hand. It was only an exploratory attack, the American unsure if he could maintain his hold – but the second strike, with his other foot, was more confident. The carbon shard Eddie was holding snapped off at the base as Simeon's heel stamped down on his knuckles. The Yorkshireman swung and fell a few inches as more wires in his left hand ripped away before the remaining ones again just barely caught his weight.

Simeon lowered himself further, about to smash his foot down on the other man's head—

Eddie stabbed the composite spearhead deep into his calf.

Simeon screamed, almost losing his grip. Eddie twisted his makeshift dagger deeper into his flesh, then tugged at his ankle as hard as he could. The American's hands slipped down the pointer's edges. 'Time's up!' Eddie yelled—

The cultist finally lost his hold and fell – only to slam to a stop after barely a foot. Another protruding carbon spike had caught him, impaling him up through his abdomen and behind his ribcage. He shrieked, blood and stomach fluids gushing from the wound.

A loud detonation from above. The whole clock shuddered as if kicked by a giant. Eddie looked past the flailing American to see flames belch out of the hole, dirty smoke spewing from the widening gaps between the panels. The machinery was on the verge of destroying itself, the hub about to rip away and take the long fall to the ground.

Still gripping Simeon's leg, Eddie released his hold on the wires and hurriedly clamped his hand around the pointer's edge. He followed the American's example, pressing his insteps against its sides, then let go of the other man – and dropped.

He managed to grab the edge with his right hand as he fell,

but his palm was slick with blood. He squeezed harder, but wasn't slowing fast enough, the great pointer narrowing to just two feet wide at its tip . . . and then nothing.

Eddie plummeted towards the balcony—

The netting caught him – but it was drawn so tightly that it felt almost solid, pounding the breath from his lungs. He clawed at the nylon lines as the rebound threw him towards the edge, finding grip with one hand. Fingers clenched so tightly he could have crushed coal into diamond, he flipped over, landing hard on his back. Muscles and tendons strained to their limit, arm joints almost wrenching from their sockets . . .

But they held.

He bounced once, twice, then came to rest on top of the mesh. Gasping, he looked up. Simeon was still pinned gruesomely to the minute hand, his screams echoing down the building.

Another blast from the machine room – and the centre of the clock face disintegrated as the hub was ripped out of the motor, dragging girders and lighting panels with it. Both hands toppled forward – then the tip of the minute hand hit the elaborate golden relief around the clock's circumference and flung the entire assembly outwards, away from the tower's face.

Simeon was still screaming as he fell past Eddie. 'I should've said "Time's *down*!"' the Englishman yelled after him. Seconds passed – then a colossal crunching *boom* reached him as the clock hands smashed apart a quarter of a mile below, their unwilling passenger reduced to a bloody pulp amidst the storm of carbon shards.

Eddie caught his breath, then groped inside his jacket. The statue was still there. 'Thank God,' he said, before looking at the Grand Mosque below. 'Or thank Allah. Or Yahweh, or whatever he's called.' He rolled over to get a hold on the netting with both hands—

Twang!

The tightly stretched net jerked beneath him – and he suddenly found himself slipping towards the balcony's edge. Falling debris had ripped the mesh, and now the rest of it was tearing free from the support posts, one strand after another breaking with an insistent *ping-ping-ping* of snapping nylon.

'Oh, come *on*!' he cried, pulling himself up hand over hand, but the netting was rolling towards the void faster than he could climb. The observation deck slithered past behind his outstretched arms, followed by the balustrade—

Hands locked around his wrists.

Eddie raised his head to see al Farhan braced against the low wall, teeth bared with the strain of holding him. He shouted in Arabic; several policemen ran over and raised the Yorkshireman on to the balcony.

'Thanks,' he wheezed, looking around. The observation platform was strewn with debris, but he was relieved that the tourists had all been evacuated. He hoped the same was true at ground level.

'What happened?' al Farhan demanded. 'Where is Rajhi – and did you get the statue?'

'I got it,' Eddie replied wearily, producing it from his jacket. 'Rajhi's in the clock's machine room; he's hurt. So are some other people. You need to get paramedics up there.'

The Saudi prince issued orders, then regarded the figure in Eddie's hands. 'So that is the angel? Is it safe?'

'I think so,' he said, checking it for signs of damage and finding none. 'That's one taken care of. I hope we can do the same for number two . . .'

35

Vatican City

'You've got the angel?' Nina said into her phone. 'Thank God! What about Simeon? Did you catch him?'

'No, the ground did,' her husband answered. 'What about you? Don't suppose you convinced the Pope to postpone his talk?'

'Ah . . . nope.' She regarded the covered stage standing before the great facade of St Peter's Basilica. A figure in white robes stood within, his words resounding from loudspeakers around the vast expanse of St Peter's Square while his image was relayed to numerous giant screens for the benefit of the hundreds of thousands attending the papal audience. 'He just started.'

'Oh. Great. And I'm guessing you haven't found Anna yet?'

'No, we're still searching. Her picture's been put out to all the police and security personnel, but there are a *lot* of people here.' She turned in the other direction to survey the square. In front of the stage was a large cordoned area with thousands of seats reserved for those who had either obtained tickets or been specially invited – most near the front were priests and nuns. Beyond it, the rest of the square was standing room only, a mass of faces watching the address. 'But she might not even be this close. She could release the gas outside the square and still kill thousands of people.'

'Yeah, I know,' Eddie said gloomily. 'She could be half a mile away. Simeon was going to use a drone.'

'That might not work here. The cops have sharpshooters on the rooftops, and Massimo – he's in charge of security,' she explained, glancing at the rangy Italian as he spoke with one of his officers – 'told me they've been prepared for potential drone attacks for a few years now. So she's probably hiding in the crowd. But,' she added with a sigh, 'it's a big-ass crowd.'

Massimo Rosetti gestured for her to join him, his expression suddenly excited – and tense. 'Hold on,' she told Eddie, going to the Italian. 'What is it?'

'A guard saw her,' he replied, pointing towards one of the checkpoints at the perimeter of the seating.

'What, she's in *here*?' Nina exclaimed.

'Yes, but that means she cannot get out.'

'She doesn't *want* to get out. I told you, this'll be a suicide attack – she thinks she's one of the Witnesses from Revelation, who both have to die before the prophecy can come true. And the other one just did!'

Rosetti gave orders over a walkie-talkie. 'I have told my men to look for her in the seats,' he said, starting for the checkpoint. Nina followed, limping from her leg wound. 'Quietly, so they do not alarm her – or anyone else. If a panic starts, many could be killed.'

'Many could be killed anyway,' she pointed out before returning her attention to the phone. 'Okay, Eddie, I'll call you back. Love you.'

'I love you too,' he replied. 'And the baby!'

She smiled, then pocketed the phone. 'Do we know what she's wearing?'

The Italian shook his head. 'That will not help us.'

'But if he recognised her—'

'That is why we are going to talk to him.'

They made their way down an aisle between the banks of seats. Nina became acutely aware that Anna knew her by sight. But if she had been spotted, there was no sign, the crowd watching the Pope with rapt attention.

They reached the checkpoint, a booth with an airport-style scanner to check the personal items of those entering. Two uniformed guards manned it. Rosetti spoke to one, frowning before turning to Nina. 'He remembers the statue on the X-ray, but not the woman carrying it,' he said, annoyed.

'Why not?' she asked.

The young guard shrugged helplessly. 'She was a nun.'

'What did she look like?'

'A nun!'

Nina looked back, seeing more habits than she could count. 'Well that's really useful!'

'We must find her,' said Rosetti. 'Dr Wilde, you will recognise her if you see her?'

'Yeah, and she'll recognise me! If she realises we're looking for her, she might release the gas.'

'But you say she will release it anyway, so we must try.' Transmitting more instructions, he led her back up the aisle.

Nina looked along each row as she passed, but the sheer number of people was visually overwhelming even when she tried to focus solely on the nuns. 'Great, it's like finding one particular penguin in an entire colony.'

Rosetti stopped to speak to a small group of his subordinates, who rapidly dispersed, giving orders through their own radios. 'Every man I have here is now looking for her,' he told Nina. 'But if you could also help . . .'

'I'll do what I can.' She scanned the crowd, wondering where to start.

From the front, she decided. Cross's cult considered the Catholic Church a heretical organisation, which would make its leader practically the Antichrist in their eyes. While it made no difference in terms of the prophecy from Revelation whether he died or not, the Pope would almost certainly be Anna's primary target: his murder would be a massive blow to the faith. Nina had seen how quickly the gas spread, but if Anna were too distant, the pontiff's staff could still get him to safety.

So where was she? The first five rows, ten? The stage was at the top of the broad steps outside the basilica, at least seventy feet from the front row of seats. Movement above caught her eye: fluttering flags atop the building . . .

The wind. It was blowing roughly south-east, away from the Pope's position. If Anna was too far back, the breeze would slow the gas cloud, or even stop it from reaching him.

She tried to picture the square from above. When Miriam had broken the angel at the Mission, the initial release of gas had been extremely forceful, mushrooming outwards for about a hundred feet before the wind finally caught it. The breeze was more gentle here, so assume a radius of a hundred and fifty feet to be sure of reaching the stage . . .

The first twelve rows, she estimated, and in the sections of seating to either side of the broad central aisle. *If* her assumptions were correct. She could be wrong – about how the gas would expand, about Anna's plan.

But it was all she had. 'I'm going to check these two blocks of seats,' she told Rosetti, pointing them out.

'You think she is there?'

'Maybe. But it's just a guess.'

'I will come with you,' he said, following her.

'You do that,' she said distractedly, her gaze already sweeping the ranks of visitors. The seating was divided into eight rectangular blocks across the width of the square, around twenty chairs to each of their twelve rows. That meant almost five hundred people in the two-block section to which she had narrowed her search. Even limiting it to nuns alone left over a hundred suspects. And would she pick out Anna? With her hair covered, a pair of glasses could be enough of a disguise . . .

She and Rosetti reached the front of the crowd and moved across it. Nina surveyed the guests, slowing to check each face beneath a headscarf or habit. Annoyed glares came back at her; some not welcoming the attention, others simply irritated that she was obstructing their view.

She crossed the first block to the central aisle. 'Have you seen her?' Rosetti asked quietly.

'No, but I couldn't get a good look at all of them.' Some nuns had been obscured behind taller audience members, or had their faces turned away.

They crossed the aisle, Nina glancing sideways to see the Pope still delivering his sermon. A message crackled through the policeman's radio. 'More men are coming from the rest of the square to help us,' he said.

'Tell them to hurry up.' Nina's nervousness was rising; the attack could happen at any time. She looked over the next sea of faces. It seemed that half of them were nuns. Young, old, fat, thin, white, black, and all points in between, but the one she wanted to find was nowhere to be seen . . .

Her eyes met a nun's, just for a moment – and the woman hurriedly turned away.

Nina flinched with a shock of adrenalin . . . and fear. 'Have you seen her?' Rosetti asked urgently.

'I don't know.' She looked back at the nun, but saw only the top of her head: she had leaned forward as if picking something up from the ground. 'It could be her, about eight rows back.'

The Italian stared into the crowd. 'Which one? I can see ten nuns around there.'

'The one who's trying to keep her face hidden!' Nina increased her pace, eyes locked on the hunched figure as she reached the aisle and turned down it. The woman in question was just under halfway along the row – and as Nina drew level, she saw that the nun was pulling something from a small bag.

The angel.

'Shit, it's her!' she cried. A few visitors reacted with offended shock at the obscenity, but she didn't have time to worry about wounded feelings. 'She's got the statue! There, there!'

Rosetti pushed down the row, drawing his sidearm as he shouted a warning in Italian—

The statue was not the only thing Anna had taken from the bag.

Her arm whipped up – and Rosetti staggered, a slim black throwing knife jutting from his throat. He fell heavily on to an elderly man beside Anna. The other people nearby were momentarily stunned, then the screams started.

Nina was already forcing her way along the row. 'Down, stay down!' she shouted, pushing a panicked nun back into her seat before she could block her path.

Anna had the statue in one hand, the other tugging the carbon-fibre blade from Rosetti's neck. 'Back, bitch!' she yelled, stabbing it at the redhead.

Nina jerked away from the bloodied tip, then overcame her fear and lunged for Anna's arm. The blade caught her palm, making her gasp, but she managed to grab the cultist's wrist. 'That's *Doctor* Bitch to you!' she yelled, twisting the knife away—

Her heart froze as she saw Anna's other arm draw back . . . and hurl the statue.

It flew over the front rows of the crowd. Time seemed to slow, the angel falling towards the base of the steps . . .

It hit the ground – and shattered. Nina stared at it, paralysed with terror—

The broken pieces came to rest. She drew in a startled breath. There was no gas, no eruption of yellow poison. Anna was equally stunned, mouth open in disbelief. 'But . . . it can't . . .'

'It can,' Nina replied, realising what had happened. It was not the real angel. Cross had given Anna the fake Eddie had used to locate the Mission – and it was clear that the biochemist knew nothing about the deception. 'He lied to you. Your Prophet lied to you!'

'No!' Anna jerked her arm free and slashed the blade at Nina's face. The redhead jumped backwards to avoid it, only to stumble against a chair. A burst of pain from her injured leg, and she fell.

Anna shoved past Rosetti and stood over Nina as others in the crowd fled. But she didn't stab her, instead holding the knife to her throat. 'Back off!' she cried as a uniformed cop pointed a gun. 'Back off or I'll kill her!'

The cop retreated, but kept his weapon raised. Shouts in Italian reached Nina as more officers closed in. 'You've failed,' she said breathlessly. 'You *and* your husband. Neither angel has been released. We recovered the one in Mecca.'

Anna stared at her, anger and panic in her eyes. 'What happened to Sim— the other Witness?'

Nina hesitated, feeling the blade against her skin. But she knew she had to tell her. 'He's dead.'

The other woman did not react for a moment, as if she hadn't heard, then anguish joined the other emotions. 'Dead?' she repeated, voice cracking. 'He can't . . . No, he—' She broke off, her anger resurgent. 'Killed by the minions of the Beast . . . so now the prophecy can be fulfilled!'

She pulled back the knife, about to stab it into Nina's neck – only to hesitate after a glance at the redhead's abdomen. Then she leapt on to the now-empty seats, letting out a demented scream as she charged at the nearest cop.

He fired. The bullet hit her chest. More screams came from the crowd as she crashed to the ground.

The cop ran to her, kicking away the knife. Other armed men

hurried to join him. 'Wait, get back from her, get back!' Nina called, staggering to her feet. A brief glance told her that the Pope was being rushed into the safety of the basilica. 'Anna,' she said, crouching beside the dying woman, 'Cross lied to you – he *used* you. He always had three targets, because he thought he'd have three angels, but he had to change his plan when he destroyed one angel at the Mission, didn't he? He gave you a fake and kept one for himself, so he could attack the biggest target personally. He sent you to die as a decoy! Where is he? Where's the real angel?'

Anna turned her head weakly, coughing blood. Red speckled the white cloth of her habit. Despite her pain, she was almost smiling. 'No, doesn't matter, he's . . . succeeded. When the Witnesses . . . die, the second woe is past, and then the seventh angel sounds!'

'No it doesn't!' Nina protested. 'The seventh angel doesn't sound until after the Witnesses are resurrected and taken to heaven in a cloud – and that's not going to happen because *this is the real world*! Cross himself thinks John was hallucinating when he wrote Revelation: there *is* no prophecy, it's all nonsense. You and Simeon have died for nothing!'

'If it's . . . nonsense, then how did you find . . . the angels?' The smile twisted into mocking disdain.

A policeman clambered over the seats to check on Rosetti, surprise and concern in his voice telling Nina he was still alive. But she had no time to be relieved – or to argue theology. 'Where's the last angel?' she demanded, leaning closer. 'What's Cross going to do with it?'

'Loose it,' Anna gasped. 'Of course . . . the Prophet will release the angel . . .' An expression almost of joy crossed her face. 'And bring down . . . Babylon. The kings of the world . . . will witness . . .'

'What do you mean?' said Nina. 'Tell me!'

But the other woman's eyes grew unfocused. One last sigh of escaping breath, then she fell still and silent. 'God *damn* it,' Nina whispered.

The cops closed in around her. '*É morta?*' asked one.

'Yeah, she's dead,' Nina replied. 'And so are our chances of finding the real angel.'

36

'So Cross gave Anna the copy and took off with the real angel?' said the disbelieving Dalton over the conference call. 'Where's he taken it?'

'That's kinda what I was hoping you could tell us,' Nina said, exasperated. While paramedics tended to Rosetti, she had been taken to an office inside the Vatican to give the bad news to Seretse in New York and Eddie in Mecca, calling upon Dalton – now in transit to America in the company of a trio of US marshals – in the hope of learning the cult leader's true plans.

'I have no idea,' the disgraced politician replied.

Her frustration grew. 'Are you saying that because you don't want to incriminate yourself in front of law enforcement officials, or do you genuinely not know?'

'I genuinely don't know!' Dalton snapped. 'Until that son of a bitch dumped me in the desert, I'd planned to go back to Tel Aviv and meet some Israeli friends. I don't know where he meant to go!'

'Wait, you have friends?' Eddie said sarcastically.

'Not helping,' said his wife.

'I've still got plenty of friends in Washington,' Dalton growled. 'I can assure you that I'll be back in—'

'Just one moment, Mr President,' interrupted Seretse, breaking off to speak to someone. When he returned, despondency was clear even in the diplomat's normally controlled voice. 'I have had a message from the State Department.'

'Doesn't sound like the one you were hoping for,' noted Eddie.

'I am afraid not. They were able to reach out to the intelligence services and provide the flight plan of the jet Cross had been using, but after leaving Ovda airbase yesterday, it flew to Jordan – and is still there. Anna and Simeon travelled on to their targets by commercial flights under false passports. It would appear that Cross also left the country under an assumed identity, but so far we have not been able to track him.'

Nina put her head in her hands. 'So he could be literally anywhere in the world by now? Great.'

'How are we going to find him?' asked Seretse. 'What is his target?'

'Babylon,' she told him. 'That's what Anna said: Babylon will fall. All part of Revelation, but somehow I doubt that Cross plans to attack the ruins of an ancient city in Iraq.'

'Maybe he really hates sci-fi and he's going after the bloke who created *Babylon 5*,' Eddie suggested.

'*Eddie!* This is serious.'

'What, a terrorist attack that could kill thousands of people? No!'

'I don't know what's more terrifying,' said Dalton. 'That prospect, or the fact that you two are the best hope to stop it.'

'At least we're *trying*,' snarled Nina. 'Rather than coming up with the idea in the first place, only to have it all blow up in your face!'

'I did not come up with—'

'Oh, shut up, Mr President. Stop trying to cover your ass and *help* us! You know Cross, you know what motivates him and what he was trying to achieve. What's his endgame? His target could be anywhere in the world – but where?'

There was no immediate reply. Eddie was the first to break the downcast silence. 'So he's not going to attack the original Babylon. What else could it be?'

'One theory about Revelation was that Babylon was code for Rome,' said Nina.

'Rome was not the target today, though,' said Seretse. 'Not the real target.'

'I know. But Babylon was the centre of an ancient empire, Rome was the same in John's time, so now . . . Washington DC?' she suggested.

'I wouldn't think so,' Dalton replied. 'Cross was many things, but he was definitely a patriot. His long-term goal was to bring about the creation of a unified Christian America—'

'You mean *your* goal,' Eddie cut in.

Dalton ignored him. 'But that was by using the attacks on Rome and Mecca to build up threats from outside the country, not to attack the country itself and kill US citizens.'

'Maybe that's not his plan any more,' said Nina. 'Maybe it never was. Learning God's secrets was always his ultimate goal. If people die, even Americans, it doesn't matter because the end of the world is imminent – they'll soon be judged by God no matter what.'

'So there still is a possibility that he may attack Washington?' asked Seretse.

'Anything's a possibility with that maniac,' replied Dalton. 'But right now, the balance of power in DC is with people who would tend to side with him. Wiping out Congress wouldn't get him what he wants.'

'It'd get a big cheer from everyone else in the country, though,' said Eddie. Nina could tell he was grinning without needing to see him.

'You'll forgive me if I don't find jokes about killing political leaders amusing,' Dalton snapped.

Nina sat up as his words prompted a thought. 'Anna said something else before she died,' she said. 'It wasn't just that Babylon would fall. It was also that the kings of the world – the leaders – would witness it. But there's only one world leader in DC . . .'

She jerked bolt upright as another possibility came to her. From the startled gasp over the speaker, the same thought had struck Seretse. 'The General Assembly!' the diplomat cried. 'The world's leaders are coming *here*, to New York.'

'The UN is a tower where all the world's languages are spoken – just like the description of Babel in Genesis,' said Nina. 'Your Fortress America, Dalton – you said it wouldn't be subject to United Nations treaties. And Cross hates the UN even more than you do – he wants it removed from American soil. Gassing the place in the middle of a General Assembly would be one way to do that. And taking out most of the world's leaders would stand a pretty good chance of bringing about the apocalypse!'

'But he'll still be an angel short,' Eddie noted. 'The one he meant for Mecca's still in one piece.'

'He doesn't care. He already justified scrambling and skipping over the parts of Revelation that didn't fit his timeline as a result of John the Apostle's hallucinations, and I think he's jumping right to its end on the principle that if he brings about the fall of Babylon, everything else will come to pass as well – and then he'll learn all God's secrets. Oswald, is there anything you can do to increase security?'

'I am not sure if anything more *can* be done,' Seretse told her. 'I can warn the Secret Service and the police about Cross, but the streets around the United Nations complex are already cordoned off. The first of the world leaders have begun to arrive.'

'What time does the Assembly actually start?' Nina asked.

'Most of the delegates will be arriving over the course of the morning – President Cole is expected at one thirty. The session opens at three p.m.'

'That'll be when Cross is most likely to do it,' Eddie said. 'When they're all in the same place at the same time.'

Nina checked her watch, adding in the time difference between Rome and New York. 'That's only just over eight hours from now! It's not even enough time to get us back to the States.'

'You want to come back here?' Seretse asked.

'Absolutely I do! Eddie and I stopped the attacks in Mecca and Rome – well, okay, Eddie stopped one of the attacks, and the other one was a decoy,' she admitted. 'But we still might be able to help. At the very least, we've both seen Cross before. We spotted his Witnesses; we might be able to find him as well.'

'But it's all academic, isn't it?' said Dalton in a biting tone. 'Italy to New York is at least a nine-hour flight. Even if you chartered a business jet, there's no way you could make it before the session starts.'

'There's one way,' Eddie cut in. 'Be hard to arrange, but you might actually be able to help with that, Mr President. If you really do still have friends in Washington.'

The politician was surprised, both at the suggestion, and at the Englishman's sudden politeness, or at least lack of open hostility. 'What do you mean?'

'Yeah, what *do* you mean, Eddie?' said Nina, curious.

'I mean, Mr President, that if you still had enough pull with the CIA to get rides on their black flights, then maybe you've also still got some pull with your old mates at the Pentagon – like you did when you got us access to Silent Peak.'

Dalton had once arranged security clearance for the couple to enter a top-secret government archive. But it had come with a price. 'Uh, that didn't work out too well,' Nina reminded him. 'For any of us.'

'He's not going to betray us *this* time, though, is he?' said Eddie. 'Not since he wants to keep his arse out of jail, and out of the hands of his cellmate Bubba Manlove.'

'I promised I would do everything in my power to find Cross

and stop whatever he's planning,' Dalton said stiffly. 'What is it you want, Chase?'

'A lift.'

'A lift?' said Nina, wondering what he meant.

She saw the answer for herself an hour later.

'Have you ever been in a fighter jet before, ma'am?' asked United States Air Force captain Tyler Fox as he escorted her across the concrete apron of Rome's Ciampino airport.

'Can't say that I have,' she replied with trepidation. Standing before her was a slate-grey aircraft, an F-15E Strike Eagle: her transport back to America. Whatever contacts Dalton had, they had come through in spectacular fashion.

'I'll go easy on you, then. Especially as you're pregnant. I've never had a baby on board my aircraft before! It sure isn't standard operating procedure, but I understand it's real important you get to New York asap.'

'Yeah, it is.' She looked down at her olive-drab flight suit and the helmet in one hand. 'I feel like I should call myself Maverick or something.'

'*Top Gun* is navy, ma'am,' said Fox, with a hint of disdain. 'The air force shows 'em how it's done.'

She smiled. 'What is it with you military guys? The air force can't stand the navy, and my husband's ex-army special forces with very strong views on flyboys. Or "crabs", as he calls them.'

Fox grinned back. 'Friendly competition, ma'am. Well, usually friendly. But we all pull together when it comes to the crunch.' They reached the idling aircraft, where two uniformed ground crew were waiting. 'You were lucky to get me, I gotta say. We're normally stationed in England, but we've been doing NATO exercises over Turkey and the Black Sea these past few days. I was kinda surprised to get called for taxi duty, but hey, if you need to get back home in a hurry, there ain't a faster way than riding in an Eagle.'

The ground crew positioned ladders so Fox and Nina could climb into the cockpit. Her pilot took the front seat; she went to the weapon officer's position behind him, waiting nervously as her harness and oxygen system were secured. 'You had the safety briefing, right, ma'am?' Fox called over his shoulder.

'Yeah, the Cliffs Notes version.'

'These things are very reliable, and tough – one of 'em once landed with an entire wing shot off! If anything does happen, just do what I tell you and you'll be fine. But I doubt there'll be any trouble.'

The ground crew finished strapping her in, then descended and removed the ladders. Fox closed the canopy, running through a truncated series of pre-flight checks and communicating with air traffic control before addressing her again, this time through her helmet's earphones. 'Okay, we have take-off clearance. We'll be refuelling three times over the Atlantic, but since we'll be going supersonic as much as possible, the total journey time should be under four hours.'

'How fast will we be going?' she asked.

'Top speed of an F-15E is classified, I'm afraid,' he said, humour in his voice, 'so please try not to look at the air speed indicator during flight. But I can tell you we'll be reaching speeds in excess of Mach 2. *Well* in excess.' Another exchange with the control tower. 'All right, here we go.'

The whine of the idling twin engines rose in pitch, and the Eagle started to move, bumping along the taxiway. Nina flexed her hands nervously, trying – and failing – to relax. The impending take-off was not her only worry. Four hours was less than half as long as a commercial flight would take, but it was still cutting things fine. By the time she arrived in New York, there would be under three hours before the General Assembly's first session began, and it was entirely possible that Cross planned to attack before then.

The main runway swung into view ahead. 'Okay, Dr Wilde,' said Fox, 'we're good to go. You might want to brace yourself.'

She did not like the sound of that. 'Is it going to be a fast take-off?'

'You need to get to New York in a hurry! Are you ready?'

Nina gulped, crossing her arms protectively over her stomach. 'Yeah,' she said, dry-mouthed.

'Then hang on to your butt . . . I mean, your *hat*, ma'am.'

The engines rose to a shriek, even through her helmet's soundproofing – then a thunderous crackling roar joined the cacophony as both afterburners ignited, raw fuel pumping into the jet exhausts and blasting out of the twin nozzles in a spear of flame. The F-15 shot forward like a rocket. Nina gasped as she was thrust back into the seat. The acceleration of an airliner was nothing compared to the jet fighter's, and the G-forces kept building as the plane hurtled along the runway. Almost before she could register it, the Eagle was airborne, Ciampino dropping sharply away, and the pressure on her body grew even stronger as Fox pulled the nose up to what felt like the vertical. 'Oh my *God*!' she squeaked.

'Are you okay?' Fox asked.

'I don't know! What are we doing, ten G?'

'Only about two, ma'am.'

'Two!' she cried. 'Is that all?'

'I deliberately kept it low on account of your condition. But I can ease off if it's too much.'

'Please, be my guest. I'm not supposed to ride roller coasters while I'm pregnant, and this doesn't seem much different!'

'I guess I won't be showing off any barrel rolls for you, then.'

Her glare bored through the rear of his seat into his skull. 'No thanks.'

Fox chuckled, then had another exchange with air traffic control. The F-15 eased out of its climb, Nina looking out of the cockpit's side to find with surprise that the fighter had not even gone steeper than forty-five degrees in its ascent, never mind vertical. Rome receded below, the Vatican clearly visible at its heart. 'Okay,' he told her, 'we're going to a cruising altitude of forty-five thousand feet. I can't go supersonic until we clear the Italian coast, and I'll have to drop back below the sound barrier while we fly over France, but once we reach the Atlantic, I'll put the hammer down.'

'How about that,' she said quietly, putting her hands on her bump and speaking to its resident. 'Most people don't get to fly supersonic in a jet fighter in their entire lives, but you've done it before you're even born.' A smile, mixed with a sigh. 'I really, *really* hope your life isn't as interesting as mine.'

She leaned back as the F-15 banked and headed west.

Travelling at supersonic speed turned out to be surprisingly unexciting. The Strike Eagle's breaching of the sound barrier was marked with a jolt and a split-second burst of vapour whisking past the cockpit, but the flight afterwards felt no different from that preceding it. Their traversal of the Mediterranean seemed to take only minutes, then the plane slowed to make a high-altitude pass over south-western France before the empty grey curve of the Atlantic appeared ahead. Fox accelerated again, continuing for twenty minutes at full speed before slowing once more to rendez-vous with a hulking KC-135 tanker aircraft. The manoeuvres required to link the two planes for refuelling did nothing for Nina's stress levels, but Fox made the connection with practised ease, and before long the F-15 was on its lonely way again.

With nothing but ocean far below, there was little sense of motion. The unchanging view and the constant rumble of the engines, added to Nina's general exhaustion, soon became soporific. She drifted into sleep, waking as the plane juddered. 'What was that?' she said, blinking in alarm.

'Nothing to worry about,' Fox replied. 'We just caught some turbulence from the Extender.' She leaned to look past him, seeing another KC-135 growing larger ahead. 'We're about to gas up again. Once we're done, it's non-stop all the way to New York.'

'How long will that take?' she asked, shocked that she had managed to sleep through the second refuelling.

'Just under an hour. Oh,' he added, 'and if you look back and to your left, there's something I think you'll want to see.'

She craned her neck to peer back over the F-15's wing. 'There's another plane!' A sleek grey shape was approaching, its twin tails suggesting that it was a second Eagle.

'That's right. It's not one of ours; it's a Saudi bird. It set off before we did, and from what I've been told, it's hauled ass at the redline the whole way to catch up, on the direct orders of the Saudi king himself. I was actually ordered to slow down a bit, because you both need to land at the same time.'

'And who's aboard it?' she asked, smiling because she already knew the answer.

'I'll switch radio channels so you can talk to them yourself.'

Brief electronic chatter in her headphones, then she heard a familiar voice. 'Ay up, love.'

'Ay up yourself,' Nina replied with a huge grin. 'So I guess Dalton came through for you too.'

'Most of this came from the Saudis,' Eddie told her. 'Funny how they roll out the red carpet when you save their holy city from being gassed. Are you okay?'

'Yeah. I just hope we can get to New York in time to do something – and that we actually *can* do something.'

'Got to try, haven't we? Won't be setting much of an example for the kid if we don't.'

'Maybe, though when most parents worry about being a good role model it's usually about whether they eat too much junk food, not how many terrorist attacks they've stopped!' She watched as the other fighter drew closer. 'Huh, I just realised something.'

'What?'

'What I'm doing – it actually fits with Revelation. The woman who took refuge high in the wilderness was pregnant, and according to the text she was given "two wings of a great eagle". I'm pregnant, this wilderness is about as high as you can get, and this plane *is* an Eagle! Maybe there's something to the prophecy after all.'

'Hope not,' Eddie said. 'Wasn't she called the Woman of the Apocalypse? That's what we're trying to avoid!'

'Ah. Yeah. Good point. That's what I get for trying to be smart.' The other F-15 was now near enough for her to make out the figure in its rear seat; she waved at him, getting the same gesture in return. The sight made her smile, before her mood fell again. 'Do you think we'll be able to stop him?'

'Course we will,' said Eddie. Even over the radio, he had recognised the gloom in her voice and adopted a more upbeat tone to counter it. 'We stopped Simeon and Anna; we can find Cross too.'

'*You* stopped Simeon,' she pointed out. 'The only reason Anna didn't kill everybody in St Peter's Square is because Cross tricked her. Yes, I found her, but I didn't reach her in time. If her statue hadn't been a fake . . .'

'Doesn't matter,' he insisted. 'It's the results that count. You know how you said you'd been seeing a shrink to figure out if everything you'd done was worth it? Well, this proves it is. We saved thousands of lives today – and Christ knows how many more in the past. We've stopped *wars*, Nina. *You've* stopped 'em. And yeah, I know we've both lost people we cared about because of it . . . but we might have lost a lot more if we hadn't. Like you told me in the tunnel, this is what you *do*. And it *is* all worth it.'

Nina smiled, accepting his words as truth and feeling that a weight had been lifted from her. 'Thanks, honey. I didn't need to pay for a shrink after all, did I?'

'Just call me Dr Frasier Chase.' She could almost see his grin even across the gap between the two fighters.

The aircraft moved into position behind the KC-135, Nina's the first to connect to the refuelling boom extending from beneath its tail. The procedure was completed quickly and cleanly. The Saudi F-15 then took its place before both Eagles, now fully fuelled, dropped away from the tanker. 'You ready?' Eddie asked.

'Not entirely, but . . .' Nina took a deep breath, then gave him a thumbs-up. 'Let's make everything worth it.'

The F-15s ignited their afterburners. Side by side, they raced into the empty sky.

37

New York City

The two military jets touched down at LaGuardia airport, much to the surprise of observers and the infuriation of those waiting to land as the airspace was cleared for their arrival. Nina and Eddie were quickly ushered to a waiting helicopter, taking a moment to embrace and kiss before boarding. Seretse was waiting inside the cabin. 'Welcome home,' he said, shaking their hands.

'Good to be back,' Nina replied. 'Although I really, *really* need a pee! Four hours strapped into a chair is no fun at all.'

'Some people pay good money for that,' Eddie said with a smirk as he took his seat. 'Any news on Cross?'

Seretse shook his head. 'Nothing yet.'

Nina fastened her seat belt as the chopper wound up to take-off speed. 'Are we going to the UN?'

'No, Brooklyn.'

'Brooklyn? What the hell's in Brooklyn?'

'A surprising amount,' Seretse replied with a faint smile. 'I know that as a lifelong resident of Manhattan, you may find that difficult to comprehend.'

She huffed. 'Funny man.'

'But the regional headquarters of the Secret Service are located there,' the diplomat went on, 'and they are in charge of security outside the United Nations complex, so that is where we are going. Hopefully you will be able to provide them with useful information.'

'Let's hope.' She looked out of the window. The helicopter cleared the boundary of LaGuardia, heading south-west across the relatively low-rise sprawl of Queens towards Brooklyn. The towers of Manhattan rose on the far side of the East River. Her home; but it was again under threat.

The flight did not take long. The chopper touched down in Brooklyn Heights' Columbus Park, a convoy of black SUVs waiting to whisk them to the Secret Service offices a short distance away on Adams Street. Seretse took a phone call as they arrived. 'Air Force One has just landed at JFK,' he told Eddie and Nina as they went inside. 'In light of the threat, President Cole will be taken to the United Nations by helicopter rather than in a motorcade.'

'That's good,' said Nina, relieved.

'A number of the world leaders are travelling there by road, though,' he continued, dampening her mood. 'They are still at risk.'

Eddie shook his head. 'If Cross hates the UN so much, he'll make the attack when they're all there. They'll be like his Pokémon – gotta catch 'em all.' Seretse and Nina exchanged puzzled looks. 'Oh, come on. Nina, you'll *have* to learn something about pop culture once the baby's born!'

'I can't wait,' she lied. 'You're right, though. He'll want all the kings of the world to witness the fall of Babylon – and if he can kill them afterwards, so much the better to bring about the apocalypse. But he'll probably have a hard time getting close enough to do that.'

'No probably about it,' said a new voice. A broad-shouldered, harried-looking bald man in his fifties marched to meet the group, the coiled cable behind one ear giving away that he was a member of the Secret Service. 'Dr Wilde, I'm John Talsorian, USSS special agent in charge of diplomatic security at the General Assembly.'

'USSS SAIC?' said Eddie. 'That's a lot of esses.'

Talsorian gave him the briefest of dismissive glances. 'Mr Seretse, good to see you again. If you'll come to the briefing room?'

'You sound confident about your security,' said Nina as they headed through the building.

'The place is locked down,' he replied firmly. 'We were already on high alert even before this threat warning, and now it's been taken to maximum. Nobody can get within three blocks of the UN without being checked by either the Secret Service or the NYPD. The FDR drive is closed, NYPD river patrol has the East River fully covered, and we've got helicopters flying circuits watching all the rooftops. Beyond that, if anything tries to breach the city's airspace, there are Air National Guard F-16s ready to scramble from Atlantic City; they can intercept in six minutes.'

'What about submarines?' Eddie asked him, deadpan. 'A mini-sub could get into the UN basement through the old fire hydrant pipes. I know, 'cause I was there when it did.'

Talsorian's expression was now one of outright contempt. 'Who are you again?'

'This is my husband, Eddie Chase,' Nina said. 'And you should listen to what he has to say – well, most of it. He's already saved thousands of lives just this morning, so he knows what he's talking about.'

The Secret Service agent seemed unconvinced, but he said nothing, instead bringing the group into a crowded room. Roughly half its occupants were in conservative dark suits, the others in tactical gear. A pair of large screens mounted on one wall displayed a map of the area around the United Nations complex – and a photograph of Ezekiel Cross. 'All right, listen up,' said Talsorian as he stood before the screens, facing his agents. 'This is Nina Wilde; you may have heard of her, she's a famous archaeologist, but right now that's not important. What matters is that she has information about the man we're looking for. Dr Wilde?'

Nina was taken aback by the brusqueness of his introduction, but the agent was clearly already under pressure, and there *was* a time factor involved. She regarded the image of Cross, which she estimated was at least ten years old, possibly from his CIA file, before turning to her expectant audience. 'Okay, I'll tell you what I know. This man is called Ezekiel Cross; he's an ex-CIA agent turned religious fundamentalist, who was responsible for the gas attack in Antigua that killed almost a hundred people. He tried and failed to carry out an attack on a much larger scale in Mecca earlier today. He also used a similar attack on the Vatican as a decoy; I believe that his real target is the United Nations.'

Talsorian cleared his throat impatiently. 'Dr Wilde, my people have already been briefed – we know all this. We need you to tell us something we *don't* know. Like: where is he now? How is he planning to make the attack?'

'I . . . don't know,' she admitted, his tone immediately putting her on the defensive. 'I can tell you that even though he has associates, at least four other people, I think he'll try to carry it out personally. He wants to watch Babylon fall, see the Biblical prophecy he's obsessed with come true—'

The agent interrupted her. 'You *think*? Do you know for sure? You're not a profiler.'

'No, I'm an archaeologist—'

'This isn't ancient history. This is happening right now, and we need concrete information.'

'The only concrete in here's inside your skull,' Eddie snapped. Talsorian didn't even look at him, merely pointing in his direction. 'Remove him.' A pair of burly men in tactical gear advanced on the Englishman.

Eddie raised a hand in warning. 'I wouldn't.'

'Agent Talsorian,' said Seretse placatingly. 'Mr Chase may also have useful information. If you could please hear them out?'

Talsorian scowled, but gestured for the two agents to return to their seats. 'Okay, then. Let's have it. What can you tell me about Cross's associates?'

'Ah . . . not much, I'm afraid,' Nina said. 'He has a bodyguard, a big guy called Norvin; his pilot, Paxton—'

'Norvin? Is that a first or last name?'

'I don't know. But they're all American, and I can't imagine it's a common name. And there was another man called Hatch, I think.' She described them as best she could, Eddie adding his own recollections.

'Got a hit on Paxton,' said a female agent, tapping on a laptop. The pilot's photograph flashed up on the big screen beside Cross. 'Daniel Aldo Paxton, age thirty-nine, ex-USAF, qualified to fly pretty much anything.'

'That's him,' Nina confirmed.

The agent kept typing. 'Not enough info to narrow down the others.'

'Is that all you've got?' Talsorian asked Nina. 'Well, it's something, I guess. Okay, get Paxton's picture out there alongside Cross's, and see if you can find a link between them and those other names. All right, let's get back to it.' The agents stood and began to file from the room. 'Mr Seretse, Dr Wilde . . . Chase, thanks for your help.'

'Wait, that's it?' said Eddie. 'That's all you want from us?'

'That's all you've got,' he replied. 'Unless you've any other insights? Some sort of *Da Vinci Code* thing from the Bible telling us where he's going to strike?'

'I'm afraid not,' Nina told him.

'That's what I thought. Okay, I've got work to do. Mr Seretse, I'm heading back to the UN – you're welcome to join me.'

Seretse gave Nina and Eddie an apologetic look before replying. 'Thank you. That would be most helpful.' He turned to the couple. 'I am sorry. After all the effort involved in bringing you back here . . .'

'It's okay, Oswald,' said Nina. 'We did what we could.'

Eddie gave Talsorian an annoyed glare as the Secret Service man spoke to the agent with the laptop. 'Even if some dickheads apparently don't want our help. So now what do we do?'

'We could go to the UN and help look for Cross,' suggested Nina. 'I know it's a long shot, but . . .'

Seretse shook his head. 'I am afraid that will not be possible. You do not have security clearance. After all,' he reminded the archaeologist on seeing her surprise, 'you no longer work for the United Nations.'

'So there's nothing else we can do?' said Eddie.

'Unfortunately not. Hopefully you have done enough already. You foiled the attack in Mecca, and from the failed attack in Rome realised that Cross's true target was the UN. That may be enough.'

'Only if you find him,' Nina said unhappily.

'I have to have confidence that we will,' said the diplomat, drawing in a weary breath, 'because the alternative is too terrible to contemplate.' Talsorian called his name. 'I must go. All I can suggest for now is that you return home. Although I would also suggest taking a route that gives the United Nations as wide a berth as possible. The traffic in Manhattan will be quite appalling.'

'Don't suppose we could hitch a lift in your helicopter?' Eddie asked. 'Just land in Central Park at the end of our road, nobody'll mind.'

Seretse smiled. 'I suspect that would not be the case. Nina,

Eddie, goodbye, and thank you for all you have done. I hope that when I next speak to you, I will have good news.' He shook their hands, then departed with Talsorian and several other Secret Service agents.

'Bloody idiot,' Eddie said, glowering after the departing SAIC.

'I can kinda see his point,' Nina had to admit. 'He's got his hands full trying to protect over a hundred world leaders in one of the busiest cities on the planet, and then we turn up and tell him there's a new threat, but don't actually give him anything that could help. I mean, he was right: I *don't* know if Norvin was that guy's first or last name.'

'Got to be his last name. Who the hell would call their kid Norvin?'

'You wanted to call ours Arbuthnot,' she reminded him with a grin.

'That was if it was a boy. Now I know it's not . . . although actually, it would still work.' He rubbed his chin thoughtfully.

'No it wouldn't,' she insisted. 'Come on. Let's get out of here.'

That was easier said than done. Even outside Manhattan, the gridlock caused by the closure of roads around the United Nations had worked back through the bridges and tunnels to the island. Traffic was moving at a crawl, or not at all. 'This is going to take ages,' Nina sighed, looking out from their cab at the East River below. The driver had taken the Manhattan Bridge, assuring them it would be the quickest route, but they had been forced to a halt only a short way over the crossing.

Eddie peered past her. 'So they did ground that thing for the summit.' He pointed at the river's eastern bank about a mile away. The great twin-humped shape of the advertising airship was now moored at the Brooklyn Navy Yard rather than plying up and down the East River. 'Harvey told me they would.'

'Harvey?'

'You know, the chopper pilot. I got kidnapped just after having a flying lesson with him.' He indicated the buildings closer along the shoreline. 'That airship was one of the first things I saw when I escaped – the place they were holding me was just down there. When I went up on to the roof, I saw it landing at the Navy Yard.'

'It's a hard landmark to miss,' said Nina. She returned her gaze to Manhattan, and the unmoving traffic. 'Maybe we should have stayed in Brooklyn until the roads quieten down. Whatever Oswald might think, I do know the place isn't *entirely* uncivilised.'

She looked back at her husband, only to find that he hadn't heard her joke, instead frowning in puzzlement. 'What is it?'

'The guy who tortured me, Irton – he'd *been* to the Navy Yard, he had a parking receipt or something in his wallet. And when he was talking to Cross . . . what did he say?' His forehead scrunched as he dug into his memories. 'Something about there not being much security on certain days.'

'What did he mean?' Nina asked.

'I dunno. But . . .' He stared back at the airship. 'Cross won't be able to get near the UN on the ground or by water, at least if that arse from the Secret Service was right about his security. And the air's covered by the NYPD' – he indicated a couple of helicopters circling midge-like in the distance – 'and the National Guard, so anything that tries to get close'll be shot down. But that airship, I read about it: the whole thing was designed so it *can't* be shot down, not easily. It's massive, and it's got loads of different compartments for the helium, so even if you blow holes in some of them, it'll stay in the air. But it can fly at something like sixty miles an hour, so it could reach the UN in a couple of minutes – the National Guard's planes wouldn't be able to catch it in time.'

Nina cocked an incredulous eyebrow. 'You think he might be

planning to attack using an *airship*? Who is he, Count von Zeppelin?'

'Yeah, I know, it sounds like the ending of *A View to a Kill*. But if he stole the thing, he could fly right over the UN and drop the angel on it – and nobody would be able to stop him.'

'The Secret Service did say Paxton could fly practically anything,' she recalled. 'Would that include airships?'

'It's a big balloon with propellers on it. Can't be too hard. We should check it out.'

'Or we could tell the Secret Service to check it.'

'You think Talsillybugger'd pay any attention to us? It's just a theory, and a pretty fucking daft one at that. But . . .'

'But it's just insane enough to be true?' she finished for him. They exchanged looks. 'Just when I thought it was all over . . .'

'We need to hire a fat lady to sing for us,' Eddie said with a grin. 'Okay, so how the hell are we going to get off this bridge?' He checked the road. They were on the upper deck, two narrow Manhattan-bound lanes with concrete barriers hemming them in on both sides, and no sidewalks. Nor was there any easy way to climb down to the walkway on the lower deck. 'Huh. Might have to rethink this.'

Nina looked ahead. The traffic was still stationary. 'God knows how long it'll take us to get across the river. And then we've still got to come back the other way.' She reached for the door handle. 'We'll have to do it on foot.'

The driver turned in alarm. 'Hey, hey! You can't get out on the bridge.'

'No, you can't,' Eddie added. 'Seriously! It's at least a quarter of a mile back to ground level.'

'It'll be a lot faster than driving across and then turning around. And you were the one who wanted to check out the airship. If Cross really is planning to use it—'

'That was just a theory! And like I said, a daft one at that. How often am I right about this stuff?'

'Way too often. Come on.' She opened the door and hopped out.

'No, lady, wait!' the driver yelled. 'Get back inside!'

'Nina— Oh, for Christ's sake,' Eddie said in exasperation. He thrust some banknotes through the cab's pay slot, then slid across the rear seat to follow her.

She had emerged on the roadway's right, beside one of the barriers. A railing behind it meant that she was in no danger of falling over the edge, but there was very little space between the concrete wall and the oncoming vehicles. 'Nina, wait!' he shouted as she hurried towards Brooklyn. She didn't stop; with a dismayed shake of his head, he ran after her. People in the stationary cars regarded them boggle-eyed as they passed.

He quickly caught up with his limping wife. 'Are you fucking insane?'

'I'm pregnant,' she shot back. 'If anyone asks, I'll tell them it's hormones!'

'At least let me go in front of you.' He squeezed past. 'I'm not having you use the baby as a bumper!'

They crossed the shoreline, descending the bridge's long ramp until they were finally able to climb over the barrier to a footpath below. 'You okay?' asked the Yorkshireman as he helped Nina down.

'Yeah, just winded,' she replied.

'And the baby?'

She gave him a strained grin. 'She's survived gunfights, explosions and jumping over cliffs in boats in the past few days. Jogging for a quarter-mile's the least of what she's been through.'

'You're bloody mad. You know that, don't you?'

'Must be why we work so well together.' Another smile, this time filled with genuine warmth, then she looked eastwards.

'We're only a few blocks from the Navy Yard here, aren't we?'

'Yeah, but it's a big place, and the airship's on the far side,' Eddie reminded her. 'We need another cab.' They followed the path to a road passing beneath the Manhattan Bridge's lower end, soon spotting a yellow taxi and hailing it. They climbed in and set off for the north gate of the Brooklyn Navy Yard.

From the bridge, the airship had appeared huge; from the ground, it was like a mothership from another world. The conjoined helium envelopes of the Airlander dwarfed even the largest passenger airliners. The mere sight of the gargantuan craft caused Nina a moment of cognitive dissonance, her brain's gears grinding as they tried to process the existence of something that seemed impossible. 'Damn, that's . . . *big*,' was all she could say as their cab pulled up at the gate. There were buildings between her and the airship, but its sheer scale made them appear no more than shoeboxes.

A security guard leaned out of a booth. 'Where ya goin'?'

'There,' Nina said, pointing at the behemoth. 'We've got an appointment.'

The guard didn't seem interested in her cover story. 'Yeah, yeah. Take the second right on to Gee Avenue, you can't miss it.' The gate rose.

'Has anyone else been to see it today?' Eddie asked him.

'Loadsa people wanna see it,' he replied with a shrug. 'Some guys went to the company offices maybe a half-hour ago.'

'How many guys?'

Another shrug. 'Four, five? I dunno, I wasn't really payin' attention.'

'Keep up the good work,' the Englishman told him sarcastically as the cab pulled away and made a right turn.

'You think it could be Cross?' said Nina, peering anxiously ahead.

'Maybe. Or maybe not. A lot of people come here; like he said, it's kind of a tourist attraction.'

The taxi drove past docks on the river's edge. Ahead was a low building, and rising behind it, moored on an expanse of open ground, was the vast beetle-like airship, its broad stern towards them. Their driver stopped in the parking lot. 'You want me to wait?' he asked.

'No, that's okay,' Nina answered. The couple paid him and got out, then regarded the building. A sign reading SKY SCREEN INC. was affixed to the wall, an arrow directing visitors around to the structure's other side. They followed it. The airship came into full uninterrupted view, an almost comically small gondola mounted under its centreline seeming as if it were about to be squashed flat beneath the elephantine mass. The whole vessel was so large that one of the roads to the piers beyond had been blocked off to give it room to land. Its flanks were covered with a grid of LEDs that in flight turned it into a colossal *Blade Runner*-style animated billboard, but today they were dark.

Eddie looked up at the craft. 'This thing's not supposed to be flying,' he said. 'So why're the engines going?'

Nina saw that the propellers were slowly turning, diesel engines rumbling. 'Maintenance?' she offered, not convinced.

'Let's ask.' They headed cautiously for a door. Eddie opened it, flinching as an electronic bell made a loud *beep-boop* noise. 'So much for the element of surprise,' he muttered before raising his voice. 'Hello?'

No response for a few seconds, then: 'Yo! Come on in.'

'Wait here,' Eddie told Nina, wary. He entered a reception area. It was empty, but a large photograph behind the desk of the airship at night told him he was in the right place. Another doorway went through to an office area overlooking the airship's landing pad.

'Anyone here?' he said. The office was apparently shared by the airship's flight and ground crews and those who sold advertising space on the giant craft's sides, a nest of cubicles surrounded by whiteboards and flip-charts showing sales figures and targets. But there was still no sign of any staff.

He rounded a battered couch, noticing an overturned coffee cup on it. A faint rush of cold air told him that an exterior door had been opened. In the far corner, a fire exit swung shut—

He froze. Poking out from behind one of the cubicle dividers was a foot, a man lying on the floor. There was a dark, glistening stain on the cheap carpet tiles nearby. Eddie instantly knew it wasn't spilled coffee.

Another door opened, this one behind him—

He dived behind the couch as Washburn burst out of a back room, gun in hand. Bullets punched through the sofa's back, spewing shredded foam stuffing over him as he scrambled towards a small desk bearing thick ring binders of paperwork.

The scar-faced man skirted the couch after him, seeing the Englishman go underneath the table. He bent lower to take a shot—

Eddie jumped up – bringing the desk with him. He hurled it at the gunman. Washburn fired, but the round hit only wood and paper. An instant later, wood and paper hit *him*, the table knocking him to the floor and landing on top of him.

The gun was still in his hand. Eddie rushed over and stamped a heel down hard on his wrist. A pained gasp, and the pistol thumped to the carpet. The Yorkshireman snatched it up. Washburn shoved the table away – only to take a bullet to the head from his own weapon.

Shouts from outside, Nina's voice amongst them. Eddie ran back through the reception area, checking for further enemies before emerging.

His wife had gone.

But he could still hear her. He hurried to the corner of the building and looked across the landing field—

To see Cross dragging the struggling Nina with him as he and Norvin headed for the airship.

The cult leader had a gun to her head, using her as a shield. Eddie whipped up his own weapon, but knew he couldn't shoot at Cross without risking hitting her. He aimed instead at Norvin, but before he could fire was forced to jerk back as the bodyguard sent several shots at him.

Another man sprinted towards the airship's cabin. Eddie recognised him: Hatch. He had released the mooring lines, the cables now hanging limply from the bulbous envelope. Paxton was visible at the controls in the gondola.

Norvin fired again, forcing Eddie to retreat further as bullets smacked off the wall. When he looked back around it, Hatch had reached the cabin, Norvin following him aboard. He saw Nina shout, but couldn't hear her over the noise as the propellers revved. Cross pulled her inside, and the door closed.

Eddie ran into the open, raising his gun. He knew it wouldn't deflate the airship, but the envelope wasn't his target. Instead he took aim at one of the engines. There were two pusher propellers mounted on the stern, and he opened up on the nearest. The fibreglass cowling cracked apart.

The gondola's door slid open again, Cross leaning out – with a sniper rifle.

Eddie immediately abandoned his attack and sprinted for cover. A bullet tore the air barely a foot behind him with a supersonic crack. He threw himself behind a parked van as another shot exploded brickwork in his wake. Before Cross could fire again, he hunched into a tight ball behind the front wheels. The whole vehicle jolted as a third round struck the engine block.

The airship's propellers grew louder. Eddie looked up to see it pulling away from him. He fired his remaining rounds at the second engine, but this time caused no visible damage, and even with its cowling broken the port engine was still running.

The airship gained altitude, slowly at first but with increasing speed as its forward engine nacelles tilted downwards to provide extra lift. It cleared the landing field, turning north over the East River towards the United Nations.

With Nina trapped aboard.

38

'Watch her,' ordered Cross as he went to the front of the cabin. It was equipped for sightseeing, ranks of aluminium seats on each side of the central aisle. Norvin and Hatch shoved Nina into a window seat opposite the door, the hulking bodyguard squeezing beside her to block her in as the other man took the place directly behind.

'So this is your plan?' Nina said over the buzz of the engines. 'You're going to drop the angel on the UN and kill the "kings of the world"?'

'Babylon will fall, Dr Wilde,' Cross replied. He put down his rifle and took the eagle-headed statue from a bag. 'The prophecy will come true.'

'But it *can't* come true,' she insisted. 'We stopped Simeon's attack in Mecca, and his statue's been secured. It'll never be loosed, which means the sixth angel's instructions can't be carried out. Until that happens, it's impossible to fulfil the prophecy.'

Cross glared at her, eyes wide in mania. 'It doesn't matter! The Witnesses are dead. That means the seventh angel is about to sound – and when I destroy Babylon,' he held up the figurine, 'the end time will come!'

'No it won't!' Nina shot back. She realised how dangerous he now was, clinging to his delusion even as it crumbled in the face of the evidence, but she couldn't help challenging him. 'You're picking and choosing pieces of Revelation to suit yourself! What happened to the seven angels who pour out their vials of plague over the earth? What about the Beast, and the dragon? Where are they? You're ignoring anything that doesn't fit your interpretation!'

'I found the angels!' he shouted. 'That proves my interpretation is *right*. I saw through all the layers of hallucination and metaphor in John's writing – I saw the *truth*. The only truth! God's word was revealed to me, and now I'll reveal it to the world!'

'You're insane,' was the only response she could manage.

Fury clenched his face. 'You'll soon see,' he growled. The airship was now passing over the Williamsburg Bridge, the United Nations complex visible on the west bank a few miles ahead. 'The gas will kill everyone at the UN. "And the kings of the earth, who have committed fornication and lived deliciously with her, shall bewail her, and lament for her, when they shall see the smoke of her burning."'

'And how are they going to do that if they're all dead?' Nina demanded. Cross did not reply, instead regarding the view ahead with growing anticipation. 'You can't answer that, can you? You've lost it.'

He stalked back down the aisle, getting in Nina's face to snarl: 'After Babylon falls, so will you, Dr Wilde.' His gaze flicked towards the cabin door. 'Right on to its ruins from five thousand feet up!'

'Look, just get everyone out of there!' Eddie yelled into the phone at Seretse. 'The airship'll be there in a few minutes!'

'A full evacuation in such a short time will be impossible,' the alarmed diplomat protested. 'There are thousands of people here; even if we get the leaders out first—'

'Just do what you can,' Eddie snapped before ending the call. He stared helplessly at the receding Airlander, which was still gaining height, then had an idea. He found another number in his contacts and hurriedly dialled it.

Infuriating seconds passed. He watched the airship retreat – then a shrill of engine noise told him that he was through. 'Harvey! Harvey, it's Eddie Chase – can you hear me?'

'Eddie? Yeah, sure,' Harvey Zampelli replied, sounding puzzled. 'Where you been? I phoned you a coupla days ago, but—'

'Harvey, we've got trouble,' the Yorkshireman interrupted. 'Where are you?'

'Right now? Just comin' back from a tour of Liberty Island.'

'I need you to pick me up. I'm at Brooklyn Navy Yard, the airship landing field.'

'Pick you up?' the helicopter pilot exclaimed. 'Eddie, I got passengers, I can't—'

'Can you see the airship?'

A moment's pause. 'Yeah. Hey, I thought it was supposed to be grounded 'cause of that thing at the United Nations.'

'It was, but someone's stolen it to *attack* the UN. Harvey, they've got Nina, my wife, aboard. I've got to get after them!' When there was no immediate reply, he went on: 'You said you owed me a favour. Forget flying lessons – this is it. A lot of people will *die* if I can't stop this!'

'You're not kiddin', are you?' said Harvey, worried. 'Okay, I'll come find you. Not sure how I'm gonna break it to my passengers, though.'

'Just get here,' Eddie said. He stared upriver once more. The airship was still heading relentlessly towards its destination – but had now been noticed by the forces guarding it, helicopters changing course to intercept.

Paxton listened to a message through his headphones, then turned to Cross. 'They're ordering us to turn back to the Navy Yard and set down.'

'Of course they are,' Cross replied, surveying his target

458

through binoculars. The United Nations was now only two miles away, and the Airlander had reached its cruising speed: two minutes' flight time. 'There's a lot of activity on the ground. They know we're coming.'

'They're evacuating,' Nina told him. 'The VIPs'll be out of there before you can drop the angel.'

'In two minutes? No, they won't. There are one hundred and sixty-five world leaders attending the General Assembly, and they'll all be fighting over who gets to escape first. I know how these things work. The Secret Service won't let anyone else leave until President Cole's been secured, and they haven't even gotten a *police* helicopter on the ground, never mind Marine One.' He raised the binoculars to check the sky ahead. 'Paxton, NYPD choppers coming in.' He indicated a white-and-blue Jet Ranger heading towards them.

'I see them,' Paxton replied. 'What do you want me to do?'

'Stay on course. I'll deal with them.'

'I'll have to slow down,' the pilot warned. 'The wind at this speed'll throw your aim off.'

'I can handle it. Just hold us steady.' Cross went to the port-side door and opened it. Wind rushed into the cabin, the rasp of the propellers rising to ear-splitting volume. He squinted into the slipstream. 'Come right five degrees so I can get a clear shot!'

Paxton obeyed, turning the Airlander slightly to starboard. Cross leaned against the door frame as he aimed the rifle through the opening at the nearer of the approaching helicopters. 'Steady, hold it steady,' he called, fixing the cross hairs in the telescopic sight on his target. 'Steady, and . . . *now*!'

He fired. Even over the roaring engines, the retort made Nina jump. For a moment, it seemed that he had missed – then the leading helicopter slewed around, dropping into a corkscrewing descent.

Cross hurried to the front of the cabin to watch as its fall picked up speed, spinning like a sycamore leaf until it smacked down on the river. The rotors sliced into the water's surface and kicked up a great swathe of spray before the downed aircraft rolled over and began to sink. 'You got it!' Paxton crowed.

'There's still another one.'

The second helicopter started a sharp climb, taking a course that would pass directly over the airship. Paxton leaned forward to follow it, then turned in alarm to Cross. 'He's going to use his rotor downwash to force us down!'

'Will that work?'

'Against a ship this big? Probably not, but it'll throw us around and make it almost impossible to steer.'

Cross returned to the door with his rifle, but the Jet Ranger was now out of sight above the airship's bulbous twin prows. The cabin shook, forcing its occupants to brace themselves. Nina held on tightly to the seat in front as the Airlander rocked despite Paxton's best efforts to stay level—

She felt something protruding from the aluminium frame. A latch. The lightweight seats were designed to be easily disassembled and removed . . .

The idea that formed was quashed as the Airlander wallowed, pitching sickeningly like a ship on stormy seas as the chopper's downdraught pounded it. Cross grabbed a ceiling strap. 'Up, take us up!' he roared.

Eddie shielded his eyes from flying dust as the red, white and blue tour helicopter swept in to land. He scurried beneath the whirling rotor blades. 'Come on, everyone out!' he yelled to the passengers. Even after Harvey had explained the situation, they were still bewildered and frightened. 'You'll be a lot safer on the ground, trust me!' He helped them down. 'Sorry about this, but I'm sure Harvey'll give you a refund.'

'Refund?' said the pilot as Eddie clambered into the front seat and donned a headset. 'They got a longer flight than they booked – they should be payin' me!' He checked the passengers were clear, then applied throttle and raised the collective control. The LongRanger left the ground and turned up the East River.

'There's the airship!' said Eddie.

'It's kinda hard to miss,' Harvey replied sarcastically. Even from almost two miles away, the Airlander still loomed like a floating football stadium. He frowned, spotting something above it. 'The hell's that guy doing?'

Eddie saw an NYPD helicopter flying directly over the enormous airship. 'Must be trying to force them down.'

The pilot grimaced. 'Hell of a chance he's taking. If the airship comes up underneath him, the displaced air'll maybe cause a vortex ring!' The Yorkshireman gave him a blank look. 'That's a bad thing.'

'What about the airship? Can he make it crash?'

'Only if he completely wipes out on it, and hopefully he ain't that stupid. Probably the most he'll do is slow it down.'

'Good enough for me. The longer it takes it to get to the UN, the more chance there is of evacuating everyone.' The LongRanger cleared the Williamsburg Bridge, rapidly closing the gap to the airship as the huge craft veered right, its nose tilting upwards – towards the buzzing fly above it. 'Oh shit! They're going to hit each other!'

Harvey stared at the police helicopter in horror. 'Move, you asshole, *move!*'

'Full power!' screamed Cross. 'Ram him!'

Paxton shoved the throttle levers to maximum. The engine noise rose to a scream, the airship forcing its way through the downdraught—

A muffled *whump* reverberated through the vessel as it hit the police helicopter's skids. The impact threw everyone around in their seats. Paxton struggled to maintain control, wrestling with the joystick.

Nina pulled herself upright, her hand again finding the latch. This time, she tugged it. It opened with a *clack*, but the noise was drowned out by the roar of the propellers. The seat back came loose, aluminium tubing sliding freely inside its frame. If she raised it, it would detach.

But she kept it in place as Norvin levered himself up beside her. She now had a weapon, however improvised: what she needed was the right time to use it.

Paxton pulled back the joystick. The Airlander pitched upwards once more – and another blow shook the cabin.

'That guy's crazy!' said Harvey, unable to look away from the slow-motion collision.

'The chopper pilot, or the airship pilot?' Eddie asked.

'Both!'

The police helicopter reeled drunkenly as it bounced off the Airlander's upper hull, the tips of its main rotor coming perilously close to the envelope's Kevlar skin. It levelled off, trying to climb out of trouble, but the airship rose after it like a killer whale. The pilot finally decided that discretion was the better part of valour, accelerating away before turning to flank the enormous craft from a safe distance.

The Jet Ranger's rear door opened and a cop leaned out – holding a sub-machine gun. He opened fire, shots spraying the airship's port lobe. The envelope was tough, but designed to resist impacts from birds and hailstones rather than bullets. It puckered and ripped, helium gushing out with a piercing shrill.

But the airship was not slowed. Only one of its internal compartments had been violated, and the others provided more than enough buoyancy to keep it afloat. Magazine empty, the cop withdrew.

'Now what's he doing?' Harvey asked as the helicopter descended.

Eddie saw the cop return to view, holding a different weapon. 'He can't shoot down the airship – so he's going to shoot the pilot!'

A red light flashed insistently upon the instrument panel. 'We're losing helium,' Paxton warned.

'How bad?' Cross demanded.

The pilot checked the display. 'Only looks like one cell.'

Cross looked to port, seeing the helicopter drop back into sight. He hefted the rifle and went back to the door. 'Hatch, give me cover fire. I'll take him out.'

The cult leader braced himself against the bulkhead. Hatch unslung his gun and crouched alongside him to take aim at the helicopter—

The police sniper saw them and fired first. The round ripped through Hatch's thigh. He screamed and fell through the opening, tumbling into empty space.

But Cross had now locked on to a target of his own – and pulled the trigger.

The sniper lurched, then toppled out of the Jet Ranger. Nina gasped in shock, flinching as he jerked to a stop in mid-air, hanging from a safety line. The helicopter jolted violently with the abrupt shift of weight. It peeled away from the airship, the wounded cop throwing the aircraft off balance as he swung back and forth.

Cross tracked the chopper as if about to shoot the pilot, then drew back inside the cabin, returning his attention to the view ahead. Nina lifted the loose seat back slightly. He was barely six feet from her, beside the open door. If she could reach him, she was certain she could push him out . . . but Norvin was a wall of flesh obstructing her. 'Don't try anything,' the bodyguard rumbled, as if reading her mind.

She looked away, seeing that the airship had been knocked from its flight path by the helicopter. Roosevelt Island bisected the river ahead, the UN complex off to one side. 'Bring us back on course!' Cross called to Paxton.

The pilot adjusted the rudders, the behemoth angling to the left. 'We'll be overhead in a minute,' he announced.

'Excellent.' Cross returned to the front of the cabin, putting down the rifle and collecting the angel. He gazed down at the approaching tower of the Secretariat Building and the broad domed sweep of the General Assembly beyond, the ground around it a seething mass of people. '"Thus with violence shall that great city Babylon be thrown down . . ."'

Norvin glanced back through the rearmost window as the airship turned. 'Prophet!' he cried in sudden alarm. 'There's another chopper coming in behind us!'

Harvey's helicopter was gaining fast on the airship. Eddie picked out the mooring lines hanging over its sides. 'Get above it,' he said. 'I'll jump down on its top!'

'You'll *what*?' said the Bronxite in disbelief.

'Those cables – I can climb down one and get to the cabin.' The lines were affixed to the upper part of the hull; Eddie was sure he could reach one before the envelope's curvature became too steep for him to keep his footing.

'The hell you can! There must be an eighty-foot overhang between the side of the blimp and the cabin.'

'I can swing that far. I've done it from bridges—'

'That ain't a bridge! It's a floating bag of gas doin' sixty knots! Eddie, I know you've done some wild shit – I've *seen* you do some of it – but there's no way you can swing from the side of that thing like Spider-Man and jump into the cockpit. You try it, you'll be killed. Hell, even just *thinking* about trying it'll probably tempt fate!' Harvey briefly took his left hand off the collective control to finger the gold cross around his neck.

'I've got to do something,' Eddie protested. 'How about slicing it open with the rotors?' Harvey's expression told him that was a very bad idea. 'Okay, maybe not— *Shit!*'

He saw movement in the cabin's open door: Cross aiming his rifle—

A hole exploded in the windscreen – and Harvey jerked back with an agonised shriek as a bullet tore through his upper left arm. 'Jesus!' Eddie cried, feeling hot blood on his face and neck.

The pilot's wounded limb flopped nervelessly to his side. He clapped his other hand over the torn flesh, trying to contain the gush of blood . . . and the LongRanger pitched sharply towards the river.

Eddie grabbed the co-pilot's controls. 'What do I do, what do I *do*?' he yelled. But Harvey's only response was a keening moan. 'Shit! Two fucking lessons! That's all I've had!' he shouted at the universe in general. 'Two fucking lessons and I have to fly a fucking helicopter that's – that's about to crash into the United fucking Nations!'

The LongRanger had overtaken the airship, heading straight for the Secretariat Building. Eddie increased power and tried to gain height, pushing hard on the rudder pedals – but they refused to move, Harvey's feet wedged against his own set in his pained paralysis. The green glass tower loomed ahead; even at its maximum rate of climb, the chopper would still hit its upper floors. 'Harvey! Move your feet! Move your fucking—'

He changed tack, leaning over to deliver a solid punch to Harvey's jaw. The pilot fell limp. 'Sorry,' Eddie told him, cringing, but the duplicate pedals were now free to move as the other man's feet slid off the main set. The LongRanger's tail swung around – and the helicopter veered away from the skyscraper, the rotor tips slicing within mere feet of the windows.

★ ★ ★

Cross watched the LongRanger begin its uncontrolled descent, then put his rifle on a seat near the door and reclaimed the statue as the Airlander approached the United Nations. '"And the earth was reaped",' he said, returning to the opening ready to throw the angel out at the crowds below – then he froze as the chopper swung crazily back towards the airship.

Eddie gasped in relief at having avoided the crash, only to realise he still had no idea what he was doing. 'Okay, okay,' he said, desperately trying to remember what Harvey had taught him. 'Centre the stick, level out, keep the throttle at . . . at something, fuck knows what.' The East River and Brooklyn beyond blurred across his view as the helicopter continued its sharp turn. 'Stop spinning, that'd be a good start! Okay, level the rudder pedals, and— *Fuuuuuuck!*'

The Airlander's swollen hulls loomed in front of him.

He jammed the chopper into a dive. Nausea rose in his stomach as it plunged, the rotors whisking just below the port lobe—

A sound like a concrete block being thrown into a wood-chipper – and he was flung hard against the door as the helicopter whirled like a top.

The LongRanger had hit one of the airship's mooring cables.

Squeals of rending metal sounded behind Eddie as parts of the overstressed rotor assembly disintegrated. The steel-reinforced line had tangled and jammed the rotor head – and the engine's torque was instantly transferred back to the fuselage. The dangling aircraft spun around, its forward momentum swinging it upwards behind the Airlander's stern before gravity pulled it back down like a pendulum.

But the airship was also affected. Even with its huge lift capacity, it still had to be properly stabilised in flight, and the sudden addition to one side of almost a ton of corkscrewing metal threw it wildly off balance.

The savage lurch as the helicopter snagged the mooring line sent the airship's occupants flying. Paxton was hurled over the instrument panel, his flailing foot kicking the throttles to full power, while Norvin crashed to the floor in the central aisle. Nina ended up on her side in the bodyguard's seat, clutching the now-detached seat back.

Cross came off worst. The impact flung him against the thin Plexiglas window in front of the door, smashing it. He dropped the statue, which skittered under the seats. The cult leader lunged after it – only to reel as the swinging helicopter jerked the dirigible sideways.

He fell backwards through the open door, barely catching the sides of the frame with his fingertips. The Secretariat Building rolled past behind him as the craft overflew the United Nations complex. 'Norvin!' he screamed. 'Help me!'

'Prophet!' Norvin yelled, scrambling to the door. 'I'm coming, hold on!' He gripped his leader's arms and hauled him back inside.

Cross collapsed on the seats behind the door, eyes wide with shock – then his expression became one of alarm as he saw something behind his bodyguard. Norvin turned—

Nina smashed the seat back into the big man's face. He stumbled over Cross's sprawled legs – and fell through the open doorway, plummeting over seven hundred feet with a terrible scream.

Cross jumped up at Nina – only to crash back into the chair as her makeshift club swung again and hit with a bang. 'Fasten your seat belt, asshole!' she yelled, snatching up his rifle.

He froze as she pointed it at his chest. 'Put it down, Dr Wilde.'

'The hell I will,' she replied, glancing over her shoulder to see

Paxton pushing himself off the console. 'Tell your man to land this thing, or I'll shoot you.'

'You're not a murderer.'

'No, but you are. And you're a direct threat to the world's security.' The United Nations complex dropped out of sight beyond the open door as the airship continued into the city. 'I'll do whatever I have to in order to protect it.'

'*Protect* it?' he spat. 'Corruption, decadence, blasphemy – evil and ungodliness everywhere? This is the world you want to protect?'

'It's the only one we have!'

'It needs to be cleansed! Babylon must be destroyed to bring about God's kingdom on earth! The prophecy will come true – I'll *make* it come true!'

'You're not God's prophet,' Nina shouted back. 'You're a delusional lunatic!'

Hatred glinted in Cross's eyes. '"The fearful, and unbelieving, and all liars, shall have their part in the lake which burneth with fire and brimstone . . ."'

'Shutteth the hell up,' she snapped. Paxton finally dropped into his seat; she looked passed him. 'Hey, pilot guy! Take this thing down right now, or I'll shoot your boss—'

Paxton gasped in fear, but not at her threat. Nina looked back – to see the black glass monolith of the Trump World Tower looming directly in the airship's path. 'Shit!' she gasped, grabbing the nearest seat.

The pilot yanked back the joystick. The Airlander pitched upwards, the forward engine nacelles pivoting to speed its ascent. It swept over the corner of the seventy-two-storey tower's roof, narrowly clearing it – but still demolishing a couple of communications masts as it climbed. Nina gripped the chair more tightly, holding her breath as the building's edge passed barely a foot beneath the gondola . . . then they were clear.

Paxton reduced power and put the airship into a hard turn back towards the river. 'Hey!' she yelled at him. 'I told you to set us down! If you don't, I'm gonna—'

She was thrown to the floor as the vessel slammed to an abrupt stop.

39

The crippled LongRanger's engine cut out: whether through some safety mechanism or simply because it had been destroyed, Eddie neither knew nor cared. But the helicopter's insane whirl was slowing, the blur through the windows resolving itself into the skyscrapers of New York.

A tall black one whipped past, and again, and again, closer each time—

'Shit!' he yelped, seeing the helicopter's reflection in the dark glass growing ever larger. He grabbed Harvey – as the aircraft smashed into a penthouse apartment like a wrecking ball.

Its tail was ripped off and fell away, but the main fuselage ploughed through the condo's windows, scattering ultra-expensive furniture as it bowled across the living room. The mooring line snapped taut as the airship pulled away from the tower, dragging it backwards – but the remains of the rotors wedged against a freshly exposed steel girder above the demolished windows. The cable strained, but held, the makeshift anchor yanking the Airlander to a sudden halt.

Eddie opened his eyes . . . to find himself looking straight down at a sheer drop through the broken windscreen. Only his seat belt kept him from plunging to the sidewalk over eight hundred feet below.

And his position was far from secure. The mooring line rasped against the girder as the airship tried to pull free, rocking the cockpit. 'Oh, *arse*,' he gasped, securing one foot against the column supporting the instrument console. 'Harvey, are you okay? Harvey!'

The pilot stirred weakly. 'Oh man, what . . . what happened?'

'My third flying lesson didn't go too well. Harvey, we've got to move – this thing's going to fall any second.'

'Fall? Whaddya— Whoa, *shit*!' Harvey cried as he opened his eyes. 'Jesus Christ!'

'Yeah, you'll meet him in a minute if you don't get out! Go!' Eddie unbuckled his seat belt, balancing precariously on the support column as the other man frantically released his own restraints and barged the door open. Harvey piled out – and the helicopter lurched with the shift of weight.

The Englishman scrambled across the cockpit, batting aside dangling headset cords and diving after the American—

A shrill of buckling metal – and the fuselage toppled over the edge behind him as he hit the carpet.

Heart racing, Eddie looked up to see a stylishly dressed woman in her fifties staring at him in stunned amazement. 'Hi,' he said. 'Sorry about the mess. There's a bloke called Oswald Seretse at the UN, he'll pay for the damage . . .'

Her gaze went back to the gaping hole in the wall as a shadow fell over the room. Eddie turned to see the airship drawing closer. Without the lift from the engines at full power, the craft was being pulled downwards – and back towards the building – by the helicopter wreckage.

Nina grabbed a seat just in time to arrest her slide as the cabin pitched backwards. But she had dropped the rifle, and it was now slithering down the aisle.

Towards Cross.

She caught it with one hand – as Cross lunged at her. He landed on her legs, catching her shrapnel wound. She cried out in pain as he clutched at the gun. 'Give it to me!' he roared.

'Go to hell!' she snarled, pulling one leg free and thrashing at his chest. He grunted in pain, but still managed to grip the rifle. He forced the barrel towards her head and clawed at the trigger—

She let go of the seat.

They both skidded down the central aisle, slamming against the seats behind the open door as the swinging helicopter made the airship roll sideways. Nina grabbed the rifle with her free hand, pushing it away from her – as Cross found the trigger.

The boom of the rifle at close range was agonisingly loud. Nina felt the muzzle flash scorch her hair as she screamed – but it was Paxton who was hit, the bullet striking him squarely in the back of the skull and exploding his face across the windshield.

Eddie watched in horror as the airship reeled towards the tower. If it hit the roof's edge side-on, multiple buoyancy cells would be slashed open at once and it would fall out of the sky like an airborne *Titanic* as the helium escaped, taking Nina with it—

The behemoth rolled, a whale turning on to its other side. The wreck of the LongRanger had swung away from the tower as it fell, but it was now coming back, changing the airship's centre of gravity.

The helicopter would smash into the building several floors directly below him. And the Airlander was still approaching, blotting out the sky . . .

'Get back!' he told Harvey and the penthouse's occupant as he judged the movement of the mooring cable, waiting for the impact—

What was left of the chopper pounded against the featureless black glass face of the Trump World Tower. The fuselage was flattened by the blow – and the rotor assembly disintegrated, the central shaft tearing loose. The cable whipped free as the heavy debris fell away.

Eddie burst into a run – and leapt out of the window at the quivering line.

He seized it with both hands, swinging away from the building as the airship, shorn of the helicopter's weight, shot upwards. Pulling the cable to his chest, he used his feet to secure himself in place, passing it under one foot and back over the other.

First Avenue rolled past far beneath him as the Airlander angled back towards the United Nations. 'Okay, maybe Harvey was right about this being a fucking stupid idea . . .' muttered Eddie as he started to climb.

Cross pulled himself over Nina, using his weight and greater strength to shove the rifle down to the deck with one arm, then clamped the other hand around her throat. '"True and righteous are his judgments, for he hath judged the great whore!"' he snarled.

'Don't you . . . call me a . . . whore!' she gasped as he squeezed, clawing at his arm with her fingernails. 'You Bible-thumping prick!' She drew blood, making him flinch. He leaned away from her, trying to force the rifle out of her grip.

Realising there was no way she could keep hold of the weapon, she instead let go of it, lashing her now-free hand at his eyes. Cross gasped, reflexively jerking back to save his sight.

But his hand was still wrapped around her throat. He pulled her upwards – then slammed her head back down against the deck, once, twice. Nina's vision blurred, pain overwhelming her. Cross squeezed harder, forcing a choked rasp from her mouth . . . then he let go.

A thin line of blood running from the corner of his eye, he collected the rifle and stood. Terror surged through the breathless Nina as she thought he was going to shoot her, but instead he hurried past her to the controls. The engines' roar grew louder as he increased power, aiming the craft back towards the United Nations.

Eddie was still climbing the mooring line when he heard the propellers speed up. He looked ahead. The airship was heading for the plaza outside the General Assembly. The crowd was spreading, people running for the exits to First Avenue, but it seemed that for every person who had fled, at least two more had replaced them as politicians and diplomats and officials spilled from the complex's buildings. Several helicopters were hovering nearby, one a heavily modified Black Hawk in green-and-white livery: Marine One, the transport of the President of the United States. But despite the efforts of the Secret Service and UN security to clear a landing space, the panic at ground level was making it impossible.

Aware that he was rapidly running out of time, he brought himself a few last feet higher and secured himself. He was not far below the gondola; from this low angle, he had a partial view of its interior through the large windows and open door. No sign of Nina, but he saw movement at the front—

Cross! He was at the controls, looking down through a gruesome film of blood on the windscreen as he lined up the airship with the plaza. Then he stood and moved down the cabin. The Englishman felt a brief fear that he was going to throw the statue from the doorway, but instead he went past the opening, turning from side to side as if searching for something.

There was only one thing it could be. The last angel.

Time was up.

Eddie kicked his legs back, then thrust them forward, building up momentum as he started to swing from the line. His original plan had been to reach the gondola's door, but Cross was armed, and would shoot him before he could recover from the landing. Instead he aimed at the cult leader himself. One of the windows was broken, revealing it as flimsy Plexiglas; if he had built up enough of a swing to reach the cabin, he would be moving fast enough to smash straight through another thin acrylic panel and hit the man behind it.

He hoped.

Another sweep brought him closer to his target. Two more would do it. He fell back, the wind whistling in his ears as he swept backwards, then in again towards the airship's underside. The boundary of United Nations territory passed below. One more swing to go, the gondola just feet away as he reached the top of his arc . . .

Nina clutched at Cross's leg as he moved back down the aisle, but he pulled away without even seeming to notice. She struggled to roll on to her side, feeling a new wave of pain as she raised her head.

The cult leader was looking for the fallen angel. She could see under the seats from her position on the floor, spotting the statue a few rows back from the open hatch. Breathing heavily, she started to pull herself up, feeling dizzy as her head throbbed again . . .

A dark shape moved past the doorway, just for a moment, before falling away. Nina blinked, not sure what she had seen. It hadn't been another helicopter – it was much too close, only a few feet from the gondola.

But the mystery object vanished from her mind as Cross finally found the object of his search. He bent down – and grabbed the angel.

Eddie kept his eyes fixed upon the American as he dropped away. Out as far as he could go, the Airlander's bloated flank hanging above him like a solid cloud . . . then he whooshed back at the gondola, bringing up both legs as he hurtled towards the window.

The cult leader stood, holding the angel in one hand. He turned – and saw the Englishman rushing at him like a cannon shell—

Eddie hit the window – but it didn't break.

The entire panel popped out of the frame with a crack of ripping rivets, the impact propelling it across the cabin to hit Cross like a transparent bulldozer blade. He flew backwards, the rifle spinning from his hand.

But Eddie's swing came to a premature halt when he slammed against the window. The cable jerked from his grip. He dropped, the backs of his thighs hitting the edge of the opening – and pitching him backwards out of the cabin.

Pure instinct saved him from a long and fatal fall as he bent his knees to slam his heels back against the inside of the wall, hooking his legs over the sill. He jolted to a stop, hanging upside-down from the gondola's side.

He was anything but secure, however. Pain burned through his hamstring tendons as the angular metal edge ground against them. He flailed his arms, searching desperately for a handhold, but found only smooth aluminium and empty air – and he could no longer hold his position, his own weight pulling him downwards—

Someone grabbed his ankles. He squinted up at the window – seeing a familiar face with a halo of wind-blown red hair looking back.

'Eddie!' Nina cried. She pressed herself against his legs to hold them in place and stretched an arm out to him. 'Eddie, grab my hand!'

'No, get back!' he shouted. 'It's too dangerous, you'll fall out!'

She took a firm hold of the window frame with her other hand and leaned out, determination clear in her voice. 'I'm not letting you go. You've got diapers to change, mister!'

Somehow Eddie managed a crooked smile. He strained to

476

bend at the waist, raising his arms towards her waiting hand. 'Come on, come on!' Nina cried, stretching out further. Their fingertips brushed . . . then hooked together, husband and wife gripping each other as hard as they could.

She leaned back, pulling him upwards. He managed to get hold of the window's sill with his free hand and hauled himself upright, his legs finally sliding down into the cabin. There was a red-painted handle set into a recess above the window where the gondola was attached to the envelope. He reached for it, wanting a firmer handhold as he lowered himself inside, but then made out some warning text above it: PORT SIDE ENVELOPE RIP – DO NOT PULL EXCEPT IN EMERGENCY. He hurriedly reconsidered and gripped the top side of the window frame instead.

With both hands now secured, he worked his lower body through the opening. 'Are you okay?' Nina asked as his feet touched down.

'Yeah,' he gasped. 'Thanks.'

'If I'm going to be a good mom, I want support from a good dad!'

They both smiled, then Eddie looked back outside. They were now directly over the crowded plaza, the Secretariat Building looming ahead. 'We'll turn this thing out over the river—'

'No!'

They both looked around at the shout to see Cross back on his feet. He was clutching the angel – and had retrieved the rifle, pointing it at them. He sidestepped to the door, raising the statue ready to hurl it to the ground. '"There will be no more delay!"'

His finger tightened around the trigger—

Eddie's hand snapped up – and pulled the emergency handle.

The results were literally explosive.

On a smaller airship, the envelope would have been ripped by physically tearing away a cable embedded in the material; a craft the size of the Airlander, however, required something more powerful. A line of detonation cord ran the length of the port lobe – and it took only a split second for the controlled explosion to slice open a gash in all the helium compartments.

A hurricane of escaping gas blasted out, the airship rolling as it lost buoyancy on one side. Eddie was flung back through the window, swinging from the handle with only the grip of his fingers keeping him from falling. Nina shrieked as she was thrown against the wall, one hand snatching a ceiling strap as her other stretched out to grab her husband's legs.

Cross staggered as the floor tilted beneath him. He dropped the rifle and tried to catch a seat, but too late—

He hit the bulkhead beside the door. The statue flew from his hand. He clawed at the door frame as he toppled out of the cabin and managed to halt his plunge, hanging on by his fingertips.

The airship's roll worsened, venting helium gusting over Eddie as he hooked his ankles back over the window frame. Below, the Secret Service had finally created a cordon large enough for Marine One to land, the helicopter touching down to pick up President Cole. Cross's target was still in danger, Nina realised. 'The angel!' she cried, pulling her husband in as she tried to spot the statue. 'If it falls—'

It was on the floor – and rolling towards the opening.

'Eddie, hold on!' she cried, releasing him and diving for the angel. She snatched it up just before it tumbled out into the void—

A hand grabbed her wrist.

Nina shrieked as Cross tugged at her arm, his right hand in a death grip on the door frame as he tried to drag her through the opening. The plaza circled beneath him, the deflating airship banking into a turn. 'Give me the angel!' he snarled.

'No!' She jammed a foot against the bulkhead, but Cross's weight was drawing her inexorably towards the open door.

'Why?' he shouted over the wind. 'Why are you protecting this corrupt world?' Another tug, and her foot slipped back, only her toes holding her in place. 'What's in it that's worth saving?'

Nina tried to pull away, looking down at him over her stomach. The sight of the small bump gave her a sudden surge of strength . . . and an answer. *'My daughter!'* she replied, smacking the statue down hard on his right hand.

Bone broke with a flat crack. Cross yelled, losing his grip and swinging away – but he still had a firm hold on Nina's arm, dragging her after him—

Eddie grabbed her, pulling her back. She gasped in pain as her shoulder joint took the cult leader's full weight.

But Cross did not give up, still struggling as he tried to dislodge her. '"The hour of judgement is come!"' he roared. '"Blessed are the dead which die in the Lord!"'

'You want blessing?' Nina yelled back. 'Bless *this*!'

She slammed the statue back down against his clutching hand.

The force of the blow hurt her wrist – but the pain Cross felt was far worse. He cried out, straining to maintain his hold . . .

And failing.

His hand slipped over hers. One last desperate grab at her fingers, then he was gone, reduced to a dot in moments as he plunged towards the plaza. He screamed all the way down, people below scattering as they saw him fall—

On to Marine One.

The helicopter was on the ground while President Cole and his closest staff were bundled aboard, its main rotor spinning just below take-off speed. Cross plummeted into the whirling blades – and was reduced to a wet haze, what little remained of him spraying out over the aircraft and across the plaza.

Nina grimaced as she saw Marine One's white livery turn crimson. 'Jesus!'

Eddie drew her away from the door. 'Red, white and goo,' he

said – in a high, duck-like voice. He had inhaled some of the escaping helium, affecting his vocal cords. 'Buggeration and quackery! That's not right.'

She embraced him. 'Are you okay? Apart from the voice, I mean.'

'I'll live. What about you?'

'Same. For both of us.' She put a hand on her belly. 'This has *so* not been good for my cortisol levels.'

Eddie squeezed her, then looked outside. The crippled airship was spiralling down towards the plaza at an increasing rate. 'We need to get this thing under control. And stop grinning, this is serious.'

'I can't help it,' Nina replied, finding his high-pitched voice incongruously amusing.

He huffed, then clambered to the front of the cabin. A tug at Paxton's seat belt buckle released the dead man, who fell sideways from his chair. 'Okay, how hard can this be?' Eddie asked himself as he took the pilot's place and examined the controls. Joystick, rudder pedals, throttle levers; the basics, at least, were much simpler than a helicopter's. He looked through the blood-streaked windscreen, the Secretariat Building coming into view as the Airlander circled.

Nina joined him, keeping a tight hold of the angel. A monitor revealed that the port lobe had now lost most of its gas, and what remained was venting fast. 'The helium's almost gone on that whole side.'

'We'll hit the ground pretty hard at this rate,' he warned. 'I'll try to get us to the UN's roof before we lose it all.'

He took the joystick. The airship turned sluggishly towards the green glass tower. Nina judged their speed and the distance they still had to travel against the rate at which the Airlander was descending. 'We won't make it – we're falling too fast!'

Eddie shoved the throttles to full power. 'That's the best we can do.' He pulled the stick back in an attempt to gain height, but to no avail. 'Fuck!'

Another smile, despite the situation. 'That's not what ducks say.'

'They do in Yorkshire!' The rooftop passed above the level of the cabin. 'Shit, we're going to hit it!' He forced the stick and rudders hard over, trying to turn away from the building—

The gondola swung clear – but even largely deflated, the airship's port lobe still overhung its side. It caught the roof's edge, the torn composite fabric scraping along it and tearing away antennae and satellite dishes. Eddie and Nina clung to their seats as the Airlander lurched to a stop, debris cascading down the face of the Secretariat Building.

The cabin tipped back towards the horizontal . . . and continued past it, rolling in the other direction as the starboard lobe, unable to support the trapped craft's weight on its own, continued to wallow towards the ground. 'Now what do we do?' Nina cried.

Eddie saw a glossy green wall rushing towards them. '*Hang on!*'

The gondola hit the tower's side. Glass shattered, flying shards spraying in through the airship's doorway and missing windows. The airship creaked and moaned as it settled, then everything fell silent as Eddie shut down the engines.

'We need to get out before this thing falls,' he said, voice starting to drop to its usual deep timbre. He helped Nina from her seat, and the couple made their unsteady way along the tilted cabin. It had come to rest practically inside one of the UN building's offices, the glass broken and the window frames buckled by the gondola's lower edge. 'Hop up.'

Nina pulled herself out of the door as her husband pushed from behind – and was startled to recognise her surroundings. Eddie emerged behind her to react with similar shock. 'Bloody hell. We just can't get away from here, can we?'

They were in the office of the Director of the International Heritage Agency, which until six months earlier Nina herself had occupied. 'Stepping right back into my old office? You think that's an omen?'

'It'd better not be,' Eddie rumbled, clearing his throat as his voice returned to normal. Feet crunching over glass, he led her away from the windows. 'We've got other stuff to do. More important stuff.' He switched on a lamp and checked his wife for injuries. She had acquired new cuts and bruises, but internal damage was his greatest fear. He put a hand on her lower body, feeling the small swelling within. 'God, I hope she's okay . . .'

'She is,' Nina told him.

He looked up at her. 'You sure?'

'Yeah, I am.' She smiled. 'Mother's intuition.'

He grinned. 'It took all of this to finally make you realise you were cut out to be a mum?'

'What can I say? We don't lead a normal life.' She kissed him. 'But yeah, I can be a mom, I know it for sure now. I even picked a name for our little girl.'

Eddie nodded. 'What is it?' he asked.

Nina hesitated, then said the name that had dominated her mind for what seemed like an aeon. 'Macy.'

Simply saying it out loud made her feel as if a tightness around her chest and heart had been released. She drew in a nervous breath, awaiting his response . . .

It was a gentle smile. 'I thought it might be.'

'Yeah?'

'Yeah. I know how you've been feeling – and I know you must have been worried sick that naming our baby after Macy would be . . . disrespectful. But it isn't. I think it's honouring her.' He put his hands on her arms, the smile widening. 'And

Macy would have been chuffed as nuts to know we'd named our kid after her.'

Nina glanced heavenwards. 'Maybe she still is. Who knows?'

'Who knows,' he echoed. 'I know one thing, though.'

'What's that?'

'We should start now if we want to reach the apartment before it gets dark.' He looked back at the window, the view of Manhattan blocked by the hanging mass of the crashed airship. 'Traffic'll be a nightmare.'

Nina laughed. 'And I get the feeling a lot of people will want to talk to us.' She kissed him again. 'Come on then. Let's go home.'

Epilogue

New York City

Five Months Later

'Welcome home,' said Eddie, unlocking and opening the door. 'Both of you.'

'Thanks,' said Nina with relief as she entered the apartment, her newborn baby in a sling against her chest. The little girl – *impossibly* little considering the size of her bump after nine months of pregnancy, she still couldn't help thinking – had been asleep during the ride from the hospital, but was now starting to stir again. 'Hey, honey,' she cooed. 'This is where we live! It's Mommy and Daddy's home – and now it's yours too.'

'Mummy,' said Eddie with a grin as he followed her in.

'*Mommy.*'

'Mummy!'

'Am I wrapped in bandages? Then it's Mommy. Although *you'll* be wrapped in bandages if you say it again,' she warned him jokingly.

He leaned in closer to his daughter. 'Mummy's bad-tempered and violent because she's got red hair,' he said in a stage whisper. 'You want to be more like Daddy.'

'What, going bald?' In fact, they weren't sure what colour the baby's hair would eventually become, as it somehow managed the feat of seeming blonde, dark or even red depending on the light. 'Don't listen to Daddy – he's British, he talks in a weird way. And he's from Yorkshire, so that makes him even weirder.'

'Tchah!'

'See what I mean?'

Eddie took off his leather jacket. 'Okay, then. Let's show the little one her room.'

They went through the living room, pausing en route at the shelf of mementoes. Nina gently shifted the baby to see one photograph in particular: that of Macy Sharif. 'Macy . . . meet Macy.' She didn't know which Macy she was addressing, but decided it didn't matter. Macy Laura Wilde Chase blinked her wide green eyes in response, then made a soft mumbling sound that her mother decided meant *hello*.

Eddie smiled. 'Macy would have loved that. Big Macy, I mean.'

'I know.' A moment of sadness as she regarded the picture of her friend, then she looked back at her namesake. 'When you're older, I'll tell you all about her.' Her gaze moved again, this time to the photograph of herself with her parents. 'And I'll tell you all about my mommy and daddy, too. They would have been so happy to meet you . . .'

'You okay?' Eddie said softly, after a moment.

'Yeah.' There was a hint of sadness to her voice, but it vanished as she regarded her daughter once more. 'But that can wait for another day. Let's get you into your bed.'

They continued to another room. What had previously been the study was now a nursery, the desk replaced by a crib containing a Moses basket. Nina went to it, taking a deep breath. 'Okay, I practised this with a doll, so hopefully I'll manage the real thing,' she said, gingerly unfastening the sling with one hand while supporting the baby with the other.

'You'll do it,' Eddie assured her. 'Trust me, you're not going to drop the baby. You could be juggling hand grenades and you *still* wouldn't drop the baby!'

'I hope you're right . . .' The sling came free, and she took Macy's weight with both hands, carefully lifting her out and lowering her into the cot. 'Yes! I did it! I actually did it – and she didn't even cry!' Macy squirmed in her new bed, but didn't make a sound. 'Oh my God, Eddie. Look at her. Isn't she beautiful?' She felt tears swelling in her eyes.

'Yeah, she is,' he agreed. 'My baby girl. Wow.' He made a sound that was half chuckle and half disbelieving gasp. 'I'm a dad. I'm a bloody dad!'

'That only just sank in, huh? I *thought* you looked a bit spaced out at the birth.'

A grin. 'Having her here at home is what did it. We're an actual *family* now.' He reached down to stroke his daughter's cheek; she wriggled in response. 'So are you ready to be a mum?' he asked Nina. 'Or a mom, even.'

'Yes,' she replied. 'I'm ready – I really am.' The admission was entirely truthful, and it felt good. 'Though I know it's going to be hard work. She's quiet now, but . . . well, you heard her at the hospital before I fed her! I don't know how she fits such big lungs into such a tiny body.'

'At least we can concentrate on her. Your book's finished, and you've optioned the movie rights to Grant, so we don't need to worry about money. You don't have to go chasing after any more archaeological bollocks for a while.'

Nina laughed. 'Just because I've become a mother doesn't mean I'm going to stop doing what I do.'

'Yeah, I was afraid you'd say that. Oh well . . .' He let out an exaggerated sigh, then wrapped his arms around her, looking down at their sleeping baby. 'It doesn't matter right now, does it?'

'No, it doesn't.' She smiled, then kissed him. 'We've just started a whole new adventure.'

Turn the page for an exclusive sneak peak of

Nina and Eddie's adventures in the next

WILDE & CHASE novel

THE MIDAS
LEGACY
ANDY
McDERMOTT

Out in Hardback and Ebook

Autumn 2016

<u>headline</u>

The Midas Legacy

Nina and Eddie emerged from the auditorium, to be immediately greeted by several journalists. 'Dr Wilde!' said one, recorder raised. 'So, *The Hunt For Atlantis*, the movie based on your life story – what did you think of it?'

Nina was about to let them know her true feelings, how her hopes for a serious, sober account of archaeological discovery had been quickly dashed by a parade of gunfights, train crashes and exploding helicopters, but the sight of the movie's producer nearby – and the thought that she had signed a contract that specifically forbade her from criticising the film before release – persuaded her to be more diplomatic. 'It was . . . interesting,' she managed. 'A lot was changed from my book, which was what *actually* happened, but it was all still very . . . exciting.'

'Hey, I thought it was great,' said Eddie. 'Some of the stuff in the movie was different from real life, but you can never have too many explosions, right? And the gist of the story was the same.'

'Insofar as Atlantis was being hunted for, yes . . .'

To Nina's relief, some of the stars of the movie chose that moment to appear, immediately drawing the journalists away with the promise of more famous prey. 'Thank God,' she said 'Can we go now?'

They headed for the exit. Nobody tried to catch them, Nina gave silent thanks that archaeologists were low on the celebrity totem pole—

'Dr Wilde? Nina?'

'Goddamn it,' she muttered before turning to see who had called her name.

To her surprise, it wasn't a member of the press but an elegantly dressed old lady with a VIP guest badge. Despite her age, the woman's green eyes were bright and intelligent, regarding the redhead with a contemplative, almost approving air. 'Hello?' Nina said after an uncomfortable silence.

'I'm sorry,' the woman said. 'It's just that . . . I hadn't been prepared for how much you look like Laura.'

At hearing her mother's name, spoken by a complete stranger, Nina felt unsettled. And as she looked back at the woman, the feeling grew – because she was now also experiencing an odd sense of *recognition*. Something about the elderly lady was familiar, almost disturbingly so. 'Do I know you?'

'No, I'm afraid you don't. But I did know your mother – and we need to talk about her.'

'What about my mother?' Nina demanded. 'Who *are* you?'

The woman smiled. 'My name is Olivia Garde. I'm your grandmother.'